SATIN CINNABAR

HISTORICAL MYSTERIES COLLECTION

BARBARA GASKELL DENVIL

Cover design by
It' A Wrap

ALSO BY BARBARA GASKELL DENVIL

HISTORICAL FOREWORD

When I started writing some years ago, I set my books during the medieval period, and quite quickly made the choice to translate my books into modern English. "Thou art a scoundrel," just didn't appeal, and no one would have wanted to read it. I certainly wouldn't have wanted to write it. However, this leaves the author with a difficulty. Do I use entirely modern words, including slang, or do I create an atmosphere of the past by introducing accurate 15th century words and situations.

I made the choice which I continue to follow in all my historical books. I have been extremely strict concerning historical accuracy in all cases where I describe the background or activities. I do not, on any page, compromise the truth regarding history.

Wording, however, is another matter. For instance, all men (without titles) were addressed as "Master ----" But this sounds odd to our ears now. Only young boys are called master now. So I have adopted modern usage. 'Mr. Brown," has taken over from 'Master Brown". It's just easier to read. I have used some old words (Medick instead of doctor for instance) but on the whole my books remain historically accurate, but with wording mostly translated to modern terminology, which can be understood today, and hopefully allow for a more enjoyable read.

I was once criticised for saying that something had been bleached. (I didn't imply that they went to the local supermarket and bought a plastic bottle of the stuff, paying on credit card). But yes, in that age bleaching was a common practise. They used various methods including sunshine and urine. But it was bleaching all the same.

Indeed, nowadays most writers of historical fiction follow this same methodology.

Also a quick word of warning… Most of my books do contain small amounts of sexual content. As with all elements of my writing, I try to make them as realistic as I can, and as such have chosen to included this aspect of relationships too. If you choose to skim over these parts, there are not too many, and I hope you can still enjoy the rest of the story.

Regards

Barbara Gaskell Denvil

For
Gill

CHAPTER ONE

S o this was it.

The sun blazed and the slow heat shimmered across the mullions. But the weather's kisses were drowned behind the explosion of canon, the tramping and the shouting, which all told the story she and all the local villagers had been so terrified of hearing.

Kate stared from the window. The sunshine promised a day of beauty, warmth and delicious satisfaction. But the noises she could hear far out from the rolling hills and marshy valleys, gave an agonisingly different promise.

The invading army had trudged all the way from their landing in Wales, to the final slaughter of a blood caked battle to the death, known as inevitable. When the invader's troops clashed with those of the English king and the men of his realm, anyone within earshot would also be in great danger.

She had been warned, of course, her father had told her, the villagers had told her, the priest had told her, and most of the staff within her father's great mansion had warned her.

"My dear young lady," his lordship had said ten days past, although she was not his dear young lady in truth, "this inconvenient problem comes closer each day. No, I have no intention of joining this nonsense nor risking my life in such a manner. We all know his royal highness our blessed king will win against this exiled invader. Our Lord God will see that the result is righteous and proper. King Richard will conquer the interloper."

As the only child, and a female child at that, Kate was well aware of her position. Papa spoke to her occasionally but no father to daughter friendship was ever likely to arise.

So she had said simply, "Yes, Papa."

"I shall remain in my rooms," his lordship had continued. "And you, Katherine, if you have any sense at all, will stay in yours. Even our own courageous Englishmen are not always on their best behaviour after a bloodthirsty fight. It fires them up, you know."

The butcher's wife had been more specific. "You runs and bloody hides, m'lady, when them lads come roaring from the battle field lookin' fer summit else to stick them swords into."

Kate's solution had been decided several days ago, but she had continued to hope that the battle would eventually take place further away. Now she knew that was not going to happen.

Rummaging on the cluttered floor of her garderobe, were the clothes she had borrowed from Papa's young friendly page. Calling her maid, she begged for assistance to dress herself in these old clothes and look as much like a boy as she could.

Ellie blushed and swallowed hard. "Oh mistress," she mumbled, "I never helped dress a boy afore. I ain't sure how some of this stuff goes on. And besides, me lady, you doesn't know if them soldiers don't attack little boys and all?"

"Indeed they may." Kate shook her head. "But whatever the danger for a young boy, ten times that danger will land on a woman. I've had so many warnings, I could say it all in my sleep. There will be hundreds, probably thousands, of soldiers getting away from the battleground. Some will be deserters and they'll be searching for a place to hide and maybe steal food or livestock or anything of value. Even worse will be the soldiers from the losing side escaping afterwards. They'll be looking for places to hide too. But everyone has told me that it's the winning side who are the most dangerous. This wild killing and winning goes to their heads, as if they were drunk to the point of insanity. They come marching to any place near enough, where they rape and pillage, slaughter and destroy. So, do you think I'm going to sit here like a patient young lady in my finest clothes waiting for the first man to break down the door, smash the windows and drag me off to his friends in the mud?"

"Oh, for pity, my lady, don't say such a thing." And she burst into tears.

Kate passed her a kerchief. "I refuse to be a baby," she said. "I shall dress as a boy, and here are clothes already for me. But you have to help, Ellie, and perhaps it would be a good idea if you did the same thing. I'm sure some of the scullery boys would be happy to share some spare clothes."

"Mistress, I could never do such a thing. It would be most improper. How could I appear in hose, with my legs showing and no skirt? I wouldn't even know how to put them on."

"Well I don't care," Kate told her made. "Ellie dear, most of this is just easy to guess. First there's the braise. Ladies don't wear these things, but personally I think it's a very good idea. I don't know why someone hasn't invented braise for ladies. And look they just tie up around your middle. Quite easy. Now for the hose, I think this will be more difficult to pull on. They seem go all the way up to my sit-upon and I think they have to tie round my waist too. I'm used to stockings, but those stop just below my knees."

She was sitting on her bed, taking considerable interest in these new garments, but far-off she could hear the horrific noise of battle and death. It was impossible to enjoy this new experience while hundreds of young men out there in the sunshine and the wind, were dying in pain.

Imagining such bloodshed and agony, made her feel sick. And the fact that all this was taking place so near her own home, made it far worse.

Quickly Kate returned to the problem of the hose. These were a little too long for her, since they came from a pageboy taller than herself, but she was able to pull up the fine black wool and tie the ribbons tightly around her waist. Noticing that there were small baggy loops left around her knees, she tried to hitch these up but that didn't work, and she decided it didn't matter. With Ellie's help, she

3

began to pull herself into a tight necked shirt and the buttoned doublet which went over. She was used to long embroidered, dangling and beautiful sleeves, pinned on and sewed over the tight inner sleeve. But no pageboy war such finery, and Kate was a little shy to see that now both her arms and legs were almost revealed by such tight and clinging clothing. She did not change her mind however, and so Ellie helped her pin up her long curls beneath a little hood, looking slightly incongruous, but was the only way she could hide her maiden hair.

Slipping on her shoes, she knew herself ready. "Oh mistress," squeaked Ellie, "take something for protection. Take a knife. Take a sword. Take something."

Again, they heard the thunder of horses galloping, men running, and the battle cries, beneath the scorching August sun. Kate bowed her head, praying silently. "I'll get a knife from the kitchens," she muttered. "And I'll see what seems safest as the day goes on. I can hide in my garderobe. I could even hide under my bed, or out in the shade might be safest. Which horrible soldier is going to think he'll find anything to steal or rape in a hay shed?"

"A little knife won't be strong enough against a great big sword," Ellie whispered.

"I'll find a pitchfork."

"Tis too dangerous to think about, milady," said the made, her voice trembling as much as her hands. "I doesn't even know which side might be winning."

"If it's King Richard's side, which means our own side," Kate pointed out, "the danger will not be quite as bad. Wandering soldiers tramping home after such a terrifying and bloody experience, may still want to rape and thieve. But the greatest danger will come if the other side wins. They will hate us all until their leader gets them in order. And depending on the leader he may not even bother. Once satisfied by pillage, he may find his men easier to manage."

"I don't know nothing about who he is," Ellie muttered.

"Nor me," Kate said to the window, staring again at the peaceful sky beaming across her own garden. "But I know it's some exile who wants to be King of England. Well, this isn't a very nice way of saying hello to everybody. *I'm your new king'.* Not with half of the people dead."

"Tis too horrible to think of my lady."

"Anything could happen now." Kate remained at the window. She refused to admit, even to herself, that she was scared, even of leaving her bedchamber. "I shall just have to wait and hope desperately for the best."

Her only mirror was small and damp stained, but Kate was able to see a smudged blur of her own reflection and was relieved to discover that a young boy was staring back at her. He looked as though he had dressed in a hurry and was certainly no lord. But, she thought, this would do, and as long as she didn't stand under the brilliance of the sun, she might be safe. Indeed, she began to enjoy the sudden small lurch of excitement. The lurch of fear felt very similar, but she was finding men's clothes considerably more comfortable and felt a strange sensation of bodily freedom.

Yet the faint pleasure swirled into desperation as she heard the thundering of galloping horses not so far distant, the echoing screams and felt the reverberation of cannon fire. Then she realised that horses could also scream, and rushed to the garderobe, leaning over the privy and heaving in pity and disgust. Clutching at her stomach, she hurried down the great staircase and through the wide corridors to the back shadows of the kitchens where the staff were trembling and clutching to each other.

"My lady is it over yet?" whispered the cook.

"I don't know," Kate whispered back. "But some of the noises are fading. I hope – I just desperately hope it's almost over."

"My poor husband," sighed one woman, "is out there. May the Lord help him. T'was the lord o' our half acre farmland as mustered him, and he said as how he'd willingly fight for our righteous king, But what if he's wounded? What if he loses a leg or an arm? Dear Lord, what if he's killed?"

Such dreadful thoughts. "Dear Ethel, be strong. He'll need you when he comes home."

"But what if he never comes?" she wailed.

It was true, Kate thought. Anything could happen now.

CHAPTER TWO

Convinced of his death, he was unsurprised at the depth of his grave. Black sweltering weight forced down upon him and the heat, being airless, was inescapable. Deep buried and suffocating, he recognised the prerequisites of hellfire, for death was the inevitable consequence of life, its ultimate curiosity, and in battle, its culmination. The darkness remained absolute, the furnace insufferable and the pain unrelenting. Seeping to him from beyond his tomb, the sounds of nightmare intruded and concentrated.

Alex smelled old blood crusted in the heat, a sour coppery smell that gagged at the throat. He assumed the blood was his own. A sudden spasm jabbed his shoulder and he gasped, gulping for breath. A reaction which inspired a question. Breathing, therefore, perhaps, after all, not dead. Buried not as corpse, but alive. And if not dead, then how to rediscover life.

Blinking, slowly accustomed to the dark, he found a face above him, a splintered snarling bone, divided where once there was nose and mouth. So Alex knew himself alive but lying crushed beneath the slain, stiffening in blood and thick in shit. But having survived, would not survive much longer. Some things were immediately imperative. Therefore escape the grave, discover the battle's end and know which cause claimed victory.

One arm was clamped beneath the faceless dead, his armour dented and the buckles broken. He moved his other hand, punched up and explored air. The air felt fresh against his fingers, sun-balmed and pleasant. Squashed within the stink of other men's deaths, the sweat of their futile desperation and the agony of their slaughter, Alex found more breath and the strength to struggle. He wrestled, elbow and knees, the clank of fist on metal and the soft moist squelch of open wounds and limbless joints. Some of the weight rolled away.

It was the blood of the ruined face which he wore and the same man's torn chain mail ragged against his jugular. Then more bodies. One by wretched one, each unrecognisable lump of voided debris flung aside, Alex freed himself from corpses and crawled out into sunshine.

He spat bloody sputum. He looked, and saw the nightmare, and heaved. The dreadful wailing of the dying and the pain wracked injured spread across the strewn fields to either side. Meadows of blood, of limbs amongst the little wild flowers, a hacked mutilation of bodies filling ditches, now hillocks of humanity.

Thrusting away the broken steel, he searched himself for wounds. He could still not see clearly. Eyelids gummed with blood and pus, head spinning, he sat and breathed through the rolling acid nausea. Whimpering nearby, wails of entreaty, guttural pleas for water, for aid, and for a merciful death. Echoes, the sudden flutter of feathers; ravens and kites smelling slaughter, come to scavenge. England's great battlefields fed the birds of the skies as well as the power hungry, lords of vendetta and misrule, and the great knights shouting of righteousness while satisfying ambition, avarice and insatiable need.

Alex remembered the last words he'd heard before falling. "The Stanleys. Stanley has turned against us. Rally to Richard or we are lost." Lost then. Alexander, younger son of the eighth Baron Mornington, began to climb out of his armour.

The heat dazzled, and he found the first injury. An arrow had pierced his upper arm beneath the paldron, shaft from a mercenary's crossbow and the quarrel imbedded. He searched the entry and began to ease it loose. The wounded muscle screamed below ripped flesh but finally, impatient, he dug his fingers in and wrenched the bolt away and flung it, biting his lip, keeping his silence. His arm bled freely and steamed a little under the sun.

Then he shrugged off the broken harness and chain mail, unbuckling greaves and baldric, finally pulling off hauberk and spurs. He had worn his king's badge. If the Stanleys had brought victory to the Tudor bastard, then showing the white boar meant death. Life was suddenly precious. His armour was too expensive to leave, but what had once been designed to save his life might now condemn it. He left behind all proof of his name and rank and struggled, sweating, to his feet.

He saw his father first. The old man was smiling. Lying flat on his back, he was open-eyed, gazing into the cloudless blue above. His basinet had tumbled off and lay beside him in the wet grass. His scalp remained within it; his smiling head quite open, as an old jug might lose its lid. The brains had oozed a little, grey globules sticky in blood.

Alex, weak legged still, caught his breath and stumbled. He knelt in the trampled mud and closed his father's eyes. A smear of brains stained the edge of his cuff. He leaned forwards again and removed the old man's gauntlets, holding the cold fingers for a moment before taking the ring from his thumb. He had never really known his father, so often away at court or fighting his own family squabbles over property rights and inheritance. Honour thy father, but do not necessarily love him. Alex left him for the ravens. And the looters. It was much the same thing. They were all scavengers.

The household had fought together and Alex recognised other faces close by, family retainers, stall holders and local farmers who had answered the muster and taken up arms for their country and their king. The three Bowyer brothers, best archers in the county, slumped in a heap as if they embraced. At their feet the blacksmith's boy, just ten years old, who had come to distribute arrows from the supply wagons. He still clutched the sheave he'd been delivering, but someone else's arrow now protruded from his eye. Face up, staring at the birds, in his clasp the fine goose fletching quivered a little in the breeze, from his eye the quarrel's metal caught the glitter of the sun. The child had vomited his own teeth.

The fighting had been fierce under Norfolk's banner. Alex trudged the boundaries where the standard had been raised. But no time to search for friends he could no longer help. The dead lay thickest there and his own people were only a small part of the human debris. He turned and hurried on.

The tramp of boots behind him was sudden, heavy and immediately ominous. Neither of the heralds certainly, who would have already made their counts and listed the titles of slain nobility. The able bodied victorious then, come to claim their own dead, to dispatch any of the enemy still groaning, and manage some quick looting before digging the burial pits. Consecrated ground in some nearby church yard for their honoured companions, communal holes for the unnamed enemy; England's own.

Alex crawled under cover. Holes in his hose. Knees bleeding. Everything bleeding. Shrubs, bushes, the scrub of a hot English August. A fine day with the harvest already gathered and stored safe in the barns, while the country waited for news of their king. A fine day for dying.

The ground was boggy, ditches churned by horses' hooves, a farmer's new ploughed soil ruined, daisies gaudy with blood. A young man, little more than a boy, doubled over, face in his own spew, whimpering, too tired for agony. The seepage of his intestines escaped between his grasping fingers. Alex stared a moment, then moved away. The boy would be dead soon enough from the brisk surgeon's knife or the grave diggers shovels, if not before.

Like breezes through the forest, the passing of the looters quietened the last piteous wails, echoes fading like forgotten shadows. A flash of black feathers, the mew of a disturbed kite, and Alex pushed a path beneath the blackberry hedges. He stood on men, crossing over their bodies with the squelch of raw yielding meat. He had not expected to find his brother.

No time then, for John to enjoy his new won title, just a brief moment's inheritance and a bloody death. The new Baron Mornington had been decapitated. Still clutching his sword, the body was sprawled in its proud polished armour. The head, having lost both basinet and casque, seemed confused. Caught on thorns, its loose pretty curls fluttered like little banners. Alex sat down heavily in the mud.

He had barely known his father but he had loved his brother. The hero of two years older, the shoulder for comfort after mother went, advice and example, sweet smiles and whispered promises. A child's trust. No time now for tears, Alex kissed the soft pink cheek and crawled into deeper cover.

The battle had been fought across the fields and into marsh, through ditch and muddy stream, on where the rising land sang golden and the shadowed tree line cut through little valleys, and where the placid country was previously divided only by hedge and hamlet. After days perhaps, a villager would find a head, half rat eaten, squashed amongst his garden cabbages. A body, sliced through, might be found in the soft mud behind some crumbling church wall, or a decomposing corpse face down in a green slimed pool. A child would find a broken arrow to keep as a memory of when his father was slain, a hole made by cannon shot would spoil the line of next year's plough. There would be pieces of armour, lying empty or nursing hacked bloody flesh, continuing to reflect the summer sunshine and the aimless clouds in their bright blue sky.

The noise of the men behind him gone now, French dialect from the bastard Tudor's bastard foreign mercenaries, and the moment for a quick run across from the first manor down the lanes and on to the next town. Not Atherstone where the king's camp was doubtless being torn apart by French soldiers, and Stanley's traitors with their sweaty fingers in the royal linen, but the hamlet of Witherley with no walls to withstand raiders, deserters or the frantic escape of the routed vanquished. Like himself.

He came in as the sun hit the roof tops and sent the thatches steaming. Doors locked, shops closed, people huddled terrified and silent. Furtive noises in the tiny cobbled alleys, running boots, sudden squeals and two men dragging a woman into the shadows, skirts up, first rape and then the knife. In battle scarred countryside the villagers suffered from both sides; excitement of the victors, bitter resentment from those cowed, the profiteering of camp followers, deserters on the run, and every man a looter.

He'd find neither open inn nor generous farmer's wife. Alex kept to the back streets and out again into the fields beyond. He clambered down into the leaf tangled brook and washed the blood from his face and hands. The sun was still hot and dried him quickly. He kept walking, slowly now, and increasingly weary.

For three hours on a hot August morning, he had battled for his life and the rights of his king. One footstep away from a total stranger, the continuous swing of sword, battle hammer and axe, each blow in desperation to kill him before his stroke killed you. And after him, once he fell, another stepped across his heaving back and took his place, and raised his metal against you. The ache of the fight returned now, muscles throbbing, legs shuddering, with no further fear of capture to keep him alert. The wound in his shoulder no longer bled but the pain still stabbed. Alex held that arm up with the other, cradling the elbow across his chest. He wore only what had been beneath his armour and its padding; a linen shirt, plain knitted hose, soft ankle boots. He'd kept his belt and the knife wedged into it, but he had left the sword; his family crest on the hilt too dangerous. His father's ring was tucked tight in his codpiece, gold hot against the moist skin of his groin. The nausea was returning.

Far across the cut stocks of the shorn wheat harvest there was a barn. There he slept with the little whiffle nosed rats scurrying amongst the straw. Smells of cattle, the latest litter of kittens, puppy piss and a tub of stale mutton lard stored for tallow. Curled safe and warm, sore shoulder resting on the softest hay, it occurred to Alex that he was now the new Baron Mornington himself. He was not likely to mention it to anyone until he knew more of what had happened that day. If marked traitor and attainted, no doubt he'd lose not only his title but also his home within the week. It would make little difference now. He'd already lost everything else.

Alex found he was crying. He slept with the tears still wet on his cheeks and his brother's smile hovering through his dreams.

He woke with a pitchfork in his face and a pair of very dark brown eyes peering at him over the handle.

A scruff nosed page boy in a grimy doublet, hose baggy round the knees, hair stuffed incongruously under a man's faded liripipe hood, and a voice not yet pubescent. Brandishing the pitchfork like a spear, shoving so the points seemed menacing, the boy said, "You're trespassing. Who are you?"

Alex managed to heave himself up without groaning. His shoulder hurt like hell. So did his head. He was dizzy, had a knife-sharp headache and felt sick. He mumbled with a careful lack of clarity, "Alex. Um. Gypsy."

"Alicks?" demanded the page boy. "A poacher then?"

Alex nodded faintly. "Um." Admitting to poaching might be almost as dangerous as admitting to the losing side of a war.

The boy sniffed, and seemed perturbed not to find a kerchief. He wiped his nose on the back of his hand and wedged the pitchfork handle under his arm. Most unexpectedly he said, "Well, that's alright then," and sighed.

It occurred to Alex that the boy looked as though he'd been crying. Since he knew he'd been crying himself, it seemed to help. He relaxed and shuffled back a little into the shadows, hiding the blood stains on his shoulder. "I'll go then," he muttered. "And no more poaching, I promise. Not on your master's land anyway."

A slow violet dawn crept through the open barn door and turned to dazzle behind the boy's head, setting him in sudden silhouette. "My? Oh, yes." The boy frowned. "But you'll have to stay here while I call my – master. He'll want to make sure you're – not dangerous."

Alex raised an eyebrow. "Your master's here then, and unscathed? So not away, fighting for his king?"

The boy blushed slightly. "We thought - ." He paused and scowled. "Anyway, that's his business, not yours."

Alex had raised himself slightly, squatting back on his heels, knees bent and poised. He took a deep breath and launched himself immediately. The boy fell back and the pitchfork clattered to the ground. Alex grabbed him and swung him round, one hand trapping both the child's wrists hard against his chest. Alex then made a very interesting discovery.

"Well, brat," he said, "more to the point, who are you?"

CHAPTER THREE

"Tom the page. None of your business. Let me go." Alex politely removed his hand. The situation was too dangerous, he felt too ill and there was no time for appreciating a servant girl's breasts. She glared back at him.

Alex shook his head. "Don't be stupid. You expect me not to know the difference? Who are you really? A laundry maid?" He allowed her to pull away but still kept a firm grip on her wrists. "So you let me go. And then I'll let you go," he said.

She wriggled, trying to twist her hands free. "If you try to – do anything," she hissed, "I'll – I'll kill you."

"Try to do what?" He frowned. "Rape you? Is that what this unconvincing disguise is about?"

She brought her knee up fast. Unhampered by skirts, hopping on one foot, she aimed straight for his groin. Stepping quickly aside, he grabbed her leg, wrenched it higher and toppled her backwards. She fell back on the straw, him heavy on top. She started to squeal. Alex released her wrists and clamped his palm hard over her mouth. She fisted him in one ear and gripped his hair in one desperate handful.

"Little fool," he muttered. "I'm not going to rape you. I wouldn't have the energy if I wanted to." It wasn't the right thing to say but his head hurt. He tried to look stern. Alex had some experience with laundry maids, though they didn't usually struggle this much. He grappled, trying to catch the hand that was tugging at his hair. She brought her knee up again and this time he wasn't prepared.

"Shit." He rolled off her, doubling over. The whole Lancastrian army hadn't hurt him that much. His father's ring felt sharp, disastrously imbedded. Alex turned his back on the girl, extricating himself. She struggled up and kicked from behind. He swung back, grabbing her again. "Keep this up," he said, hearing his own voice shamefully breathless, "and I will hurt you. For God's sake woman, I'm exhausted. I've stolen nothing and I've no desire to touch you. Just let me go."

She had noticed the wound in his upper arm. Exertion had made it bleed again, a weak trickle of scarlet down his sleeve. "You're not a poacher," she accused in a hoarse whisper. "You're one of them." She was reaching for the pitchfork.

Alex sighed. "I can't understand your particular predilection for poachers," he said plaintively. "Have you ever met one? Louts, most of them. Besides, if they get caught, they get hung by the justices. So no, I'm not a poacher, and yes, I'm one of them." He tried a reconciliatory smile. His fate, if caught, might also lead to a hanging. "But I promise I'm harmless. Now can I go?"

She had the pitchfork in his face again. "My father warned me about the soldiers," said the girl. "Thieves and ruffians and murderers, he said. Welsh pirates. French mercenaries."

"Good God, girl, do I sound French?" One point of the pitchfork hovered perilously close to his eye. Alex moved his fingers reluctantly towards his belt, where his knife was wedged out of sight. "Now, before I'm forced to hurt you, for pity's sake, just stand aside and let me go."

She shook her head. Her hood had tipped loose and a good deal of thick brown hair was escaping. "To come back and murder us all in our beds? Certainly not." Alex noticed that some of his own hair was still caught around her fingers. It explained the abrasions on his scalp.

He said, "I've no intention of coming anywhere near the house, and besides, I presume you've someone more fearsome indoors to protect the household, not just one loopy maid servant waving farm implements around?" His groin had stopped throbbing but his head hurt more. He'd had enough. "One more warning, and that's it. Use your brain, if you have one. What good would it do me, to murder you all anyway? I just need to get far away without arousing your lord, whoever he is. Now, move away from the door and give me a few minutes before you raise the alarm. That's all I ask."

"Soldiers are all murderers," the girl said, biting her lip. "They can't help it. That's what they're trained for." And she lunged. Alex knocked her out.

His fist aimed up beneath the pitchfork and clipped her neatly on the jaw. She crumpled with a small sigh. There had been little noise but the dawn was brightening and he expected the imminent arrival of milk maids, farm hands, hounds let out for exercise and all the paraphernalia of a busy manor on a fair fresh new morning. Alex stepped over the girl and reached for the open barn door. A small hand grabbed his ankle from beneath and tugged. He tripped.

The girl grunted. He had fallen heavily on top of her and was now sitting on her chest. Alex shook his head and pushed his knifepoint tight up under her chin, staring down into large brown eyes. They looked startled and distinctly moist. "You," he said, "are an insufferable nuisance."

The girl wheezed, struggling for breath. "Get off."

"Not until you promise to be good," said Alex, pressing his blade a little harder. One tiny bright bubble of blood sprang to its point.

She showed no obvious indication of obeying. Struggling desperately, she kicked both legs, wriggling to free her hands. Alex resisted the temptation to slap her. He grabbed out behind him, reaching out blindly to stop her kicking, then found his hand hard up between her legs. He cursed, and wrenched away. As she began to squeak, he planted one hand flat over her mouth again, and glared down at her. "Girls aren't supposed to wear doublet and hose. There's a good reason for it." Her answer was a wild eyed mumble. "I'll let you speak," Alex said, "if you promise not to scream." She nodded. After a moment's pause, he took his hand from her face and shrugged. "Who the devil are you anyway?"

He was still sitting on her chest. She gulped for breath. "I told you. I'm the laundry maid. I work in the - ."

"Presumably the laundries," he suggested. "What I meant was, what's your name?"

She scowled. "I don't give my name to poachers. Or dirty common soldiers. Or all and sundry."

Alex raised an eyebrow. "First wash girl I ever met who didn't. I don't believe you're a scullion at all. You're probably not even a servant. I'd say you're the local farmer's daughter. Does your father know you run around in your brother's clothes?"

She managed a deep breath. "I don't have a brother."

Since this seemed the matter of least relevance, Alex sighed and began to climb off his captive and back onto his feet. "Alright. No doubt it's frightening enough, being a girl, with an army running loose through the paddocks. But whoever I am, hopefully I've reassured you I don't intend any harm. So, are you prepared, whoever you are, to let me go without squealing and waking the neighbours?"

"Intend no harm?" demanded the girl with indignation, now struggling to sit up. "After you've knocked me down and squashed me and made my neck bleed. I could be dead."

Alex closed his mouth on the automatic response. He had heard footsteps.

Boots on cobbles, then voices. "Where the devil is she? Find the damned nurse maid." Roaring; "Kate." More scuffles, mutterings, hurried feet.

A softer voice, "My lord, I beg you to be more circumspect. Anyone could be around. Today, of all days, my lord."

Alex looked at the girl. "Nurse maid?" he suggested.

She was hopping from one foot to the other, one finger to her lips. "Please," she whispered, "keep quiet. Don't tell them I'm here."

Having been about to say the same to her, he was suddenly amused. "Me? Rescue you?"

He turned towards the way out but the girl had grabbed his arm and was pulling him back into the barn. "Hush. I won't tell if – you don't." The big brown eyes were huge again.

The doors swung fully open and a wide shouldered man in a

16

leather apron peered in. "Sara? Miss Kate?" The door rattled, sunshine burst in, a horse neighed from a distance.

"The stables. She'll be in the stables."

The barn doors were pulled shut and closed with a thud. The sudden depth of shadows within increased into green echoes. The girl relaxed, slumping down in the straw. Alex stared down at her with bemused sympathy, fury lessening.

"So now I'll never get away," he said. "Not until the household calms down at any rate. So you're the nursemaid? You look too young." He thought for a moment, and smiled. "Or are you Miss Kate?"

Her expression was more frightened than angry. "The – the nurse maid. I'm – Sara. But there're such tales about what the soldiers did when the French marched through." She tried to hitch up her hose, which were wrinkling even more under the knees. "They say terrible things happened. Mercenaries you know, and the soldiers decimating the fields and livestock, and threatening anyone who got in the way. We heard such stories. So when we found out who won yesterday, we were terrified. I knew I had to be prepared. Pretending to be a boy seemed safest, but when father heard what I wanted to do – "

"Father?"

"He – he works in the household too." Sara sniffed and still couldn't find a kerchief. "He's the Steward," she decided. "So I have to behave. But what's more important? Being a lady, or being alive?"

"I imagine," said Alex, "dressing like that might save you from rape, but hardly keep you alive. Especially running around being a damned nuisance, which is what you've been doing. French gallows fodder out for rape and pillage would have spitted you on the instant. The most sensible thing you could have done was hide indoors."

She frowned. "Not all girls are such miserable cowards," she declared. "I came out to see if everything was safe, and heard you snoring. You could have been anyone. I had to protect the family."

Alex raised one eyebrow. He hadn't known he snored so loudly. "Protect your own mistress perhaps," he said. "But not many nursemaids take it on themselves to protect a manor full of able

17

bodied servants. Since I gather none of them were off fighting – which they should have been."

"Everyone thought the king was bound to win without any extra help," the girl insisted. "And he should have. What happened anyway? How could he have lost?"

The misery of the battle hung at the back of his mind, dark clouds of confusion and horror, damp vapour like an imminent storm. He had been trying not to think of it. "I don't know," he said, immediately bleak. "You may know more about it than I do. Was the king taken prisoner? Or did he get away?"

He knew the answer already. Richard had been a fighting king. He would have fought to the death.

Sara sniffed again, blinking from the shadows. "We only got rumours. Then we locked the doors and wouldn't let anyone else in. But they say he's dead. The king's dead."

Alex nodded. "Then I certainly need to get away. Richmond's army was made up with debris from French gaols, criminals, mercenaries and Welsh bandits. And the fucking Stanleys of course."

The girl flinched. "What would they do?" she whispered. "If they caught you? Rip you limb from limb?"

Alex smiled faintly. "Something like that."

"Well," she decided, lowering her eyes, "you'd better go. I'm - sorry I delayed you."

He was already at the doorway. The two wide planked doors were now firmly closed. Alex heaved, then kicked. "Shit."

The girl flinched again. "Push harder. There's no noise outside. It's quite safe. Everyone's off looking for me. That is – for Miss Katherine of course."

"Push harder?" Alex glared at her over his shoulder. "Who do you think I am? Fucking Hercules? They've been braced from the outside." He turned, staring up and around, looking for a window, skylight or side door. There was nothing. He stood over the girl. "Is there some hidden way out? Come on, use your sense. What happens now?"

"Happens?" The girl shook her head. The liripipe hood dislodged further. "How should I know? I don't spend my life exploring the secret entrances of barns. You'll have to stay here until someone

18

opens the doors again. Then you can run away. It's all very well for you. It's me who'll get into trouble."

Alex itched to hit her. "Serves you right for being irritating and stupid. And pull your hose up, or they'll end up around your ankles, and then I will jump on you."

"You wouldn't dare," she hissed under her breath.

"Well, there's a fine lack of logic." Alex slumped down beside her on the straw and lay back with a sigh. "I'm surprised anybody still employs you. But you're right about one thing. I'll have to wait here until someone unbars the doors and then make a run for it. The only consolation is knowing you'll get beaten."

The girl gazed at him sorrowfully. "I will too. Tell me about the battle."

A searing memory of his brother's face, perplexed and bleeding, hanging from a thorn bush, silenced Alex at once. "No," he said.

"Was it horrible?"

Alex thought of several sarcastic answers but said only, "Yes. It was horrible."

The girl nodded. "You're wounded too. I think I made it bleed again. And you smell awful."

Alex didn't doubt it. "I was buried under bodies. Sudden death in battle, bodies tend to – well, never mind. You don't smell too good yourself. Whoever owned that doublet before you stole it, dribbled his soup."

The barn was stuffy, the straw scratched. Recent exertion had made them both sweat. "Little Tom. I've never watched him eat soup. And I didn't steal anything. What is it that bodies do in battle that smells so bad, then?"

Alex stared at her with dislike. He had a strong desire to upset her, which he no longer resisted. "I suppose it doesn't occur to you that you've probably caused my imminent death? My arrest at the very least. And bodies, to whet your lurid imagination, usually void their bowels during a violent death. There's more shit on a battlefield than blood, and plenty of guts and brains and heads rolling around as well. Go for a quick walk up the lanes since you're interested, and have a nice long look. Most will have been cleared away by now but there'll still be a satisfying mess to gape at. And if I end up in the Tower and lose my head because of your stupidity, I shall curse you with my dying breath."

"Well, that wouldn't surprise me," glared the girl. "You curse all the time anyway. Your language is appalling. And if anyone's stupid, it's you. Common soldiers don't get put in the Tower even when it's treason, and don't have their heads chopped off. That's only for lords."

"On which you're no doubt an expert."

She turned her back. "My imagination may be – lurid – but at least I have one. You're just a – man! You can't even appreciate the difficulty I was in. You try getting raped one day."

"Hopefully not." Alex scowled at the back of her head, reluctantly staggered to his feet and stretched. His shoulders and head ached dreadfully and he was beginning to wonder if he had some internal injury as yet unrealised. "Listen. If you want rid of me, there's just one thing to do. You'll have to bang on the door and shout. When they come to let you out, I'll get away. I assume the longer you keep hidden, the worse it'll be for you anyway. You might as well get it over with."

The girl looked up at him in silence for a few moments. She had lost her hood entirely, and her hair was thick brown, darker in the lightless barn shadows. Her eyes looked bruised. She nodded slowly. "If you promise not to kill anyone on your way out."

"The only person I'm tempted to kill is you," said Alex with a deep sigh. "Rid yourself of the conviction that every man is out to deflower you and murder your entire household. Just get some idiot to open these damned doors, and I'll run. I promise not to kill a soul. I haven't even got a sword."

"You've got a knife."

He shrugged. "Which I need, so don't bother asking for it. I may have to spend some time on the run, and no doubt I'll end up becoming a poacher after all. Just stop talking nonsense, and go and bang on that door."

He reached out one hand towards her and she took it, allowing him to hoist her up. She made a quick attempt to readjust her clothing, sniffed, gave up, and approached the doorway. "Will there be other soldiers around, do you think?" she asked tentatively. "I mean – from the – Tudor side?"

"I doubt it." Alex shook his head. "That bastard Richmond'll be busy handing out rewards. None of his people need be running wild, and they've looted their fill already. No, you're safe enough. You can go and climb back into your skirts."

"Well," she said, timid again, "thank you I suppose. I mean, you did hurt me and my chin's really sore where you hit me. There'll be a horrid bruise. But I did attack you first. So I wish you – good luck. I hope you get away. I really do."

He was faintly surprised. "So do I. The alternative isn't pleasant. But I've friends I can aim for. Now – Sara, or whatever your name is – "

"Sara Whitstable."

He suddenly took her very small fingers in his own, and briefly kissed her knuckles. "Goodbye then Sara Whitstable. I hope they don't beat you too hard, or turn you out on the streets."

She stared in amazement. "Oh. Yes. Good luck then – Alicks." Then she turned away, took a deep breath, straightened her shoulders and started to thump both fists against the doors, calling to be released.

Alex grinned, clutched his knife, flattened himself back against the wall, and stood poised to run for his life.

CHAPTER FOUR

The September sun was already climbing close to midday as Alex
entered London, the Cripplegate a seething busyness of shove
and slam. A great gloom still lay over the land, fear and suspicion rife.
News of the battle had arrived spasmodically and even now, with the
new king installed at Westminster Palace, rumour still rebounded
louder than fact. The first weeks of consternation, astonishment and
rabid terror had subsided into sullen disappointment. Farmers and
merchants glowered and muttered as they crossed from Moorfields
into the city. A covered litter was edging under Cripplegate's low
arch. The drover gazed up, nervous for the height of his leathers as
the sheep pushed through behind, the drover cursing, herding the
beasts on towards Smithfield. The litter was piled with stinking hides
and unwashed fleeces. Alex moved his foot quickly and the metal edge
of the wheel just missed his boot. He held his breath and hurried
between the skinny scurrying sheep; wool steaming, rain drops
drying under a pale sunshine.

London was the last place he'd wanted to come, but Burton House
seemed his last chance. Alex strode down Muggle Street.

The Steward glared down from the high step beyond the
gatehouse. "Be off with you, lout, or get around to the kitchens

through the stables. No begging at the main entrance. Be off, or I shall call the Watch."

"Don't be a bloody fool, Jenkins," scowled Alex. "It's me."

Jenkins stared. "My lord – is it really you? Forgive me, but the household is in chaos, and – but come in, come in my lord. I shall inform the earl."

"He's alive then?" Alex stepped quickly inside.

The Steward lowered his voice. "The new young earl is thankfully alive, my lord. But Lord Edward was taken at Bosworth, falling at Norfolk's right hand." He lowered his voice even further, and Alex strained to hear him. "Now Sir Merevale has been arrested, and kept at the Tower."

So he had come a long way, tramping across half of England for three weeks, hiding, searching out allies, accepting repeated rejection and disappointments, stealing clothes, poaching, going hungry and finally arriving utterly weary, and all for nothing since the danger here was the greater, yet his friends still could not receive him. Briefly, he spoke with the new earl. Full twenty years younger than himself, the child was restless and frightened.

Alex stood, his back to the huge empty hearth where the summer's dried flowers had turned to little more than dust, dead and colourless petals floating from their jug. The child sat, fidgeting with his doublet lacings and smoothing his fingers down the ridged pink silk of his hose. Alex looked dubiously down at the boy who had been his own father's Godchild.

"Everyone's so scared. And you look - "

"I look terrible," said Alex. "I know. I've been through ditches and thorn bushes and slept under trees, with pigs waking me up poking for acorns in my ears. Three weeks ducking and hiding. I could hardly go home for a change of decent clothes, could I? I stole a shirt hung out to dry on a hedge, but it didn't fit. I swapped with a swineherd I met while poaching."

The very young earl blinked. "It sounds awfully exciting."

"Damned uncomfortable," Alex shook his head. "And every friend I went to for a good night's rest at the very least, has been attainted or arrested, and the others are rallying out in the north and east, trying to organise rebellions. Perhaps that's where I'd better aim for next."

"Oh, hush," the child begged. "You never know who might be listening."

"What, even the servants?" Alex demanded. "Don't you even trust them now? Well, your lordship, if that's the case, you'd better throw me out and be done with it."

The boy blushed. "Please don't call me that. I hate it. When Nurse Cissy calls me that I throw pillows at her. Besides, I suppose you came to see Uncle Merevale, not me."

"Damned lot of good it's done me," Alex sighed, "since I hear he's languishing in the Tower. But you should be proud of your title, Stephen, and proud of the father who handed it on to you. Jenkins says he fell at Norfolk's right hand. That makes him a hero."

The boy squirmed, staring down at the hole he had just made in his hose. "It makes him a traitor. They nearly attainted him. My mother went to the king herself to beg for our estates on my behalf. It's – it's – shameful."

"It's the new bastard king that's shameful," said Alex briskly. "And to think of dating his reign from the day before the battle, so he can accuse every man of treachery who was simply loyal to his anointed monarch, and stood up to fight for his king and country - that's bastard cruelty. And the cowards who are letting him do it - there's the shame."

"I – I don't want to seem like a coward," murmured the new Earl of Burton, staring uncomfortably at his visitor's torn and stained shirt. "At least you could take some of Uncle Merevale's clothes."

"Very courageous of you Stephen. But it wouldn't serve. I'm safer dressing like a yokel until I'm sure of my own position."

The boy nodded. "Henry Tudor, I mean the new king, he's at Westminster. They say he watches everything. He doesn't trust anyone. So I don't trust anyone either. That's what my tutor says anyway, not that it stops him beating me, even now I'm an earl."

"Of course." Alex paused, thinking a moment. "If you really want to prove your courage, you could put me up here for a few days. I'd stay in hiding of course, and pretend to be the boot boy if you like."

Stephen blushed, fidgeting again. "But the servants would know. It wouldn't be safe."

"Alright. Hire me as a servant then." A wry grin. "Employ me. Forget the wages, just give me a bed and food. I'll scrub your floors."

"Don't be silly," said the small Earl of Burton. "I can't employ Mother's own cousin in the sculleries. Anyway, I don't suppose you know how to scrub floors. I wouldn't. And the servants would still guess. Besides, mother wouldn't like it."

But it had given Alex an idea. "So they've hauled Merevale off to the Tower," he said. "But what about your grandfather? And what about your uncle Daniel?"

Stephen shook his head and stared at his lap. "Maman's father was killed in the battle, next to Papa," he whispered. "Uncle Daniel's been attainted. He's in the Tower too."

"Shit," muttered Alex. "I need to speak to your mother."

Stephen looked up, frowning. "She won't want to talk to you."

"She'll have to," said Alex.

The Dowager Countess of Burton declared she was not at home, but Alex marched into the small solar with Stephen at his heels, and glared at the woman sitting bleak eyed, her curled paper work abandoned on her velvet lap. She looked up with a myopic glare. "It's not my fault, Maman," said Stephen quickly. "He insisted."

"Hello Lizzie," said Alex. "Now for the Lord's sake, don't start squealing. I need information, and I need help."

"I don't ever squeal, Alex," said the woman coldly, "which you should know perfectly well, under the circumstances. Information, I'm prepared to give I suppose. But help is out of the question. Even your befuddled brain should see I'm not in a position to offer help to anyone, even myself."

"Not what I heard," said Alex. "You pleaded with the bastard Tudor and got little Stephen his title back."

The countess nodded. "Which had to be done, however unpleasant. That man's little more than a commoner, after all. But with my husband slaughtered on the battlefield and both my brothers in the Tower, I was forced to do something for my son, even though it hurt my pride. As for my poor brothers, I did what I could for

Merevale too, but was told very curtly to be satisfied with one act of merciful leniency, and not to try his majesty's patience with begging for another. His majesty indeed. Alex, I could have spat in the man's face."

Alex grinned. "Well, at least you tried to help. Good for you, Lizzie."

"As for information," the Lady Elizabeth shook her muslin widow's cap, "terrible stories still spread through the streets, and we can never be sure what is true. But my dearest husband was killed defending Norfolk from that wicked de Chandee and I believe my dear father died there at his side. I was permitted to bury them both with decency, at my own expense of course. Just think Alex! I was kindly permitted to bury my own husband and father. As if it was a noble favour, grace of his majesty."

It was a small bright solar on the upper floor, and a little casement window looked out over the back stables and the squashed roof tops of Cripplegate's tenements beyond. Alex stared at the spotless sky and the sudden flash of the martins. He said, "It's a bad world sometimes, Lizzie. And such a fine summer! I keep expecting the sky to darken, as if God might at least acknowledge this damnable disaster, or proclaim some fitting punishment and recompense. He sends a pestilence soon enough, with far less need for threats and warnings than we have now."

"But it's a pestilence we do have, Alex," said the countess, looking up as though startled. "Haven't you heard? This is something quite new, which the medicks have never encountered before. They say those foul foreign mercenaries brought it with them from France. The sweating sickness, they call it, but it attacks both sides, Tudor's traitors and our own loyal men alike. Folk have been known to drop dead suddenly in the streets. The Lord Mayor, dear man, died of it a week back. They elected a new mayor at once, but he is sickening now they say, and expected to die within the day."

Stephen tugged at the ragged hem of Alex's shirt. "You might be carrying it too Alex. Did any of the soldiers breathe on you?" He backed off slightly, avoiding possible air borne vapours.

"Breathe on me? During hand to hand battle?" Alex turned back in disgust to the countess. "What the devil do you teach the boy, Lizzie? And what about Danny? He's in the Tower too then?"

The Lady Elizabeth nodded. "Indeed. Arrested and attainded, so my poor father's title has been lost entirely. I don't believe Daniel played any very large part in the battle to be honest, and we expect him to be pardoned and released sometime soon. But he won't get the title back and where will he go? Poor Mary is beside herself."

Alex frowned. "And what more do you know of Merevale?"

Elizabeth sighed. "He was in the cavalry charge, riding behind the king himself. He was taken captive as the king lay murdered. Mel won't be pardoned so easily."

"I heard about the charge," said Alex. "I spent a few days with Lovel in sanctuary over in Colchester. I got some of the news there, but Lovel's utterly distraught you know. He can't believe Richard is truly dead, and the whole country come to such dread and disaster. And every story you hear contradicts another."

"Rumour is always more salacious than truth, so far more popular," nodded the countess, "and there's still such confusion. Who knows what happened up there in the miserable north. You were there, for goodness sake Alex. You fought at the king's side. If you don't know what happened, how can you expect anyone else to understand?"

"I fought at my father's side, and never saw the king," said Alex, sitting down suddenly. "You can't imagine it, Lizzie. The howling and slashing, the black whiz of the arrows so thick they hide the sky. The hideous injuries and the pain. With seven thousand or more on either side, we ranged over at least two miles of Leicestershire's damned muddy fields and marshes, slaughtering each other in any way we could. Nothing made sense. I've a bandaged arm though I wasn't badly hurt, but I was knocked senseless and woke up buried under half a dozen dead bodies. The battle was over and me still too weak to know what was going on. I didn't even know which side had won until I heard the damned grave diggers speaking French."

Elizabeth blew her nose into her kerchief and fiddled with the little square of paper curls in her lap. "You didn't see – dear Edward?"

"No." Alex shook his head. "And you wouldn't want to know about it if I did. I'm glad his body was brought back at least, for a decent burial." He paused, then said, "Did you hear what happened to John, and my father? They were both killed, you see, but I was on the run and never claimed their bodies."

Elizabeth reached out and patted his hand. "Your uncle Godfrey did. They're both buried with honour at the parish church in Mornington. But your father was prominent in the king's cause. He's likely to be posthumously attainted, Alex dear. You'll have no title, you know. And the manor, well, it'll be taken by the crown I suppose, and all your lands too."

"I expect it." Three weeks hiding, searching out friends, some information at least he'd collected, though always more rumour than fact. He was presumably nameless and homeless, and without a penny unless he begged the new king for a pardon and a conciliatory pension. Which he had no intention of doing. "Listen Lizzie. I know I can't stay here. You wouldn't want me, it'd be most improper under the circumstances – especially after – well, never mind about that now. And you have to stay in Tudor's good graces for Stephen's sake. But I need to go somewhere for a few days. Damn it, I've hardly slept or eaten for a month. What about Mary?"

"Daniel's wife? But she loathes you, Alex." The countess dropped her paperwork in alarm. She gazed at it in dislike and left it crumpled where it lay. "Of course, she loathed Merevale most, which is why my brother came here to live. But she always blamed you for leading Merevale astray. Which you did, Alex. And anyway, daily she expects to be flung from the house."

Alex retrieved the countess's paper embroidery for her, though most of the curls were now detached and it hardly looked worth saving. "If she's scared, she's vulnerable," he said. "I can use that. Besides, she'll need someone she believes can protect her. Who better than her husband's cousin?"

"That's very manipulative of you Alex," said the Lady Elizabeth. "Though I don't believe Mary's ever vulnerable. Besides, if you insist on looking like a yard rakyer, you can hardly protect anyone."

"Now, I imagine a rakyer is just the sort of person who could protect his women folk," said Alex, "not that I've ever had the pleasure of acquaintance with one. But with the possibility of a warrant out for my arrest, I'm hardly likely to go flouncing around in damasks and velvets just yet. And I need a few days to rest, before deciding what to do next. Getting past these wretched rumours and finding out a scrap of truth would help."

"You could climb into the Tower dungeons," suggested Stephen suddenly from behind the chair, "and rescue Uncle Merevale. You could visit the lions in the Tower menagerie at the same time. I've always wanted to see the lions. Then you could climb up a wall and get Uncle Mel out."

Alex had forgotten he was there. He smiled faintly. "I'll save that for next week," he said. "In the meantime, I think I'll visit Mary. Not unlike a lioness, come to think of it."

CHAPTER FIVE

From Muggle Street directly south, Alex took the short cuts through the alleys to Ludgate and the quickest way back out of the city.

A woman was crouched in the puddles of piss, a handful of bean pods laid on a leaf at her feet. Someone threw her a farthing, but did not buy her beans. They were mouldy and withered; had been collected perhaps from the gutters beside Neville's Inn's rubbish heap before the raykers came.

A few half naked children were tormenting a mangy dog, kicking it down Noble Street, bums out of their lacings and no braies or hose beneath. Alex dodged. He'd have sworn at them once. Now he was simply glad he'd recently eaten, when it was clear they had not. The Dowager Countess of Burton had given him manchet and pickled eggs for a quick supper before he left, and it had tasted like a feast.

Two men pushed a barrow piled with turnips, leeks and cabbages, its front wheels squelching through ox dung down the unpaved lane. They were eagerly watched from several doorways. Turnips rolled easily, anything could tumble from a rumbling cart. Alex turned right into Pissing Alley. Outside St. Paul's the stink swelled in the warm afternoon sunshine. A child stood on one corner, singing for her supper. Her song faded, a tremulous squeak within the tumult. Two men had picked a fight, one with his fingers in the other's eyes, both cursing and spitting. A woman threw a bucket of water over them. Traders were screaming their wares, piled trays hanging from their necks, one selling wooden clogs, another with tinder boxes, a third offering ribbons bright under the sun. A goat was nosing the spilt offal in the gutters. A cat darted in to steal the knotted guts from beneath its hooves, then ran off, flabby intestines flying out behind.

The open square around St. Paul's steamed with a multitude of lawyers gathered for late business, shouting for clients and shouting at their clients, representatives of the Guilds arguing the precedence of law, solicitors clutching their gowns in the sudden wind, a pair of ecclesiastical secretaries in furious debate, three monks heading for the cloister library and kicking at a woman in their path, huddled there and sobbing into her shawl.

The steeple shadow was lengthening across the cobbles, the long autumn day announcing its eve. Alex cut through the Cathedral; it wasn't raining but there was still a long way down to The Strand and it was convenient to avoid the long walk around the boundaries. Two bodies were slumped drunk inside the wide porch. Alex stepped over them. One, a child of about eight, looked up bleary, hiccupped and vomited over his father's outstretched hand. Within the great shadowed church, other children were playing in the long empty aisles between the pillars, one tap-tapping at a hoop, hopping and wobbling up towards the pulpit. The elderly priest's muttered sermon sounded plaintive. A small congregation had gathered for evening vespers and were grouped below the pulpit, straining to hear what little they could, though two women had become distracted by some argument and one man left to see what the itinerant traders were selling beneath the statue of Our Lady. The priest moved on to the Latin litany and most of the congregation yawned and wandered off, the men's hats tucked beneath their arms. The two women who had been arguing about the merits of the Italian silks on display in the Budge Row draper's, noticed their men departing, clamped their hands to their butterfly headdresses, gauze flying, and hurried to catch them up. The priest sighed and fumbled for his rosary.

The East Minster; St. Paul's vast vaulted height was chilly even on warm afternoons and someone had lit a small fire of twigs by a pillar. A couple of vagrants held their hands to the little blaze and the smoke puffed up in a sooty billow. Alex suddenly recognised someone he knew. Hurrying, turning quickly across the nave to obscure himself within the rising smoke, Alex tripped over a piglet. It was getting dark but a thousand tall candles soared wavering lights. The shadows fluttered like the women's veils, winged devils watching from behind the pillars, the great death and devil murals obscured in the haze. The sun was low now in the west and the rose window at the eastern end slunk into a sullen gloom. Alex pushed the mighty doors further open and stepped outside, hurried across the pavings and between the portico pillars, bumping into a woman pissing on the bottom step.

It was far lighter outside and the air fresher, though London's smoke still hazed the thatches and drifted in dark and dirty tributaries towards the clouds. Alex strode a little faster through Ludgate and down towards the Fleet.

Once outside the city walls, the noise lessened at once. A collier's barge was sweeping down the Fleet towards the Thames, the wherryman heaving, bringing a steady slurp of excrement up from the shallow depths. The smell of coal made Alex's nose itch, but the stink of shit was greater. The Fleet was more shit than water.

With immediate relief, Alex headed down The Strand. Palaces, gardens, bird song from the trees and suddenly a glorious peace. He was walking into the sunset. The Earl of Sheffield's mansion had once belonged to a bishop, before becoming an Archbishop had inclined the cleric towards something grander. Now it was due to belong to someone else again. Alex turned towards the stables at the back. The setting sun played crimson stripes down the tall chimney pots and turned all the windows gold. He entered the house through the bakery and kitchens, sending the under-cook into a flurry.

He marched on through with the turn-spit, three kitchen boys and the apothecary running and shouting behind. It served to produce the mistress on the spot, and the Lady Mary appeared in a quaking terror from the small solar.

Knowing how much she had always disliked him, and how disreputable he was now looking, Alex expected a tirade and a demand for the ostlers to march him off the property. He had not expected the lady to clasp him around the neck and dissolve into pitiful tears on his very grubby shoulder. He had an idea she was using his collar for a kerchief. Well, no doubt it had already been used for worse in its past. Alex smiled. "Ah," he said. "You might be interested in what I have to say after all."

"Dearest Alexander," she sobbed, voice muffled.

"Damn it, that's going too far," he said, extricating himself. "It's simpler when you admit to disliking me."

"But you came, just when I was so desperate," sniffed the lady. "I prayed, you know Alex. I've been on my knees in the chapel this hour past. And then you arrive, just when I'd given up hope. I was sure I could never manage alone." She stood back and gazed at him, face tear stained. "You have come to help, haven't you Alex?"

Alex nodded. Without being precise as to whom he intended helping, it was, after all, true enough. "Eviction?" he frowned. "Yes, they'd want you out pretty smart, I suppose. Where's the title going, do you know?"

The newly disentitled Countess of Sheffield collapsed into a chair. "Some aged brute who made up part of Richmond's court in exile," she said. "A man I've never met. A – commoner."

"Well, evidently not anymore," said Alex briskly. "But since I imagine you've been thoroughly involved with your own problems, you may not have heard about me. I can't just openly move in and take charge, you know."

Mary's perfect chin trembled. "I've thought only of – dear Daniel, these weeks gone," she whispered.

"Well, thinking of dear Daniel," Alex said, "no doubt you've realised he's likely to be pardoned sometime soon. He may not get any of his estates back, but he'll be given some position if he swears loyalty, and a pension to go with it perhaps." The Lady Mary looked as though she was about to cry again. Alex said, "Dammit Mary, your grandfather was a well-known Lancastrian sympathiser. Use your influence. Have you tried to see the new king?"

"Since my poor Grandpapa was slaughtered at Tewkesbury fighting against King Edward, his influence certainly never did me any good at the time," she said at once. "Now – well, I've been eight years married into a good Yorkist family. And yes, I've begged an audience with the new king. As yet his majesty has chosen to ignore me."

Alex thought if she fluttered her extraordinarily long eyelashes at any man, blinked the huge blue eyes and trembled the perfect chin beneath the perfect mouth, she would get her way instantly and without hesitation. He simply said, "Keep trying. In the meantime, where do you intend going once you leave here?"

Mary clasped her hands meekly in her lap. "To dear Elizabeth. Young Stephen is the new earl, but it's his mother still makes the decisions of course."

Alex nodded. "Actually, I've just come from there. Not that they let me stay. In fact, Lizzie didn't even admit she'd agreed to take you in. Too scared I'd demand the same, I suppose."

Mary wiped her bright blue eyes with her kerchief. "That's hardly surprising under the circumstances. But you're welcome to stay here Alex. Oh yes, I'm well aware there's probably a warrant out for your arrest. But as long as you stay in disguise, you could be most helpful. Wretched Thompson the butler went and died of this horrid sweating sickness the troops brought with them, and Daniel's secretary went off to fight at Bosworth and got killed. His silly squire too. The cook was French so I had to dismiss him, and there's barely a soul left to help me pack up. Most of them have run away and I couldn't pay them anyway. There's boxes everywhere and I cannot remember where anything is anymore. And what shall I take? Elizabeth hasn't space for all the furniture, but I hate the thought of leaving it to the thief who's stealing our title. And I've to be out in less than a week." She paused, frowning slightly. "You can't come with me of course, so after that you'll have to go and find someone else to take pity on you."

"After that," said Alex, not overly keen on the reference to pity, "I can manage my own affairs."

The kitchens were less than half manned, the long benches unscrubbed and the irons and trivets left dirty and discarded beside the hearth. Two cauldrons hung over the low fire but the roasting spits had already been dismantled. The under-cook remained, sweating over the pots. A desultory turn-spit sat at the cook's feet beside the grate and the kitchen boys slumped, elbows on the big table. The apothecary was counting the remaining nutmegs. An insistent smell of stale cabbage water, soot and mutton tallow soap suds, hung from the beams like old cobwebs.

Every face glared as Alex stomped in. He was unused to kitchens, or to ordering his own supper, but since he'd lately been more in the habit of eating nothing at all or finding roots in the forests, he had no objection to making himself at home in a kitchen, and would have cooked his own food himself had he been ordered to do so. Instead, the cook slopped some pottage into a bowl, first wiped out with a corner of a damp apron, and set it for him. Alex sat at the kitchen table, something he had never been required to do in his life. "Right," he said between spoonfuls, "might as well get to the point. Presumably you've gathered I used to be an acquaintance of the earl, - but things change. In times of war – well, there's a new king and we all know what that means. So – you're shorthanded and the lady of the house is moving out." He grinned, putting his spoon down with satisfaction. "So I'm – Alex. The new pot-boy."

The apothecary looked sour. "And may I enquire, young man, as to whether we treat you as one of us? Or as a gentleman of respect? To work with someone without knowing how to give or take orders, might prove an inconvenience."

"I've no objection to a bit of respect," smiled Alex. "But you can give your orders, for what they're worth. I'll mostly be helping the lady organise her departure. But anyone comes calling, I'm the pot boy, and I'll do the work of one." He thought for a moment. "Not that I've the slightest idea what a pot boy's expected to do."

The elderly turn-spit sat hunched beside the coals. With his spit taken down, he seemed particularly despondent, as if the eradication of his duties diminished him. One long finger, indelibly blistered, extricated itself from his nose and pointed at Alex. "Better go find yerself a bed, then," he said, lifting his chin up a little from his knees. "Wot with the staff mostly dead or run off, we's beds aplenty."

"Best avoid the pallets on the top floor under the roof struts," advised one of the kitchen boys. "Damp they are, and them big chambers is full of rats."

"The lesser menials," the apothecary informed everyone and no one in particular, "should by rights take what slumber they may here in the kitchens. Straw pallets beneath the benches, until such time as promotion leads directly to the stairs above."

The turn-spit grunted. "We did. Afore, we did, that is. No need no more."

"Then I'll be off to find a decent room for myself," said Alex, getting up. "And see you all tomorrow."

Safer to keep to the servants' quarters rather than sleeping in the main wing, at least the lack of staff permitted Alex a tiny chamber to himself, directly below the apothecary's larger chamber above, with a palliasse of acceptable proportions. The filling was old wool, accumulated into damp lumps. After forest undergrowth, soggy with worms and burrowing things and gritty with stone and twig, the lumpy mattress felt soft as duckling down and utterly tantalising. Alex slept the night through and couldn't care less whether he snored or not. If his night-time grunting floated up to disturb the apothecary's slumbers, then Alex was not in the slightest bothered.

The waking hours also passed quickly. Packing up the house and organising the eviction seemed easy work inspite of the remaining injury to his shoulder, but Alex had his mind on other things entirely.

Two days later the turn-spit died. Alex only discovered his name when he fell. "Quick. See to old Ben." Ben had been humping the loaded chests out to the cart, and had complained of a headache. A fine excuse, the cook had said.

Alex packed the chest he'd been carrying onto the wagon, and turned back to see what was happening. The turn-spit lay askew in the yard, twitching, trying to hug himself as if frozen with cold, but the fever had already broken into the glisten of fiery sweat across his face.

"Don't touch the man," yelled the apothecary.

"The pestilence," squealed a laundry maid, and ran.

It started to rain. The trees were half stained gold, the rich colours of spices and mustards, autumn leaves turning dry as vellum. Down by the stables where the two sumpter horses, heads down, waited to be harnessed to the cart, the beeches were already hazy in metallic rose and the bent willow fluttered in pure Seville orange. The rain pattered on the cobbles and slurped into the holes between damaged pavings. It rained on Ben, who lay forlorn under the clouds, trying the stop his shivering, trying to struggle to his knees.

Alex knelt beside him, putting one arm beneath his scrawny shoulders, raising him. The man whimpered. "Hush, I'll get you to your bed," Alex said. "Can you walk?"

Half carried, Ben was taken to his pallet behind the steps from the brewery cellars. The turn-spit was sweating so readily that Alex felt both his hands slimy and wet, and wiped them on the soiled woollen blanket. He sat on the edge of the mattress and held a cup of watered ale for the old man to drink. Most of it ran from his mouth in spittle. Alex went back to the kitchens. Everyone had stopped work. "Same as what happened to the butler," whispered the cook. "One day Thompson was right as cockerels in the pit, next he was gone. Sweating like belly o' pork in the pan, and covered in nasty spots, he was."

Alex sighed. "Do you intend leaving the poor bastard there to suffer alone then? Dammit, he's not my friend. You do something about it."

The cook shook his head. "I won't go near him. And he's not my friend neither."

Alex turned to the apothecary. "Your job, I assume."

"There is neither draught nor potion can do anything against the sweating sickness," Reginald Psalter said, "for that's what it is, I fear. And the treatment of those incurables is not my interest nor my duty, unless the afflicted was one of their lordships."

Alex finished loading the wagon alone and hitched up the horses. The hired wagoner was late, so Alex took a deep breath and returned to the small lightless hole over the cellars at the back of the kitchens.

It was immediately hot. The old man's sweating seemed to have drained the air, filling the tiny space with a bilious stench of dying flesh. Alex brought a candle stub from beside the brewery vats, lit it and held it up. Ben screwed shut his eyes, turning away from the small flame. Alex sat again beside him on the sagging mattress. The wool and straw were imbued with the sweat and the smell. In the candle light, Alex saw the disfigurement across the man's face and body. He seemed swollen and an inflamed rash of wide black spots was eating his skin. There was bloody pus at his lips. He still shivered as the sweat dripped and slid across him, turning the blanket that he clutched to a darkened rag.

Alex sighed. He had watched men die in battle. Battle was worse. He had stood face to face with men as young and desperate as himself, and hacked, over and over, until his sword struck through basinet and brigandine, dividing a man's life in two bloody halves down skull, chest and pelvis. Disease was not as hideous as battle.

But it was more mysterious. Alex had no idea what to do for the man. He brought him ale, but Ben, pleading to drink, could not swallow. The turn-spit had been sick for less than half a day. He lay now in the puddle of his own body fluids, waiting patiently, as he had been taught to do all his life, for the next uncontrollable turn of destiny. Alex left him to die

CHAPTER SIX

That night the Lady Mary came to his bed. Her gossamer blanchet floated azure to match her eyes. Alex sat up in a startled hurry and stared at her. A full moon silvered through the unshuttered window.

She closed the door quietly behind her and stood a moment in the small empty space beside the bed, her feet bare on the dusty boards. Alex sighed. "Go away," he said.

She seemed ghostlike, a pearly phantom in the moonlight, blurred by the window's grime. Then he could feel her breath warm against his cheek. Her movements were stilted, a little stiff, as she climbed onto the bed beside him, pushing her toes under the covers. She smiled and laid her head on his shoulder. He was naked apart from the soiled bandage around one upper arm, and beneath her blanchet, so was she. She undid her ribbons and the moonlight caught the rise of her nipples. Alex stared down at her.

"This is absurd," he whispered. "Are you so desperate, then?"

"Aren't you?"

Alex slipped a slow arm around her, his fingers brushing across her breasts. The top of her blonde curls, tickling a little, shone beneath his chin, as gossamer as her blanchet. "It's been a long, long time," he said softly. "Yes, I suppose I'm desperate. But it shouldn't be you."

The warm swell of her breasts lay heavy beneath his hands and he could feel her heartbeat, fast as rat's paws in the dark. She murmured, voice muffled by his neck. "Why not me, Alex dear? Am I so – terribly – unattractive?"

"Fishing for compliments, Mary?" He chuckled. She was probably the most beautiful woman he had ever known. She was the most beautiful woman most men of her acquaintance had ever known. There had never been any doubt about her perfection and she had never doubted it herself. Alex's fingers crawled up, sliding around one wide soft aureole. The nipple was already hard.

"It's not compliments I need." She giggled, a mewling sound like a kitten. "Are you any good at it, Alex? Lizzie said you were. Prove it to me."

Alex grunted, irritated. "I promise you, Lizzie wouldn't know. I can't refuse you now, but don't threaten scandals, Mary, or I'll throw you out, however much it hurts me."

She reached up suddenly, biting his ear lobe. Her voice was all breath. "Don't be a fool Alex. Now give me what I want."

He grinned and pushed her roughly to her back, leaning over her, thrusting one knee between her legs, pulling the crumpled edges of her open gown away from her shoulders. He did not kiss her. Instead he kissed her nipples, rubbing his tongue across their rise. She arched her back, pushing impatiently against him. Stroking down from breast to belly, Alex pressed the heel of his hand against her groin, and opened her legs with his own.

She pulled away quite suddenly, wriggling from beneath him. Alex caught his breath and stared at her, pausing, fingers tight in the thick golden curls above her thighs. She stared back up at him, blinking, bright diamond tears spangled in her lashes.

Alex removed his hand, rolled off her and lay back on the deep pillow, staring up at the flaking ceiling plaster. He carefully quietened his breathing. He said, voice still slightly hoarse, "A fine moment to change your mind, Mary."

She curled, drew her knees up and turned towards him. "Stupid boy. I haven't changed my mind."

He closed his eyes and took a moment to control his voice. "You're crying."

She snuggled closer, one knee curled over his legs, nudging upwards, her hand slipping across his chest. He could feel the wet touch of her tears against his arm. He lay quite still, unmoving, breathing deep. "Can't you close the shutters, Alex? I like the dark. Your horrid little bed has no curtains."

He shook his head. "And the window has no shutters." He wiped gently beneath her lashes with his thumb. "A woman of your beauty doesn't need to hide in the dark. Now tell me, why are you crying?"

"Shouldn't we all be crying, Alex?" she whispered. "It's a city of tears. Such misery, such hollow eyes."

He relaxed and drew her close, his arm strong around her. "That's true enough. The battle, the sickness. The city's in mourning for many reasons. And you've lost your husband, and your home. I understand, my dear. But you shouldn't have come here tonight."

"I can ask for comfort too, can't I?" Her fingers crawled down, discovering the muscles over his ribs, then further down to the hard flat belly.

Alex kept his gaze on the ceiling. "Comfort, yes, perhaps. But you're sure you're not going to regret this in the morning, Mary?"

Her voice changed imperceptibly, hardening into momentary anger. "I don't make mistakes. I never ever regret anything, Alex."

Alex turned and leaned over her suddenly. "No? But I might." Her fingers were moving fast now, groping down into his groin. He grabbed her wrist and held her off. "You're my cousin's wife," he said fiercely, his breath hot in her eyes. "Your husband's in the fucking Tower. What the devil do you expect of me?"

"You know perfectly well what I expect of you." Her voice sounded shrill. "Aren't you capable, Alex? How sad. You were capable when you raped poor Elizabeth, and she's your cousin too." She pulled her hand from his and leaned over suddenly, pinching at his nipple. Her finger nails were filed, and sharp. Then she bent, and bit. Her nice even white teeth met in a snap.

41

"Shit." Alex shoved her way.

She rebounded and snatched between his legs. He grabbed her again and threw her backwards, pressing one leg over her. She bounced slightly on the mattress lumps. His hand was at her crotch when she said, as if absently remarking on the weather, "You've a most uncomfortable bed, Alex."

He sighed and lifted himself up a little on both knees, staring down at her. "I'm the pot boy, remember? Do you usually give your servants your best four posters?"

"No," she said, "but I don't usually give them my body either." She sniggered. "Sometimes of course, but not usually." She grabbed his neck and pulled him back down.

He wanted to hit her and his groin ached with wanting her. The moonlight striped her in silver and turned her hair pure gold. The ringlets tumbled around her ears, framing her face in glory. The curls below her belly were frosted in saffron. He held her down with both hands firm on her shoulders, nudged her legs wide and entered her hard and sudden. She grunted and thrust back. He lay heavily on her, one hand gripping her buttocks, the other over her mouth. She cried out, twisting her head and trying to escape from the flat of his palm. He pressed harder, silencing her. He came almost at once, a furious compulsion he made no attempt to control. He had done little to arouse her but felt her climax join his, her hips jerking violently against him.

He relaxed his hand over her mouth, letting her breathe. At once she reached up and bit his shoulder, just above the bandage. He gulped and pulled away. One final thrust and he fell on top of her, panting. Her hair was in his eyes and his mouth. He lay there a moment, catching his breath before finding the energy to roll away.

Alex woke shivering and cold. His fingers, thighs and belly were sticky, his whole body damp with sweat. The first thing that occurred to him was the sweating sickness and the dying turn-spit. Then he felt the woman beside him and remembered.

The moonlight had withdrawn from the angle of the little window, leaving the chamber slumped in gloom, but a first paling of dawn had eased beyond the clouds and a slight wind was rattling the casement.

Alex peered through the shadows at the Lady Mary, and smiled slightly. Even unconscious, the amazing blue of her eyes hidden and the rounded lower lip slack and open in a sleeping pout, she was almost perfect. She would have been perfection itself, except that she was dribbling slightly. It looked like snail slime across her little pointed chin.

Alex wedged himself up on one elbow and wondered what to do next. She was due to leave later that day, and as long as she didn't gossip to Lizzie, which seemed unlikely, he felt the whole business was likely to be quickly forgotten. He reached out one careless finger and stroked her nipple. Her breasts were large and held unusually high, with the soft creamy nipples of a younger woman. In many years of marriage to his cousin, she had never conceived a child, and was therefore unlikely to fall pregnant with his. He sighed, turned, and climbed rather noisily from the bed, bouncing a little from the mattress.

He ignored the chamber pot and trotted naked to the upper-story latrine cubicle, leaving the bedroom door slightly open behind him. The corridor was black and he felt along the walls, trying to remember if there were any steps, loose boards or protruding nails.

When he got back, his bed was empty. It had worked then.

He sat awhile, propped against the pillows, breathing deep. He felt sore. His thighs felt bruised, there was crusted blood across one side of his chest around the nipple, Mary's bites and ripping scratches had left bruises and tiny wounds, and the arrow wound in his arm had begun to throb anew. It was some time before he bothered to rise again and get dressed.

The Lady Mary Corby, once Countess of Sheffield, departed her home shortly after midday dinner, mounted her palfrey and followed the last wagon piled with her belongings, heading east towards the city gates. There was no longer an ostler at the house and only one very small urchin for a groom, so it was Alex who helped her mount and saw her off. There was no flicker of acknowledgment between them of what had happened the night before. Alex said, "Give my regards to Li – no, on second thoughts, you'd better not. Just give my love to young Stephen."

She looked down at him from the saddle. "You'll stay on a while then, Alex, and see the house respectably passed over? At least until the new staff arrive?"

"I will," said Alex, squinting up into the wind. "I've no objection, and I need somewhere to stay. The new man will have no idea who I am after all. And you know what else I shall be doing."

"Trying to help Merevale. Yes, I know," she frowned. "Though I doubt you'll have much luck. How is one convicted felon going to plead for another?"

"Nicely put, Mary." Alex stepped back as the lady kicked her heels and the palfrey blinked, pulling in its head and shaking its mane. "But if I stay anonymous, I might manage something, and I intend keeping in contact with Lovel out east while I'm about it. In the meantime, if you get permission to visit Daniel, try and get word to Merevale for me, will you? Tell him I'm working on his behalf."

The house was cavernous with echoes. The dust swirled into empty corners, carried by draughts and the wind down the chimneys. Some of the great rooms stood quite vacant, others still furnished with the heavier objects the lady was unable to take with her. Out through the wide alcove windows facing south, the great river flashed in the sun beyond the sloping gardens. The water was choppy with wind gusts and busy with the endless business of the barges, showtes and lighters, the continuous crossing of traffic from north to south and from the west out towards the sea; taxi barges carrying impatient passengers, wherries with their small cargo, lighters delivering messages and letters. And a little over one mile east stood the great Tower, banking the shadowed river. Somewhere there in the cold damp lay Merevale, imprisoned for loving his king.

The under-cook had left shortly before his mistress, clinging to the bench on the wagon. The apothecary, being the only servant of seniority remaining, rode beside the lady, escorting her in place of groom or guard. Reginald Psalter, though awarded the honour of accompanying his mistress and taking the spare mare, was pink faced and glowing with pride, and, being an inexperienced rider, white lipped with nerves. Alex, considered a tall young man, was accustomed to looking across the tops of people's heads and addressing them downwards. The apothecary was a good deal taller. Alex, for once, looked up. Now, hunched upon the saddle, the thin man's legs were bent up like a frog's, his large feet splayed to balance against the stirrups. He gripped the reins with studious suspicion and eyed the horse's wide neck with considerable dislike, but the mare was placid and elderly, the master's good horses having already been sent ahead to the Lady Elizabeth's. Mister Psalter gazed across from his mount, sleek back steaming a little in the gentle sun, to the figure of the lady, straight and trim in her saddle. His expression changed, his cheeks flushed and his eyes glittered with the thrill of respect. The lady's palfrey snorted, dancing a little with impatience. The apothecary reached out one hand as if to steady her, realised the incongruity, and slumped down again, awaiting orders.

As trained and senior servants, the apothecary and the under-cook would be absorbed into the Earl of Burton's household. Those remaining in The Strand, including the new pot-boy, would not. Three kitchen lads, two laundry maids, and a brat of indeterminate age who had begun his training as a page but who was now the stable urchin, would await the arrival of the new Earl of Sheffield and their probable dismissal into immediate destitution.

Reginald Psalter looked down at Alex one moment. "Young man," he said. "I have greatly extended my energies in your education. I believe you have absorbed some intelligence with the art of spices, treacles and sugars from watching my own humble efforts, manipulating subtleties to please their lordships. And in particular, the ladies." He attempted a benign smile while keeping a grip on the reigns. "I hope to leave these premises knowing I have improved your lot, and that even in my absence, you may benefit from my example."

Alex sighed and trotted back upstairs to his room. Squashed beneath the servants' stairs, rickety and lacking balustrade, the disadvantages of his bed place were also its advantages. The dimensions ensured the likelihood of his keeping his privacy. He heard each footstep going up and those going down. The window, though its lack of shutters had bothered the Lady Mary, did not bother him. It watched over the stables and back courtyard, another surety of information.

45

Beside his swinging palliasse was a small chest for his belongings. He had no belongings. He had arrived only with the clothes he wore, some of which had never been his own. He owned only his father's signet ring and a small ivory hilted knife. But the little chest, carefully locked, was now half full. It contained the silver and other small items of value which he had been systematically stealing from the Lady Mary ever since his arrival.

CHAPTER SEVEN

Having no coin for the wherryman, Alex approached the Tower on foot, walking across the city from Ludgate. Following the river and skirting the docks, he arrived at Tower Hill by early afternoon. The shadows of the great white keep spread already dark. The battlements were spangled in sunshine, but below the huge stones remained chill, nestled within their dominating shade.

Alex quickly crossed the moat at the Byward Tower through the western entrance, shivering beneath the first portcullis where the warmth of the sun was immediately eliminated. With the necessity of airing, repairing and refurbishing the royal apartments for the imminent coronation, the new Constable of the Tower was conveniently preoccupied. Alex went directly to the offices of his resident assistant, with whom he had an appointment. He smiled, opened the satchel he was carrying, and passed over the silver standing cup, ostentatiously decorated with a bevy of naked cherubs and inlaid with ruby glass. It was the second time he had bribed the man. It was his second visit, and likely to be a long one.

Sir Merevale Corby had been poorly housed. The battle of Atherstone near Market Bosworth had brought many captives to the Tower, and what had once been a grand palace was now little more than a prison. Once bright with music, it had instead become a place of dread. The stench of cold and misery invaded, as surely as Henry Tudor's foreign troops. In the main keep the more comfortable apartments secured the young Plantagenet blood, those relations of the late king previously living in grandeur at Sheriff Hutton Castle. Within a few hours of success, the new king had ordered those possible contenders to the throne and rivals to his position as conqueror, brought south, and imprisoned for the duration of his pleasure.

"It's a damned dungeon," said Alex, wrinkling his nose. "You must be devilish stiff, Mel. Do they let you out for exercise?"

Merevale sat on the bed, one boot up on the damp turn of the blanket. The pallet had been shoved back against the wall to allow a little more central space, but the condensation slipped down the rough stone like tears. His hair was uncombed and his bandages blood stained, though the blood was old and dark now. He shook his head. "Once. But there's too many of us. The guards only have time for the ones who pay."

"Yes, well, that's where I come in." Alex passed over the satchel, lighter now, but still substantial. "Buy yourself some decent food and some exercise, coz. Buy yourself a better chamber, if you can. There should be enough there to satisfy the guards."

Merevale sat up straight. "On no account, Alex," he said. "You risk arrest yourself. I'll not take what few goods you have left. For God's sake, keep whatever property you've managed to salvage."

Alex grinned. "Your property, cousin, not mine." He was standing by the tiny window, a slit in the massive stone, unshuttered and open to the winds. "At least, not yours perhaps, but certainly your family's. I've been helping your sweet sister-in-law to move house. Stealing isn't a skill I would've considered cultivating in the past, but it's a talent I'm acquiring."

"Filtered from father's hoards?" Merevale smiled and relaxed. "But everything belongs to Danny now and he's in here himself. Or has he been pardoned? Do you know?"

"No." He didn't know. "But that'll come soon, if not already, and Mary's onto it. She'll have him out if she has to jump onto the wretched king's lap and crow. It's you who'll be abandoned, my friend, and this was your father's silver even if you aren't entitled to inherit it. He'd have used his entire fortune to get you out, if he was still alive. I brought some pieces here a few days past, but it wasn't enough for them to let me in. Just got you a charcoal brazier and some roast mutton."

Merevale slumped back against the damp stone, his eyes slightly glazed. "So that's where that came from? And the one morning's exercise too no doubt? But they won't be letting me free, you know that don't you Alex? I've no title to attaint nor fortune to take, so they'll want my head. I don't care. Riding the final charge beside Richard, that was honour enough for a lifetime."

"Stop being so bloody noble," frowned Alex. "As long as I manage to keep my own head, I'll be damned if I see you lose yours."

Merevale shook it, proving its solidity. "Why should I care now, coz, with my king murdered and that bastard smug on England's throne? Tudor's already shown us his mettle, dating his reign from the day before the battle; making his thefts and attaintings sound legal."

"Idealism won't help you, me or the country now," said Alex. "It's pragmatism that'll keep us free to fight again." He lowered his voice to less than a whisper. "Lovel's still out east. Once I've got you out of here, we'll join him." He smiled, speaking normally again. "So in the meantime, enjoy your brother's unexpected generosity, Mel, and buy yourself an upper chamber, food and wine, and whatever else will serve. There's some of his clothes in the sack too. Dress fine and be damned."

"Both Dan and Mary would grudge me it, if they knew," glowered Merevale, shaking his head again. He reached into the satchel and unearthed a bent candlestick. "At least take something for yourself, Alex, something you can sell. Are you penniless, for God's sake? You look like hell."

"Yes, of course I'm penniless," Alex grinned. "You think I dodged home after the battle for a hot bath and a collection of the family treasure? But I look like this from good common sense, rather than misfortune. And it won't serve me to get picked up by the Watch on the way home with a measure of the Sheffield silver tucked in my sack. It was risky getting here, but it seemed worth the risk. I won't double the trouble. I'll have you know I'm a pot-boy at your old family home, and need to keep my position."

"At least you always make me laugh, Alex." Merevale showed no imminent indication of laughter.

Alex nodded. "Laughably shameful, as my father always told me, God rest his soul." He turned, hearing the gaoler's key in the lock. "There's no death warrant signed yet, Mel. I asked. That means I can maybe get you out. I won't bend my knee to that Welsh bastard for myself, but I might for you. And you look like hell too. Put on a clean shirt and buy yourself a decent dinner."

The wind had gathered force throughout the day, churning up the river from the Narrow Sea and forcing the tidal surge into white tipped maelstroms beneath the Bridge. As Alex strode down Lower Thames Street, the chimneys on the tall houses to his right began to rattle. He hurried. Chimney pots often fell in stormy winds, and a force of so many bricks from such a height could kill. It would be a ludicrous way to die after all. And he was desperately tired. Not with walking, but with thinking. He had hoped to be back in Lancaster by now but that was as far away as ever, while the risks to his own life and freedom were greater in London, and Merevale's safety as precarious. Henry Tudor's victorious army was still lodged in the city, along with the sickness they'd carried with them, and it made for a raucous, dishevelled capital, dangerous streets both before and after curfew, and the chance of being caught up in one of the many brawls and arrested without even his identity known. He hunched his shoulders against the spite of the gale and glowered into his shirt collar. He hoped De Chandee would take his mob back to France with him soon, and then the Welsh would disband while the Lancastrian lords sent their troops back home to their wives and the meagre winter rations due their station.

It had been a fruitful summer before the outrages of the invasion. There had been a plentiful ripe harvest for those who worked the land. Alex sighed. His own father's estates had enjoyed the best growing season for many a year, the sheep would be fat and the barns full. He wondered who would be there to enjoy it, and what newly-honoured bastard would wear his title, and feast from the results of his father's good management.

The bells had started to ring as he reached Ludgate, the gates ready to close for the night. Alex hurried through. It was then he saw the stream of traffic, horses, litters and wagons rumbling the cobbles towards The Strand. He followed, keeping to the evening's shadows. They led him to his own new adopted home. The robber of the Shefffield title had come to stay.

First the staff. Enough for a house twice the size. There'd be dismissals.

He was met at the stables by the remains of Mary's ragtaggle servants. The child groom and the laundry maids were in tears. Sent off on the spot. "But wer'll I go, sir?" sniffed the boy. "Got nor ma nor pa. Must I sleep in the gutters, sir?"

"Plenty do," nodded Alex. "Had I means to employ you, I would. Instead, it's likely I'll be following you onto the streets. Bed down with the horses tonight, then get up to Cripplegate when the gates open in the morning, and see if the Lady Elizabeth will take you in."

The horses were being stabled and fed; a spare handful of rouncies, a fractious charger and six placid hired sumpters. Wagons were brought through from the courtyard to the back doors and the furniture unloaded. A stream of carters had been employed, journeymen shouting contrary orders in contrary dialects. One cart tipping on the cobbles, half a dozen strong backs shoved to brace against the wobble. "Get this righted. And quick, before the light sinks altogether."

"Light the torches, boy. Sharp to it. Are you a simpleton? Where's your common sense?"

Alex grinned. He was suddenly reminded of being a child at home again, and his father screaming orders, accusing him of laziness, telling him he was a fool. He turned quickly, retrieving the long torches from the stable sconces and an oil lamp from the back door. He found a tinder box and lit the flames, flaring wild in the wind. Then he pushed up his sleeves and began to help unloading. Remembering to be a servant was as good a game as any. Gathering the three remaining kitchen boys, Alex organised a chain, passing chairs, coffers, kitchen equipment and bedding from cart to house.

Then he felt three plump fingers down the back of his shirt collar, and whirled around. "Who are you, boy? What business have you here?"

Alex frowned, guessing status. Faced with a fat man, tall, well-groomed and proud of his bulk and his livery, Alex guessed Steward, secretary or gentleman usher. He bowed, hiding his smile. "Sir. From the household of the late Earl of Sheffield, sir. Not needed, sir, where the lady of the house is going now, I stayed to pass over the property to the new lord, sir."

The fat man nodded. "You were in charge then, boy?"

Certainly dressed as he was, he couldn't pass for a Steward himself. A pot-boy, earning him nothing but beatings and no time free to work for Merevale, seemed suddenly inappropriate. "Alex – Bowyer, sir. Clerk of the Spicery, sir. Hoping to be taken on by the new lord, sir." He wondered, momentarily, if he could remember a single relevant thing about spices. What he had learned from Reginald Psalter had barely interested him at the time.

The fat man frowned, seemingly unconvinced. "Well," he decided, "I'll keep you on trial, and see how you get on. It's a post the master needs filling perhaps, but you seem mighty young for a senior clerk. So get yourself to the kitchens, say I sent you, Master Hewitt is serving a hasty peas pottage for supper, and then to bed with you. I'll put you to the test in the morning. Be at my offices by half past five."

"Yes, sir. Thank you, sir." Alex trotted off, grinning. He caught up on the news, the gossip, the names and positions, as he spooned his pottage in the kitchens.

Mister Hewitt, a man he would certainly never have employed himself, was a cook who understood more about hunting than food, and could therefore roast an excellent venison but not raise a pestell or a pippin pie, nor set a galantine or a syllabub. A country cook used to a small country manor and the tastes of the minor gentry, a man who organised his kitchens by shouting and bullying his scullions, and saw nothing amiss in coughing heartily into the pottage. Alex ate his supper with little appetite.

"And you, boy, you tell me you've experience with spices?"

Alex looked up. "Mister Hewitt? Indeed I have sir. Cassia bark from far China, sir, and saffron from the fields of Moorish Spain. Exotic peppers from India, as precious as diamonds, and cloves, dragon's blood and nutmegs."

"Ah, well," said Hewitt, obviously impressed. "Dragon's blood, you say? And how do you get that then? You don't need to leech the beasts, or milk them I hope, since the gardens here don't seem that large."

Alex hiccupped gently. "Dragon's blood is better known as cinnabar, Mister Hewitt. It's found in the ground, near the great volcanoes of southern Italy. A useful mineral, in fact, and used for – many things." Poisons, for instance. The apothecary had warned about using too much. Alex said nothing more and returned to his bowl.

He passed the test the next morning. After a restless night repeating everything he could remember, which was little, about spices and medicks, he was punctual for his appointment with the principal Steward. With a fast talking mixture of what he'd always known, what he had picked up from Lady Mary's apothecary in recent days, and what he simply invented, he astonished Mr. Shaddle with facts both amazing and sublime. Mr. Shaddle had never heard of dragon's blood either.

"Cinnabar, Mister Shaddle, sir. The source of mercury, and used as a pigment for dying as well as in cooking. We've no need to add dragons to the stables."

"Well, I'm glad to hear it," said the Steward, stretching his doublet lacings. "Sounds like you'll do, young man. But the last household was very lax, it seems, and you look more like a pot-boy than a respectable clerk. I shall have to get you some decent livery."

The recently knighted Earl of Sheffield arrived a week later. The staff filed into the great hall, standing stiff as polished armour against the panelling. Edmund Tranter had stayed close to Henry Tudor in Brittany and France, a voluntary member of the Lancastrian court in exile. He was little known in England and his household newly set up. His servants did not know their master, and little of his reputation. They had been employed in Yorkshire at the ancient manor of the Tranter family, serving his lady mother, and after her death, a

53

dwindling fortune and a vacant house. They were as curious to meet the new earl as was Alex, but for different reasons.

He did not look like a man, Alex thought, likely to be interested in dragon's blood. Alex kept his head down. A clerk of the spicery might have warranted a brief introduction but the earl was uninterested not only in spices, but in his entire household. He strode past followed by his entourage, velvets and gold tissue sweeping the boards as surely as a broom, and nodded only to the Steward. The staff were dismissed immediately and filed dutifully back to the kitchens.

"Did you see?" demanded Mr. Hewitt. "Fine as sixpence."

"Well, of course we saw, and would have cost a deal more than sixpence," said Mr. Shaddle, sinking to the long bench with a sigh. "I'll have you know I went down to Grasschurch Street two days back, and saw the price of Italian silks in the draper's there. Sixpence wouldn't buy a single thread. One length of ready dyed silk velvet with gold on gold, was held up for fifty pounds before bargaining."

The kitchen boys drew in their breath and lowered their eyes. Mr. Hewitt coughed into his cauldron. "So we've a fine lord, lads, and worth a merry penny. Reckon back in Yorkshire, the Tranter household never seen silk velvet, nor that shiny gold stuff the lord had his doublet of. Good worsted we had, and strong linen, and wool of proper superior quality. Seems London likes the fancy cloths."

"Our master's an earl now," sniffed the Steward. "And we should be proud of it."

The new Earl of Sheffield was short, thin, and extremely bandy. A clipped blonde moustache hid a receding lip and the rest of his hair was grey but he did not dye it, nor pad his calves within his hose. His confidence needed no bolstering. He made no attempt at personal contact with his servants, but let it be known through Shaddle that any boy, girl, man or woman of whatever rank, except of course Shaddle himself, would be beaten if caught stealing, watering the wine, swindling the portions, lying in bed past four of the clock each summer morning and five o'clock in winter, or in any way shirking his duty, committing immoralities, making excuses to miss Sunday Mass, or otherwise bringing disrepute to the house of Tranter. Alex smiled.

He bought his own spices. What clerk of the spicery, he queried loudly, would risk the acquisition of such a precious commodity to lesser persons without the expertise to judge quality? There was a small shop in Bucklebury Street, once recommended by Reginald Psalter, where Mistress Darrelby sold the best spices, herbs, bark, nuts, sugared almonds and camphor oils, but Alex discovered a far cheaper commerce direct at the wharves, where the Venetian galleys and the great trading ships arrived from the Indies and further east. It was not, however, with the intention of buying spices that Alex usually left the house. He returned each time with some purchase, not wishing to attract suspicion, but in the meantime he visited the Tower.

Merevale had been moved to a larger chamber higher in the great Keep, where the damp pervaded a little less as the autumn sun baked the stone, and although the small window was unshuttered, it was enclosed with glass. The brazier was larger, the bed was no longer a simple pallet but a feather mattress and there was a small desk and chair. Alex sat on the chair. Merevale eyed him with faint concern. "It's an improvement, I'll grant you that coz. But what in heaven's name makes you want to dress like a scullion?"

"I'll have you know," said Alex with asperity, "that scullions don't look like this at all. They're lucky to get more than a shirt and some folded underpants beneath for modesty. I'm no longer a pot-boy. I've promoted myself to a clerk of the spicery."

Merevale frowned. "Our old house never had a spicery."

"Well, it does now," said Alex. "I've invented one. Rather small, but quite serviceable. I have the key around my neck now, and I keep the cupboard well stocked. After all, buying supplies is my only excuse for leaving my duties and coming to visit you."

"What duties?" demanded Merevale. "What do you do with spices anyway?"

Alex shook his head. "I've very little idea. I chuck some at the cook from time to time and he feels mighty important adding pepper to the sauce. Since his sauces are all vile, the pepper helps. The staff are all from Yorkshire and don't know a mustard seed from a cardamom pod."

"Neither do I," admitted Merevale. "How the devil do you know these things, anyway?"

"I spent a week as pot-boy to your apothecary, before they all went off to Lizzie's," said Alex. "Reginald Psalter. A mine of information. Besides, I knew a little already. Always wanted to go to sea and sail to exotic places such as the Spice Islands. Being the younger son, you know. Well, you would know. You're one too."

"Never wanted to go to sea though," said Merevale. "Just used to complain to my mother for having given birth to me second. Daniel inheriting everything never seemed quite fair. And now," Merevale sighed, "poor Danny won't get a penny either, nor title nor honour."

"The new man," interrupted Alex, "isn't impressive. Not his fault he's got legs the shape of Ottoman scimitars, but he ought to wear longer surcoats. In a short doublet, his codpiece looks as though it's suspended in mid-air."

"I don't want to hear about him," sniffed Merevale. "Just tell me if the wretch dies. Is he likely to, do you think?"

"Seems fairly robust," Alex shook his head. "But he must be at least fifty years old if not more. No one knows much about him of course. Yorkshire born, old Lancastrian family fell out of favour after Tewkesbury, been in Brittany these twelve years past. Certainly not fussy about his food, since our cook is a pestilence on two legs. Do you want me to get rid of the new earl? I've access to a good variety of poisons now."

Merevale stared. "I thought you said you looked after the spices?"

"Same thing," grinned Alex. "And I've no idea which are which half the time. It's quite interesting."

"Well I'm glad you've found an honest trade at last," sniggered Merevale. "Better than going to sea anyway. Sailors usually drown, I hear. Have you met the new king yet?"

"Well, as it happens," smiled Alex, "I've an appointment with an usher at Westminster next week. I tried to get in to see Sir William Stanley but my lowly status was somewhat of a disadvantage as you can imagine."

"Good God, Alex," said Merevale, "Stanley could recognise you. You couldn't take the risk."

Alex laughed. "I'm teasing, coz. It's his offices I need, not the man himself. I bribed the usher with a ghastly great silver platter, inlaid with gold. Worth a fortune. Quite hard to steal, as it happens. But the new Earl of Sheffield has Yorkshire tastes."

No word arrived of Merevale's death warrant though the block had already been used by others, for King Henry needed to secure his position. Alex met his appointment at the usher's office in Westminster Palace, kept his head low and his eyes averted, thick black hair well covered by the cap of his light blue livery. He was unusually articulate for a kitchen servant, but when a country's loyalties swung sharply after conquest and its politics became influenced more by hypocrisy and fear than care for the common weal, many men's station altered and the palace usher, more interested in bribes than suspicions, asked few questions.

It was then announced that the coronation of the new king would take place on the thirtieth day of October, in the year of our Lord 1485. The moon would be at an inauspicious angle to the new sovereign's natal sun, but Henry was not concerned. He wanted his official title ratified as quickly as possible, with secret whisperings as to his unsuitability and lack of bloodline to inherit all squashed. Alex remarked that one day later would have been more appropriate, since that was All Hallows Eve when witches and devils were free to ride aboard.

That same day Sir Merevale Corby was brought word of his pardon and release from the Tower, on condition that he take the oath of allegiance to his new monarch. He would not, however, be permitted to return to the home of his youth, claim any of his past wealth, or attend the royal court. Everything confiscated by the crown.

The following day the new Earl of Sheffield, Lord Edmund Tranter informed his secretary, who informed the Steward, who informed the rest of the staff, that a lady would shortly be arriving at the Strand palace. Mistress Katherine Ashingham was Lord Edmund's newly affianced bride. They were indeed already joined by proxy, a legal binding having taken place between relatives of each party, a somewhat incongruous pairing of Lord Edmund's great aunt with

Mistress Katherine's young cousin, conducted by the clerics of the parish church and fully witnessed by the Sheriff of Leicestershire and his two principal clerks. The true wedding would take place the morning following the Feast of the Kings, one week previous to the Coronation and three weeks after her arrival.

In the meantime, the young lady, having journeyed all the way from Leicestershire, was naturally to be accorded great honour and places must be found for the housing of her staff, since she would arrive accompanied by her personal dresser, four maids, a page, and her official chaperone and nurse, Sara Whitstable.

In the meantime the Earl of Sheffield, seemingly unimpressed by the imminent arrival of his future wife, whom he had never actually met, dressed in his riding finery with a well plumed hat and spurs of solid silver, and went hunting.

CHAPTER EIGHT

"Who?" It was not a name he had forgotten. Alex had not thought of it in any way over the preceding weeks, but on hearing it again, he knew exactly who was meant. He remembered very dark brown eyes and small breasts firm beneath his hands.

With a new king jealous of his throne, families were on the move, alliances reforged, new loyalties affirmed. Where once a man would not have countenanced his daughter's barter, now titles sprang lesser men into new prominence, and what had seemed an unthinkable match became suddenly respectable. The lords of the great Yorkist families quickly sought Lancastrian affiliations. Henry Tudor, promising to marry old King Edward's daughter, now claimed a coming compromise; uniting the two rival powers. The people were disbelieving and unimpressed. It was quickly clear that those rewarded were not to be men loyal to York, and the future queen herself was kept unmarried, uncrowned and out of sight.

The marriage mart, the price now of far less consequence than aligning with the new king's favourites, was an immediate scramble across the country. That it brought a name Alex remembered to the place he now used as a temporary hiding place, was a small and unexpected pleasure, but not so surprising. Marriageable maidens of good family had always been a useful commodity and the country boasted few enough. Men newly titled needed heirs. Few of Henry Tudor's friends were married since exile and a lifetime under threat allowed little more than dalliance with an inn keeper's slatterns. Alex was well aware that the same would doubtless now apply to him. A pretty nursemaid might serve him well for the short time he intended remaining close to the city.

As it happened, Alex was also absent from the house when Miss Katherine, her servants and her entourage arrived, having taken himself to the Tower, there to take custody of one released prisoner.

Fresh from imprisonment, Merevale was neither stiff nor weak, his cousin's bribes having taken care of good food and exercise, a soft bed, warm blankets and a frequently replenished brazier. But the light hurt his eyes, the soles of his boots were cracked, and climbing once again into the saddle reminded his back muscles of old wounds. It was his first time on a horse since the last dreadful charge which had lost the Plantagenets their England. Merevale blinked away memories.

A silver candle snuffer bought the two hired palfreys and two thick cloaks, with change for pies at an Ordinary, manchet rolls and a mug of ale each. "Pasties at fourpence ha'penny?" said Merevale in disgust, stuffing pastry crumbs into his mouth. "Since when did they cost that much?"

"Since this bastard king started squeezing the whole country with his damned new taxes," said Alex. "But it's worth the price to eat a decent meat pie again. You should see the rubbish they serve in The Strand now."

Merevale licked his lips and wiped them on the linen with which the pie had been wrapped. "Well, for pity's sake, come back and eat with us," he said. "This absurd pretence of servants and spices cannot serve in private, Alex."

Alex grinned, remounting. "Not too sure about that. Lizzie doesn't want me at her place for obvious reasons, and Mary won't be keen I imagine. There's news of your big brother being freed tomorrow or the next day, and the household will be in turmoil. Go and add to it, Mel. I'm off home. As it happens, there's a nursemaid coming to stay some time today, and I've an interest in meeting up with her again."

Merevale eyed his cousin with disapproval. "A nursemaid, Alex? I thought you stopped chasing the serving girls back when your voice dropped."

"Since I'm a servant now myself - ," he shook his head. "And no, don't say it. I'm keeping up the charade for the time being, Mel. You may have been courageous enough to do your stint in the Tower, but you had little choice. I was lucky to escape the battlefield, so I'm not handing myself in now. He's a spiteful man, this new king, far as I can make out, and there's no saying who he'll forgive and who he won't. Yes, yes, I know you'd plead for me but it'd be an absurd risk, and downright unnecessary. Besides, once you're settled, I'm off to Colchester to join Lovel."

"And meddle with nursemaids in the meantime?"

"Why not?" Alex pulled the collar of his new cloak around him, keeping the October wind from his neck and his neat livery well hidden beneath. "An irritating brat, but she intrigued me. I don't play too deep, you know me, but it's been a frustrating two months in more ways than one. Go off to Lizzie's and placate your sister, coz. And give her my love."

"Is that an allusion to playing too deep?" smiled Merevale, turning towards the Cripplegate stables.

"Oh well, since you once objected to my trying to seduce your sister."

Merevale dismounted, frowning up at Alex. "Seduce her? Damn it, Alex, you abducted her. I was obliged to hate you for a whole year. It was most inconvenient."

"All her own plan, as you know perfectly well," smiled Alex, dismounting beside his cousin. "And I'm excessively pleased I failed, otherwise I'd have been married to Lizzie these nine years gone, and that would have been far worse than having your father threatening to decapitate me, and my own father beating me bloody." He passed the reins of his palfrey to Merevale. "Now, these are old tired stories and should be forgotten. It's the future we need to think about. Take my horse too, will you coz, and get both the beasts back to their owner. It won't do for me to turn up at Sheffield House on horseback."

The Burton House ostler and two grooms ran over to take the horses.

Merevale nodded. "A junior clerk of the spicery, hiring a pony to go to market? Shocking indeed. They might suspect you of stealing."

Alex, ignoring his cousin, shrugged out of his cloak and handed that over as well. "And the same goes for this. Now, on foot and without your company, I'm safer in my livery. But keep it for me. I might need it later."

He did not wait to greet any of his family, hearing the squeals of welcome for Merevale fade quickly behind him. He strode away, crossing the city north to south and heading back towards The Strand before the gates were locked.

Back at his own stables, the hounds were milling, tails wagging and noses deep in their water bowls as the kennel boys brushed them down. Lord Edmund was back from the hunt beyond the Piccadilly orchards, and had no doubt now deigned to meet his arranged bride. Alex entered the house through the kitchens. He carried no parcel of spices this time to excuse his absence, but sufficient chaos disguised his entrance. The kitchens were hot, scullions running, one boy shovelling charcoal to the fire, logs already spitting, eyes smarting from the smoke, the new giro-rosto assembled, oiled and turning.

The cook was spinning his own circles in the centre of the long boards, a demented obstacle for the interweaving boys to avoid. "His lordship's given word to Mister Shaddle," moaned Hewitt, "and we've to serve three courses, with a full complement of subtleties for the ladies. Subtleties, indeed. I doubt we've a sugar loaf in the whole pantry. Then he suggests eel cakes poached in almond milk with grated cinnamon. And how am I supposed to cook that?"

Alex laughed. "Well, I can supply the grated cinnamon. And the almond milk too I suppose, given time. As for eels - "

"None." The cook was quivering, though whether from indignation or panic was unclear, but his tears were due to smoke and temper rather than misery. "Roast venison I have," he said. "And hare too, ready spitted. But I sent one of the lads down to the river to see if any eel boats had come this far up, and not a one. His lordship brought pheasant back from the hunt today, but they'll need hanging for a week at least before I can even pluck them."

Alex shook his head. "You knew these people were expected. Didn't you order in extra supplies of any kind?"

"Of course I did," scowled Hewitt. "Perch and smelt, and some plump pullets with six baskets of salads and roots. But they're supposed to be too tired from travelling all day. They shouldn't be hungry. That's not even lady-like. And I hear Miss Katherine rode all the way from Leicestershire, and never entered the litter once. It's all most upsetting."

"Well it's a three day's journey at least," smiled Alex. "I imagine they took today's dinner at some country hostelry. Now it's supper time, they'll be stiff and dusty and I doubt any of these people are up to eating three courses. Lord Sheffield just wants to show off his new wealth and status. Serve your venison and stuff a pullet with prunes. I'll get you almond milk and grated cinnamon, and make cakes out of the chicken livers instead of eels. As for subtleties without sugar, do you have berries to bake in pastry? A custard sauce perhaps?"

Hewitt stared in newly discovered awe at the clerk of the spicery, and nodded slowly. "Must have been a proper grand kitchen you served in afore, lad, I must say."

Alex turned. Through the smoke and the shouting, a small pink faced boy was standing in his way. The child was round cheeked and thrilled with importance. "I'm come with a message," he announced with a deep inhalation. "Sent by your Steward with a message from my lady."

Since Alex had never seen the boy before, he said, "And you're Miss Katherine's page I presume? Well, get on with it."

The page clasped his hands behind his back and closed his eyes for accurate repetition. "I'm to fetch a cup of hypocras," he said with care. "Warmed but not hot. And I've promised not to spill it."

Alex raised an eyebrow. "Wise, undoubtedly. Do you usually spill things?" He averted his glance from the child's stained stomacher with a slight shudder. "Although I've certainly never met you before, I have a feeling I've met your doublet. Would you be Tom?"

The boy blinked, smiled and nodded eagerly. "But I'm getting better and I don't drop too much anymore. And your Mister Shaddle says to give me a tray to put the cup on. A silver tray."

Alex wondered if there were many left. He'd stolen most of the smaller ones. "I shall arrange it," he said. "Wait here and don't get in the way. Your mistress's supper has the kitchens in turmoil."

"But she won't want supper." The boy shook his head urgently. "Never does. Besides, my lady's staying in her chamber. She said so. 'I'm not leaving my bed till I have to, Tom,' she said. 'I don't want to see this miserable hole nor its miserable owner again until tomorrow morning at least.' Just wants a cup of spiced wine, she does, and a hot brick to warm her feet. Sara's getting her that."

Alex grinned. "I see," he said. "Though it's perhaps a touch inadvisable to repeat your mistress's words quite so openly to his lordship's staff. And speaking of Sara, if it's a Miss Sara Whitstable you mean, I believe I know her. Had the pleasure of her acquaintance just over two months ago. Tell her if she needs anything, to come and see me personally. I'm the clerk of the spicery. Name of Alex."

The boy screwed up his nose. "What, soppy Nurse Sara? Oh well, if you say so."

Alex passed on the news to the cook and the rush towards a grand supper subsided into damp sparks. Shaddle was informed, and further instructions sought from the earl's secretary. Eventually it was the kitchen staff who sat down cheerfully to roast venison, perch baked in splendid sauce, chicken liver cakes poached in almond milk with a sprinkling of grated cinnamon and wild blackberry pies in a (rather burned) vanilla custard. They thoroughly enjoyed themselves, though the new nursemaid ordered only a light posset of the almond milk to be taken in her mistress's chamber, and did not join the party.

Mid October was bitterly cold. The hot summer, shuddering on past the great battle, had subsided into a mild but windy autumn. The Thames had flooded as usual and the lower gardens had become more quagmire than pleasure palace. Hewitt said he would not be surprised to find swans sailing right into his kitchens, surrendering themselves for the roast. Then winter came with a hiss. The soggy paths shrank hard and white and the cobbles were slippery with rime. With the new king's soldiers still lodged in the city, the terrible sweating sickness had now taken the lives of more citizens across the country than had the mighty battle. Two lord mayors and a handful of aldermen gone, without enough left standing to elect replacements. Shops closed up, priests died at the very moment of delivering the sacrament of penance, slumping inert over the gasping bodies of the stricken, and funeral processions gave way to hasty burials. Mutterings of divine justice were silenced with threats and imprisonment. Newgate also sweated and its inmates died without recourse to either doctor or priest.

The church bells had tolled until the small hours and the ringing from Westminster had echoed right down The Strand. It had not been a restful night. Alex opened his eyes, yawned and rolled out of bed. It was still black outside, his small window glimmering faint with the last aura of a dying moon. He shivered and grabbed his livery, dressing fast in the dark. Footsteps outside and a creak on the stairs. It must be gone five. He grinned, thrusting his feet into his worn out shoes. He wondered happily what on earth he would do if anyone ever attempted to beat him for arriving late for work. It was not something he could imagine himself accepting placidly, whatever his need for anonymity. Besides, in a week or two he intended making his way east to join the rebels. He brushed the dust from his pale blue shoulders, shoved his cap over his hair and plodded dutifully downstairs.

Warmth at least; the bustle of the kitchens with the fire already blazing huge. The clerk of the spicery had little to do so early on a frosty morning. Alex helped himself to a mug of ale, a crust of cheat and a stool close to the hearth.

A child's voice he now recognised, interrupted his thoughts from behind. "Master Bowyer?" It was an effort, sometimes, to accept his pseudonym although he was now called by it often enough. Alex could certainly not remember why he had ever chosen that particular title since he had usually avoided the obligatory archery practice in his youth.

He turned towards the page. The child was bobbing about in the vicinity of his knees. At that hour in the morning, it made Alex feel slightly queasy. "What now, boy? Stand still, for pity's sake."

The boy hopped to the other foot and attempted to stabilize. "It was you, as asked, Master Bowyer. For Miss Sara, that is."

"That I know her. Yes," said Alex with patience.

"Well," insisted the boy. "She says she doesn't."

Alex finished his breakfast ale and put the earthenware cup down on the table. His toes were only just thawing out. The shoes belonging to his livery were thin leather and deeply cracked over a lifetime of use by at least seven different pairs of feet not always of the right size. He missed his own boots. He sighed and turned back to the child Tom. "She might not associate the memory with the name," he explained. "We met under what you might call unusual circumstances. Nor was I a clerk of the spicery at that time. It's a position I've – acquired – fairly recently. The damned woman can't have forgotten me already. She'll remember me when she sees me."

A hesitant cough interrupted him. Alex looked up. A thin woman was peeping down at him from below the peak of her muslin cap. Her hair, kept severely back from her brow, was permitted only a brief frizzy freedom above her pink tipped ears, which jutted at an unfortunate angle from her head. Her pale eyes seemed myopic and her mouth timid.

"I am afraid not, young man." She clasped and unclasped her fingers and attempted a smile. "I should remember, I assure you," she murmured, "had I ever encountered a young gentleman like yourself. I am quite sure I have not."

Alex stood, bowing briefly. It was a more bitter blow than he had expected. "I apologise ma'am. Presumably there was more than one Miss Sara Whitstable residing in Leicestershire."

"Unfortunately, it would seem so," said the lady. "But perhaps, since we are now acquainted indeed, we can remedy the discrepancy – of non-acquaintance, that is."

His disappointment was palpable. "I'd be delighted, ma'am." Alex said politely and turned back to the wide welcoming warmth of the fire.

CHAPTER NINE

I t was conceivable that six months might pass during the practice
of normal duties before the clerk of the spicery happened to
encounter the lady of the household. Alex's tiny room was little more
than a closed alcove beneath the rise of the back staircase, where
access to the fourth storey angled from steps arriving at the third.
Only the staff used these dark and narrow stairs, leading directly from
the kitchens and pantries and avoiding all contact with the grand hall
and principal chambers. Additionally, at this stage of her introduction
to her new life, the young bride would be unlikely to take the
remotest interest in the running of the house or the supervision of the
servants. Although already legally married by proxy to the earl, her
nuptials had not yet taken place and she remained fully chaperoned
by her ladies. Nor was the clerk of the spicery expected to serve the
household in any manner directly, or to answer any summons. There
was, therefore, no reason whatsoever for the earl's kitchen staff to
meet their new mistress. Instead, Alex began his own preparations.

After two nights when his mattress seemed twice as
uncomfortable and his room twice as cold, Alex realised that his self-
interest had, absurdly, been interrupted by thoughts of someone
utterly unconnected to his future plans or to the necessity of his
imminent departure. He decided that, slow witted and complacent as

he had undoubtedly become, he still had wit enough to guess he had once met not the nursemaid Sara Whitstable, but the daughter of the manor, Miss Katherine. And though she was no longer in disguise, he definitely was. They seemed interesting circumstances. The fact that she was about to become the Countess of Sheffield, indeed already held that title in principle, interested Alex far less. Husbands had never interfered with his pleasures before.

Francis the ninth Baron Lovell along with the Staffords and a growing band of those knights still stubbornly loyal to the deceased King Richard, had taken sanctuary at Colchester Abbey. Since Alex had every intention of joining their muster before any challenge to the new Tudor king was mounted, his time was limited. But time enough for flirtation, and some mild revenge for the girl's infuriating behaviour in the past and her insistent interruption of his placid night's sleep at present.

"I've an almond milk posset for - your Miss Sara," Alex informed Tom. Tom had been lighting the fire in his mistress's chamber and had scorched his thumb. He was dispatched to the kitchens for goose grease and sympathy. Without a resident apothecary, it was Alex who administered both. "With grated cinnamon, as she seems to like it," he placed the cup on a small silver tray, the last of its description. "You can take it up to her once I've finished this bandage."

"I don't know why you keep sending Nurse Sara things," Tom objected. "She's sure she never met you. Besides, all that milk makes her belch."

Alex smiled. "Then what drink does her ladyship prefer, and I shall send that to your mistress instead."

Tom shook his head with scorn. "My lady doesn't want anything. She says she doesn't like anything. She says it's a miserable place with miserable people and miserable food."

"So she's determined to be miserable?" suggested Alex, who wholeheartedly but privately agreed with the summary.

Tom nodded and examined his generous bandage. "That's going to make it even harder to carry this tray without spilling anything. Do I have to take this horrid posset all the way upstairs?"

"You do," said Alex firmly. "Then bring the tray back. We're running out of them."

It was common knowledge amongst the staff, that the lady took very few meals with her lord and avoided his company when possible. Rumour, embellished with a little slander, was helpful towards relieving the relentless toil and tedium of the kitchens. Although impressed by the new grandeur, few of the servants yet felt any particular loyalty to their lord. Only Shaddle openly disapproved of the gossip, and silenced the pleasures of conjecture.

"The wedding feast is to be held in just a few days from now," announced Shaddle with a faint shudder of suppressed panic. "You've been living the easy life, all of you. No more. No more chattering in the corners. No more slipping off early to your pallets before midnight. No more lying in bed past four in the mornings. No more begging a half day off for some dying mother, nor sweating sister. No more sneaking off to the latrine for breaks. You'll line up for early mass, then eat your breakfasts on the run, with a bare half turn of the sand for midday dinner."

"Quite right, Mister Shaddle," smiled the clerk of the spicery. "And I shall scour the markets, day after day, for the necessary refinements of exotic flavour. I shall leave no darkest corner of London unexplored. Be assured, the feast will include the most expensive spices."

Shaddle regarded his least explicable underling with mixed emotions. "Are you telling me, Master Bowyer," he said eventually, "that you intend being out of the house more often than not?"

Alex smiled reassuringly. "Naturally. Not much I can do in the kitchens until the spicery is fully stocked."

"But the grinding, the grating and the pounding? All the preparations?" suggested the Steward. "Not that I've any complaint about the standard of your work, lad. But all day every day at market? Is that really necessary?"

"Oh, I'll be back from time to time," Alex nodded cheerfully. "But you're right, Mister Shaddle. We need to do our very best, each of us within our own speciality. And that means me out in the cold, discovering the city's finest ingredients. I shall have a miserable back-breaking time of it of course. But anything for the reputation of the Sheffield title."

Shaddle frowned. He had a feeling he was being duped. "And all these fancy drinks and sweetmeats you keep sending up to the lady's nurse, lad? Is that part of your duties too?"

"Indeed it is," smiled Alex, shrugging on his livery surcoat, ready for a quick departure. "What better way to keep a lady happy than please her faithful nurse. I can hardly send gifts to the lady herself, which would be most improper. Besides, she keeps saying she doesn't want anything. I believe she's missing her family. So please the nurse, and you please the lady. Please the lady, and you certainly please the lord."

"It sounds very convincing to me," interrupted Hewitt. The cook had received considerable and unexpected assistance from the clerk of the spicery over previous days. "Fair fast coming as good as an apothecary, he is," Hewitt added. "Young Alex'll make a mighty useful member of staff I reckon, an' we let him go his own way."

The West Cheap, London's principal highway, encompassed the extremes of Goldsmith's Row on into the stench of offal puddings and the bloody gutters of the Poultry. Alley pocked shadows led off, but the main road was wide and grand and fully cobbled. Houses five storeys high leaned their protruding gables, as if bending over to listen to the ladies' gossip in the street below. The visible sliver of sky narrowed as the richer quarter ran east into the butcheries of the Poultry, on past the unfortunates chained in the stocks at Cornhill, and down towards the bustle of The Bridge. Alex pushed through the crowds, the stall holders screaming their wares, the sudden rush of an officer on horseback sending every shopper scurrying back against the walls, barrow wheels squelching through mud and refuse, and the loud incessant fury of bargaining and barter. Stray dogs, ribs deep furrowed, foraged the rubbish heaps, and squabbling ravens picked along the gutters, flapping up in constant disturbance from passers by, back again to catch another thrown chicken head.

Early enough to risk the emptying of chamber pots from the upper storeys while passing beneath, Alex pushed up into St. Margaret's Lane and found the Blossom Inn still closed. He swore at the darkened windows, discovered he was standing in the exact same commodity with which his cursing made reference, and turned. Merevale chuckled. "You're early," he said. "And if you have to wear nasty cheap shoes that look as if they've been fashioned out of cabbage leaves instead of leather, then at least watch what you stand in."

"I had to get out of the house," Alex scowled, scraping his heels against the tavern's doorstep. "They were expecting me to work. The damned place is getting dangerous."

"How's the nursemaid?" inquired Merevale. "She doesn't seem to have put you in a placid temper."

Alex grinned suddenly. "I got the wrong woman. Wretched female told me so many lies when I met her, I had no idea who she actually was."

"A woman who lies?" Merevale twitched his surcoat collar into place, thick sable up around his ears. "How unusual. Should suit you very well, coz."

"Might, if I ever get hold of her," admitted Alex. "Turns out she's the affianced bride of my lord and master, the bastard who now wears your family title. Not an entirely willing bride, I gather. But then he's not a prepossessing specimen. Must have been a shock when the poor girl first met him. Whoever arranged the marriage, had no particular care for the girl's sensibilities."

"Well, that's normal," frowned Merevale. "Why should they? You do say some odd things sometimes, coz. Don't tell me you'd like to marry the wench yourself?"

Alex blanched. "Good lord no," he said, kicking at the tavern door. "Don't be absurd Mel. I've not the smallest notion of commitment on any score except Lovel's, not that any sane woman would have me. Now, is this damned inn going to open its doors, or do I have to kick them down?"

The upper storeys were creaking in the wind, the strange whine of old wooden beams stretched beneath too much weight, like the masts of the carracks and carvels moored along the Thames. The door opened in a long black crack and a pink nose tip peeped out. "If the gentlemen were wanting – "

"Yes, we were," said Alex. "What sort of customers do you get, for goodness sake? It must be gone eight."

"Be it seven on the grain," muttered the voice within. "We was open earlier for the break-fast ale, but it's the habit to shut for a bit when the carriers come wi' the rolling of the barrels. We opens again when the cellars is put to rights."

"Well, put them to rights, and be quick about it," said Merevale. "It's bastard cold out here."

The tavern keeper, unimpressed by Alex's shabby livery, eyed Merevale's damasked velvets and hurriedly opened his doors wider. "There's a fire already high in the small back chamber, gentlemen, if you've a mind - "

"What's it like, living with Daniel and Mary again?" Alex asked, as they sat either side of the hearth, wine cups filled.

"They both behave as though they're the only suffering souls in the whole country," Merevale glowered. "There's half the old nobility either attainted or under threat of attainder, great houses standing empty and idle with their servants thrown out on the streets, a thousand women sobbing into their kerchiefs for the slaughter of their husbands and sons, and as many dead from this new sickness. But my big brother carries on as if Henry Tudor and his foul army invaded England purely to annoy Daniel and deprive Mary of her luxuries."

"I was wondering," nodded Alex, "whether you've had time to make your own decisions, coz? Are you coming to join Lovel with me, or not?"

Merevale frowned. "It's risky, talking like that. They'll pick you up if you're not careful, Alex." He leaned forward and lowered his voice. "Tudor has a new network of spies, they say. He's a man who knows how to watch his back. He's no fool, to think himself popular, or truly welcomed as king. A throne gained by conquest and not by the right of bloodline, needs to be constantly protected and a long life in exile taught him ruthless severity. He'll rule with a harsh hand, this one."

"Unless we get rid of him," said Alex.

"People adapt," sighed Merevale, draining his cup. "The merchants are gaining new trade now France is an ally. You're part of a household loyal to the new king coz. Don't you hear the news with a Lancastrian bias?"

Alex laughed. "I'm a servant, Mel. The only news I hear is whether Hewitt's burned the porridge again. But don't tell me you're feeling tolerant towards the bastard who flung you in the Tower?"

"Tolerant, never." Merevale leaned back and stretched his boots up to the raised hearth. "But after one visit to the Tower, I've no desire to return on a permanent basis. Yes, I'll join you and Lovel once I hear there's a proper army mustered, with some hope of success. Until then, I'm staying out. Keep me informed, coz, should you hear anything, and I'll try and get news myself when I can. But the attainder means little to me you know. So, now there's nothing to inherit! But as the younger brother, I was never going to inherit anything anyway. Perhaps we should both sail the seas after all, coz."

There was a spit of snow in the air as they left the inn and Merevale pulled the edges of his surcoat across his doublet. The sable spangled a little, the soft fur catching the damp white crystals. A gentleman dressed in the first style of elegance would not normally allow himself to be seen in amicable company with a servant, and Merevale shoved the spare cape he carried at his cousin. It was heavy wool with a high collar but no fur trimmings. "Take this and warm yourself, Alex," he said. "For goodness sake, hide your miserable broadcloth. And I'll have you know, that insipid pale blue doesn't suit you at all."

Alex took the cape he had originally bought himself with a stolen candle snuffer, and wrapped it around his shoulders. "I'll let the new Earl of Sheffield know you don't approve of his choice of livery," said Alex. "I'm sure he'll change it at once."

The two men turned back into Cheapside, continuing up towards Goldsmith's Row and the Shambles. The snow began to gust into flurries, settling in a fine white dust across the stalls of salads and roots with their grand fat cabbages and curly pig tailed parsnips. Alex was looking for something to buy, to account for his long absence from the kitchens. Merevale said, "Do you mean to start bargaining for little packages of things, while I have to stand and watch?

Honestly, coz, you always were eccentric, but this is becoming unhealthy."

Alex grinned. "Go away then, Mel. I can't go back with nothing; I've been gone all morning. There's a seld run by an old witch of a woman along here, has the best whole mace I've seen in the city." He pointed to a striped cover and a dark wooden barrow beneath, glittering with tubs of coloured powders.

Merevale eyed his cousin with some concern. "I do believe you're starting to enjoy this stuff, Alex. For God's sake watch yourself or you'll be taking it up as a profession, and even turn respectable. And this place stinks. What the devil is a mace anyway? It looks like donkey excrement."

Alex rubbed an appreciative finger over the dark fibrous skin of the fruit. "Very useful friendly thing, mace," said Alex fondly. "Skin makes sacking. Flesh makes medicinal jams. Grate it for breads and beers, crumble it for medicks, grind it for powdered spice. Then the kernel hidden inside is the nutmeg." He grinned up at Merevale, who was looking shocked at this amount of knowledge being freely forced upon him. "It's amazing what you learn in an average kitchen."

"Yes, amongst the pig swill and smoke, I hate to think," murmured Merevale. "You'll smell of it all soon, coz, and then I shall have to carry a nosegay."

Alex smiled politely and sniffed the pervading perfumes of London's largest market. The stench of gizzards, blood and shit, the soot and belching reek of fumes from the chimneys above, and the central gutters of decaying rubbish from the stalls and shops, masked the subtle tang of the spices on offer before them. "In future I shall endeavour," he said, "to wash the unnatural odours from my person before daring to come and meet you, Mel." He picked up the mace he'd chosen, and then a small cask of treacle syrup, fumbled in his purse for the silver pennies required, and then decided on a twist of ground turmeric to add to the substance of his excuse. "It's your own fault, coz," he continued as they walked away, crossing the main thoroughfare up towards Cripplegate. "I only came back to London to pull you out of the bloody dungeons, and no doubt I'd have left again by now if I wasn't hoping you'd join me."

"Of course I'll come. Eventually," grinned Merevale. "Just give me a few weeks to enjoy my freedom before you get me arrested again."

"At least you live in style and comfort in the meantime," Alex pointed out. "Unlike some of us."

The gentle puff of fish scales rose from Friday Street, running south as Alex and Merevale turned north. Both sides of the thoroughfare were packed with the business of buying and selling; stalls and barrows jutting out haphazard into the street and leaving little space for customers to avoid the filth in the central gullies. Shop owners sat in their doorways, shouting prices and services, brushing the snow from their laps and shoulders. A scurry of young pigs was being herded by the swine boy up towards their slaughter at the Shambles, passing a small herd of geese, feet black tarred, pattering down from the Newgate to their destiny at The Poultry. Fresh winter meat being scarce, late arrivals from out of the city were essential, but simultaneous passage was invariably unfortunate. The geese took great exception to the pigs. Rearing up and hissing, they flapped huge wings into the faces of the women haggling over twine, trivets and tonics. A stall keeper rushed out from his awning and waved a kerchief to chase them off. He got a mouthful of feathers and a yell from the goose boy. Beyond the squealing and hissing, with a piglet escaping into an ironmonger's and a goose trapped beneath a barrow's wheels, Alex turned, hearing a distant but more urgent sound.

Below the stone Eleanor Cross, a group of ruffians was jeering at a young servant girl who had clasped something protectively into a fold of her apron. One of the boys spat and threw a stone. The girl faced away from Alex, but he saw her stumble back and guessed the stone hadn't missed. The three urchins capered, prising up the muck at their feet, kicking it upwards so the shit spun in wet muddy drops, spattering against the girl, her clothes and her face. She seemed frustrated, unable to fight back due to whatever she held in her apron. She ran at one of the boys, trying to stamp on his toes, then turned to another and kicked him in the shin. Her pointed toe left a large patch on his bare hairy leg and he clutched at it, hopping and shouting.

Alex began to stride forwards. "Leave it," begged Merevale,

receiving the small parcels that Alex thrust at him. "You'll start a hue and cry, see if you don't. For pity's sake, must you always get involved?"

But Alex, unarmed himself, had pulled Merevale's sword from its velvet scabbard and was already amongst the boys. He turned quickly, pivoting on his heels, thwacking one urchin across his backside with the flat of the blade, another across his grubby knees, and stabbed the steel point straight at the nose of the third. Faced with a large, muscled and angry armed man, none made attempt at retaliation and all three snivelled loudly, running off at once into the dark side streets. Alex turned to the girl in the rather soiled servant's gown, with her crumpled apron bundled up in her hands and her little cap askew over her brown curls.

"You," said Alex in sudden surprise.

Huge brown eyes regarded him reproachfully. "You," said the countess.

CHAPTER TEN

He was tempted to reach out a snow damp finger and wipe off the little droplets of mud and muck that freckled her face. He resisted. "Dressing up in someone else's clothes again? Getting into trouble again? You really are the most annoying girl. And what the devil have you got wrapped up there?"

He pointed at the bundle she had made of her apron, which appeared to be wriggling. She glared at him. "None of your business. You've no right to question me at all. Go away."

Merevale had sauntered over. His obvious station kept the crowd at a distance and only curious glances followed his approach. He said, in a voice that attempted authority, "Causing a disturbance is punished severely, you know. I could have you put in the stocks, young man."

Alex grinned at his cousin. "My apologies, sir. It's the lady's nurse from the house where I work. She was attacked, and not her own fault, sir. I'll take her home now, with your leave."

"Um. Yes," said Merevale, mouth twitching. "Though I'll have my sword back first, if you don't mind."

With a slight bow, Alex presented it hilt first to its owner. "I'll be off then."

Since the girl showed no intention of accompanying him, Alex took her elbow. She pushed him away. He persisted. "You've no idea who I am," she said through her teeth. "You'll end up in trouble if you try to do anything to me, I warn you. And since I suppose you sort of rescued me, in fairness, I'll give you the chance to get away now."

Alex smiled fondly, meanwhile removing her forcibly from the gaping interest of the crowd and ducking into the unpaved back streets. "I know exactly who you are," he said cheerfully "You're a damned nuisance, that's who you are. You're also Mistress Katherine Ashingham, and you'll end up in just as much embarrassing trouble as I will, if you're taken by the constable dressed like that."

She gaped at him, standing firm a moment and resisting his grip. "How do you know my name?" she demanded.

Bread Street was narrow and dark, leading straight through into Candlewick, and the central gutter, being cluttered, left little space for two to walk side by side. It was no longer busy, most of the baker's shops having closed after early sales. It was now dinner time and the shoppers were hurrying back to warm themselves, eat a hearty midday meal, and escape the increasing snow fall. Mistress Katherine shivered. Alex pulled her on. "Because I work for your new husband," he said with a grin. "Poor man. He doesn't know what misery he's in for."

"How dare you talk to me like that," she accused. Hurried roughly down the sloping street, she nearly tripped over her maid's shoes. "And let me go. I'll have you – whipped." Since he ignored her and continued to drag her onwards, she had another thought. "If you work for him," she said, a little breathless now, "that means you work for me. I'll – I'll dismiss you."

"No you won't," said Alex. "Because I'll quite cheerfully blackmail you. And since I've just saved your life – or your virtue – or possibly both – I consider you appallingly ungrateful."

"I could have handled those horrid boys myself, if you hadn't butted in," she told him. "But I would have been grateful – if it hadn't been you. You nearly got me beaten last time. In fact, come to think of it, you're the reason for my being married to that ghastly Edmund creature in the first place."

Alex stopped suddenly and turned to face her. "Really? How ironic.

Tell me how that happened. Or am I simply to blame for all your problems?"

She looked up at him, snowflakes on her eyelashes. "After they opened the barn door and you ran off, they took me to my father. He was furious. Said I needed taming, and hadn't learned manners or decorum. He even said it was my mother's fault, which was terribly unfair, since she died when I was three."

"He presumably meant growing up without a mother," smiled Alex. "Probably true. You certainly don't behave like any other ladies I've ever known."

"And of course, being a common soldier and a poacher and a servant, you've known hundreds of ladies," she said with pronounced scorn.

"Yes," Alex nodded cheerfully. "Hundreds at least. Many intimately." He began to walk on without releasing his grip on her elbow.

The lady scowled, trotting unwillingly beside him. "So my father said he'd received an offer of marriage for me. He'd intended turning it down, but now he wouldn't. He said if he couldn't control me, then maybe my husband could. So it's totally all your fault. And then to find you actually work for him. It's – it's - "

"It's quite amusing," said Alex. "And what the devil have you got cuddled up in that absurd apron anyway?"

He stopped again, frowning at her, then reached down and flicked back the edge of the linen which covered her parcel. Two minute furred faces peeped out at him. "You collect rats?" he said with some surprise.

"Stupid man," said the Katherine. "They're kittens. I'm taking them home."

Alex laughed. "Pulled from the rubbish dump? What an odd girl you are indeed."

"Those horrid boys were going to use them as footballs," she glared. "I rescued them and kicked the boys instead. And it's none of your business. Besides, that wretched house is full of mice and rats. We could do with something to clear them out."

"The size these are at the moment, the mice would eat them," said

79

Alex. "They'll need hand rearing for a month at least. You're a country girl. You should know."

"I do know," said the lady with suppressed annoyance. "I used to look after lots of abandoned animals at home. Though why I'm telling you anything, I don't know. You can escort me back to that beastly house if you must, but you've no right to question me. Nor touch me. And certainly not criticise me."

"I can't imagine anyone knowing you without the irresistible temptation to criticise you," said Alex imperturbably, without releasing his grip on her elbow. "And what's this new disguise about anyway? Stealing Sara's clothes and walking off alone into the Chepes. A remarkably stupid thing to do. You've obviously no idea how dangerous London can be."

"Oh not with gallant knights around like you to save us, surely?" said the lady with elaborate sarcasm. "Besides, you can't know how disgustingly dull that horrid house is. Just sitting around, day after day with nothing to do, waiting for the inevitable wedding. I wake up feeling sick every morning. I had to get out."

"So go to church," suggested Alex, "and pray for salvation. You've enough sins that need forgiving, after all. Or just walk in the gardens. Sit down by the river and watch the shit go up and down with the tide. At least have the sense not to go to the busiest and most dangerous parts of the city. You'll be wandering the Southwark stewes next."

"I've no idea what they are, or maybe I would," said the lady. "It's frustrating being so close to London, and not seeing any of it. All my life I wanted to see London. It always sounded so exciting."

"Like battles," nodded Alex. "The other big thrill you wanted to know all about, if I remember. You'd better get these nonsensical ideas out of your head before the marriage or the charming Lord Edmund might get into the habit of beating you too."

They were skirting around the outside of St. Paul's since Alex wished to avoid the throngs of congregation, itinerant sellers, lawyers and solicitors, ecclesiastical clerks, monks and vagrants. Miss Katherine, however, stopped mid stride and stared upwards. The wooden spire soared gloriously above her into the swirling snow. "I always wanted to see the East Minster," she said, faint with awe. "My father says the steeple's one of the tallest in England. And he said the bells are just magnificent. Isn't it all wonderful?"

Alex shook his head. "Makes a useful short cut when it's raining," he said. "If you want to stare at clouds, you should have come here before, instead of the damned market. Then you'd have been safe, and I wouldn't have bumped into you."

"To tell the truth, I meant to," admitted the Miss Katherine. "But I got lost. I just ended up following the crowd, and then I saw the kittens."

"Since you never seem to have the smallest compulsion to tell the truth," said Alex, "I've no reason to believe anything you say. However, London's an easy place to get lost in, when you don't know your way around. Now, will you stop peering up like a country bumpkin, and come with me. I'm missing my dinner."

"Please can we go inside?" pleaded the lady. "Just for a quick look?"

"No, certainly not," said Alex, pulling her away. "It gets as crowded inside as outside, and on a day like this they'll have fires lit all through the nave. The smoke'll be noxious and it'll be a shocking squash and I don't want to bump into anyone I know."

The lady glared up at him. "Oh yes, I'm sure you know all the lawyers and priests. Just like the hundreds of ladies you claim you've known. Just what do you do, anyway?"

They were leaving St. Paul's behind, its great steeple almost obscured now by the thickening snow storm. "Clerk of the spicery," said Alex with a grin. "Impressed?"

Mistress Katherine craned her neck around, staring back for one last gaze at the mighty cathedral. Then a sudden thought occurred to her. "You mean you're that dreadful man who keeps giving my nurse indigestion? All those horrid little possets with cinnamon and badly crushed almonds? I thought it was some decrepit old servant who wanted to pay court to my Sara. So just why have you been chasing after my nurse?"

"To get to you," said Alex simply. "Now, keep quiet while we go through the Ludgate. This particular gatekeeper's always on the lookout for the wrong sort of people heading out towards the court and the bishop's palaces. Just remember you're a maid, and keep walking."

"I should tell him about you then," muttered the lady. "Tell him you're abducting me."

"You'd be in as much trouble yourself," Alex pointed out. "Besides, I was out on honest business I'll have you know, and then rescued a stupid serving girl who'd antagonised a group of street urchins."

"Honest business?" objected the lady. "All this time, just for those three little packets you're carrying? Besides, you stole that man's sword."

"What man? Oh yes, – him," smiled Alex. "But I gave it back. Now just behave like a lady for once, and keep quiet. Then I'll smuggle you into the house through the kitchens without anyone knowing who you are."

The Strand, wide and well paved, was a whirl of gusting snow crystals. The walls of Sheffield House were soon before them. The house was grand, its height and girth plastered rosy in between the squared black beams, great oriel windows along the first floor, then tiny squashed mullions above in shiny green swirls, the whole blurred by the early November storm. Alex took Katherine by the shoulders, stood her firm in front of him and looked disapprovingly at her. "What's the matter now?" she demanded.

Alex licked his thumb and began to remove the spatter of little black spots from her face, including a large splodge from the tip of her nose. She wriggled. "Stand still," he commanded. "Even a disreputable maid servant isn't going to approach her mistress looking like that. And even young Tom's doublet fitted you better than Sara's gown. It's too tight, too long, and too old. The cape looks as though it once belonged to her grandmother and the cap's creased to hell. It's been very badly starched and now it's wet, it looks dreadful. Didn't your father ever put his hand in his purse for some decent livery? All your staff seem to be wearing little more than rags."

The lady allowed her face to be wiped clean, but scowled, blinking between onslaughts. "As if you look any better," she accused. "Your livery is horrid. That baby blue looks more like marchpane than broadcloth. Your cloak doesn't match the rest, and your hose are laddered."

Alex grinned. "The cloak isn't part of the livery. I shouldn't really be wearing it, but it's too damned cold. And you shouldn't be looking at my hose."

Hewitt stared in some amazement as his clerk of the spicery pushed the young woman, her head kept low, through the back pantries towards the front of the house. Neither Shaddle nor any of the principal staff were present, and the kitchen boys carefully took no notice, heads lower than the lady's and eyes averted. Alex saw his captive onto the main staircase, and returned to the kitchens.

"And just wot were that all about?" demanded Hewitt, as Alex unlocked the spicery cupboard and stored his packages.

"One of Mistress Katherine's personal maids," said Alex. "Met up with her in Cheapside. Escorted her home. It's snowing."

"You mean she were out there all on her own?" demanded Hewitt, now considering himself an experienced sophisticate. "Most improper. Don't these country people know to send maids out in pairs?"

"They've no notion how dangerous the city is," smiled Alex, coming over to the table and helping himself to pottage from the cauldron. "She'll learn."

"Well, we've all had to do that, master Bowyer," agreed the cook. "Lucky you recognised her, though I don't know how. We never sees none of the lady's staff."

"A chance meeting," grinned Alex, "while buying mace." He ladled the pottage into his bowl, took a spoonful and pulled a face. "Your pottage is a little better than usual, Mister Hewitt. Congratulations."

Hewitt hid a proud smile. "Well, it were well done of you to bring the young girl back safely, Master Bowyer," he said. "I hope you managed to finish all your own business too. Must have been a great inconvenience for you."

Katherine scurried up the stairs, keeping to the shadows. Although it was now snowing very heavily and the day had turned dark, Lord Edmund had not yet ordered the candles lit. Since he was in his study with his secretary and three of his friends, the light on the stairs and in the main hall did not interest him. He invariably ordered his servants to conserve expense when possible, habits learned in exile from his master Henry Tudor.

Up the stairs and along the wide corridor, the lady flung open her chamber door, rushed inside, upended her apron folds, and threw herself on the bed in a collapse of giggles.

Sara Whitstable rushed over, concerned. "Thank the Lord you're back, my dear," she said. "I've been worried sick."

"Mind those kittens," said the lady, rolling onto her back. "Such tiny little things. See how pretty they are? But they'll need a lot of looking after, and you have to help me."

Sara Whitstable sat on the edge of the grand bed and took one of the minute balls of fur into her hand. "Well, with all the mice in this house, we can do with them," she said. "But I warn you, my dear, you have to stop these wild adventures. What if something had happened, with you wearing my clothes and all on your own? I should have been beaten too, you know, as soon as I admitted you'd taken my gown and apron with my knowledge."

The lady smiled up at the high tester of her four poster bed, huge swags of embroidered velvet in crimson and gold. She addressed the air. "I'm sorry you were worried, Whitsy," said the lady. "But I've had the most fascinating time."

CHAPTER ELEVEN

M istress Katherine Ashingham became the Countess of
Sheffield, standing beside her husband in the chapel porch
attached to the church of All Saints. It had stopped snowing but a fine
silver sleet frosted the air and the wedding guest's shoulders, and
seeped through headdresses and cloaks. The countess was not
accompanied by either of her parents, her mother being long deceased
and her disillusioned father, having presided over her marriage by
proxy, was no longer required.

The bride wore a gown of silk tissue, elaborately patterned in
scarlet with gold loops. The separate sleeves of satin dyed with
cinnabar were taken from another gown and worn over an
undersleeve of fine blue velvet. Her bodice was low cut and the sable
trim nestled against the swell of her breasts, a fine transparent gauze
tucked across her cleavage. The huge openings of her sleeves were
also trimmed in sable, and hung almost to her hems. Her stomacher,
heavy gold damask, divided bodice from skirts, which fell into a
sweeping train caught up by her young page, dressed in his proud new
livery, and held over his arm while trying not to crease the soft fabric
between his nervous fingers. Her hair line and her brows had been
severely plucked and her thick brown curls, no bridal display of

maidenly hair, was pinned up beneath a pillbox bonnet with the short starched veil flicked back.

She looked distinctly unhappy.

Although the lady was accompanied by her much favoured Nurse Sara, none of the earl's staff were invited to witness the ceremony. Lord Edmund was accompanied by a considerable crowd of friends, of which he seemingly had many, it being distinctly politic to fraternise with those now in royal favour. Some of the guests were already somewhat intoxicated. The bride glared at all of them, and especially at her husband.

The minuscule priest blessed the union, kept his unblinking blue eyes on his crucifix, shook holy water from pockmarked and trembling hands, ignored the ribaldry from the young men present, and then slammed the church doors on them. The bridegroom bent and made some semblance of kissing his wife. She was aware of the scratch of moustache, the glitter of pale grey eyes and the smell of stale beer. She was then allowed to walk with her nurse while he strode off to laugh with his friends. They arrived back at the house separately, the bride making a deliberate choice to dawdle along the street, even though this meant getting rather wet and very cold.

This day the Earl of Sheffield had decided not to follow youthful fashion, so did not wear the very short style of doublet designed to display every curve of a good thigh and a well turned calf. He had dressed instead in sumptuous tradition, in a long skirted doublet of emerald baudekin, threaded in gold over a dazzling silver tissue shirt collared in lettice, and beneath a full length surcoat of mustard velvet lined in black taffeta and again trimmed in lettice. His hose, though knitted in fine pea green silk, still managed to wrinkle at the ankles and the curvature of the shin bone was unfortunately accentuated by long crimson stripes woven into the stocking. He marched into his own hall and called for the feast to be set.

An enormous fire hissed and spat across the hearth, dazzling its scarlet shadows along the panelling, while the rest of the hall was lit with a hundred pure beeswax candles shimmering from the tables, the sconces and the central chandelier.

The bride sat at the ladies' table with four of the gentlemen's wives and stared into space muttering inaudible pleasantries when addressed. The bridegroom sat in the grand gilded chair at the longer table, surrounded by his friends. He began immediately on the wine, being the best malmsey, followed by liberal muscatel and vernaccia, and finally a sweet Malaga sack. He seemed to consider the fancy food incidental.

Since Hewitt was the principal cook as on all occasions, this was perhaps understandable. The sumptuous addition of every spice the obliging clerk of the spicery could produce, grind, grate, slice or pound, added considerably to the remarkably rich colours, the most unusual perfumes, and the general indigestion.

There were three hearty courses, starting with roast boar in a mustard and pepper coating, pickled lampreys, lobster in splendid sauce (somewhat over-cooked), frumenty (almost solidly gelatinous), eels (badly boned) in a bed of grated turnip and cloves, and bull's testicles stuffed with onions, parsley and ground nutmeg. The second course was a little lighter, with galantines (rather runny) and a compote of dates and prunes with ginger, a large pike with a furious expression and a dusting of cinnamon which made its scales appear leprous, beans cooked in almond milk and crab meat encroute (burned around the edges) with crushed grapes and a thick mace jam.

The final course consisted only of small custard pies and subtleties, having been constructed, in the absence of anyone specialised in the art of sugar carving, by the clerk of the spicery. The subtleties tended to droop a little in the heat of the hall and what had begun as a pheasant in flight, soon resembled a butchered thrush collapsed upon its nest.

Indeed, the clerk of the spicery, noting that most of the gentlemen guests, including the groom, were completely cupshotten, had decided to add himself to the list of official servers, and made a point of warning the bride, whispering into his collar as he filled her wine cup, that the crab meat was a little off, the pickled lampreys shockingly over-spiced and the custard pies underdone, which meant they'd spurt as she ate them, spilling an inevitable drool of hot custard into her cleavage.

The countess's page boy, now smart in pale blue livery courtesy of his new lord, stood the entire evening behind his mistress's chair and tried to keep a stiff back and not snigger at inappropriate moments.

The Lady Katherine maintained a wooden expression and gazed with determination into the distance during the feast, eating little, and picking only at the melting subtleties with a slight uncontrollable twitch of her dimples.

The feast finally over, cups raised in toasts with frequent allusions to potency, virility, bulls in heat and stags in rut, the earl stood and came over to his bride, bowed – though not too low in case he fell over – and informed her it was time to retire to bed. She blushed, which seemed heightened by the firelight, and stood, holding up her train. The earl then led the way upstairs, surrounded by his friends who had relapsed into bawdy song. The lady followed, accompanied by the other women and her nurse, who pushed rather improperly to her side and thrust a helpful arm around her waist.

It was the first time Lady Katherine had ever seen the earl's bedchamber and at first she seemed a little unnerved. The room was large and entirely painted in vivid and contrasting colours. The bed hangings were chequered in gold and scarlet and the lavish bed cover was checked vair; squirrel fur in squares of black and white. The ceiling beams were crimson with gold studs, the plaster azure with gold studs, and the huge mantle green marble, with gold studs. A fire had been set, the windows shuttered, and the chamber sweltered.

The earl waved a peremptory hand at his friends. "And we'll have none of that undressing in public business," he said. "We'll celebrate our marriage quite well without you lot. Off with you now. I believe I can scramble out of my wedding finery all by myself thank you." The young men looked disappointed. Seeing the bridal pair stripped and settled in bed beside each other in suitable embarrassment was part of the guest's prerogative. The earl shook his head. "I'm too old for that nonsense," he said. "Go down and finish the calvados."

This being a satisfactory alternative, the men trooped from the room, taking their wives with them and leaving Katherine and her nurse standing uncomfortably beside the door.

The earl came over and stood, looking his bride over. Katherine curtsied, keeping her eyes on her toes. Lord Edmund turned to the nurse. "Alright, alright," he said. "You can go now. I'm quite capable of undressing myself and my wife too. Come back in the morning and you can take her back to her own chamber. For tonight, you're no longer needed."

Alone with his wife, the earl took her hand and led her to the bed. He then stretched himself on the fur cover, crossed his ankles, put his hands behind his head, and regarded her with vague intensity.

"Well, now my dear," he said, distinctly slurred, "never did learn much about women, you know. The Breton whores are a rough bunch, tell the truth. And the French, well the brothels there are so damned diseased, you'd scarce trust your prick anywhere near them, not more than once a month at any rate." Lord Edmund sighed, lost in sweet memories for a few moments. Then he opened his eyes again and smiled. "Fact is, I'm as pissed as a fart now anyway, so I doubt I could get it up. Just get yourself undressed like a good girl. I'll give you a hand if you come over here and stand still. Then let me look you over and see what's on the menu for the future, and then we can both get to sleep."

Downstairs in the great kitchens, the fire was guttering. The kitchen boys had finished the washing and scrubbing and were curled on the damp boards in the corners, eyes drooping, waiting for permission to scuttle off to their pallets. Hewitt, red faced and shirt sleeves rolled up, was sitting beside the hearth, gulping down the large quantities of malmsey which had been left in the cups. He was exhausted.

"If'n his lordship wants more feasts like that," he rumbled, "We'll need to take on extra staff, I'm telling you. Well nigh killed me, this lot did. All them courses and nicky knackies, stuffing this and stuffing that. I don't mind telling you, Master Bowyer, I couldn't have done it without you. Grand spices in everything there was, just like proper nobility."

"Glad to have been of service, Mister Hewitt." The clerk of the spicery was lounging on the high backed chair at the head of the table, one leg up on the scrubbed wood, the other swinging. "I think it all went very well," he said softly. "His lordship should have been suitably impressed." He was smiling, his face half lit by the last tongues of flame as the fire spat into soot, but his eyes remained strangely hard, as if the smile could not find them.

The Lady Katherine did not wait until the following morning to be collected by her nurse. She waited only until there was heavy snoring from the prone figure beside her, then slipped quickly from the bed, pulled on her blanchet, grabbed the rest of her clothes into a bundle, and scurried bare foot along the cold passages back to her own chamber. Abandoning pride, she clambered into bed and burst into tears. Her nurse leapt, startled, from the truckle where she slept at the foot of her mistress's four poster, and rushed to comfort her. Katherine sobbed on her shoulder.

"Did he - " murmured Sara, "did he do something terrible, Kate dear?"

"He's a drunken sot," sniffed the lady. "He's insulting and ugly and rude."

"I don't believe men can help being ugly, my dear," suggested the nurse. "Indeed, most of them are, I've noticed. But insulting? What on earth did he do?"

"He didn't do anything," Katherine admitted, sitting up and blowing her nose with the kerchief Sara offered her. "But he took all his clothes off – which was hideous. And he made me do the same. Then he sort of – poked me. Here. And then he made rude remarks and went to sleep with his mouth hanging open. How can I ever let him touch me again?"

"He didn't - " ventured the nurse, "actually – as they say – make love to you?"

"He wouldn't know the meaning of the word," snorted Kate. "But that's the good part. I'm so blessedly thankful he didn't. But he will next time, when he's not so soused. There's only one thing for it."

It was a frosty mid-morning and Alex was pounding cassia bark very hard when the summons came. He had no very precise idea of what to do with ground cassia bark once he had it, but slamming the pestle repeatedly into the bowl suited his mood perfectly. His restless and uncomfortable imagination, which had kept him awake and strangely overheated for most of the night, was now sternly repressed by the strenuous use of the pestle. The brown powder splattered flecks along his fingers and under his finger nails. He spread his fingers in disgust, and returned to the pounding. A mistimed blow spun against the side of the bowl and Tom the page took a quick step back as the mortar sped across the table towards him.

"Catch it, don't run away from it," complained Alex. "What do you want anyway?"

"Why's everyone so pissy this morning?" remarked Tom. "And after that nice party too. I suppose you've got a headache as well."

Alex raised an eyebrow. "Tell me."

"It's – Sara," said Tom, reverting to the glazed expression he adopted when trying to recite a message correctly. "Miss Whitstable is suffering from a feverish headache. Miss Whitstable needs a curative tonick. Or a draught of something. I've forgotten what it was she actually asked for. But then she said something about bleeding."

Alex appeared startled. "Good Lord," he said. "I don't know the first thing about bleeding anyone and I don't own a fleam. Tell her to lie down somewhere and get over it."

"That's not very helpful," objected Tom. "You might at least offer a posset."

Alex leaned both elbows on the table and sighed. His mind was not on Nurse Sara's sufferings, but on the Lady Katherine losing her virginity to the wrong man altogether. "I suppose I could concoct something or other," he muttered.

Tom shook his head. "Don't you know anything? Aren't you supposed to know?"

Alex sat down and scowled at the small boy before him. "I'll have you know I'm a clerk of the spicery," he said, "not a damned doctor. Alright, admittedly sometimes the two things go together, but it's a damned confusing position, what with all these bits and pieces. Evidently it also involves wax, and candles and parchments and all sorts of other things I'm not in the slightest interested in. But when it comes to bleeding people, forget it."

"Well," said Tom, hands clasped behind his new smart pale blue back, "she wants you to come upstairs and see her. Prescribe something. Be helpful."

Alex sat in silence for a moment. The summons was unexpected.

Various ulterior motives suggested themselves. Eventually, warily, he said, "Upstairs where?"

"The mistress's chamber," said Tom loftily. "Right away."

"Ah." Alex stayed where he was. "The bedchamber?" Elderly maidens, especially once their charges were married and off their hands, could get strange ideas.

Tom said, "That's right. She's sick. You expect her to be running around the garden?"

"Oh, very well," Alex sighed. "I'll bring some hypocras. But you have to come with me, whelp, and stay at my side. I might need you."

The air tight tun of prepared hypocras stood in the driest part of the upper cellars, easily tapped for frequent use. Alex stomped down himself to fill a large jug, and brought it back up to the kitchens where Tom was waiting. The immediate perfume of cinnamon, cloves and nutmeg permeated the air, overtaking the previous scents of mutton tallow soap, turpentine, scrubbing bleach and vinegar. The scullions put down their brooms and looked up in appreciation. "Alright," said Alex to Tom. "Lead on."

The lady's chamber was barely lit. Although nearly eleven of the clock, the shutters had not yet been taken down from the windows and only one candle had been lit, placed in the far corner beside the entrance to the garderobe. Alex peered around for somewhere to put the jug. He was then aware of the door shutting behind him with a snap, and turned quickly. Tom had deserted him. Alex felt a distinct unease. It was not, in fact, the first time he had ever been forced into a compromising situation by a female, but in the past he had always been capable of making his own choices. This time he was a servant. He was fully aware, though never before at first hand, what trouble could come to a servant in such circumstances.

The woman lying within the deep shadows of the velvet bed hangings, began to sit up. Alex regarded her with misgivings. "I've brought hypocras," he said at once. "I really don't see what else I can do. I must warn you, I'm not a trained physician."

"Of course you're not," said the Lady Katherine. "You're a horrid soldier. You don't even know anything about spices. The stuff you served up to me yesterday was absolutely awful. Spices here, spices there, an absolute pestilence of pepper and mace. But that doesn't matter. I want to talk to you."

Alex grinned, put the jug and cup he carried down on a small table, and walked over to the bed. He pushed the two tiny scraps of wriggling kitten from their nest beside the pillows and then sat most improperly on the edge of the mattress, looking at the lady. Although it was dark and her face was deeply shaded, he could see her eyes were large and moist and her eyelashes were spangled with the damp of tears. Her face looked a little puffy. She was clutching a heavy blue brocade bedrobe up to her neck, and her hands were trembling.

Alex stopped grinning and sighed. "Tell me at once. I'll do what I can to help."

The Lady Katherine blew her nose. "Will you really? I mean, I know I get on your nerves, but you're the only person I can turn to. And I'll do my best not to let you get into trouble because of it."

"Good of you." Alex resisted the temptation to pat her hand. She was searching for a clean kerchief, which he saw folded on the cabinet beside the bed, and passed it to her. He took a deep breath. "So, brat, tell me what you want from me."

It was not the way Katherine was used to being addressed, especially by the staff, and she paused mid nose-blow. Then she hesitated, fumbled with her kerchiefs, eventually stuffed them both under the pillows, clutched her blanchet tight beneath her chin again, adjusted her knees beneath the bed covers and stared down at her lap. She took so long in discovering the courage to admit what she wanted, that Alex, sitting patiently watching her, began to get some interesting ideas. In fact, it was something of a disappointment when she finally spoke. "I want you to keep him drunk," she said in a rush. "All the time."

"The gallant Lord Edmund?"

The lady nodded vigorously. "Yes. And please don't ask for explanations. Can you do it?"

Alex frowned. "It's the Steward who controls the cellars and the wines. The only wine I deal with is the hypocras, because of the spices. Incidentally, I think you'd better have some. In fact, if you've got another cup up here, I'll have some myself."

There wasn't another cup. Alex poured the wine and passed it to the lady. When she had finished, he refilled the cup and drained it. "You're a very odd servant," she said, watching him. "Which is why I bet you could do it, if you wanted."

"I don't see why you can't just embroil your own staff in your dubious schemes," Alex said, pouring a third cupful. "I suppose you know I could get flayed for doing this."

She shook her head. "If you get caught, I'll take the blame," she insisted. "I'll confess I made you do it."

"You've no idea, have you," smiled the clerk of the spicery, downing the remaining hypocras. "We'd both get flayed, and I'd certainly lose my position. Mind you, I've no particular objections on that score."

"I won't let them hurt you, really I won't," she said. "I'm not that useless."

Alex grinned. "That's true. I've seen you in action." He sat down beside her on the bed again and this time patted her knee through the blankets. "Yes, I'll help."

The lady leaned back against the pillows with a shuddering exhalation of relief. "Oh, thank you," she breathed. "And you won't tell anyone else? Or ask me why?"

He grinned sympathetically. "I don't need to ask why. I'm not that lacking in imagination. I can guess. And I'm certainly not such a beetlehead as to tell anyone else."

"You see," she said with a sniff, "my ladies have been sent off because – he – said they were too expensive. Now I've only got Sara and Tom and my little dresser, who's no good at all. And how could any of us manage such a thing?" She was searching for another kerchief. "Do you really think you'll be able to do it? Without the Steward or – or Edmund – or anyone knowing?"

"You may think I'm ignorant with spices," said the clerk of the spicery, reaching for another kerchief from the pile, "but Shaddle thinks I'm a veritable genius. So does our cook. So I get a reasonably free hand with what I want to do. Incidentally, I'm not actually as bad as you think I am, it's just that these northerners believe a knowledge of spices to be the next best thing to the priesthood, and are all utterly over-awed. The more coloured powders I add to Hewitt's concoctions, the more impressed they all are. And I don't care. I don't have to eat it."

He held up the third clean kerchief for her to blow her nose, and then leaned over and tucked it beneath the pillow for her. She managed a smile. "Well, your hands are certainly covered in mucky powders. In fact, your finger nails are filthy."

"Just cassia, nothing more disreputable, I assure you." Alex paused, considering a moment. Then he said, "Are you really sure getting him drunk is going to do the trick? That is, men have been known, when suitably cupshotten, to become – what you might call more insistent, not less."

The lady blushed and retreated back into the shadows of her bed hangings. She looked carefully down at her lap. "I – think it will – work. And anyway – it's all I can think of."

"Well, as it happens, I can't think of anything else myself just yet," Alex admitted. "Except for poisoning the bastard, or stabbing him in the back. Though while getting whipped and sent off I can probably cope with, being hanged for murder, I can't. So pissed to the gills it must be."

She blinked, and nodded. "I do thank you. Very, very much. And I'm sorry to be such a nuisance. But – the more – insensible you can make him, the better. I mean, best if he can't even stand."

Alex chuckled. "You know, if you ever have the courage to actually admit the lurid details of the problem, I could probably advise you. But no doubt you won't. No matter. I shall do my best. In the meantime, while I won't be telling anyone about this conversation, I gather both your nurse and your page know everything."

"Oh no." The lady shook her head. "Just Sara. I always confide in her. But Tom's only nine or ten. He thinks this is just a game."

"Well, you'd better tell him it's a damned serious game, and not to go putting his foot in his mouth. The child already has the brain of a flea." Alex stood, with a faint waft of ground cinnamon. "And I'd better not get caught in your room, either. Just manage to keep that headache going for as long as possible. And if you need me again, send Tom down to say you need bleeding. I'll come up and visit you with my fleam. That's enough to frighten everyone else away. Either that, or a strong emetic."

She giggled slightly, half smile, half sniff. "Sara always says I need a good purge."

Her curls were thick and loose around her face, the first time he had seen her that way, and her eyes still looked moist. Alex leaned down very suddenly, and lightly kissed her cheek. "Yes, I know," he said, straightening up. "Most improper. But so is getting me up to your bedchamber with no one else here, and you wearing nothing but a bedrobe. And don't go getting indignant. Of course I can see you're not wearing anything underneath. You should disillusion yourself of the idea that I'm another country bumpkin with no experience of anything except poaching and common soldiering." He turned for the door, gathering up the empty jug and cup. "By the way," he added, "you'd better remember not to drink anything his lordship gets served from now on. I don't intend to poison the bastard, but I'll have to put more than wine in his cup. And since getting him legless every day may not be entirely practical, I suggest you start adopting some very poor health.

CHAPTER TWELVE

Alex strode down Lower Thames Street and concluded his shopping quickly in the large pungent shop behind the vintner's wharves. He then cut due north and headed for Cripplegate. Burton House was bright with fires and candles, and was considerably more welcoming than the house he had left a couple of hours back.

The Steward, however, took a step back when he saw the younger son of the late Baron Mornington on the doorstep, wearing the ill-fitting and slightly soiled livery of a servant. "Damnation Jenkins," demanded Alex. "Let me in quick before I freeze."

Merevale grinned as Alex swept into the lower solar, and deposited his packages on the table beneath the candelabra. "More little coloured powders, coz?"

"No, as it happens," said Alex, stretching himself into the chair before the fire. "Calvados, special strength, a couple of Uisge Beatha and a little poppy syrup."

Merevale nodded knowingly. "That bad is it? Planning to stay sotten and insensible under the kitchen table until they throw you out? Probably a good idea under the circumstances."

"Not for me," smiled Alex. "I've orders to keep a certain gentleman away from a certain lady's side. Goodness knows if it'll work, but she seems to think it will."

Merevale was immediately interested. "When did getting pissed ever keep a man from a woman's bed?" he demanded. "And who the devil is this misguided female anyway?"

"Now, that would be telling," said Alex. "Tell me about yourself instead, Mel. How is it with a house full of relatives? Haven't Daniel and his gentle wife sent you into permanent inebriation yet?"

"Almost," agreed Merevale. "But at least it's better than the Tower. Mind you, coz, I used to enjoy staying here with just Lizzie and the children. Always got on well with her husband you know. Burton was an affable man, and generous too. Now though it's Lizzie's property and little Stephen's officially the earl, Dan thinks himself the man of the house and throws his weight around. Not that Mary shows any signs of trying to keep him from her bed." Merevale sighed. "Or anyone else," he added, "Mary's not too fussy. Just prefers not sleeping alone it seems."

Alex raised an eyebrow. "Got you too, did she?"

Merevale laughed. "And you? Well, I might have guessed. Pretended not to like me in public, but she's been chasing me since I was only interested in chasing tadpoles. Not that I'm complaining. But you're getting very coy yourself, Alex. Keeping quiet about your little nursery maid, are you? Or is it the lady you spoke of before?"

Alex shook his head. "Nothing to do with either. It's some other girl I got to know. Nice girl. Just got married. Evidently had a horrendous experience. It was arranged of course, never knew the bastard before, and now she wants him kept at a distance. Honestly Mel, these girls are told nothing beforehand. It must come as quite a shock."

"Doesn't sound as if you're talking about a servant at all, coz," decided Merevale. "Come on. You used to confide in me. Who is she?"

"I'm not in a confiding mood," Alex smiled. "Nor do I intend to be. And it's no good thinking I've such loose morals as all that, because I haven't. Not all the time, anyway."

Merevale snorted. "Getting religious, coz? After what you did to Lizzie?"

Alex regarded his cousin with growing impatience. "I never touched Lizzie," he sighed. "I accept that little episode's left me with a reputation I'll never live down, but you know I never touched her."

"I know nothing of the sort," said Lizzie's brother cheerfully. "In fact, I'm sure you did. Lizzie would have made you. Now – who is this bastard who raped your lady friend?"

"God knows why I ever open my mouth to you," complained Alex. "She's not my lady friend and I never accused the bastard of rape. He married her, after all. I don't know what the problem is, she didn't tell me. I just assume he was violent, or has strange fancies. You know – tying her up and spanking her - or making her act like a horse. I knew a groom once who admitted – anyway, that's not quite the point. This girl asked for my help, that's all. No innuendoes. Poor little thing was quite upset. Now, do keep out of it Mel. It's not something I intend discussing."

"So – why did you come to see me?" Merevale asked.

"For civilised conversation about something other than puddings and sugars and possets and spices. I can see I needn't have bothered," said Alex. "And I've an idea I ought to be leaving London as soon as possible. Any decisions yet, Mel?"

Merevale nodded. "Yes, I told you so before," he said. "Next week, if you like, after the coronation. I have to stay for that. Lizzie's supposed to attend as the dowager countess and keep young Stephen from tripping over his gown. She's terrified, and furious she'll have to bend her knee again to that Tudor bastard. Besides, Danny and Mary are spitting mad they won't be invited. I suppose I ought to run away beforehand, but it seems fair to stay and placate the family. Then I'll happily leave with you, sometime before the Christmas season starts at least."

Alex nodded. "Good. A servant's life is getting me down. I've ground cinnamon so deep under my finger nails, I can't scrape it out. Besides, I think I'm getting too involved with – other things."

"The nursemaid?" Merevale grinned. "Go on, admit it. So you plan on abandoning her to her fate instead? And letting her amorous husband ravish her after all?"

"I can't keep him off her permanently," Alex sighed. "He's three times her age, but the bastard could live another thirty years. Anyway,

I told you I wasn't going to discuss it. I'll come again in a day or so, and we can make proper arrangements for the ride north. I'll need a horse."

"What, run out of stolen silver?" Merevale said.

Alex returned to the house before curfew, and went immediately to see Mister Shaddle in his offices. He closed the door carefully behind him. The Steward looked up and smiled. He approved of his clerk of the spicery.

The dark panelled office was murky with smoke and the stink of two small tallow candles. The Earl of Sheffield had spent a considerable amount on his public wedding and the celebratory feast that followed it, but had no intention of maintaining unnecessary expenses while in private.

Alex, both hands on the desk, leaned over, peering through the drifting haze at his superior. He said, "I've something to discuss, if you don't object, Mister Shaddle. It happens that his lordship called me up to see him this morning for a quiet word."

"Ah, yes," nodded the Steward with a conspiratorial wink. "I heard one of the pages was sent to get you after Mass. I imagine his lordship wanted to congratulate you on the use of spices in yesterday's feast."

Alex coughed slightly. "Something of that sort," he said. "Thing is, he was particularly pleased with the wines and sherry. Complimented you most highly, Mister Shaddle. I hope he told you so himself. But he feels that married life will put a greater strain on his – masculine - resources. And with the coronation coming up – he asked me, in utmost secrecy of course, if I could add a little substance to his wine occasionally. I've bought everything he suggested. I wondered, with your permission of course, if you'd permit me to serve him personally from now on, when his cup needs a refill."

Mister Shaddle looked perplexed. "Is this normal in grand houses down south, Master Bowyer? You're the clerk of the spicery. An important position indeed, but with specific boundaries to your duties, lad. I shouldn't feel comfortable passing over any of my butling responsibilities, you know. And as for filling cups, you're neither footman nor serving girl nor page."

"Oh well," smiled Alex. "I've no objection to helping out." He straightened up, wiping the tallow fumes from his eyes. "His lordship spoke to me in strict confidence," Alex continued. "Naturally, I've no wish to usurp any of your official duties, but overworked as you are - -. Of course it was my expertise in spices that made his lordship guess I'd understand spiced wines and liquors. Naturally I wished to inform you about it all first, but strictly speaking, his lordship may have preferred that I did not. Not wishing to inply that his virility requires any aphrodisiac you see. You being the principal member of staff, and a man of considerable respect, that is."

"I shall mention nothing to a soul, Master Bowyer," said the Steward, breathing deep. "Though I have to confess, it all sounds most odd. However, no doubt you know exactly how these city nobility manage their households, and I'll not interfere. You do as you think best, lad."

Lord Edmund was distinctly uninterested when, during supper served that evening in the great hall, a new face placed his wine cup at the side of his trencher. Nor did he notice that his cup and his platter were both pewter, and that the usual silver had disappeared. He was not in the habit of striking up conversations with his menials, nor of gazing at them. He drained his cup, enjoyed what was in it, and stamped for more.

Alex watched him drink a third cup, smiled most improperly at the Lady Katherine who was regarding him closely, and left the hall in a saunter. The two page boys standing behind the respective chairs of their master and mistress, looked at each other, shrugged, and went back to picking their noses.

The lady, accompanied by her page and her nurse, retired early but his lordship, involved in animated political discussion with one of his friends, remained at the table for another hour. The candles were guttering when he finally rose and, leaning heavily on his friend's arm, aimed for the main staircase. Alex was again on hand. Jug in hand, he approached his master with a benign smile and another cup.

"Would your lordship care for a warming curative?" he suggested with a slight bow. "I understand it's common procedure amongst the nobility these days on retiring, my lord. Being winter, that is. They say it'll snow again tonight. Better than a hot brick in bed any day."

Lord Edmund was already sufficiently warm. Warm enough, indeed, to overlook the entirely unexpected behaviour of a servant he had never seen before. He noticed only a pair of blurred dark eyes and the bobbing attraction of a full cup. He grabbed it on the way out and managed a nod. Alex went back to the kitchens.

Two days later, although not specifically summoned either by her ladyship or her ladyship's nurse, Alex grabbed Tom and told him to take a message upstairs, saying he wished to see the countess. "Tell that damned woman I need to talk to her," he informed the page.

Tom blinked in surprise. He was helping himself to a platter of honeyed wafers which Hewitt had produced for experiment, but had discarded on Master Bowyer's prompt advice. The page coughed hot biscuit flakes. "I'm supposed to tell her that?"

"Well, not the damned woman part," smiled Alex. "Ask her if she's ready for the enema she wanted me to prepare this afternoon."

Tom shook his head. "I don't believe you. She'll throw me downstairs."

"Done it before, has she?" said Alex. "Well, just tell her that her loyal servant the clerk of the spicery desires a quiet word. She'll agree, don't worry."

"Oh well," admitted Tom, stuffing the errant wafer crumbs into his mouth, "It sounds like a silly game to me, but you grown-ups always have a daft idea of fun. Now, back at the house in Leicester, one day the old man – I mean the Lady Katherine's father – he was running down the corridor after one of the laundry girls - "

"Hurry up," interrupted Alex, "and come back to get me as soon as she's alone."

Slightly less than an hour later, the Lady Katherine gazed haughtily at Master Alexander Bowyer, an expression she'd been practising for some time earlier in the day. She was unsurprised when he neither bowed nor appeared impressed. "What?" she demanded. "And watch out, you're about to stand on a kitten. Anyway, it's all very well, but you aren't supposed to order me around, you know. I was busy."

"Rubbish," said Alex. "What was so important? Embroidery? Paper curling? Plucking your eyebrows? Or ardent prayer?"

"You're nearly as horrid as he is," said Kate. She smiled suddenly. "But I do thank you. Honestly, it's been working very well. I am grateful, truly I am. It's just that you're - so - "

"I know perfectly well what I am," said Alex, striding over. The lady was sitting on the cushioned window seat and he stood looking down at her. She was wide eyed in the pale November sun, tinged green by the glass mullions. "Anyway," he added approvingly, "you look happier than you did the last time I saw you in private."

Katherine blushed slightly and gazed into her lap. "I am, thank you. Is that what you wanted? For me to say thank you? I know I should have - "

"Good lord no," Alex snorted. He reached down a peremptory hand and tilted her chin up towards him. "Listen, child. I need to warn you, I can hardly go on doing this for your entire married life. I'll give you what I've been using, and instruct you how to spice your lord's wine yourself. I'll even get hold of a few stronger drugs for you to use in extremity, if you think you can manage not to bungle it and kill the old fool off. But I'm not staying. You'll soon have to cope on your own."

The lady stared up at her most unorthodox servant in dismay. "But you said you would," she whispered.

Alex sat down abruptly next to her, pushing her up slightly to make room. She wriggled obediently aside and groped for her kerchief. Alex sighed. "The trouble is," he said gently, "even someone as idiotic as your husband is going to sober up eventually, or at least want to know why he's permanently pickled even when he only drinks a cup or two. And the thing is, I really have to leave. After the damned coronation at the latest. I've other things to do, even more important than worrying about your conjugal exploits."

The Lady Katherine blew her nose and nodded. "I understand. But there's no need to be crude. You swear and curse all the time you know. It's terribly improper, especially in front of me. But - well - I suppose under the circumstances, it doesn't matter." She sniffed and clutched her kerchief. "You haven't been dismissed have you - I mean - for getting - his lordship -? "

"Pissed?" grinned Alex. "No. Don't worry, it's nothing to do with you. I just need to be somewhere else before Christmastide. Now, do you need lessons in how to keep your charming husband away from your bed, or at least get him to behave decently within it, or are you still too timid to talk to me about the details?"

"I couldn't possibly," said Kate, severely startled. "And it's horrid of you to take advantage of the – situation – and say things you shouldn't. But – well – I'm sorry you're going. Very sorry. Can you keep filling his cup at least until you go? And then if you give me - whatever you use – I shall try and do it myself afterwards."

Alex nodded and looked at the lady of the house with mild amusement. She stared back at him, trying hard to keep her composure. "You'll manage, child," he said, suddenly taking her hand and squeezing it reassuringly. "Since you can't very well confide in me, I can only guess what you're having to put up with. But married life really isn't that bad, you know, once you get used to it. The earl seems more of a fool than a villain, and you'll learn how to handle him. Give him an heir, that'll keep him happy, and you too no doubt. One day I'll try and come back and see how you're getting on."

Instead of pulling her hand away, the countess clutched at Alex's fingers. "You – you think I'm going to have a baby?" she whispered urgently. "Do – do you know about these things? Sara doesn't know either, and I'm frightened. Do I look as though I – I mean, does it show on my face or something - that is, can you tell?"

Alex sat in blank silence for a moment. Having struggled for some nights to banish the girl's face from his dreams, he was distinctly over tired, and now wondered abruptly if he was imagining things. Finally, since she remained clutching his hand, Alex put his other arm fully around her and laid her head against his shoulder. He murmured very softly to the top of her head, praying that no one was about to enter her chamber without knocking. "My dear girl," he said. "That isn't something I can tell, nor anyone else at this early stage. Since you've only been married five days, it seems unlikely, though no doubt it's possible. But that's nothing to be frightened of. His lordship'll have resource to all the best doctors, and they'll see you safely through it, I promise. But you won't be able to know, one way or the other, for some time yet; three months at best. Not that I'm an expert on these matters, for God's sake. As you know full well, I'm not even a genuine clerk of the spicery. I'm a soldier and a poacher, and you most certainly shouldn't be in my arms."

The lady sniffed against his rough broadcloth shoulder. "I know. I'm sorry." She sat up a little and searched again for a kerchief. "And I'm not usually this pathetic. I'd really like to go and kick that beastly little man where it hurts. But that's impossible. I feel so ignorant. And he's sent my ladies away, not that they were any use anyway, and even Sara's useless. She never was married, you see, and she gets upset if she sees I'm upset. So there's only you."

"Then heaven help you," sighed Alex. His fingers discovered the thick brown curls down her back, and absently caressed the hollow at the base of her neck. He took a deep breath. "I suppose I'll have to stay around a little longer," he said to himself.

The lady's delighted response was lost beneath a flurried tapping on the outer chamber door. The child's voice was a hoarse and indignant whisper. "It's him," Tom said through the panelling. "He's coming."

Alex cursed under his breath and strode at once to the door, pulling it one finger's width open. "Where is the damned man?" he demanded. "Have I time to get out of sight?"

Tom giggled. "Yes, if you run. And if you get caught it serves you right - " But Alex was gone.

CHAPTER THIRTEEN

The Earl of Sheffield and his young wife transferred to the royal Palace of Westminster during the Thursday morning before the official coronation. There was no opportunity for the Lady Katherine to speak in private to her clerk of the spicery before her departure, and she saw him only as she mounted her small hired palfrey, looking back from the mounting block and catching the sparkle of his eyes from the shadows by the pantry entrance. He bowed, disappearing again inside as her lord called to her.

"For goodness sake, Kate," said the earl. "Wake up. I've not got all day. It's the king's court waiting, not one of your brainless little friends."

The countess refrained from informing her lord that she no longer had any friends, either brainless or otherwise, since he had seen fit to send them back home to Leicestershire. Then she remembered that one friend did remain to her, but that she was about to be deprived of him too. She found rather suddenly that she needed another kerchief.

Alex sighed and stalked back to the kitchens. "Cheer up, Master Bowyer," said Hewitt, clapping him on the back with a large sweaty palm. "We've three days of peace and quiet without their lordships, and not a dumpling needs to be coddled nor stuffed nor spiced. Heaven, it'll be, and me and you lad, we can put our feet up."

"I intend going out," Alex said, "and I shall be gone some time. In fact, you can tell Mister Shaddle I'm unlikely to be back tonight. I'll see you tomorrow evening."

Hewitt stared. "Out? Until tomorrow? Without even asking? Honest to God, Master Bowyer, pardon the expression, but you've the nerve of the devil. At least ask Mister Shaddle if he'll allow it."

Alex shook his head. "I don't give a damn. Tell him I've important messages to carry for his lordship. Perhaps he'll believe you."

Alex left the house and walked briskly in the opposite direction to that taken by the Earl of Sheffield's party. His livery was disguised beneath the heavy cloak and he had changed his cheap servant's shoes for his own worn buskins, in which he had first made his arrival in London nearly two months previously. The streets were rimed and patches of snow still lay, part iced, part brown slush, against the angles of the houses and in shadowed alleys. Snow had not fallen again that night, and now a sullen grey light leaked from a reluctant dawn. The city was more slunk in resignation than Alex had ever known it, and though only one day from the coronation, there was little activity. The city clerks and aldermen, those who had survived the continuing nightmare of the sweating sickness, had already organised the hanging of the tapestried garlands and banners across the route of the morrow's procession, but there was no gathering of crowds from out of town, nor practising of trumpets and clarions. The raykers had been under strict orders that night and the central city's gutters were well cleaned, but there would be no running of wine from the principal conduits nor singing and dancing around blazing midnight bonfires.

The gulls wailed, sailing the great carracks in from the Narrow Sea and up the winding passage of the Thames to the scent of the fish wharves and Marlowe's Quay. The church bells rang and the congregations scurried home from early Mass until the mid-morning quiet soon hung like a funeral bier.

That morning Henry Tudor travelled by royal barge down river, to be officially greeted by the Lord Mayor and Aldermen and then conducted to the Tower where he would stay overnight in prayer, preparing for his grand entrance through London towards

Westminster Abbey the following day. It was likely that he knew his unpopularity, since it was said he'd demanded a bodyguard for the entire city crossing, the first king in history who felt the need of protection as he rode past his own subjects on his coronation day.

Alex was through the Ludgate and halfway to Cripplegate before the young Earl of Burton and his mother were even fully dressed. He arrived on Jenkins's doorstep while the Steward was ordering the bird droppings scrubbed from the stones by one of the pages, and as the chimney pots puffed out a hearty gust of black sooty smoke above.

Lizzie was descending the main staircase at the far end of the hall. She had made a regular attendances at court when Richard III was king and his brother Edward IV before him, excited to be the grand Countess of Burton and wife of the benign and elegant earl. But this was a new king carrying a sombre weight of expectation. Under recent threat of attainder, Lizzie's appearance was now crucial.

Seeing her, Alex stopped and bowed. "You look grand, coz," he said. "Don't worry. You won him over once. You'll do it again."

"I wish I didn't have to go at all," she said, "but I must, for young Stephen. He needs the king's approval, even if I don't. Come into the side solar, Alex, where it's warm. I want to talk to you."

"There'll be a fairly good attendance at the Abbey," nodded Alex, following her through the long doors. "The old nobility are eager to prove their loyalty, and the new lot eager to prove themselves worthy of Tudor's favour. You won't be the only hypocrite, my dear. There'll hardly be a genuine smile in the chapel."

Lizzie sat by the fire and lowered her voice. "Careful what you say, Alex. We've taken on new staff now Mary and Danny are living here too, and I don't trust every strange face. They say the king's spread a pox of spies across the whole country."

Alex nodded. "I've been warned before. But I don't want to think about the bastard, Lizzie. Knowing he'll be anointed with God's grace tomorrow makes me wonder about God's sanity." He sat, spreading his legs out to the flames. "And don't fuss about blasphemy either. If I spend an eternity in hell fire, then no doubt I'll have Henry Tudor for company."

The dowager countess ignored these remarks and frowned, gazing into space. "I'm not usually pleased to see you Alex," she said. "But this time I am. It's about Daniel and Merevale." She turned, frowning at her cousin and one time suitor. "Danny's been wretched ever since getting out of the Tower," she said softly. "It must have been so terrible in there, so I'm hardly surprised he came out unwell. But now there are so many undercurrents, it's like living underwater. He can barely speak a polite word to me, and nor can Mary. They both resent it so much of course, that I managed to save my poor husband's title for Stephen – while they've lost everything. And what's worse, Dan blames Merevale. You see, Mel was a hero in the battle, and rode in that fatal cavalry charge everyone still talks about. Daniel hardly lifted his sword from what I've heard, so he considers the attainder to be more Mel's fault. Frankly, I consider it more likely to be a reflection on our father. He was utterly loyal to Richard, and would have died fighting his heart out, as I'm sure my darling Edward did." She paused, and smiled. "I don't want to bring back terrible memories, Alex dear. But did you – do you know how - ?"

"Oh, good God, Lizzie." Alex sighed and leaned back heavily in his chair. "How can any man explain a battle? I was no hero, you know. I meant to be. But I was knocked down, and out cold before I'd had a chance to kill more than three or four of the bastards. My father's people were seconded into Norfolk's vanguard, and we marched half a mile under the onslaught of Tudor's arrows. His mercenaries only had crossbows but the Welsh are great archers, you know; and how many of us went down then, I've no idea. With your ears echoing inside your helmet and your hair stuck to your head with sweat, all you hear is a thunder of feet and the clank of steel. Then suddenly it's chaos. Their van flanked ours, forcing us into a tighter formation with the sun directly in our eyes. Then everyone's running, and instead of marching, you just hear screaming." He did not look at his cousin but stared into the fire, as if he saw the battle stretched there before him. "I had all my trust in my father," Alex said, "and John of course. And even more, there was Norfolk. I thought him the greatest soldier in the country after King Richard himself. But all butchered. All gone. Thank God I never saw the king killed. I couldn't have borne that."

Lizzie sniffed and fumbled inside her stomacher for a kerchief. "But you escaped," she whispered. "We must thank God for that."

Alex shook his head. "I was ashamed of it at first," he said. "I don't even remember the stroke that felled me, but I woke up buried under a round baker's dozen of bloody corpses. I thought I was dead. You can't imagine it Lizzie, climbing out from under the butchery, and seeing the even greater spread of the slaughter lying there steaming under the sun. Flat ground to every side, heaped with bodies and limbs and heads, and the moaning, whimpering agony of the dying."

"Hush, Alex." Lizzie stood abruptly, pulling her train up over her arm. "One of those moaning could have been Edward. I don't want to hear any more of your tales. It's too dreadful."

Alex reached out and caught her wrist. "I didn't mean to upset you, coz," he said. "But living with the memory's a black weight, you know, and there's been no one I can talk to since getting back to London, what with being in strict hiding and playacting the dutiful servant."

"But you talk to Merevale," nodded Lizzie. "And that's precisely what I wanted to see you about. I was telling you how Danny and Mary are impossible guests, with their bitterness and blame. They're playacting too – only they play the grand nobles, always trying to make me feel small, and they patronise little Stephen because he still holds a title. Well, there's more than that now. After a frightful quarrel with Dan and Mary screaming at each other about who's more culpable, Mary ended up tiptoeing into Mel's bed. I heard them myself. And I'm quite sure Daniel did too."

"Oh, for God's sake." Alex still saw the dead strewn across the fields and marshes. He still heard them. He snapped back to Lizzie's voice. "What the hell can I do about that?"

"Take Merevale away, and as quickly as possible," said Lizzie.

Alex smiled. "I will. I always intended to," he said. "And I've a favour to ask you in return."

Lizzie turned towards the door. "Under the circumstances, Alex – "

"Don't be a fool, coz," he said. "It's nothing like that, though no doubt you'll misjudge what I tell you anyway. But sit down a minute. I want you to talk to – a female friend of mine - who needs advice. I'll explain - "

A little later, Alex watched the dowager countess and the young Earl of Burton ride off with their tiny entourage, heading through the courtyard and out into Noble Street towards Westminster Palace. Then he went back quickly into the draught layered hall and climbed the stairs two at a time, avoiding the back solar from where he heard Daniel and Mary's voices raised in argument. He did not bother knocking on his cousin's bedchamber door, but entered quickly. Merevale was stretched on the bed, glaring silently at the window.

Merevale said, "Bugger off, if you've come to gloat."

"I'm tired," said Alex, throwing himself onto the bed with his back to one of the end posts, facing his cousin. "I spend half my life tramping for miles across this damned dirty city just to visit my only remaining family, and the other half of my life working in the smelly, sweaty kitchens of the house your father once used to own. Personally I don't give a damn if you cavort naked with your sister-in-law at all hours of the day and night. But don't sulk about your life to me, because I've had enough. It's not as if you'd want to go to this wretched coronation, even if you were invited. So cheer up, or I shall bugger off."

Merevale grinned. "Lizzie told you, did she?"

"Yes, and for once I feel sorry for her." Alex watched the remaining shards of mud and ice slip from the soles of his boots onto his cousin's brocade bed cover, but made no attempt to move. "I've promised her to take you away soon after the coronation. Not that I imagine she'll be any happier with just Mary and Dan for company, but at least she's less likely to have a bloody dismemberment to cope with. However, the thing is – I can't leave immediately. It'll have to wait a week at least."

Merevale raised an eyebrow. "The nursemaid? You've got her in the family way I suppose? Can't she palm it off on the new husband?"

"You know," said Alex with faint dislike, "there are times when you show a remarkable lack of sensibility, coz." He crossed his ankles, watching with satisfaction as the damp stain on the bedcover darkened beneath his boots. "No. It's nothing like that. But the lady in question needs a little platonic support. In fact, I've asked Lizzie to have a word with her. I'd probably do it far better myself, but she's much too timid to confide in me to that extent."

"What? Lizzie?" exclaimed Merevale, aghast.

Alex sighed deeply. "Don't be a damned pillicoot. No. This – girl. She's in considerable need of intimate womanly advice. Anyway, I feel obliged to stay around for a few days. Then I'll take you off to join Lovel's eventual muster."

"I know what it is," said Merevale, sitting up. "You're in love. Disgusting though it is, I can see some female's finally got to you. Acting like some damned Sir Galahad - it's just not like you, coz. And you can call her a nursemaid all you like, but you'd never be asking Lizzie to have a private chat with some little maidservant."

"It's you who keep calling her a nursemaid," objected Alex. "Frankly, I'd prefer not to talk to you about her at all."

Merevale laughed. "But you do, coz, you do. First sign of infatuation, when you can't keep some mention of her off your tongue. Besides, your mother and mine were sisters. You ought to tell me everything. Not that you need to. It's the new little countess, isn't it? The chit who's stolen dear Mary's title. The new Countess of Sheffield. Now, I thought you were a servant in that household. How did you manage to woo the lady?"

It was a sombre room, large and deeply shadowed. The window was wide but shallow and looked out to the back of the house, avoiding the noise of the crowds but catching instead the smell of the stables. The colours were dark, blues and greens with the wood deep stained. The bed hangings were painted with old scenes of heroic legend; the siege of Troy and the rigours of Sparta. Since the bed was covered in a brocade of forest green dyed four times in the deepest of woad and weld and then trimmed in wolf, there was little light in the chamber, inspite of it being nearly dinner time. Merevale's room seemed to Alex more like a cavern than a restful retreat, and inspite of the small fire in the grate, he shivered.

"Since I intend sharing your bed tonight, Mel, I'll forgive you your rudeness, your intrigues, and your damned dreary taste," he said. "But I hope your charming sister-in-law doesn't come visiting at midnight, since she'll have to squeeze her perfect complexion between the two of us. And forget trying to find out anything about my women friends or my sentiments. They're both subjects I intend keeping to myself from now on. You're wrong on all counts, and that's enough said. Now, come on and let's get some dinner. I'm starving. I presume they still feed you here?"

"Staying the night?" said Merevale, cheering up immediately. "I'm delighted. I thought I'd have to spend the evening with my miserable brother. Teasing you is much more entertaining."

Alex swung his legs from the bed and stood. "I've been told I snore," he smiled, "so I hope I keep you awake."

Merevale led the way out into the cold corridor towards the hall, where perfumes of a light midday dinner had already settled. "You intend to sit down in your damned servant's livery, I suppose coz?" he said over his shoulder. "That will certainly puzzle the staff."

"Which reminds me," said Alex. "I need to see Reginald Psalter while I'm here."

Merevale's feet echoed down the stairs. "Who the devil's he?" he demanded.

Mary did not come to the grand table for the midday meal. Watching her sister-in-law ride off to court had given her a headache. Daniel presided over dinner and gazed with extreme disapproval at his cousin's irregular appearance. He pointed out that at least while visiting the Burton household, Alex should borrow some of Merevale's clothes. He then spent the next hour explaining in some detail the difficulties he was suffering from himself.

"Of course," Daniel informed him, "my father's estates are all stolen by the crown. Some insipid overseer's in charge. As if a country clerk has the knowledge to run fifty acres of prime farming land, and manage the forests too. There's magnificent hunting in those woods, with boar and deer, and game birds and good fishing. It'll all be gone to ruin in a year, you'll see."

"No, it bloody won't," Merevale interrupted. "It's all going to this Edmund Tranter I reckon, or some other bastard traitor to England. As soon as parliament's called after the coronation, the lot will be parcelled out as bribes to keep Tudor's backers happy. The Stanleys will get half the country, as payment for their bloody treachery to

King Richard." He turned to Alex. "Your father had even more prime land, coz. Have you chased that situation up yet?"

Alex was busy enjoying his dinner. It was a considerable time since he'd enjoyed food, and he was making the most of it. Servant's rations had left him with a solid hatred of turnips, parsnips, pottage, gruel and porridge, and on the rare occasions when the staff had been able to help themselves to the lord's leftovers, the state of Hewitt's cooking had given Alex an even greater disgust. Now he put his spoon down with a sigh. "No," he said. "What happens in the northwest is always a mystery in the south, and there's no one down here who knows a damn thing yet. Once parliament sits to ratify Tudor's miserable intentions, then I imagine I'll get to hear something of my fate." He cut himself some more roast pheasant. "In the meantime, my uncle Godfrey took charge of the family funerals after the battle. The poor bugger presumably thinks I'm dead too – corpse unidentified. But that's the way I want it to stay for the time being. Hence the livery."

"Then you're taking a risk coming here at all," frowned Daniel. "But you always were damned irresponsible, Alex. I used to say to father; nothing you ever did would surprise me."

Alex paused momentarily, then lowered his head and proceeded with his meal. "Your condemnation shatters me of course, cousin," he said softly, spooning a glazed onion and sage sauce over the slices of pheasant on his platter. "But I imagine I'll survive it. At least I'm not simply bemoaning my state. I intend doing something about it."

Merevale interrupted. "Best not discuss business now, coz," he said. "Not in front of the new servants and so forth." He grinned. "Tell us about this new Earl of Sheffield instead. Now that'll amuse dear Daniel."

Alex was about to decline, then noticed Daniel's furious expression, and immediately decided to comply. "Well now," he said. "Since neither of you yet had the pleasure of meeting the charming creature who's taken your family house and title, I suppose I ought to fill in the relevant details for you." He finished chewing and smiled at his audience. "Lord Edmund," he continued, "is originally from Yorkshire. Nothing wrong with that. York was King Richard's most loyal city, and they say even now the aldermen are trying to make

Tudor's accession difficult. Publicly denouncing the treatment of the late king's body and other matters. But that's where Richmond is of course."

Daniel scowled. "That's right. Tudor's father was Earl of Richmond before the family was attainted and exiled. Another Edmund, damn them all."

"Which brings us back to the inestimable Edmund, now Earl of Sheffield." Daniel flinched. Alex smiled and continued. "He's not prepossessing of course, but then nor is the new king. More to the point, dear Edmund's a fool. He's attempted no changes, has no ambitions to improve the property, just enjoys showing off to his new friends – all equally foolish. I've heard them trying to discuss politics a few times, but you'd think they were talking about cleaning out the chicken coop, or the latest bout of bear-baiting. The man's bought all the most expensive materials his tailor could find in the cheaps, and swaggers around in mismatched foolery, drinking himself blind. He clearly hasn't discovered where Smithfield's is and still hires his horses, broke backed rouncies too. The sort of man who pisses directly into the hearth and then wonders why the fire's gone out."

"And the wife?" said Merevale abruptly.

Alex turned calmly to his grinning cousin. "I barely know the woman," he said. "Very young, I believe. Whereas Lord Edmund is at least fifty years of age and probably more. No one has any idea of gracious living, the kitchens are run according to the standards of a Southwark hostelry, the cook has the talents of a scullion with ague, and the earl doesn't even realise since he's no notion how to behave himself."

"Which is why dear Alex is drugging the man," laughed Merevale, who was fast becoming inebriated himself. "Slipping strong liquors and poppy syrup into his ale, and using the poor bugger's own housekeeping money to buy them. Probably means to poison the bastard, and get back your title for you Danny."

The short silence was interrupted by a deep sigh. "Thank you Mel," sighed Alex. "An accusation of intended murder is exactly what I need in front of the servants just at the moment. Also no doubt interesting for your brother. A considerable aid in my attempts to stay quietly incognito."

"Oh well," shrugged Merevale. "Danny doesn't ever take me seriously, do you Dan? And besides, what does it matter? Nothing's going to happen, is it?"

CHAPTER FOURTEEN

I t was after dinner that Alex searched out Reginald Psalter. He caused considerable confusion, striding through the kitchens demanding to see the apothecary; dressed as a servant himself and wearing the livery of another household while being a gentleman guest of their lordships upstairs and clearly a person of quality. He was recognised by the under-cook, who had originally been employed by the Earl of Sheffield, the same earl whose sons now resided upstairs, and whose title had been claimed by the friend of the new King Henry.

"Afternoon, Wem," nodded Alex, now as equally at home in kitchens as he had ever been in the grand castles and halls of the nobility. "I'm after Psalter. Where is he?"

The undercook bowed, wiped his hands on his apron in confusion, straightened up and frowned. "Master Bowyer, it's mighty opposing when you comes here a-visiting their lordships. We've not the remotest idea how to address you. And one of the new brewery girls was proper upset and got the hystericals after seeing you at dinnertimes today. Came sobbing down here to tell us there was a servant boy sitting high and mighty at the table, discoursing with the master, and demanding a sharper knife for the carving of the pheasant. It cannot be done, Master Bowyer. Sir."

Alex laughed. "I apologise. But you've no idea how low your old kitchens have slunk since your departure, Mister Wem. The new cook from the north has the knack of roasting I'll admit, but everything else is cooked to ruination. Just be glad you've left. In the meantime, it's a pleasure for me to taste your pies and sauces again. Now, I need to talk to Psalter."

"Mister Psalter, if you don't mind, Master Bowyer," said the apothecary, emerging from the open brewery door. He no longer wore plain broadcloth livery but was dressed in mahogany duffel, a long skirted doublet collared high beneath his chin. His sleeves shone with a film of grease and wear and his shoes were cracked, but he used his considerable height and looked down on the young man who had once been a lowly pot boy in his kitchens. "Although I consider it quite improper of you," he said with a sniff of disdain, "to inconvenience respectable members of the staff here in this manner, Master Bowyer, I shall accept the invitation to speak with you. In private perhaps?"

Alex grinned and nodded. "Private indeed, Mister Psalter. The cellars maybe, or wherever you keep your supplies now."

"I must tell you I have been promoted personal physician to the young earl," said Reginald Psalter. "Apothecary and medick. I therefore have my own study. Follow me."

"I've been promoted myself," grinned Alex, trotting behind. "I'm now the clerk of the spicery. Thought I'd ask your invaluable advice on certain matters, Mister Psalter. Who would know more about potions and spices than yourself?"

The little studio was a dark panelled alcove between the locked pantries and the serving entrance to the hall. The apothecary lit a folded spill with a tinder box from the desk, and carried it, shielded from draughts, to half a mutton tallow candle in the dark corner. The candle flared, spat, smoked, and illuminated the cobwebs hanging from the beams above. Mr. Psalter sat on the stool behind the desk. The sudden light illuminated a pair of deep twinned scratches down the back of his neck.

Since there was no other seating, Alex perched on the edge of the desk, swinging his legs. Reginald frowned, but accepted the impertinence. "Now, how can I aid your education in spicery, Master Bowyer?"

"I have a friend," said Alex carefully, "who suffers from certain difficulties, having been wounded – during the battle – and now needs sleep and prolonged beneficial rest, being the quickest path for a quicker recovery. And a little relief, of course, for the pain. He's tried some of the stronger liquors, but the poor man can't stay intoxicated permanently. He's twice taken a little tincture of the Oriental poppy and naturally that works very well, but he's nervous about possible unwanted aside-effects. He's hardly a doctor himself, you see, any more than I am."

"Dangerous stuff, Master Bowyer," nodded Mr. Psalter. He tentatively patted the back of his neck where the scratches were still presumably tender, aggravated by his collar. "The poppy is often far safer when taken as a suppository, you know."

Alex grinned. "That might be a little difficult to administer," he said. "Any other suggestions?"

The apothecary leaned forwards, elbows to the desk, tented his finger tips and regarded his guest with appreciation. "At least you knew where to come," he said generously. "I doubt you'd find a greater expert in all London than myself. If your friend is a man of means, then he should employ a physician of course, but I gather, since you speak of the battle, that the person in question is not free to move around easily. In hiding perhaps?"

Alex nodded. "You understand perfectly, and I'm obliged," he nodded. "But since I'm free myself to visit the wharves and the cheaps on his behalf, though naturally our funds are limited, perhaps you can give me a list of what to buy?"

"He should first have his urine examined," said Mr. Psalter. "That's most important. The clouds in the urinary balance are the best indication to almost every ailment. Of course, it's a little more difficult when the patient is a lady, but that can be managed too with a little careful diplomacy. Take up the urine in a jug or chamber pot - "

Alex interrupted him. "Out of the question," he shook his head and disguised a smile. "Besides, there's no need. I know quite well what's wrong with the poor fellow. He was wounded, that's all. The cuts have healed, but he's in pain. Needs to sleep for a week. Repeatedly."

"There could be infections," insisted the apothecary. "A sedative effective to a healthy man might be positively fatal to someone suffering from the palsy, or with a fevered infection. The grated root of the Mandragora soaked in a little sweet malmsey may help a strong man sleep, but for a child or a young woman, it could be poisonous. This is not a simple matter, Master Bowyer. I should hate to prescribe something which could damage someone's humours."

Alex sighed. "Life is never simple, Mister Psalter," he said. "Believe me, this is a strong man with no fever and well balanced humours. But I won't risk doing him any actual harm. If you don't feel you can advise me, then I must leave him to suffer unaided."

"I'd never countenance such a thing, young man," frowned the doctor, fingers tapping again to his neck. "I shall prescribe within reason. Henbane, for instance, in minute quantities, can be efficacious to a troubled sleep. Mixed with a little marigold water it should be drunk slowly, or combined with mandragora and applied to a cloth held beneath the nostrils. The poppy syrup is the strongest aid to a healthy rest of course, but should be well diluted, and only the tincture of pure narceine used from the calyx of the flower. Now, the wounds must be cleansed with alum, though that can be rather expensive – though some may be obtained by the impecunious from the dyeing vats - "

"The wounds are already healed," said Alex quickly.

"And your friend doesn't suffer from the strangury, I suppose?"

"Good Lord, why should he?" demanded Alex.

"No, no." Mr. Psalter shook his head, though appearing disappointed. "Just that I've recently devised my own treatments, and I admit I'm rather proud of the results." He leaned forwards, gazing hopefully up at Alex, who was still sitting on the desk. "You may remember our unfortunate turnspit at the Sheffield Palace, Master Bowyer. The wretch who died of the sweating sickness shortly before I left. Well, as you must know, there have been numerous cases of that terrible malady since, and one of the main causes of eventual death, according to my prolonged examinations, has been the strangury. Of course, I was unable to help poor Ben, but I've attended several cases since. As for the women, well, I've not attempted any intervention, as can easily be understood with clarity of reason. But with the men, they sweat so mightily, losing all the liquids of the bile and phlegm through the leakage of the perspiring skin, that they accumulate a terrible thirst - though cannot stomach the intake of ale or even boiled water. I have considered," the apothecary leaned confidentially closer, "that if the afflicted soul should be forced to urinate copious quantities, then these leaky humours would be expelled in the usual manner and there would be no bodily fluids left for the sweats. He would immediately be cured."

Alex raised an eyebrow. "Sounds arse over cock pit to me, Mister Psalter."

"Not at all," said Reginald firmly. "I have tried it twice. Once it worked perfectly. The second time, admittedly it did not, but I believe the patient died from other causes. You see, I command the patient to lie down, and to tell the truth, he is usually quite prone anyway by this time. Then I take his masculine organ between my fingers and insert a copper rod first smeared in hot pigeon dung, through the small hole and up into the bladder. This can be manipulated to remove possible blockages. It's a method I admit I've already seen used by chirurgeons for the treatment of kidney stones, but I've adapted it myself to purge this terrible new disease. I hope you're impressed, Master Bowyer."

He wasn't. Alex escaped from his flea bitten tutor, feeling rather queasy, back upstairs to Mcrevale's rooms, silently repeating to himself the particular doses of henbane and mandrake recommended to induce a suitably safe but comatose reaction.

Inspite of the luxury of lying again on a feather mattress, well aired and covered in fine crisp clean linen, Alex himself did not sleep well that night. He had frequently stayed in busy hostelries while travelling the country in the past, having to share a bed with four or even five strangers; merchants and gentlemen of good profession, most of whom slept naked by tradition except for those bashful souls who retained their braies, laces dangling, and all of whom snored, muttered, snorted and tossed all night. None of this had ever bothered

Alex. Now in a bed wide enough to sleep ten and inhabited only by his cousin aside from himself, Alex was disturbed by every movement, felt over hot and even missed his own lumpy wool palliasse back in the servants' quarters in The Strand.

The room seemed swathed in dismal doubts, a sheen of murmuring shadows. The ashes in the hearth had lost even their faint glow but the window shutters remained down and the moon, escaping its clouds, pearlised the chamber's floor boards in metallic polish. Now just one night previous to that of the king's coronation feast, and shrugging off October bluster, the cold light swung into frame, peering through the mullions into the bedchamber.

Merevale, highly embarrassed, had admitted that since his imprisonment in the lightless damp of the Tower, he now insisted on keeping his windows permanently unshuttered and his bed curtains open. In any case, he slept deep. Alex shut his eyes and turned his back on the intrusion of moonlight.

Alex saw ghosts. The unnamed dead buried near Bosworth rattled their bones through the silver puddles of diffusion. He saw his brother's face, hanging bloody from the thorn bush, and it sighed, tears filling the sad brown eyes. Then he saw his father, armour stained with gore and mud, limping across the field, crying for his slaughtered king.

Alex blinked, turning again, found Merevale's outstretched leg, and swore under his breath. He felt suddenly cold; an absurd memory of childhood and his puzzled loneliness after his mother's death. He shivered and turned again. He could no longer remember his mother's face. It was some years that he had searched the back of his mind for her lost expression, but found only empty spaces. The only memory, which he relived unwillingly in his bleakest moments, was of her voice. "Goodnight, my own baby prince," and the warmth of her kiss on his forehead. She had been often ill, shut away in the western tower birthing his six little sisters, not one of which had survived babyhood. Then, when he was ten years old, she had finally died in childbirth and his seventh baby sister died with her. Childish memories, even through the adult years, carry power.

And then, as the moonlight glanced across the bed, the face that came to mind was not his mother's, but the girl Katherine's, dark eyes again but wide and sad, not heavy lidded but thick fringed and wary, moist with repressed tears. And for a very long time the face would not leave him, and he still could not sleep.

The two small chambers allotted to the Earl of Sheffield and his countess at court were dark and draughty. Lord Edmund had ordered a fire lit but it had smoked and the down draught from the chimney filled the chamber with an intermittent grey haze. "Damned miserable place," objected the earl. "We should have stayed at home."

The Lady Katherine had been curious to see the great internal wonders of Westminster Palace but she dreaded being left unprotected in a strange place with her husband, forced to accept his probable advances, and presumably finding him both inevitably sober, and avidly impatient. They had been married almost a week. She said faintly, "We could always go home again now, my lord. It's not very far."

"Stupid girl," scowled the earl. "What nonsense you do have in that silly head of yours. Your damned father should have warned me about your insipid brainlessness before I accepted the marriage arrangement." He was standing in front of the smoking fire, the back of his surcoat hitched up high behind him, warming the back of his legs at the last spit and flare of flame. "Now, call that idiot maid of yours," he said, "and get yourself undressed."

Katherine sighed and reached for her bedrobe. "Is it so late? Very well. I'll get undressed in the other room."

"No you damned well won't," said her husband. "Six long nights I've passed as a married man, and not fucked my wife once. Now, I'm a fair man and I'm not saying it's your fault. In fact, you may have been wondering if I was ever going to get around to it, but the fact is, it seems I've less head for wine than I used to have. I've been pissed for a week, and I admit it. My own fault, no doubt. But I've drunk nothing at supper tonight, and made a great point of it, just in case. Went against the grain too, since it's all at the king's expense. But it's high time I satisfied my marital duties, my girl, and you'll get undressed right here in front of me, to get me stiff."

Katherine was sitting on a low settle beside the guttering fire. The belching smoke made her cough. She looked carefully at her clasped hands, fiddling with her kerchief in her lap. "My lord. The trouble is, with all the excitement – moving - and the court - and thinking of the coronation - and the food was so rich too and not what I'm used to – and of course it isn't that - I'm not – but I mean – I did drink a little wine myself. You see, I have a terrible headache. In fact, I feel quite ill."

"Oh, never mind that," said the earl cheerfully. "I won't care if you're a bit unresponsive. Virgins and all that, not that I ever got into a virgin before as it happens – but I wouldn't expect a lot of heaving and squeezing from you. Of course the whores know just what to do for a man, but I'm not lacking in imagination and I suppose you won't have a clue. So I'll just do my usual, and you can learn as we go along. You'll feel fine after I've finished. I expect it'll be just as good as a medicine."

Katherine blinked. "But the servants - "

Lord Edmund shook his head. "No doubt they're used to it. Well, maybe not your silly little page, or that daft old creature you call your nurse. Come to think of it, not that pathetic maid of yours either. But we'll pull the bed curtains. It's not as if I'm planning on a full audience."

"But they'll hear," whispered Katherine, blowing her nose.

"Who cares about that?" demanded his lordship. "None of their damned business what I do with my own wife. Now, be a good girl and don't keep me waiting. At my age you know, it can't be done every night. In fact, getting it up at all can be a bit of a struggle, but I expect that's normal at fifty odd. The whores usually do a few things to get me started, but I see I shall have to manage on my own with you, this first time at least. But I've promised myself, after a week of getting constantly pissed and missing out on having my prick stuck in, I'm determined to have you tonight, and that's that. So get your stuff off, there's a good girl, while there's still a bit of warmth in this pokey little fire. Otherwise you'll catch cold and we don't want that, do we? You'd be most unattractive, with your skin all pimpled up in the chill. Like a plucked goose. It could put me off altogether."

Katherine stood up and straightened her shoulders. She glared at the earl with all the disgust she already felt for him, which he did not seem to notice, and held both her damp kerchief and her blanchet tightly against her. "I shall obey you, as I must my lord," she said quietly, "but I have a right to some consideration. I shall undress, with my maid's assistance, in the side chamber. I trust you will already be in bed when I return." And she swept, with all the dignity she could retain, from the room.

She took a very long time getting undressed. She unclipped each tiny hook from each little button with a sigh. Her maid, ordered to stand aside, watched sadly. Katherine shook her curls, now tumbling loose. "Here," she said, finally stepping from her gown, "brush it and fold it carefully. I've only brought two." She turned to Sara who was standing by the window, peering out at the huge silver moon and its ghostly reflections on the river water. "You'll have to sleep in here tonight, Sara dear," Katherine said. "I've sent Tom to the communal page's quarters, and his lordship's two boys as well. I think I need the other chamber to myself tonight. I mean, just me – and him."

Sara and the little maid both regarded their mistress with wide eyed sympathy. She tried to smile at them, clutched her heavy brocade blanchet very tightly around her, and tiptoed back into her bedchamber.

She had hoped her husband might be already asleep. He was not. "What the devil took you so long?" he demanded. "And you look more damned dressed up in that silly robe thing than you did in your proper clothes. Get it off." He was not in bed. The earl was once more standing in front of the fire, which still flared with a few small and hesitant flames. He had put up the window shutters himself and without candles, the room was dark, lit only by the sudden fizzle of red from the hearth. Although not in bed, he was prepared for it, and was quite naked.

Lord Edmund's face, neck and hands were weathered, brown and coarse skinned, while the rest of his body was a soft and almost luminous white, reflecting the occasional spark from the embers. His greying hair was brushed very flat across his head while his small fair moustache bristled with hedgehog resilience beneath his nose. At his groin his third patch of sprouting hair was a little darker, but with an orange tinge. The long wait for his wife to return had affected his arousal and within the wiry dark orange, he remained white and limp. "Been waiting so long," he complained, "I even went and washed my hands in the basin for you. A bit greasy they were, from the roast swan at supper. Brushed my hair too. Well, it's not the wedding night of course, but might as well be, so I thought I should look my best."

The lady was feeling faint. She tried to look only at her husband's face. "I really don't feel very well, my lord - "

"Rubbish," said his lordship. "Come here, and let's have a good feel. I'll warm you up quick enough. Hopefully a bit of exploration will get me warm too, but you may need to do a few extra things. You know – sucking a bit or something. Well, I suppose you don't know what that means yet, but don't worry, I'll teach you."

Katherine backed off. "I think I need to sit down," she whispered, blanchet clasped tight to her throat.

The earl strode forwards, grabbed one of her wrists and pulled her firmly towards the bed. "You're not going to be much fun, are you?" he muttered. "Well, I suppose wives never are, if it comes to that. Plenty of whores in the city for afterwards, so I'm not complaining – but in the meantime, I just need to get you impregnated. No point getting a title if there's no heir to pass it on. So lie down, there's a good girl, and open your legs."

Katherine did no such thing. "I – won't," she said, shivering uncontrollably. "I'm – sick."

Lord Edmund released her suddenly and gave a hearty push, sending her backwards onto the mattress. "What tiresome things women are, to be sure," he scowled. "But if you won't co-operate, I shall have to force you. I didn't mean to make it uncomfortable for you, but well, they say it hurts the first time for virgins anyway, so it won't make much difference if I'm rough. But I warn you, if you struggle, I'll get one of my men to hold you down."

The earl, now noticeably more aroused, jumped onto the bed on top of her, dragging the edges of her bedrobe aside. His eyes, usually a bland and slightly blank grey, glittered suddenly in the firelight. He reached for her breast and squeezed very hard, rather in the manner of forcing the seeds from a pomegranate. Katherine gulped and rolled slightly to one side, groped a hand down to the floor and edged her fingers beneath the knotted strings holding the mattress.

As the earl pressed downwards, both hands now spreading her legs, Katherine grasped the handle of the earthenware chamber pot, swung it upwards, and hit her husband extremely hard over the head.

CHAPTER FIFTEEN

"Y ou look bloody awful," said Merevale. "If sleeping with me has that effect on people, perhaps it's just as well I never got married."

Alex remained in bed, propped up with pillows, his hands clasped behind his head. "Who'd have us, Mel? Impoverished younger sons of peers don't get too many chances at advantageous marriages to start off with – and now we're younger sons of nobodies."

Merevale shook his head. "You aren't coz. Hasn't it occurred to you yet, by rights you're now the Baron Mornington yourself?"

Alex smiled weakly. "Baron shit. If the family isn't attainted when parliament sits, it'll only be because they assume I'm already dead. Though I suppose in that case, the title would pass to poor old Uncle Godfrey. He never fought at the battle naturally. Proud Yorkist of course, but with one leg, he wouldn't have been much use. Perhaps if they let him keep the title, I should leave him to enjoy it after all."

"You're so sure you shouldn't just say to hell with it and reappear?" frowned Merevale. "The imprisonments and executions are almost done with anyway. Tudor's revenge is past its worst. Maybe it's safe to come out of hiding now."

"What, with the hope of gaining a title? What do I want one for anyway?" Alex shook his head. "I'd only be obliged to bend my knee to that bastard, and beg to keep my lands. Besides, I don't trust him. He's yet to sit with parliament. The bugger has attaintings in store yet, I promise."

"You can't want to be a servant," Merevale objected.

"I need to see to a few things here first, and then I'm off to join Lovell as I keep telling you," said Alex. "No point tempting the executioner's axe before that."

Throughout London's grand houses, staff had been given half a day off to watch the procession as the new king rode from the Tower to the Abbey for his coronation. Shops were closed. Businesses shut. Alex considered himself free for the day. Having not the slightest intention of watching the man he loathed ride to glory, he lounged with his cousin in the downstairs solar adjoining the hall after an early dinner, with a fire built high and a pale sleety daylight dampening the windows. It was Katherine who had kept him awake for most of the night, but he did not talk about that. He spoke of his next closest concern.

"Lovell's utterly distraught. I've rarely seen a sane man so out of his mind." Alex sighed, remembering the three desperate weeks between coming to his senses on the battlefield, and his eventual arrival in London. "Poor bugger was Richard's closest friend of course. I never knew him well, nor King Richard naturally, but I learned an immense respect for him those days I spent in sanctuary with him and the Staffords. And don't let anyone tell you hiding out in sanctuary's an easy matter. It's damn well not."

"Perhaps easier than the Tower dungeons," remarked Merevale softly.

"Goes without saying." Alex frowned. "For all the damned uncomfortable months I've passed since the battle, you know I never forget how much worse it's been for you, coz. I even escaped half the fighting, though not by choice." He paused, and sighed. "I've not asked – and you haven't said – but that final charge, Mel. You were part of that. You saw the king go down."

Merevale stared a moment, then stood abruptly and walked to the window. He turned his back on his cousin, clasping his hands behind him, staring out over the small formal garden beyond. "Yes. From elation to annihilation." His tightly twined fingers were rigid. "It was a grand gallop at first. No doubt you've heard some of the story. We were nearly four hundred strong, the mightiest cavalry charge any of those French buggers had seen, I'll warrant. God, the thunder of it Alex, with the king's great standard streaming ahead. The churning turf, the snorting of the beasts, the yelling of a hundred battle cries. It was a bright, hot day – well, you'll remember that yourself. The ground was steaming and the sunshine bounced off our armour like cannon balls. We saw Tudor, way ahead. Damned weasel was cowering astride his horse, surrounded by a clutch of bodyguard, as distant as he could manage from the danger and ready to make a run for it once he could see it was going against him."

"And wasn't it going against him by then?" said Alex.

"Hard to say." Merevale shook his head. "We'd already lost Norfolk, you know, and that was a terrible blow. And we'd heard something about Northumberland pretending to get confused, and taking too long to move in and cover the rear. But the fighting was still intense, and we still outnumbered them I believe. The king wanted it over. He'd planned the cavalry charge from the beginning, and we were all prepared. Then he put on his coat of arms over his armour. That was it of course – a declaration of no retreat – fight to the death." He turned at last and came back over to the hearth, looking down at where Alex sprawled in the big chair. "I wish to God he hadn't done that now," he said softly. "But at the time, it seemed right. Richard was always so committed. And he wanted to save lives. These men fighting with us are England's proudest, he said in his speech before the charge. I shall personally challenge Henry Tudor. By killing him, I can save the lives of thousands."

"And instead he lost his own," said Alex, staring up at his cousin. "But what a grand, brave way to go."

"I dream of it," said Merevale. "Night after fucking night, coz. I relive all the bastard horror of it. As Tudor saw us coming, he jumped off his horse to make a smaller target. But we saw him, and he must have seen us like a great line of dust clouds rising over the vibration of the hooves. Then one of his men galloped off for help. And that began the end."

"The pikes." Alex nodded. "I heard."

Merevale closed his eyes, as if seeing it all again. "De Chandee sent his best pikemen to surround Tudor and protect him," he said. "Swiss trained, with pikes as long as trees. A hundred or more closed ranks in a three pointed palisade, too close to break through and too late for us to swerve. We'd never seen anything like it. Half the horses were speared in minutes, steel right through their bodies and out the other side. Our own speed rammed those bastard pikes home, with men and horses screaming in agony and blood spouting in fountains. The king's charger went down at once, well, he was at the front, shouting for Tudor to come forward and fight him."

"But he broke through the pikes?" Alex had heard the stories. Whispered stories, whispered sorrow, whispered acknowledgement for their dead king's courage. "And Tudor wouldn't accept the challenge, wouldn't even face him. They say his sword stayed clean as a woman's cheek throughout the whole battle."

"I never saw Tudor," Merevale said softly. "He was well hidden, and my eyes were fixed on Richard. He did us proud, our beautiful king, but I'll never forgive him, Alex, for risking his life that day. If he'd been cautious instead of brave - "

"And ridden away to save his own life? He would never have done that, especially after displaying his coat of arms. That's the ultimate declaration within the laws of chivalry, for God's sake. He would never have retreated in shame."

"And so he died," said Merevale. "He died almost at my feet. He fought like a demon on foot, and killed a dozen I reckon, getting ever closer to that skulking coward's corner. Damn it, the king killed Tudor's standard bearer, and you can't get closer than that. But then fucking William Stanley came hurtling in to save Tudor's wretched life. Fucking traitors, both the Stanleys. It was Stanley's men that rushed the king. Richard went down fighting. I was desperate to get to him, to help him, and so were the rest of us, but the bastards held us off. I watched as they hacked him to pieces. The smell of his blood soaks my dreams."

Alex nodded. "And then they desecrated his body."

Merevale sighed. "And now Tudor dares call himself a king? He's no notion of nobility, no ideas above petty revenge and spite."

"Nobility? He hasn't a drop of royal blood in him. I've more right to sit on the throne of England than he has." Alex reached for his cup and drained it. "I'm glad I never saw any of this, Mel. I feel a terrible shame, having passed half the battle out of my wits and buried alive. I sleep badly now. But if I'd seen all that – I'd never sleep again."

Merevale took the jug from the table and slowly refilled both cups. "Tudor ordered the king's body stripped bollock naked and slung over a horse's back for transport to Leicester. He wanted Richard humiliated, even after death. But it didn't work. The body was so covered in open wounds, it showed only how brave a death he died. We were crying, all of us hauled off as captives, stumbling like lunatics, totally dazed. We didn't believe it. Richard dead. Sometimes I still can't believe it."

"I can believe it alright." Alex took his cup and stared into the reflection of the flames on the wine's surface. It looked like blood. "The country's in mourning though most don't dare show it, our best men are dead, in prison, or in hiding. And we've a new plague killing those of us left. The Sweats they call it. Shame, I call it. If there was any justice in the world, the Tudor bastard would fall sick and rid us of his miserable skin."

"There is no justice," said Merevale, drinking deep. "So from now on coz, I'll get pissed when I want, act the fool to mask the sorrow inside, and fuck my sister-in-law when it pleases me. And to hell with all of it."

The tale drifted into silence, hanging like fingers of smoke, emphasising the hiss and flare of the fire. The two men sat quietly, staring into their cups, oblivious to everything but their memories. It was when Mary interrupted them, that Alex left. The Lady Mary's laugh was high pitched, like the chimes of a chapel bell calling vespers. "You naughty boys," she said. "Why so dismal? Have you quarrelled, or is it just the toothache?"

"It's the toothache now," remarked Merevale, looking up. "Headache, gut-ache and elsewhere ache."

Mary giggled. "Fancy that. And Danny's got a fit of the sullens too. Now with Lizzie and her brat away at court, he's got no one to sulk at except me."

Alex stood, returning his cup to the tray. "Apologies, Mary, but I've appointments elsewhere. I'm leaving."

Mary's giggle turned sour. "Back to the grand Earl of Sheffield, and your lord and master, Alex? In his stolen halls with his stolen wealth."

"Something like that, Mary. That's the fall of the dice, and the fate of kings. But I hear our charming new king has awarded you and Dan a pension. You'll survive."

Mary turned with a snarl. "Don't think yourself superior Alex, just because you're too proud, and choose to stay penniless. Disguised as a servant, indeed. It's demeaning."

Alex strode to the door and opened it. "I'm off, Mel. Back to my demeaning kitchens. I'll leave you to enjoy the warmth of family solidarity."

He heard Mary's renewed giggles, and closed the door behind him with a snap.

The day had brightened a little and the sun was steaming over the wet cobbles. The streets were empty but the garlands remained, the great banners of the Lancastrian peers, the heraldry of the newly honoured and the gaudy silken colours of the city guilds strung taut across the main streets, a little limp from the sleet, spangled now in dew drops.

Alex arrived tired and despondent back in The Strand, and vainly attempted to avoid his irate superior. Mr. Shaddle, however, caught him on the stairs. "Master Bowyer, a word with you, if you don't mind. In my office, now."

Alex considered telling him to go to hell, thought better of it, and wandered back down to the hall. He stood behind the Steward's little desk, while Mr. Shaddle settled himself in the chair opposite. "Apologies for the absence, Mister Shaddle," said Alex with a wide, exhausted smile. "But I had a – matter of business – to perform for his lordship the earl."

"So Mister Hewitt informed me, lad," said the Steward. "But it won't do, not at all. It's all very well you telling me these things, and only after the doing of them as well, but his lordship's not told me nor even his secretary. How am I to know the facts? And truth nor untruth, you should still be asking my permission afore being gone all night. It's not proper at all. And don't go telling me this is how it's done by nobility in the south, for I don't believe it."

Alex nodded cheerfully. "I must admit I stretched the advantage, Mister Shaddle, with a view to watching the coronation procession. You'd hardly object to that."

"All the staff had a half day for that this morning," nodded the Steward. "But don't tell me you needed to sleep all night in the streets to be first in the queue, for there was no need. The crowds were pitiful, and I surely didn't see you amongst them."

"Just that his lordship's requirements weren't easy to obtain," said Alex with a vague attempt at a glance of puzzled ignorance. "What with the shops closed today for the new king, God bless him, there was no chance to buy what I needed." Alex shook his head sorrowfully. "Had to come back with nothing."

"If you're trying to convince me you're too much of a dolt to know that business was suspended for the coronation, Master Bowyer, then don't bother," said Mr. Shaddle. "You'd better get back to your duties now, but if this sort of thing should reoccur, I shall consider dismissing you. You've been warned."

"I shall bear it in mind," smiled Alex unhelpfully, and hurried back upstairs.

So the onetime Earl of Richmond, invader of England, completed his triumphant procession to Westminster Abbey, showing not himself to his people, but his small shadow surrounded by a careful bodyguard. Within the inner chapel and kneeling before God, Henry Tudor, the grandson of a Welsh butler and a widowed French princess, was crowned Henry VII of England, founder of a new dynasty. The ancient Archbishop of Canterbury being too infirm and too reluctant to manage more than a whispered anointing, stood aside, and John Morton Bishop of Ely and a principal architect of the Tudor success, crowned his grateful king.

With no masters to serve, the staff went early to their beds once twilight shifted deep into night. While the new Earl and Countess of Sheffield seated themselves for the coronation feast, along with the Lady Elizabeth, dowager Countess of Burton and her son the young Earl of Burton, and the entire royal court, less than a mile up river Alex found his narrow bed smaller, harder, lumpier and damper than he had remembered it, and was amused to recall having actually missed it the night before. It was a very long time before he slept, and then his sleep was fitful. The moonglow wavered through the dirty unshuttered mullions and striped the worn boards in pearly shadows. Once again ghosts walked his dreams, but it was the Lady Katherine's face which wavered constantly behind the wandering and mournful dead.

Alex was late downstairs the following morning and was absently pounding ginger with garlic, producing a perfume of interesting eccentricity, when horse's bridles jangled outside the stables, doors crashed, and the earl marched once more into his hall. He had returned in a furious temper, one full day early, with his head tight bandaged beneath his scarlet liripiped turban.

Within only a few moments an angry message was passed to Mr. Shaddle, who, not entirely complacent himself, sent it on to the kitchens by one of the page boys. It was therefore Tom who informed the clerk of the spicery that he was required, immediately, in the great hall.

"And why the hell are they back so damned early?" demanded Alex. Having banished the lady's face from his mind, nightmares of Katherine mauled by her lout of a husband had been subjugated into headache. "They're not due till tomorrow."

"Don't ask me," grinned Tom. "But his lordship wants to see you. Now."

Alex regarded the boy with suspicion. "You've a smile as wide as the Thames in flood. You know something, urchin. Tell me."

"Oh well." Tom was aware of a wider audience within the kitchens, and could not resist it. Every scullion had stopped scrubbing and Hewitt's hearty stirring of the cauldron had become strangely subdued. Even the roaring flames in the hearth stilled a moment to listen. "She hit him," said Tom.

A general intake of breath sucked the cobwebs from the beams. Alex smiled faintly. "I see. Any idea why? Was he pissed?"

"Don't think so," frowned Tom. "At least, he wasn't staggering around like he usually does. But she broke the chamber pot over his head. I don't know why. But I know she did it 'cos I had to clean up the pieces this morning."

Alex's smile tucked into dimples at the corners of his mouth. "Alright brat," he said. "I shall answer his lordship's imperious summons. Lead on."

The Earl of Sheffield was slouched in a chair in the hall, watching the fire being hastily set. He looked up as Alex bowed, and poked one boot at the page scrabbling in the hearth. "Alright, boy," he said. "Leave that for a moment. I want to talk to someone in private."

The page and Tom nodded gleefully to each other, sharing innuendos, and scampered off. "Your lordship wanted me?" inquired Alex.

"Yes, I damn well do," said Lord Edmund. Having removed his hat, one side of his bandage had slipped a little and the soft grey hair beneath showed a crust of old blood. "Seems to be you, whoever the devil you are, who keeps filling up my cup with something or other. Uncommon stuff usually, down to the spices no doubt. Well, I like it, most of the time anyway. Soothing. So I want some now."

"Is," smiled Alex politely, "your lordship feeling a trifle unwell?"

"Damn it boy, you're not blind," said the earl. "Got a bastard bad head."

"Fell over?" suggested Alex sympathetically.

The earl regarded his clerk of the spicery with considerable irritation. "Just fetch me a cup of something, boy, and quick about it. And make it strong." As Alex crossed the hall and headed towards the kitchens, the earl added, a little under his breath but fully audible, "And while I'm at it, I strongly advise you never to get married."

The Lady Katherine did not make any appearance for midday dinner and nor did she attend supper. She remained within her own rooms and was accompanied only by her nurse. She made no requests to see anyone and even her page gained no admittance to her chamber.

The nights were colder, the mornings frosty. Alex left The Strand early and strode quickly back through the Ludgate and into the city. Business had returned to normal and the usual clutter and noise took no account of kings, neither dead nor alive. The winter river was usurping its muddy banks, slurping over the lower streets and gurgling its traffic of slime, animal carcasses and excrement along the wharves. Alex, back in his servant's shoes, tramped up Lower Thames Street and through the alleys into Bell Docks, where he had previously arranged to meet Merevale.

The docks were busy with lighters bringing in the cargo from the carracks further downriver, and Alex stamped his feet, bringing the blood pulsing back into his frozen toes. He could not see his cousin amongst the bustle. He pushed into a tiny dark doorway, transacted business quickly, and reappeared into the dubious daylight with his packages under his arm. There was still no sign of his cousin, but Alex was fairly sure it was already late. He assumed Merevale had overslept and drunk too well, getting pissed being the favourite occupation of the moment it seemed, and therefore began to plod unwillingly northwards towards Cripplegate. It began to rain.

Jenkins bowed politely to the soaked and liveried scowl dripping before him on the steps, and showed the familiar guest into the main hall. Alex, not waiting for his hostess, squelched upstairs to find his cousin. The small Earl of Burton bumped into him on the stairs and grabbed his arm. Stephen said, "It's Alex. Hello Alex. You're awfully wet."

Alex shook the rain from his hat onto the polished stairs. "I wondered what was making me so damned cold."

"Well, come downstairs by the fire," said his lordship reasonably. "I can tell you all about the coronation. It was awfully grand. It went on forever. And all those trumpets."

"I hope you ate everything at the feast, since our charming new king was paying."

"Well, I did eat quite a lot." Stephen relished his memories. "Mother said to stop or I'd be sick. But I didn't stop and I wasn't sick. I had twelve marchpane balls in treacle. I'd never had treacle before, mother says it's too expensive. But I didn't like the chitterlings. They were stuffed with something horrid and brown. It tasted like what my puppy does under my bed every morning."

"Which you've tasted, naturally?" Alex turned and continued to climb the stairs. "I'll talk to you later, brat. I want to find Mel."

"He's not up yet," said Stephen. "Uncle Daniel was calling for him earlier. And Mother banged on his door twice. Then a page went up with breakfast, but he wouldn't answer."

Alex paused, frowning. "He must be sick. Hasn't anyone checked?"

"I don't think so," said Stephen. "Me and mother only got home a little while ago and everything's been busy. Anyway, you know how grumpy Uncle Merevale gets when people disturb him."

"Disturb him?" demanded Alex. "It's damned near dinner time. He's never this late, even when he's been pissed as a wheryman the night before. I'm going to get him up. Someone'd better bring some ale."

Stephen nodded and galloped down the stairs to summon aid. Alex strode the passage to Merevale's chamber, and knocked loudly on the door. Receiving no reply, he opened it and walked in.

The windows, being as always unshuttered, streamed with the gleam of sunshine through rain and the chamber was pooled with pale green light. The huge bed remained dark. The thick carved posts soared almost to the ceiling beams, and between their sentinel silence, the long curtains were fully closed. The battlefields of ancient Greece swathed the space enclosed within, Agamemnon half naked, assaulting the walls of Troy, Achilles afflicted and aptly clutching his foot, Odysseus sailing through Poseidon's raging storms, all painted across the heavy hanging linen. There was no movement from within.

Alex paused, frowning. Merevale had admitted hating the haunted darkness and so never closed his bed hangings. Nor was there need for privacy as he had no page or dresser sleeping on either pallet or truckle. Alex leaned forwards and flicked the curtains. "Mel? Are you ill, coz?"

Within the area of the bed there was a slight smell, a coppery scent, which Alex did not like. He reached closer, took a step and drew back the shadowed hangings. They swung open with a rustle of disuse and a puff of stale dust. Alex stood quite still, gazing in utter silence and absolute horror at the bed before him.

CHAPTER SIXTEEN

M erevale lay naked across the bedcover, his head towards the bed's foot, his feet splayed up upon the pillows. The dark brocade beneath him was sticky, stained and damp, its wolf pelt trimmings caught up at one side where a great black stripe oozed from bed to floor.

Merevale's neck had been sliced so deeply that his head was flung back from the neck at a grotesque angle, distorted, as if at the very moment of parting from its body. His mouth gaped, the eyes open and staring. His skin was cold and his hands, fingers grasping and rigid, clamped on nothing.

Alex stood staring in silence, unmoving. He had seen death so many times but it was as if he had never, ever seen it before. He did not move until he heard footsteps behind him, and turned. A page had been sent with a beaker of ale and a manchet roll. The child dropped both and began to scream.

It was chaos then. For some time Alex ignored them all. He sat on the bed beside his cousin, tracing the lines of surprise and pain which pulled the skin back around the lips, soothing the long fingers, and closing the lids over the shocked and puzzled gaze. Across Merevale's breast there were also smears of old blood; around the left nipple where two small scratches had left painful traces, and high on his thigh near the scrotum were bruised indentations, as if he had been bitten there.

Left alone for a moment as the family rushed for the doctor, Alex sighed, leaned down and kissed the cold face once on the forehead. "Sleep sweet, my dear friend," he whispered. "No need to be frightened of the dark anymore."

When Reginald Psalter arrived upstairs with his small box of instruments and potions, wheezing shock and wobbly legged, Alex finally left the room. He strode downstairs and out to the little garden where he stood, staring blankly at the drizzling clouds above, and breathed deeply for a considerable time. Elizabeth found him there.

"Alex?" She had been crying and her voice was now hoarse and subdued. "What does it mean, Alex?"

He had forgotten that there should, somehow, be a meaning. It seemed as though the whole world was meaningless. Alex turned and gazed at his cousin. "It means someone murdered your brother."

Elizabeth lowered her eyes. "You don't think – he did it himself?"

It hadn't occurred to him. "Merevale was never a fool, though he sometimes liked to act it. He was sane. He was – he was Merevale. Why in God's name would he do such a thing?"

"He was terribly – sad, Alex," she whispered. "After the battle, and then being arrested and that dreadful imprisonment. Seeing the king killed. Then losing the family title, losing the country estates, losing everything. Perhaps he felt there was nothing worth living for."

Alex shook his head. "Yes, he was low. He had no great hopes for the future. But I don't believe he did it himself. I'm not even sure he could have. Forgive me, Lizzie, but did you see? To cut so deep – can a man do that to himself? And where was the knife? I saw no knife."

"Did you – look?" she asked.

"Damn it, Lizzie," Alex glared. "I sat and held his hand for an hour or more. I'd have noticed a knife."

Elizabeth looked away. "He could have dropped it. Did you look on the ground?" He had not. "If not himself, then who could have?" she continued in a whisper. "And why? Alex, we keep our doors locked at night. We need to. Since the battle there's such terrible poverty, illegal beggars, men crippled and desperate."

141

Alex blinked. "I know, I see them. The city's full of widows now, you know, bedraggled and half starved, dragging themselves to the city to beg for food for their children. For lack of any other way, they prostitute themselves in the back alleys at night. I give them my salary, for what it's worth."

"Oh, Alex," sighed the dowager countess. "You don't."

"Don't be a fool, Lizzie," said Alex. "You knew me better once."

"We won't speak of that." Elizabeth sat heavily on the little garden bench and stared at her lap. "I give to the beggars too, not that I leave the house very often. There was a man sitting in the gutters on our way home this morning. I'd seen this proud new king crowned, been to court and feasted with the bastard. Then there was this wretched soul huddled in the street, with no legs at all beneath the knees and only a stump for one hand, the other hand stretched out in supplication. A soldier from the war this brave invader brought on us. I gave every coin from my purse. But you have no money, Alex."

Alex tried to smile. "I steal it, Lizzie. The odd piece of silver from the house, change from the money I'm given to buy spices. And my salary, though that's only a couple of shillings a week."

The countess blew her nose. "We're doing everything not to talk about Merevale – but we must, my dear. It's so – terrifying. And I have to try and understand. No one could have climbed in the windows you know. It's winter, they're all tight closed. And Mel's chamber was on the second floor."

"You took on new staff you said, when Dan and Mary moved in." Alex pushed the hair back from his face. It was damp with sweat, inspite of the cold. "One of them perhaps - already inside the house. Robbery."

"Check if things were searched, if his strong box was forced open. You have to find out what happened, Alex." She started to cry again. "I can't. I can't go in there again."

Alex returned reluctantly to his cousin's chamber. It was empty of life, the apothecary had left, and nothing seemed to have been moved. Alex sat for a while in the wavering gloom, then rose and took the slight body in his arms, cradling the head on its sagging neck against his shoulder. Then he laid Merevale carefully back upon the bed, gently arranging his head on the pillows, his limbs straight, his arms crossed over his breast. The body was still a little stiff, but had lost its rigidity. Alex leaned over and again kissed his cousin's forehead. He then took a clean sheet from the linen chest and spread it over the bed, covering everything. He turned and left the room, closing the door very quietly behind him.

He discovered Daniel slumped in front of the fire in the main hall. Alex stood before him, looking down. "Have you any ideas?" he inquired softly.

Daniel looked up, red eyed. "What the devil's that supposed to mean?"

"Nothing," said Alex meekly. "Only what it should mean. That someone did this, for a reason that seems obscure. Lizzie thinks he might have done it to himself. I don't believe that. I've searched the room and there's no knife. Besides, I don't believe it's Mel's style. And the cut's too deep."

"Of course he didn't kill himself," Daniel glared. "My brother isn't a lunatic. He may have been fucking my wife, but that makes him a shit, not a lunatic."

"Was Mary with you last night?" asked Alex abruptly.

"God, Alex," swore Daniel, "if you start implying - "

"I'm not." Alex moved away from the fire's heat and sat on a low chair beside his cousin. "I've no idea what could have happened. And surely not a woman. It was done with great violence. But it wasn't robbery, Dan. I've checked the room. Mel's purse is still on the old chest unopened, and there's a fair amount of silver in it. His gold collar's on the chest too, untouched. Nothing's been disturbed. The window's tight shut, and Lizzie swears no one can enter the house once it's locked up at night. So who, Dan? And why?"

Daniel stared back at the flames and remained inert for a long time. Eventually he said, "Piss off, Alex," then slumped again into silence.

Alex stood. "But you'll have to call the sheriff, Dan. Don't leave it too long."

He searched out Elizabeth once more before leaving, and found her from the sound of her sobbing. He heard Mary first, but did not enter the small solar. He knew it was Mary, for the cries were shrill and hysterical. He felt a coward for not comforting her, but that was her husband's job. He discovered the countess in her own antechamber.

It was a bright solar, light and well aired. The mantled hearth was vivid with a huge fire, and Elizabeth was crouched over it, her head in her hands. "Lizzie, I don't know what else to do." Alex squatted on his heels beside his cousin and put his arm around her shoulders. She did not shake him off. "He meant more to me than anyone else, you know. I'm not sure I can bear it. After my father and my brother – and my king. But this is worse than all of them. If I could do something - "

"You have to stay here Alex," Elizabeth sobbed. "I cannot be alone."

Alex shook his head. "You're hardly alone. Apart from all your attendants, there's Dan, and Mary. There's little Stephen. You coped with the loss of your own husband, coz. You'll cope with this too."

She looked up, suddenly flinging both arms around his neck. "But somehow this makes losing Edward even harder. I can only be strong for so much. Mel was always my favourite brother. And in my own house too."

Alex extricated himself gently. "What have you done with Stephen?"

"With my old nurse Cissy. He doesn't know anything yet. He'll be heartbroken. Of course Mel lived here for years before the battle. Stephen adored him."

"Then you have to be strong for Stephen," said Alex. "I can't possibly stay here, Lizzie. It's tempting, to be honest, and for several reasons. But I won't do it. And it would hardly do your reputation any good."

"Oh, that." The countess sighed, and removed her clutch on her cousin's neck. "Does it even matter now, Alex? I was such a silly girl, looking back now. That's not to say you weren't gorgeous of course, but no money and no prospects. A younger son, just like Mel. But it seemed so romantic."

"You were only fifteen or sixteen." Alex smiled slightly. "I was an idiot to let you talk me into it."

"You were in love with me," she said with bleak nostalgia. "And you were only nineteen yourself. Men are all babies until they pass twenty. Besides, you had to abduct me, for I knew father would never allow me to marry you otherwise. He wanted me for a rich young man with a respectable title."

"Which you got, in the end, with your patient Edward." Alex pulled up a small chair, and sat, stretching his servant's cracked shoes to the fire. "Funny to think it was my own brother discovered us, and put a stop to it. Rescued you and carried you back to your furious Papa. Poor John."

"He was so embarrassed," sniffed Elizabeth. "I did confess to John, you know. He was the only person I ever admitted it was all my idea. I didn't dare tell my father, but he guessed I'm sure. So I was whisked off and married to Edward within the month, to salvage my reputation. And thank God Edward was such a dear. I learned to love him very quickly."

"Old times, old memories." Alex smiled rather wanly. "Nobody believes I never touched you, you know. Not even Mel believed that."

"Well, you did touch me, Alex." Elizabeth blew her nose again. "Oh, maybe not the way they think, but we were half way there when John burst in on us. I was almost – well, never mind about that now. I'm a lot more sensible than I used to be, and nine years later, hopefully you are too. I'm trusting you now you know Alex dear, to find out what happened, and do something about it. I shall never sleep again until you do. And Merevale must be revenged."

She had started to cry again and Alex leaned over and put his arm back around her shoulders. "I'll do my best, Lizzie," he said softly. "But I can't stay here, and now – after this – well, I was planning on getting away from the city anyway in a week or two – I was only really waiting for Mel. London's always been a bastard filthy heap, and now –"

Elizabeth stared at him. "You shall not leave me after this Alex." She searched for a dry kerchief and blew her nose very loudly. "And you've got – dried blood on your shoulder."

Alex nodded. "I carried him – settled him more comfortably, you know." He sighed. "Alright. I may not get back tomorrow, but within a day or two at the most I will. The funeral - I'll be here for that at least.

If you discover anything in the meantime, send a message for me. I'm Alex Bowyer, by the way, clerk of the spicery. If I hear nothing from you, I'll come back anyway."

As he stood, Elizabeth stared up at him, eyes red rimmed. "Do you think," she whispered, "it could have been Danny, Alex? From jealousy. Or even Mary, in a rage because he turned her down?"

"Stop torturing yourself," said Alex at once. "No. It's not possible. Dan murder his own brother? And Mel wouldn't have turned Mary down. Besides, she's erratic, sometimes crazy, but not like that. This was a maniac's crime."

"A maniac, who's still creeping around in the house?"

"Lizzie, I have to go." He stood in silence for a moment, looking down at his cousin. Then he shook his head. "Dammit, Lizzie. Alright. I'll give in my notice, tell them I'm leaving, and come back here tomorrow. If you really don't give a jakes for your reputation, then I'll come and look after you. Hopefully I'll escape the executioner's chop for long enough to settle things here, and then ride out for Colchester. Cheer up, my dear. He's in paradise now."

She shook her head. "Purgatory, Alex. After – fornicating – with his own brother's wife! But will you truly come back? I've never been close to Danny you know, and I have to confess – I don't even like Mary."

"I'll manage what I can," Alex nodded. "And as soon as I can. In the meantime, look after Stephen and try and get some sleep."

It had stopped raining as he walked back to The Strand in a daze. A few barefoot Cripplegate brats were jumping in the puddles, but it was already growing dark and Alex started to hurry. He had little idea of the time. If he found the Ludgate closed against him, he'd be sleeping in the gutters himself. He had not mentioned it to his cousins, but it was partly self-interest that forced him away and back to his kitchens, for the sheriff would have to be called. Even a dolt of a volunteer constable would be able to sniff something amiss, seeing a young man dressed as a servant and employed as one in a different establishment, but visiting their lordships as a guest, addressed as cousin by the relatives of the victim, and being the one to discover the body. Even by telling the truth, he'd be seen as sufficiently suspicious to satisfy some simple sheriff of his probable guilt, and he could find himself hanging on the gibbet before anyone had a chance to exonerate him.

No one had eaten that day. Doubtless the servants would have been in no fit state to provide anything, and besides, appetite was the last consideration within the household. Now Alex felt faint. He thought it was more than hunger, but hunger was a part of it. He walked faster, swearing softly to himself. He had loved his dead brother. He had loved Merevale closer than a brother. And he had a difficult time imagining how Merevale might have suffered, and might still be suffering now.

The Ludgate was not locked against him but the evening was rich black and bitterly cold when he arrived at his own doors. He did not care if the Steward dismissed him for having been absent the entire day since he'd now be leaving anyway, but he dodged the bright bustle of the kitchens, intending to avoid the infuriation of questions and threats. Being thrown out of the house would not suit him just yet, he desperately needed a few hours' sleep, and he had an idea he would react with violence if anyone attempted to intimidate him now. He strode past the pantries and began to climb the dark stairs to the servant's quarters.

The wood creaked. Then a small figure raced down from the shadows, planting itself before him on the higher step. Tom was red faced and panting. "You're back. She wants you. Come quick." Alex had a sudden desire to hit someone.

"Go to the devil," he said quietly, pushing past.

Tom stared, open mouthed. "But she needs you."

Alex remembered what he had bought that morning. The packages were clutched, unthinkingly, beneath his arm. He shoved them into Tom's narrow embrace. "Give her these. Tell her to pour the whole damn lot into his cup. With a bit of luck, she'll finish him off entirely."

Tom clutched what he had been given, but turned, hopping up the stairs again. "But he's dying already," yelled the child to Alex's fast disappearing back. "He's probably dead right now. You've got to come."

CHAPTER SEVENTEEN

Katherine looked up as Alex entered the unlit chamber. She was sitting on the edge of the earl's bed, peering down at the figure within it. Her hair was tumbled and dishevelled around her face. Her eyes seemed huge. "It's the Sweats," she whispered.

Alex nodded. "Tom told me. How is he now?"

"Delirious." The countess shook her head. "We've no doctor, no apothecary to call, only you. There's no one who could help anyway. No one survives it, they say."

Alex stopped in the middle of the room, staring into the gloom. "Yes, that's what they say. In fact I know someone who – but that's no matter now. You shouldn't be tending to him, you know. It could be infectious."

"If you're frightened," said the countess, "you can go."

He smiled, striding over. "I don't frighten so easily. Besides, a quick death doesn't seem such a bad fate just at the moment. But since you can do nothing for him, it's pointless you risking the same. Here, I'll sit with him. Call a page to fetch water. And some cold meat and bread."

Katherine frowned. "I really don't think he could possibly eat anything."

"No, but I could," said Alex. "I'm starving."

Lord Edmund lay almost invisible within the bed's gaudy shadows. His hair was streaked into wet strands across his skull, and his mouth, hanging open, panted and gulped for breath. Beneath his head, the pillows were soaked. Alex grasped the woollen blankets which were pulled up to the earl's chin, and wrenched them down. Naked in the bed, he was scrawny, the muscles of an active younger man now turned to loose and sagging skin, and the sparse hairs across the meagre chest were grizzled. The entire body was pooled in the glisten of sweat. Alex said, "Do you have cloths? A bowl of water? Get some."

Katherine hovered beside him. "Do you really know what to do, then? I must confess, when I sent Tom for you, I didn't think you could actually - "

"You're right, I can't," said Alex. "I've no idea what to do, but the man's dying in a puddle of fire. It's logical to cool him down at least and perhaps that's all we can do. Maybe he'll die more comfortably." He looked back up at the girl leaning over him. "You should go to bed."

Katherine glared. "Bed? While my husband expires in the next room? What sort of creature do you think I am?" she demanded.

"Simply an unwilling wife," said Alex with a meek smile. "Don't try to pretend you care for him."

"Of course I don't," said Katherine in a furiously elevated whisper. "I loathe him. But he's still – my husband. And besides, I'd care if anyone was lying in my home, about to die in agony." She paused. "Do you think he is in agony?"

Alex thought it probable. The earl's face was flushed beneath the streaming perspiration, his eyes were blood streaked and wild and his breath gurgled in his throat. Across his chest a rash had begun to spread, the flesh beneath the weeping skin inflamed and forcing out its poisons. Alex turned back to Katherine. "Look, I've seen someone die of this before, but that doesn't mean I know anything. But I'll sit with him, and try and cool him down. If you want to stay, then you can help, but keep your distance at least. Now, where's those damned cloths I ordered?"

Two pages came, Tom with the drinking water and food, another boy with the bowl and cloths. Tom attempted to stay but was sent off again. Alex began to wash the sweat from the earl's face and chest. The cool water sluiced over him, again soaking the mattress beneath. The vair bedcover was lumpy, the fine chequered fur matted now with sweat and bile. Alex threw it off. He left Lord Edmund uncovered to the waist, and continued to work in silence.

Katherine stood shivering behind him, taking the cloths as he handed them to her and rinsing them in the bowl. She handed each, clean and wet, back to Alex as he reached for it. The cool water turned warm and scummy. Eventually Alex leaned back, sighed, and flung the last cloth back onto the floor. "It's pointless," he said.

The moon, three nights past its zenith, turned the window mullions into pearly swirls and the cold light danced across the turkey rugs in strange patterns. Alex stood, strode over and began to hoist the shutters up into place. The chamber went suddenly black. A small fire had been lit many hours before, but it lay now in a heap of ashes with a smell of smoke and soot. There was another smell in the room. From the great bed, the foul stench of death was collecting.

Alex moved quickly around the room, lighting the candles in the sconces and on the small side table. With each tiny flame, the dancing lights reflecting on ceiling and walls, the chamber darted back into life, gradually illuminated with a reminder of grandeur.

Katherine had dragged a high backed chair over to the bedside and sat there, slumped and weary. She had not undressed for bed, and was still wearing the stiff satin in which Alex had seen her before. He had thought the deep reds suited her. Now she was white faced and her cheeks and breast appeared almost ghostly against the rich colours. Alex came beside her and put his hand lightly on her shoulder. He meant to comfort her with the inane platitudes of the stranger to the bereaved, but the earl began to moan, finding his breath, and flung up both arms as if trying to escape his bed. Alex went back and sat there, leaning over to wipe the spittle from the man's mouth.

Lord Edmund had returned to delirium. The sweat pumped from him as water from a conduit, smelling of dirt and stale salts. In the new rising candle light, Alex saw that the rash across the earl's chest had entered its final stage, with tiny pricks like black pimples surging and swelling from within the inflammation. "Bitch," he moaned. "Try to kill me, bitch?" Alex reached over with the cool damp cloth, but the earl threw him off. "The dead all around," he whispered, staring suddenly up into Alex's eyes. "So many dead. Lord Henry, my dear prince, I'll come to you if I can. I'll save your life, my lord."

Alex shook his head. "Your prince survived, never fear. You can rest in peace."

"Peace?" The earl struggled to rise, staring around him. His eyes wept blood. "But if the battle is lost? The horses are upon us, don't you see?"

Alex sighed. "The battle is – won," he said gently. "Your prince is crowned king."

The earl grabbed his wrist as Alex turned, preparing to stand. "The bitch tried to kill me," he croaked. "Tell no one. But she must be watched."

Alex wrenched his hand away. "Lie still. You are unwell."

"Of course I'm unwell. My head's cracked open like eggshells." Lord Edmund had begun to drool blood flecked phlegm down his chin. The stench was deepening. "Now I'm burning. Take off the coals. I'm no Lollard. What's happening? The bitch has set the fire."

"No, my lord." Alex stood, looking down. "You have a fever." He turned to Katherine. "Have you sent for a priest?"

She shook her head. "Is it time?"

"I believe so." Alex watched her run from the room, then turned back to the earl. He sat on the chair Katherine had left, pulling it closer to the dying man. He spoke slowly and quietly. "My lord, you have the sweating sickness. There is no known cure. If you're in pain, I can help you drink some of the fortified wine I've been serving you lately. It may help you sleep. Do you understand me?"

The beeswax candles were honey perfumed but the smell rising from the bed obliterated all else, and now illuminated, the earl's body glistened with a great yellow rash, pock marked in a hundred black oozing spots.

The earl, huge eyed, nodded, groping one desperate hand. "Dying?"

"It seems likely," said Alex evenly. "Your wife's summoning the priest now. You should calm yourself, if you can."

"Drink then," the earl murmured. "You said - "

Alex went to the open door and called. Tom brought him the packets he had earlier passed to the child, then ran down for wine. Alex hoped the boy would think to bring at least two cups. He returned to the bed. Lord Edmund's eyes were closed. The rash was swelling, as if the sweat collected beneath the skin. Alex drew the bedcovers up once more and tucked them beneath the earl's chin.

Tom returned with the wine jug, bringing two cups. He asked to stay. Alex refused. "Find your mistress," he said, "and tell her not to come back. It's just a few moments until his lordship passes."

Katherine pushed past him into the room. Alex closed the door behind her. "The priest's coming," she said. "I'm not leaving until then."

Alex filled half a cup with the smuggled Scottish Beatha Uisge he had bought at the wharves that morning. It seemed a very long time ago. He topped the cup up with wine and held it to the earl's mouth. Lord Edmund, unable to close his lips on the edge of the cup, coughed and spat dark saliva, but Alex tipped the liquid slowly into his mouth and he swallowed a little, the rest dribbling across his chin to the fur bedcover and staining his moustache dark and sticky. The earl sighed, closed his eyes again and laid back. Droplets of wine collected in the corners of his mouth like tiny bright beads of blood.

Katherine looked away. "Is that – what you always give – but is it good for him?" she whispered. "Now, I mean?"

Alex smiled faintly. "More than ever. And I intend having some myself." He helped himself to a far smaller portion of the Scottish liquor, again filling his cup with wine. He held it out to the lady. "Taste it. I imagine you could do with some too."

Katherine eyed the cup with suspicion. "It won't - ?"

"It probably will," said Alex. "Just take a small sip."

She spluttered, hand over her mouth. "It's hideous," she objected, watching Alex placidly drinking the rest. "And now you're going to collapse I suppose? Drunk – as a – a - "

"Pissed as a wheryman," supplied Alex helpfully. "And no, I'm not. I don't have quite such a weak head as that, I assure you. After three or four, maybe!"

Katherine glared. "Well carry on," she said. "Be my guest."

Alex smiled. He was desperately tired, but the girl's problems and the dying earl were helping him forget Merevale and his own difficulties. He shook his head. "Silly puss." There was a well scented dreg left in the cup, and he handed it to her. "Here. Finish this. There's not enough left to make you sick, and it'll help, I promise."

Lord Edmund appeared to be sleeping. His breathing was shallow and guttural. Alex sat beside him, taking the man's hand. The skin was hot and wet. Alex leaned over, speaking directly to his ear. "My lord. Do you hear me? Will you drink more, or are you ready to sleep?"

The earl blinked and seemed to strain for something but could not answer. Alex again held the cup to his lips, allowing some of the drugged wine to fill his mouth and seep down his throat. He was crouched there, Katherine watching behind him, when the door opened and Shaddle quietly entered, showing the priest into the chamber.

It was the small priest from All Saints who had pronounced the lady wed less than two weeks previously. He pattered in as Shaddle left in a hurry, and came to the bed. Alex stood, setting down the earl's cup on the small table by the candle. "Young man," the priest looked at Alex in some surprise and clicked his beads. "Are you the doctor?"

Alex smiled. "More or less. But this is the sweating sickness, father, and no doctor has a cure. I've merely been keeping his lordship comfortable. Now I'll leave you to your business."

"My daughter?" the priest turned to Katherine. "I offer my condolences. But under the circumstances, you should not be here in danger from infection. I will search you out afterwards, if I may. In the meantime, kindly leave me alone with the patient whilst he is shriven." He knelt at once beside the bed.

Katherine led Alex along the dark passage to the small private solar attached to her own quarters. The fire was already lit, the shutters closed and the candlelight pale. She stood in front of the fire, hugged both arms around her waist and began to cry very quietly.

Alex, having brought his own cup and the jug of wine with him, offered her some. She shook her head. "It's horrible stuff."

"This is just wine. I left the Uisge in your husband's room." Alex pressed the cup into her hand. He resisted the temptation to embrace her. "Have some," he said. "You're entitled to feel wretched, you know. It's understandable, inspite of what you felt for him. I'm sorry I can't – comfort you a little more."

She blinked tear blurred eyes up at him. "I should confess." She took the cup, drank, pulled a face and hiccupped. "When I – called for you, I knew really that you wouldn't be able to help him. I know you're not a doctor. I know you're not anything really. I – just thought, well, you know, as a friend. That you'd understand. And make me feel – more able to cope."

Alex nodded. "Except that you're not supposed to have friends amongst your own kitchen staff. Amongst anyone's kitchen staff, come to think of it." He smiled. "It's most improper."

"You can't possibly lecture me on being proper," she sniffed. "You of all people. Besides, I do lots of improper things."

"Like hitting your husband over the head with the chamber pot," suggested Alex.

"Oh," she said, "you heard about that. Well – he was – utterly obnoxious. And he refused to get drunk. And I did what you told me and said I was dreadfully sick, but he didn't care. So I found the chamber pot." She gazed at her clerk of the spicery, as if hoping for exoneration. "It was empty at the time."

"Well, you won't need to worry about that sort of thing again. Not for a while anyway." Alex frowned. "You can stay a widow, claim your husband's lands, and live an idle life. Mind you, the king hasn't awarded your husband the full country estates in Sheffield yet, so I doubt he will now. You'll have to be satisfied with the Strand house. Though of course, since you've no children to pass the title on to, you may not get that either. It would be helpful if you were pregnant." He smiled helpfully. "I know we discussed this once before, and it's hardly a conversation to get involved with now, and especially not with me, but it would help if you were."

The lady scowled. "I can't imagine anything worse."

"Well the law entitles you to a fair slice but in practise widows can be involved with legal claims for years, trying to get a rightful share of their husband's property," Alex shook his head. "Especially if there's no son. Damned miserable business, fighting the law. Besides, with this new king, the law's a suspect injustice altogether. Did you come with a decent dowry by any chance?"

"He – he isn't dead yet," the countess objected. She lowered her head with a blush. "And no. I didn't, not much of one. Father managed to make a very advantageous contract and Edmund seemed too inexperienced to bargain for more. Now – can we talk about something else?" She sat abruptly on the long wooden settle beneath the shuttered window, clasped her hands in her lap and gripped her kerchief. "Or perhaps," she sniffed, "you'd like to go to bed?"

Alex smiled. "You've a singularly naive way of putting things," he said. "But no, I'll keep you company a little longer, since you need to wait for the priest. And as for your husband still being alive, I doubt if he is. I understand it must seem depressing, but since you disliked the man, you might as well see the advantages. And you can go out tomorrow and buy yourself a smart lavender mourning cap."

"That's – horrid," said the widow. "I know you've helped me – a lot – often – but you really are quite heartless sometimes. I spent hours, just sitting by his bedside watching him get sicker and sicker. I so very much needed a friend and I called for you at once, but you weren't there. The Steward said you were out. You were gone ages. And the Steward seemed to think you shouldn't have gone out at all. Aren't servants just supposed to obey orders? What were you doing, for goodness sake?"

"Poaching," said Alex.

Katherine giggled. "It's not funny," she said. "Everything's dismal and dreary and I kept wondering if I'd get sick too, and it got hot, and I was frightened to start perspiring so I opened the window and then it was freezing. And Edmund kept raving about his mother and the king and me. I don't think he even wanted me there, but I couldn't leave him. And none of the servants wanted to stay and help, and they say one of the poor little kitchen boys ran away when he heard there was the sweating sickness in the house."

Alex shook his head. "Don't worry about all that now," he said. "The priest'll arrange for the funeral, Shaddle can call in one of the charnel woman to prepare the body while the boring legalities are seen to. Then you can sleep for a week."

"It's all very well," objected the lady, "but I can't just stay in this house alone afterwards. I haven't the faintest idea what I should do. Do you think I should go back to my father?"

"If he'll have you." Alex stood by the fire, looking down at the girl whose face had entered every dream and disturbed his every night for the previous weeks. "As it happens," he said softly, "that might be the best idea. Though your father sounds as though he was fairly eager to get rid of you when he arranged your marriage to a bandy legged, addle pated old fool of a fifty year old Lancastrian. Send a messenger, and see what he says."

Katherine looked away with a mournful sniff. "You want to get rid of me too."

"Good lord," said Alex. "What have I got to do with it?" He shrugged suddenly and strode over, sitting beside the girl. "Look, my dear. I might as well admit that I do care. But that's beside the point. I'm nobody, as you so sweetly pointed out earlier, and you're the dowager Countess of Sheffield. I'll help if I can, but as it happens, I've other problems to deal with at the moment, and I won't abandon them, even for you."

She had turned towards him, gazing nervously. "You – you mean to abandon me instead?"

Alex sighed. "It's not that simple, child. You see, my cousin – died this morning – under rather wretched circumstances. I discovered his body, and the conditions will haunt me for a long time. His sister also relies on me, and – well – frankly I'd already promised her I'd leave here and go there tomorrow to help. Now – well, I just don't know. I can hardly be in so many places at once."

The countess nodded earnestly. "Your cousin? Here in London? I'm so very sorry. And his sister all alone, like me? That's terrible. So tomorrow, I'll come with you and help look after her."

Alex stared, then laughed. "Impossible, child. You're the most absurd little innocent, you know." And then he put both arms warm and strong around her as she buried her face against the shoulder of his grubby livery and burst into tears on the small dried red stain remaining from Merevale's body.

The priest pushed open the door and walked in very quietly. He stopped with an appalled and affronted inhalation.

CHAPTER EIGHTEEN

The reflections of firelight tinged the priest's long robes as rosily as his cheeks. The old man's skin was deep scarred, pitted with a hundred tiny etched circles, the familiar marks of a long recovery from the pox. The flame's crimson gilded there, catching the skin in an uneven blush. Skirting the small tonsure, his hair was white and a little fluffy like fraying threads of cotton. He seemed considerably more aged than the man he had just watched die, but he was straight backed and vehement. In one hand he held his rosary, and in the other he clutched to his chest the packets which Alex had bought that morning. He addressed the lady, carefully lowering his eyes from glare to humility. "I am sorry to have to tell you my child, that his lordship has now passed from this world and begun his journey into purgatory. You will no doubt wish to pray for his soul."

Katherine thanked him, and stared into her lap. Alex had risen immediately he heard the priest behind him. He eyed his own packages in the old man's hand. "In that case, father," he said, "I shall inform the staff."

The priest raised one finger. "One moment, young man." He walked to Alex's side, and held out the three small parcels. "Since you claim to be the doctor here, would these articles belong to you?"

Alex raised one eyebrow. "They would."

"Ah." The priest nodded. "In that case, I should like a quiet word with you."

Alex sighed. He opened the door, avoided looking back at Katherine, and showed the priest into the dark corridor. He closed the door behind him and gazed at the old man. "I hope his lordship passed peacefully?" The priest did not answer and Alex smiled. "I imagine you have questions. You might as well know, father, I'm neither qualified doctor nor apothecary. Indeed, I've done no apprenticeship of any kind but I've managed to learn something of my profession. How can I help you?"

"The earl had time to confess his sins and was shriven, so died in a state of grace," the priest said, keeping his voice very low. "But you see, my son, before I was ordained as the parish priest at All Saints, I took my vows and served my noviciate in a monastery hospital and then in the leper's hospice of St. John's, so I have some knowledge of herbs and roots myself. These purchases of yours are not the usual supplies I would expect a doctor to bring to the bedside of a dying man."

"Perhaps." Alex leaned back against the wall, studying the priest's frown, distorted into wrinkled fragments across the scarred forehead. "But if you've experience of doctoring, father, you'll be aware that a little henbane can be a medicine in small quantities, just as easily as a poison in larger ones."

The priest nodded. "Indeed, my son. That's true. But there is a great deal of henbane here, and there is a considerable amount of grated mandrake root, also a serious threat in inexperienced hands. Then there is the third packet. Was the syrup of poppy perhaps for the alleviation of his lordship's pain?"

"You could say so," murmured Alex.

"In that case," said the priest, "I assume you also have knowledge of astrological prediction, my son, since the estimable Steward at this establishment informed me that you had been absent, without permission, for the entire day. He also informed me that you returned just in time to be summoned to his lordship's bedside, having had no prior knowledge whatsoever of his lordship's illness."

"You could say that too," said Alex with a slight smile. "But you see, I'd already been treating the earl for another – condition."

"That is indeed what I feared." The priest frowned. "A condition which also demanded the use of the Scottish liquor, commonly and most erroneously known as holy water?" The priest's frown had become fixed. "This is smuggled from the north and is illegal in London, my son, as I am sure you are aware, inspite of your lack of qualifications. I smelled a good deal of this liquor on his lordship's breath, and also in the cup which stood at his bedside, from which I saw you help the earl to drink. Have you any reason to suppose that such an intoxicating liquid is efficacious to the treatment of the sweating sickness?"

"Probably." Alex's smile had also become fixed. "I imagine death and its sufferings are quite usefully treated with the Beatha Uisge, father. Not as a cure, unfortunately, but certainly as a palliative."

"I do not agree, my son," insisted the priest. "A man cannot die in a state of grace, if he is, to put it mildly, inebriated. I cannot approve."

"But his lordship approved," interrupted Alex. "And now father, if you don't mind, it's been a remarkably long and trying day. His lordship died of the sweating sickness, having all the signs and symptoms, which I hope you recognised. In any case, the staff can corroborate the facts. Whatever I did or did not do, I in no way assisted in his death, and I certainly hope you are not implying otherwise. I shall now go and attend to my duties, and then to bed."

The priest restrained him, one hand gripped to his sleeve with raised knuckles and surprising energy. "Just one moment longer, Master Bowyer." Alex paused, staring down with some hauteur. His smile had faded entirely. "May I ask, with all respect," inquired the priest, "where you obtained this – experience – you speak of in the administration of herbs and drugs?"

"Oh, the devil take it," said Alex unwisely. He thought of quoting Reginald Psalter and the apothecary's advice. Then he remembered Merevale, and thought better of it. "No, you can't ask," he said. "I'm sure your probing's well meant father, but you have no right – nor reason – to question me. Frankly I'm exhausted. The staff need to be informed, the lady's nurse sent to her side, and I need to sleep. I assure you I'm totally innocent of whatever situation you're imagining, and if you've suspicions regarding the state in which you caught her ladyship and myself a few moments ago, then be assured that was innocent too. She was upset, as you can imagine. I'm aware I abused my position in offering comfort, but it certainly was only comfort I was offering. Simple as that. Now, goodnight father."

Alex shook the priest's hand from his arm and turned down the corridor towards the stairs. The priest's voice, just slightly raised, followed him through the darkness. "Master Bowyer." Alex neither turned nor answered. "Though I saw no sign of the patient having been bled, either by use of leeches or with the fleam, I notice you have a small bloodstain on your right shoulder, my son. I believe, under the circumstances, you should attempt to wash it off." The words faded into the distance.

Alex swore roundly under his breath and strode downstairs.

Mr. Shaddle, though eager for news, remained impersonal, his anger only slightly repressed. He had been sitting at the head of the kitchen table, drumming his fingers on the wood. He sprang up as Alex entered.

"His lordship has passed," Alex informed him. "I'm afraid I've very little idea what everyone's supposed to do under the circumstances. No doubt you've far more knowledge of the proper procedures than I have. In the meantime, I'm tired out and I intend going to bed."

He turned on his heel, but Mr. Shaddle called him back. "Master Bowyer. It's a difficult time, and I'm aware that you've tried to assist both my lord and lady. However, I really must - "

Alex shook his head. "Not now, Mister Shaddle. I freely apologise for anything and everything which I've done - or you think I may have done. But this just isn't the right moment for any lectures. Let me know in the morning whether you've decided to dismiss me or not." As he strode quickly to the stairs, he turned once. The Steward was standing quite still, his mouth open. "And you'd better make sure Sara Whitstable's gone to comfort her ladyship," Alex said. "I meant to sort that out myself, but under the circumstances, it's probably better if I don't. You can see to it, I'm sure." And he then climbed the back stairs very quickly to his bedchamber, tumbled fully dressed onto his bed, kicked off his shoes, curled up and fell deeply asleep.

Habit woke him early, though the night was still star pricked. He had no idea of the time but guessed it was a few minutes until four of the morning, being the usual hour he was expected, and invariably managed, to start work downstairs. Nor did he have the slightest idea what time he had finally got to bed the evening before, but was reasonably positive the amount of sleep he had managed had been insufficient. Nor had it been undisturbed.

Merevale had come whispering into his dream, sad eyed, the wound across his throat seeping blood and tears. He had stretched out a hand, but swooping from the clouds like a great winged eagle, a faceless priest flew behind, had taken Merevale's arm and led him into the deep far shadows. Alex had called his cousin, murmuring of love and trust and loneliness, but the priest had pushed Merevale on into the darkness and then turned back to Alex with a gaze of sudden hatred. The pale facelessness lit into the pocked fervency of fanaticism and the eyes glared. The priest then lifted the wooden cross he wore around his neck and held it high before him, muttering the catechism as if warding off evil, thereby keeping Alex at a distance. The cross began to bleed.

Alex woke shivering, his head pounding. He had then risen, a little shakily, and undressed before climbing back into bed and pulling the covers over him. He had dreamed again immediately, and this time it was the lady Katherine who walked sad eyed towards him. The dreaming Alex held out his arms to her. "Come to me," he had whispered, "and be my love."

She had smiled. "And must I be a servant's wife?"

"Wife?" Alex shook his head. "I offer far greater prizes than that. I offer poverty and all the utter misery of homelessness in London's sweet shit scented gutters. I offer the dungeons in the Tower, black as hell, or Newgate's welcoming embrace. And at the end of it all, for me the gallows or the bright sharp axe. For you the sweating sickness perhaps, the great pestilence, or gaol fever amongst the rats. For death, after all, is the only sleep which cannot haunt you with dreams of ghosts already dead."

Waking with his cheeks tear stained, Alex continued to lie in bed. He was breathless, as if running, and took time to calm his heartbeat and his mind. He stretched a little, hands clasped behind his head. He found the pillow damp with sweat and smiled to himself. Contracting the sweating sickness might seem a just reward, but although he had a headache and was as exhausted as he had been before ever getting to bed, he was not, he decided, anymore unwell than he might expect under the circumstances. He did not hurry downstairs. He stayed where he was, attempting to juggle the thoughts which his mind could not reject.

The kitchens were warm and the fire was high, but there was no bubbling cauldron nor scullions scrubbing tables or floors. There was a quiet confusion. The exceedingly late arrival of the clerk of the spicery seemed to surprise no one.

Hewitt was hunched over the long table. "Honoured us with your presence, Master Bowyer?"

Alex pulled up a stool. "I had a busy day yesterday, Mister Hewitt. And it's likely to be a busy day again today. Nobody come with a message for me yet?"

Hewitt shook his head. "Expecting one, are we? From the king no doubt? Or maybe the Archbishop of Canterbury?"

"After recent events, I should say anything's possible," Alex smiled. "But message or no message, I imagine I'll be leaving you today, Mister Hewitt."

"If Mister Shaddle has ought to do with it lad, you will," nodded the cook. "Proper put out yesterday he was, with you gone all day again."

Alex sighed. "I'm afraid I make a very poor servant, my friend. And a poor doctor as well. A poor soldier, a poor cousin, a poor brother and a damned poor son too, I seem to remember. If I survive the next few days, I must try and find something I can do a little better. In the meantime, I leave you my cupboard of spices. Enjoy them, Mister Hewitt. Throw handfuls into every dish, and you'll be sure to please someone." He took the small iron key from the string around his neck and passed it to the cook. "It's well stocked, though there's one or two pots of ingredients I should perhaps discard before passing them over."

Mr. Shaddle's hand came from behind and clasped Alex firmly on the shoulder. "But that you won't do, Bowyer," said the Steward. "I spoke at some length with Father Erkenwald last night after you skulked off to bed, and he'll be back this morning, and wanting to inspect your medicine chest. So you'll be staying right here this time, and see if you can explain yourself."

"Damnation," said Alex, sitting down again. "I accept you're only doing your job, Mister Shaddle, but this is both utterly nonsensical and wretchedly inconvenient."

Mr. Shaddle had taken the spicery key from Hewitt, and now clenched it tight. "I don't doubt it's mighty inconvenient for you, Master Bowyer. Inconvenient indeed!" he said. "Especially since I've had a word with one of the scullion lads as was here before his lordship came, being a kitchen boy for the late Lord of Sheffield as lived here originally. And he says you was here just a few days then, being employed not as a respectable clerk of the spicery, but as a pot boy. Not Master at all, but just plain Bowyer. And says as well how there was something a touch suspicious about you, young man, that you came from nowhere, and had a might too much to do with the gentry upstairs." "Bugger," decided Alex.

CHAPTER NINETEEN

"You will not, under any circumstances or for any reason, get involved in this," glared Alex. "Do you understand? I forbid it."

"But you're not supposed to give me orders," said the Lady Katherine with a forlorn sniff.

"I don't give a damn what I'm supposed to do anymore," said Alex. "And since I've a very low opinion of your ability to obey anyone's orders, let me warn you further. If you dare to tell Shaddle, the sheriff or any damned interfering priest, that you were the one asking me to get your wretched husband permanently cupshotten, I shall deny it. I shall categorically deny any connection with you whatsoever."

The lady shook her head. "They'll believe me, not you. I'm – I'm a countess. You – you're - "

"Before you try to work out exactly what the devil I am," suggested Alex, "just accept it when I tell you everyone'll believe me. Not you at all. Especially that damn fool priest. You've the misfortune to be a young woman. As far as the church is concerned, women only come in three categories. Nuns, matronly self-sacrificing mothers, and lying harlots. You certainly don't fit the first two. Everyone'll assume you're unreliable and over emotional, and ignore you accordingly. They'll suspect you of lying before you even open your mouth." He grinned suddenly. "Actually, in your case, it's perfectly true."

The lady was sitting on the window seat, her kerchief clutched, as usual, in her hand. The pale daylight behind her head outlined her little cap in a streaming silver aura. She looked far more saintly than she sounded. "You're a – beast," she accused him. "How dare you tell me to – abandon you to – accusations! When it's all my fault! I won't let you take all the blame."

"You'll do as you're told," demanded Alex abruptly. "Besides, it'll all be cleared up easily if you just relapse into your natural habit, and lie through your teeth as you always used to. The priest has no legal standing and unless he drags the sheriff with him, I intend walking out. Every damned servant in this house knows the earl fell ill while I was away from the house, and they know he died of the sweating sickness. The trouble came with us being caught in each other's arms. So keep quiet, keep dignified, and know nothing. I grabbed you for comfort when you cried, sorrowing for your beloved husband. That's all. I'm simply an irresponsible idiot, which is true enough – and since I've no intention of staying here under the circumstances, they can sack me with impunity. Now – do you understand what you have to do and say?"

She nodded, still sniffing. "But you can't go."

Alex sighed. "I can't stay. That's more to the point."

He was standing, hands behind his back, in front of the fire and glaring at the lady of the house, when the door opened and Shaddle marched in, holding the way open for the priest and another person to enter abruptly.

Alex eyed the third man.

The under sheriff was proud of his position, and took it seriously. He strode forwards and faced the young man in front of the fire. He put a heavy hand on Alex's still blood-stained shoulder. "I reckon I heard you saying you intended leaving, young Bowyer. It is Bowyer, I presume? Well, as it happens, I'm afraid you're coming with me first, to answer a few questions. And if you been trying to intimidate her ladyship - nor into corroborating of your story - "

"The lady has nothing to do with this," said Alex with an impatient scowl. "I suggest the rest of us go down to the main hall. I'll answer your questions, though the whole situation's absurd." He looked back at Katherine. "Perhaps the dowager countess would like her nurse sent up?"

"I'll – I'll call her myself," sniffed Katherine. She turned to the Steward. "But no one is to be arrested, or forcibly taken from these premises without my knowledge, Shaddle. Remember that. I need to be informed of everything, and – and I have my own information to give – should it be – required."

The hall was also well lit and well heated, with a fire that filled the huge mantled hearth. Alex remained standing while Father Erkenwald sat on a low stool. Shaddle stood to attention as if guarding the main doorway, and the sheriff faced Alex across the fireplace. Stocky and red faced, the sheriff was a short man, and it was a short conversation.

"I admit to having been employed under false pretences," Alex announced at once, pre-empting questions. "I belong to no guild but since I've never practised within the city boundaries, I'm not obliged to. I know a certain amount about herbs and more about spices, however I've never claimed to be a trained doctor, nor even an apothecary. I chose to promote myself from my original position as pot boy, which was offered to me by the previous occupant here due to my being a soldier once acquainted with the lady's husband."

"Who was at that time held in the Tower, being as he fought for his grace King Richard in the great battle." The sheriff stuck his chin out and nodded. "I knows that, so's no good you inhibiting the facts. I've made inquiries, Bowyer. I know who you is. A deserter, I reckon. Run from the battlefield no doubt."

Alex smiled faintly. "Something of the sort."

"Well now," continued the sheriff with a glance at the small priest, "that's as maybe. Point is, about them poisonous substances what Father Erkenwald saw you giving the earl his lordship last night. Just moments afore he died. Working without the proper apprenticeship and without guild sponsorship, well now, that ain't the problem here, though goes against your character of course."

"I'll tell you exactly what the problem is," said Alex. "The problem is a number of people over-reaching their authority. Admittedly also myself." He spoke loudly and clearly and exclusively to the sheriff. "But there's no permanent apothecary on these premises, and it was too late yesterday to go out and call for a doctor. As clerk of the spicery, I was summoned. I gave his lordship a drink to calm the pain. It's as simple as that. The earl was already half dead when I got back here. Go up and examine the body before the women come to wash it. You'll see all the signs of the sweating sickness, and certainly no indication of poisoning."

The sheriff, feeling his lack of height, glared up at the accused. Originally quite sure of his ground, he was now feeling increasingly uncomfortable. A pot boy should not have been addressing him in a voice of accustomed command. "Poisons! Now that's a nasty business," the sheriff said with emphasis. "I've information says your master was right as rain one moment, and dying the next. And what's more, there's information you was bringing back some mighty strange stuff for some days – being gone hours without permission – the making up of secret drinks for his lordship – then seen sedoocing her ladyship as the noble lord lay a-dying. 'Tis one of the clearest cases I've come across. You're a villain and a fraud, Bowyer, and me and Father Erkenwald is going to prove it."

"Oh, damnation," said Alex, and walked out.

He had expected Shaddle to stand in his way, and even envisaged the need to knock the Steward down, but glimpsing his own doom, Shaddle stepped quickly aside. Alex strode from the hall. He first went upstairs to his chamber and made a bundle of his clothes within the bedsheet. He stuffed his father's seal ring back down inside his codpiece, and ruefully eyed the small personal chest beside the bed which still contained three items of stolen silver. Being caught carrying these off the premises could seriously undermine his health. He shrugged, left the silver in the open chest and tossed the key onto the mattress.

Having no materials for writing any note, he ran downstairs again and called loudly for Tom. The little page was in the kitchens, awaiting the next exciting event. "She's crying," said Tom. "Hard."

"The lady's husband just done died, lad," frowned Hewitt. "You'd expect a lady to sorrow and sniff a bit."

"She's not sniffing," smiled Tom gleefully. "She's howling. And it's got nothing to do with that doddery old earl, neither."

Alex hooked his fingers into the boy's doublet collar and hauled him out into the passage. "Listen," he said softly, "I'm leaving. I have to. Tell your mistress I'm truly sorry. And tell her I'll try and get back in a few days to see her, maybe escort her up north if she wants to go home to her father. Anyway, I'll do what I can."

"You ought to go and see her now," objected Tom. "She'll be furious if you don't."

Alex shook his head. "I'm on the verge of being arrested. I've no intention of being chucked into Newgate. I could moulder in there for a year before someone managed to get me out."

"Where are you going now then?" said Tom.

Alex hesitated. "Cripplegate," he said at last. "Burton House. Only tell her if you think it's urgent, and if you tell anyone else, I promise I'll feed you bloody henbane until I see you die in agony. Got it?"

Tom grinned. "Won't tell a soul. Only my lady."

"And don't tell her either," Alex said, "unless she's in trouble. Probably better for both of us if she thinks I've abandoned her. Tell her I'm a ruffian with a criminal past. What did that sheriff call me? Yes, a villain and a fraud. Well warranted too. Tell her to forget me. I'm a murderous brute."

"Oh of course," sniggered Tom. "Like she's going to believe that!"

No one stopped him on the way out and no one was sent to stop him at the city gates. Just two days before St. Nicholas and the beginning of the Christmas season, the streets were busy. Alex pushed through the crowds and made his usual way to Cripplegate, but not in his usual mood. It was bitterly cold and a sharp north wind churned up the yellow slime in the gutters, pricking the sludge with black turbulence. Alex remembered the inflamed rash of the Sweats, glared to himself and strode on.

Friday, and the fish markets were bustling. Alex cut up through Cheapside and passed the stall selling the best mace in the market, remembering his visit there with Merevale, then marched under the shadows of the Eleanor Cross, more memories of a girl clutching two flea chewed kittens. He swore under his breath and banged on the doors of Burton House.

Alex strode straight into the main hall and stopped abruptly.

Elizabeth was sitting stiff on a high backed settle in front of the hearth. Beside her sat Mary and facing her was Daniel. Facing all of them was a tall and officious stranger in the scarlet livery of the official city aldermen.

Elizabeth looked up as Alex entered, and rose, holding out her arms. Mary immediately exploded into tears. Daniel sighed and turned his back. The stranger said, "Ah. The mysterious Master Bowyer, I presume?"

Alex shrugged. "Under the circumstances," he decided, "it might be time to introduce myself properly."

CHAPTER TWENTY

R eginald Psalter created his own ghost. Being exceedingly tall, thin, and darkly dressed, his shadow crept from fire to doorway, disturbing the patterns of the turkey rug. When he lifted his arms and spread out hands and fingers in explanation, his shadow became a tree.

"But there was a knife, my lords," he said. "After discovery, I took it with me from the chamber as I left. Was it wrong then, to remove so disturbing an indication of the tribulations suffered by his young lordship? I was merely conscious of my duty to my masters. I cannot accept that to be a fault."

"No, no. Indeed not." The alderman leaned one elbow against the mantle, tapping his fingers on the tiered marble. "Very right and proper, Mister Psalter." He frowned, glancing aside with suspicious dislike at the young man in soiled pale blue livery, who was now claiming to be a member of the nobility. "But the fact is, there's a remarkable number of things here which just don't add up." He returned to the apothecary. "The knife was on the floor, you say? At the side of the bed? Where the young lord would have dropped it, from insensible fingers I presume?"

Reginald Psalter nodded gravely. "Exactly so." The apothecary was also eyeing Alex with suspicion. He did not appear to believe in pot boys who turned into lords overnight.

Alex was sitting, legs stretched, on a small chair at some distance from the fire and everyone else. He had separated himself from the proceedings. Now he said, "I should like to see the knife."

The alderman turned back to him with a deepening scowl. "I see no reason why, sir. I imagine it has been cleaned, therefore becoming one knife amongst many and in no way unusual." He raised an inquiring eyebrow at the apothecary, who nodded again. "And would by right of inheritance," continued the alderman, "now belong to the young lord's elder brother."

"I don't want the damned thing," objected Daniel.

"Then I see no useful motive in bringing it forward at this stage," continued the alderman, "thereby causing further distress to the ladies."

Alex shook his head. "I knew my cousin's possessions," he said quietly. "If this was Merevale's property, I shall recognise it."

"What would it matter?" insisted the alderman. "If the poor gentleman, God rest his soul, was sufficiently deranged to commit the ultimate sin of taking his own life, then what dagger he chose to use seems to me to be of singular irrelevance."

"You are, as is everyone these days, jumping to conclusions," Alex insisted. "I personally don't believe my cousin took his own life. How can a man damn near cut his own head off?" Mary's weeping accelerated considerably. Alex raised his voice. "What's more, Merevale disliked – the dark," he said. "Yet his bed curtains were fully closed when I discovered the body. He would not have pulled them himself."

"To disguise the corpse," suggested the alderman. "To ensure his privacy while the deadly deed was done."

"I see no sense in that," said Alex. "He knew he'd be discovered sooner or later. It was night time. He was fully undressed for bed. There was no likelihood of his being interrupted and he allowed no attendant to sleep in his chamber. So why further increase the misery by enclosing himself in the dark?"

"Ah," the alderman shook his head and crossed himself. "But

misery is the whole truth in such a case, is it not, sir? To commit that greatest transgression against our merciful Lord's earthly laws, misery must have been paramount indeed."

Elizabeth was trying exceedingly hard not to cry. She made no attempt to comfort the small sobbing woman beside her. "It's extremely important to me, you know, that my brother be – exonerated of suicide." She raised pleading eyes to the alderman. "Otherwise of course, the church will refuse to bury him in consecrated ground. It would be – terrible. And – surely – there's no – proof. Not at all."

"Of course there isn't," said Alex. "This whole business is absurd. Did nobody call in the sheriff?"

The alderman's mouth twitched with dislike. "The coroner perhaps, but if at any time I should consider an arrest to be necessary, sir, I shall take it upon myself to call the sheriff. In the meantime, this is a personal matter of concern to the noble house of Burton. The deceased gentleman, although the younger son of an attainted father, carried the bloodline of a titled lineage. This is a matter for more sensitive probing than we should expect of the sheriff and I intend discovering the truth myself. In the meantime, may I point out that your own identity, and certainly your right to question either myself or the proceedings, is in considerable doubt."

Alex's answer was never heard. His mouth was open for reply when Jenkins interrupted. Beside the wavering apothecary still awaiting permission to retire, Jenkins stood and bowed to the Lady Elisabeth. "My lady, there is a priest demanding entrance. I have informed him that the household is in the process of dealing with exceedingly private and delicate matters, and have asked him to return at a later time. He refuses to be denied. He is waiting in the ante-chamber. Because of his insistence and his holy orders, I felt it proper to inform your ladyship."

Only Alex seemed neither astonished nor impatiently dismissive.

"Oh, good gracious," said the Lady Elizabeth, "what is he after? Send the man away."

The Lady Mary clung to her kerchief and hiccupped. "Give him money. That's all they ever want."

"Blasted priests. Throw him out," muttered Daniel.

The apothecary stared at his toes and the alderman shook his head. "An unwarranted interruption, indeed. We can have no time for Mother Church at this junction. No final penance can now be performed. It is too late."

Jenkins bowed and left.

Father Erkenwald came pattering into the hall with an apologetic smile. The huge space was bright lit both by candles and from the hearth, catching the edges of the priest's wooden cross and turning its polished oak gold, his hair pure silver. He came forward, confident now, and stood directly beside Reginald Psalter. The apothecary's extreme height contrasted with the priest's tiny figure in his fluttering robes and their two shadows floated together behind them, a willow and its sapling.

"I am, it seems, acquainted with only one of those here present," the priest said softly, "and must apologise for my intrusion. However, I fear it is imperative, under the circumstances. And the actual circumstances, I must inform you, are somewhat more wide reaching than you may have supposed." At first eager to dismiss him, now even the alderman bent, rapt in attention, to the priest's words.

"But it's a most inconvenient moment, father," frowned the Lady Elizabeth.

"Inconvenient for some, I fear," said Father Erkenwald, gazing directly into the corner where Alex remained sitting in silence. "I am aware of your recent loss, and of the terrible circumstances surrounding the tragedy." The priest nodded to the ladies. "Indeed, I have come directly from another noble house where a similar loss has been experienced. The person I arranged to have followed and who arrived here, was involved also there."

The alderman stared down at the priest. "You had better explain yourself, father."

"The staff have been kind enough to inform me of all that transpired here," continued the priest. "I have been waiting in the ante-chamber for your excellencies to complete the business in hand, but upon hearing that the deceased gentleman is about to be accused and his name forever scarred with the dreadful sin of suicide, I believed the time was right for me to intervene."

Alex sighed and interrupted. "You might as well get on with it father," he said from the shadows. "You've an attentive audience. As it happens, I've been trying to tell them all for the past half hour that my cousin never took his own life."

The priest noticeably flinched. "Your cousin, my son? Am I to understand that you are in some manner related to this noble family?"

"The gentleman claims to be Sir Alexander Quyrril, only remaining son of the recently deceased Baron Mornington, killed on the battlefield," said the alderman with a twitch of the nostrils.

"Well, of course he is," said the Lady Elizabeth. "His mother was my mother's sister. He's my cousin. And Merevale's cousin. Actually, by rights he's now the baron himself."

The priest's expression remained adamantly disbelieving. "But I know this young man as one Alex Bowyer, previously employed as a pot-boy and then as clerk of the spicery at Sheffield House in The Strand, close to the little church where I administer the sacraments. There would appear to be some confusion."

"Dammit," said Alex, "I'd haul out my father's signet ring with his coat of arms to show you, but it might be a bit awkward." He grinned suddenly. "In view of ladies present, and where I happen to have kept it."

The priest, benignly sorrowful, shook his head. "The possession of a ring is no proof of anything, my son," he said. "After your departure this morning, I must tell you that the sheriff and myself took it upon ourselves to search your sleeping quarters. Items of silver were discovered, purloined from the late Earl of Sheffield's own property. Incriminating evidence which you surely cannot deny, my son. You are therefore now accused not only of probable murder, but of certain theft."

The alderman promptly gasped and put his hand over his mouth. Mary squeaked, and Elizabeth stood up, breathing deeply. "What nonsense is this, father? I assure you, I know my own cousin. He doesn't need to prove it with his father's ring, or anything else. I've known him all my life. He hasn't murdered anybody."

Daniel had been sitting on the large chair nearest to the fire. He had taken very little part in the arguments. Now he stood. He walked over to his sister and put a protective arm around her waist. "As it happens," he said, "I don't give a damn who else happens to be dead. I'm only interested in my brother." He glared at Father Erkenwald. "And you can't possibly know anything about his death. I don't know who you are or where you've come from. Most of all, I can't see what business it is of yours. But my wife and my sister have been through enough. You can take my damned cousin and this officious alderman away somewhere else and tear each other to pieces for all I care. In the meantime, I declare this whole matter finished."

Elizabeth whispered, "But Danny, about Merevale's funeral. He must be buried with full honour. Not shamefully, as a suicidal sinner doomed to hellfire."

Mary, left sitting in obscurity behind her husband and sister-in-law, now stood quickly and interposed herself between them. "And if Alex has been stealing, Danny dear, we should know about it. We are all of us shockingly poor after this new king – but to steal. Well, really!"

Reginald Psalter understood his growing irrelevance as matters ceased, he hoped, to involve him anymore, and with growing discomfiture, backed from the hall. Alex had begun to laugh. Father Erkenwald turned to him with a barely disguised sneer. "If you find this tragedy amusing, then I pity you my son. Whatever your identity, you have grave charges to answer."

The alderman stood staring at the priest. "Under the circumstances, reverend father," he murmured, "perhaps we should retire to the ante-chamber."

Elizabeth shook her head. "If Alex is going to be accused of anything, I intend being here," she said. "I want to know what's going on in my own house."

Mary turned to her with tear stained eyes. "But Lizzie dear, we all know why you're going to take Alex's side. It isn't – dignified – you know, to make it quite so obvious in front of strangers."

"Oh, shit," said Alex.

Beneath the bright starched cambric white of her cap, Elizabeth became distinctly pink. She turned slowly towards her sister-in-law. She was a little taller than Mary, her only actual advantage over the vastly superior beauty of her brother's gorgeous wife. She looked down her slightly plump nose, sniffed, raised her hand, and slapped Mary hard across the face.

Mary gasped, blinked twice, and collapsed elegantly into her husband's astonished arms.

Alex smothered a snigger. The alderman took two steps backwards, felt the heat of the fire scorching the back of his proud scarlet surcoat, and stepped quickly forwards again. Father Erkenwald coughed politely and raised a restraining hand. "It is natural," he said carefully, "for tempers to become inflamed in such a desperate situation. However, if everyone will allow me, I should like to propose a solution."

Alex grinned. "I can imagine what that's going to be. Drag me off to the Tower, I suppose."

The priest's patience flickered momentarily. "This is no time for humour, my son. I believe a case for temporary incarceration in Newgate has most certainly been identified, but the first consideration is to summon the constable. In the meantime, the ladies should surely retire."

Daniel deposited his wife back on the settle, taking her hands and sitting beside her. "Sounds sensible to me," he said.

"Certainly not," squeaked Elizabeth. "I won't accept - "

It was at this precise moment that Reginald Psalter, having almost entirely backed his way from the hall, was pushed rudely and suddenly aside. A far smaller figure hurtled into the open space before the hearth. Red faced, tear stained, and dressed in his very best gold tissue, the Earl of Burton glared at everyone and stamped his foot. A momentary startled silence was interrupted only by the intake of breath, the spit of the many candles, and the crackle of the fire.

Stephen exhaled and said, "I did it."

No one answered him at once. His mother grunted as though punched, and sat down suddenly, half on top of her semi-reclining sister-in-law. The alderman cleared his throat, opened his mouth, but could not find words. Father Erkenwald frowned, audibly swallowed, and traced the sign of the cross within the candlelit space between himself and the glowing and breathless child.

Alex rose slowly from his distant chair and sauntered over to his young cousin, stood over him, then bent one knee and knelt, taking the boy's small hands in his. He squeezed the cold fingers. "Did what, little one?" he inquired softly, smiling directly into the boy's face.

Stephen gulped. "I killed uncle Merevale."

Alex continued smiling. "I suppose you've been listening at the door," he said gently. "No – don't deny it. This is, after all, strictly speaking your house, and you're perfectly entitled to do whatever you wish. But if this confession is designed to protect and exonerate me, I'm certainly touched, but a little surprised. I know you're fond of me, my child, but I always thought you more attached to your uncle Merevale. So why?"

The small earl, unable to extricate his hands from Alex's, struggled to wipe his eyes and his nose on his gold tissue sleeve. "I can't tell you. Not here. Not in front of everybody." He stared around. "But anyway, it's true. I did it. Uncle – Alex – is innocent."

"Of course I am," said Alex, "and so are you." He was kneeling on the turkey rug with Stephen almost in his arms, when Jenkins once more entered the hall from the far doorway, pushing aside the lurking apothecary who had decided to stay after all, since matters were becoming ever more interesting.

Jenkins coughed. "My lords. I beg to announce the arrival of the dowager Countess of Sheffield."

"Who?" demanded the Lady Elizabeth, clutching her stomacher.

"The lady wishes to speak to a Master Bowyer," said Jenkins apologetically.

"Who?" demanded Daniel, looking up with a scowl. "And anyway, I refuse to acknowledge the existence of any Earl of Sheffield under the circumstances, nor his damned countess, dowager nor otherwise. I should by rights be the Earl of Sheffield. And d'you mean he's dead? This quickly? Doesn't he have any respect for the title at all?"

Mary, who had recently become surprisingly alert after her fainting fit, now promptly collapsed again with a faint whimper.

Father Erkenwald turned in fury. Where the old scars of the

smallpox circled his eyelids, they caught the dancing reflections of the firelight. His lashless glare became framed in scarlet. "What impropriety is this?" he demanded.

The alderman, uncertain as to further complications and still concerned with the young earl's confession, stepped backwards, avoiding the probable entrance of a titled lady unknown to him. Then again feeling discomfort from the proximity of the fire, he swept around. His elbow caught the mantle and knocked a silver candlestick to the floor. The candle flared, the flame threatened the hem of his surcoat, he kicked the beeswax and its polished container quickly into the hearth. His aim, panicked, was wild. He kicked again.

Alex, still holding to his young cousin, turned in astonishment from Jenkins to the alderman, and back to the doorway.

CHAPTER TWENTY-ONE

E xpecting the need to introduce and excuse herself to the Earl of Burton and his countess, whoever they might be, and explain why she needed to speak to a young man of dubious identity who had been employed in the kitchens of her home but had run away, and who had, for reasons even more obscure, taken refuge in Burton House, the Lady Katherine had dressed carefully. She had wished to appear particularly respectable.

She therefore wore a gown of lavender, appropriate for widowhood, in soft jersey folds with double sleeves and trimmings of marten over borders of black sarsenet embroidered in silver rosebuds. The neckline was higher than fashionable, and tucked in with French gorget and a chemise of bleached linen. Over this she wore a heavy velvet cloak in widow's morado, with a high collar of black squirrel.

The lady was accompanied by her page, who unfortunately, was not showing the same degree of dignity. Tom danced over to Alex and tapped him cheerfully on the shoulder. "Sorry," he said, "she insisted."

Tom and the small Earl of Burton regarded each other with interest. Stephen said, "Who's she?"

Alex sighed. He remained kneeling on the turkey rug before the fire, directly in front of the alderman who was still grappling with the disintegrating beeswax, hissing as it melted, and his host's valuable candlestick which he had inadvertently kicked into the heart of the fire. Alex ignored both Tom and the earl, and smiled up at the lady standing nervously in the doorway.

"You might as well come in," said Alex. "You'll find it a most interesting moment to have come visiting."

The Lady Elizabeth at once rose to welcome her unexpected guest. Seeing how young the girl was, her initial annoyance lapsed. "My dear, do come into the warm. It must be freezing outside. Let me introduce myself." She took Katherine's arm and led her closer to the fire. "Will you let Jenkins take your cloak, my dear?" The alderman, abandoning the silver candlestick to its ruin, moved to leave space for the new arrival. Katherine stood in front of the fire and looked down in amazement at Alex. "I'm Elizabeth," the lady continued, "dowager Countess of Burton, and my son here is the earl, Stephen. We know your title of course, my dear, but is it true you're already a widow?"

Katherine stared up at the lady, considerably taller than herself, and back down at Alex, still kneeling beside her feet and still wearing her own household livery. She took a deep breath. "Yes. My – husband died, of the sweating sickness, just yesterday," she said. "There was a certain – difficulty – involving - ". Katherine then noticed the familiar figure of the priest glaring at her, half obscured behind the body of her hostess. She stared back. "Father Erkenwald. What on earth are you doing here?"

Daniel, from the side of the settle where his wife was now sitting, sniffed. "That's something I think we'd all like to know. Damned man just forced his way in."

Mary gasped. "Danny dear! You can't swear at priests."

"Just did," glowered her husband. "None of this has anything to do with Merevale. He's all I'm interested in. And if that uninvited alderman thinks my pillicoot of a nephew garrotted his uncle, then he's even more of an idiot than everyone else."

The alderman straightened up, removed his boot from the hearth where he had again been attempting to extricate the candlestick, and frowned. "The whole affair needs careful consideration," he said. "I have the mayor's authority to continue with my questions until satisfied."

Elizabeth kissed her new guest welcome and turned to her brother. "Danny, get the young lady a chair. Bring it up near the fire. Her hands are like ice."

Alex, who had been kneeling, collapsed cross legged on the rug and grinned up at the Lady Katherine. "It's a nice house usually, isn't it Lizzie. Calm, quiet, well ordered. You've just chosen an awkward moment to come calling. But since you're here, you might as well sit down. Someone'll think to offer you some warm hypocras in a moment, if you wait long enough."

"Yes, of course," said Elizabeth at once, reminded of her responsibilities. "Just what we all need, I think. Danny, do call Jenkins."

Katherine stared down at her clerk of the spicery, still sitting on the floor at her feet. "Who are you?" she demanded.

"Oh, him?" nodded Elizabeth, clapping her hands since her brother was ignoring her demands to summon the Steward. "That's Alex."

Katherine blinked. "Just Alex? Alex Bowyer?"

"Oh, gracious no," said the Lady Elizabeth, now distracted by the alderman who had just plunged his bare hand into the flames within the hearth. "That's my cousin. He's the Baron Mornington."

Katherine opened her mouth and closed it again. Tom, on the floor now beside Alex, started to giggle. Stephen clung possessively to Alex's neck. Alex grinned. "Unofficially, that is," he said. "Just Alex will do."

"But why - ?" insisted Katherine.

"Oh, it's a long story." Alex extricated himself from both Tom and Stephen, and stood, stretching his back. "But I've decided I've had enough of kitchens to last me a lifetime. Not that my lifetime may prove very enduring, all things considered. Mind you," he smiled down at the very young dowager countess, "I can now cook a very passable capon pie, and I know exactly what not to do with cinnamon. Not so good at sugar carving though. And who knows what use any of this will be in the future."

As the Lady Elizabeth spoke to Jenkins, ordering hypocras and asking that dinner be delayed for an hour as she had no idea just how many persons might need entertaining, Father Erkenwald stood forward a little and again made the sign of the cross.

"Some of you," he said, a discreet cough commanding attention, "have expressed a natural bewilderment as to the reasons for my presence." He ignored the several nodding heads, and looked from the Lady Katherine back up to Alex. "I believe it is time for me to explain what I know."

Alex smiled. "What you think you know, father."

The priest remained standing, but turned to face the rest of the room, and in particular his hostess. "I recently witnessed the nuptials of the Lady Katherine to Lord Edmund, Earl of Sheffield, at my little church." The Lady Katherine sniffed and the priest continued. "I was then called yesterday evening to Sheffield House, in order to administer the Sacrament of Penance to a gentleman taking his last breaths, and discovered this to be the same Earl of Sheffield. His wife was at the bedside, and so was a young servant whom I was informed was, in the absence of any doctor, apothecary or gentleman barber, attending to the medicinal needs of the afflicted."

"Me," nodded Alex helpfully.

The priest's audience was suitably silent and Father Erkenwald continued. "His lordship the earl had time to confess his misdemeanours but sadly departed this world shortly afterwards, whilst I was still present. It was at that moment that I became aware of a certain unpleasant aroma tainting his lordship's final breaths. It alerted me to the fact that the earl's difficulty in speaking had not been solely due to his fatal illness, but to the fact that he was not entirely sober. Someone had been administering improper liquors. I smelled the cup at the bedside, from which I had seen this young man help his master to drink, and discovered it contained illegal substances in the form of smuggled liquors from our northern borders."

Alex sighed. "Do get on with it," he said. The Lady Katherine began to speak, but Alex put one hand to her shoulder, and shook his head.

The priest continued. "Then, suspicions aroused, I examined several packets on the table near the bed, and discovered two parcels of dangerous poisons, one of the eastern poppy syrup known to cause collapse, unconsciousness and possible death, and the original container of the intoxicating liquor already mentioned. His lordship, God rest his soul, having already expired, I searched out the young servant boy, wishing to discover the explanation for these purchases. I found him indeed, having retired in seclusion, and with the poor susceptible young widow caught unwillingly in his seductive embrace."

The rapt audience did not all respond exactly as Father Ekenwald had expected. The Lady Elizabeth snorted, and marched over to the door where Jenkins and two serving boys had appeared with the cups and two jugs of hypocras. The Lady Mary giggled and put her hand over her mouth. Daniel glowered and curled his lip in disdain and Tom and Stephen, now both sitting on the turkey rug at Alex's feet, stared at each other with growing boredom. The alderman drew in his breath in horror, but his concentration was on something quite different.

The Lady Katherine blushed furiously and unwisely said, "It wasn't unwilling."

Alex shook his head. "I suggest," he said, taking the proffered cup of hypocras, "we all have a drink first, while it's still warm. I've had no breakfast, and it's damned near dinner time." He smiled at his cousin. "Thinking of inviting the whole blasted lot of us for the midday feast, Lizzie?" Receiving no answer, he looked to his left, where the alderman appeared to be speechless for obvious reasons. "And I think," suggested Alex, "that Mister Psalter, since he's still here, which I'm sure he shouldn't be, might make himself useful and bind up the alderman's hand. I've no notion what his name is, and no desire to know, nor have I the slightest idea why he keeps sticking his damned hand into the fire. But he now appears to be in some pain." He smiled and nodded at the apothecary who darted forwards at once. "By the way, Mister Psalter, congratulations on the hypocras. A pleasant mixture, though a little light on the nutmeg. Lizzie keeps you short on the housekeeping, does she?"

"If you insist on being frivolous, my son," said Father Erkenwald with a sorrowful glance, "I must assume that you are attempting to distract attention from your own grievous guilt."

Katherine drank deep, took courage, and interrupted. "I do believe it's time I said something," she insisted. "I haven't yet had the opportunity to explain my arrival here, and everyone has been polite enough not to ask." She smiled at her hostess. "You see, I knew this – Alex – whoever he actually is, sometime ago, in Leicester, where my home is. Was. That is, my ancestral home. I didn't know who he was, and I didn't actually introduce myself either. They were difficult times."

"The battle," nodded the alderman, whilst having his burned hand bandaged by Reginald Psalter.

"Indeed," said the Lady Katherine. "He did me – a small service at that time, inspite of neither of us being aware of the other's station. So, you see, when I discovered he'd found employment in my own kitchens – apart from being rather surprised - that is, I trusted him. And actually, that has nothing to do with anything else anyway. My husband died of the sweating sickness."

"I beg to differ," said Father Erkenwald immediately. "I believe his lordship was poisoned."

"Oh, for God's sake," muttered Daniel. "Who the hell cares, anyway? Damned man shouldn't have taken my title."

"Your title?" exclaimed Katherine. "I thought this was the house of Burton."

Elizabeth sat down suddenly and drained her cup. "Yes, my dear," she said. "My late husband, killed at the battle you know, was the Earl of Burton, and now my son holds the title." She indicated Stephen, who was hugging his knees in front of the fire. "But my father was the Earl of Sheffield, and on his death, for he was also killed at the battle as so many – well, that's beside the point now – the title would normally have been expected to pass down to the eldest son, my brother Daniel." She waved a tired hand in his direction. "But they were attainted of course, a general attainder on the whole family, due to having been – loyal – well, never mind about that. Our mother and Alex's were sisters, so he's our cousin. And my brother Merevale," her voice cracked slightly, "who was only just released from the Tower, was found yesterday, in a dreadful, that is, discovered in his bed – by Alex in fact. Dead, you see. Which is why the alderman – and in such terrible circumstances."

"Poor young man probably took his own life, may God forgive him," said the alderman, tucking his freshly bandaged hand behind him.

Father Erkenwald again raised a finger. "I consider it no coincidence," he said, "that two violent deaths should have come on the very same day to both holders of the same title. Nor can I believe it a coincidence that the same young man was closely involved with both deaths."

Alex's humour snapped. He turned and stared at the priest, unblinking. "Involved, father? Please explain how you have the temerity to accuse me of being involved in the murder of my cousin and closest friend? When you have no knowledge whatsoever of the circumstances, nor even of who I am?"

"Murder?" whispered Katherine.

"Bloody murder," said Alex softly. "The man I loved most in all this filthy world, was found with his throat slit. I found him."

"A strange coincidence, my son," persisted the priest. "And as to whom you are, I find that the most sinister circumstance of all. To have been in hiding, working in kitchens when it seems you are the son of a noble house, dividing your time, each unknown to the other, between the two establishments of the Earl of Sheffield, past and present, and both dead on the same day, with you at each bedside at the very moment of passing."

Katherine shook her head a little frantically. "But my husband died of the sweating sickness. He was terribly ill while - this gentleman – wasn't even in the house. I suppose – at the time – Alex was here!"

Father Erkenwald glared at the lady. "The sweating sickness is a new pestilence, previously unknown and as yet not fully understood by the medical profession. Instead, I believe it was slow poison that killed your husband my child. The Steward at your premises has informed me in some detail how the – supposed lowly – clerk of the spicery had been supplying secret drinks to his lordship for many days, how he lied concerning his lordships' permission to leave the house on errands, being then gone for unaccountable periods, and how these drinks were made up from the spices kept in his locked cupboard. Mister Shaddle and I then examined this spicery, and found it to contain many substances known for their poisonous properties."

Katherine gulped and said, "But - "

"Perhaps you should also know, my child," continued the priest, "that the young man you are trying so hard to exonerate, has been systematically stealing from you. Several stolen items were discovered by his pallet after he ran from the house."

Katherine gulped again, and stared soulfully up at Alex. "I don't believe it," she said.

Alex smiled. "A small silver tray, a beaker, carved with the faces of the saints, quite hideous by the way, you'd have been better off without it, and a very large silver jug with a dent. Your husband probably chucked it at someone. And by the way, I didn't run from the house. I walked."

"I had you followed, my son," said Father Erkenwald. "Believing it likely that you would abscond when you found yourself accused of the murder of your master, I asked one of my brethren to wait outside and see where you went. He then returned to tell me where you had gone. It was not until I came here that I discovered the whole truth regarding the death of the tragic young man, son of the previous house of Sheffield."

Daniel, now standing behind the settle with both his hands on his wife's shoulders, was frowning. "But I don't understand what this so called coincidence is all about anyway," he objected. "I stood in line to be Earl of Sheffield, not Merevale. And if you're suggesting Alex did in the present earl in order to get me my title back, then you're quite mistaken. For one thing the king wouldn't allow it, and for another, Alex hasn't the faintest interest in doing me favours. He might be my cousin, but he was Merevale's friend, not mine. And why the devil would he kill him? Frankly, father, it's all absurd."

Alex looked faintly surprised. "I'm grateful, Danny," he said. "But someone killed Mel, you know. I swear he didn't kill himself."

Stephen, who had been picking another hole in the knee of his knitted scarlet hose, now looked up, recognising his cue. He stood up in a hurry. "I told you all already," he said loudly. "I did it."

Daniel glared at him. "And for what possible reason, you young idiot?"

Stephen shook his head. "Because – he - " He paused and stared at his toes. "I'm not telling. Just because."

The priest shook his head. "Your sentiments do you justice, my child. But attempting to take the blame in order to prove the innocence of those you love, although for the purest of motives, is a wicked lie in the eyes of God."

"And damned stupid, which is more to the point," said Alex. "It was a violent crime. You wouldn't have had the strength, little one. I don't need your help, I promise. I'm quite innocent of any of this nonsense, and I can prove it myself without you getting involved." He reached over and took the small earl into his embrace. "I don't know what you can possibly hope to achieve with this, child, but it's time to leave it to me." He looked towards Elizabeth. "Lizzie – if you'll -"

The dowager Countess of Burton came over at once, put her arm around her son and, ignoring his defiant struggles, led him forcibly from the hall.

The alderman immediately cleared his throat and attempted to summon dignity. "My lords and ladies, I believe the moment has come for me to summarise. Frankly, there seems to be no proof of anything. I'm not entirely sure on some details, but clearly I cannot announce with certainty that the young gentleman Merevale Corby, younger son of the late Earl of Sheffield, now attainted, took his own life. However, on reflection, an autopsy seems irrelevant and I shall authorise Mother Church to sanction the interment in consecrated ground, then report back to the Recorder and to the Lord Mayor. If I'm given further authorisation, I must tell you that I intend on returning to complete these investigations."

"Thank heavens, someone's leaving at last," scowled Daniel. "And you," he turned on Reginald Psalter, still hovering within the shadows of the hall, "you can damn well get lost too. I'm sure I dismissed you hours ago, and if I didn't, I should have. And as for you, father," he turned to Father Erkenwald, "you should never have come in the first place. It's dinner time. You should get back to your porridge or whatever muck you people eat, and leave us in peace to sort our own business out. Besides, I'm bloody hungry."

Katherine stood in a hurry and tripped over her hems. "I understand perfectly, sir. I should be leaving too."

Alex's hand pressed down on her shoulder, restraining her. "I think you should stay," he said. "I need to talk to you in private. Lizzie'll be happy to invite you to dine with us, I assure you."

"Certainly I will," said Elizabeth, returning briskly, having passed her son over to his tutor's care. "Is everyone else leaving? How nice."

Daniel was escorting the alderman to the doors, the apothecary had quickly scuttled off as ordered, and only the priest remained. "In all conscience, my daughter," he said, unmoving, "I fear I cannot go. I have sworn always to do God's work, and here I see God's hand, guiding me towards my duty. The worst sins of mankind have been committed, and I will not rest until I see the culprit punished." He glared towards Alex, briefly including the Lady Katherine within his hostility. "I understand I was brought to officiate at your wedding for a purpose, my child, and I also intend to officiate at your poor husband's funeral. In the meantime, I do not believe, in all propriety, just one day after your husband's demise, you should allow that young man to put his hands upon you."

Alex did not remove his hands from the lady's shoulders. "You seem determined to be offensive, father," he said quietly. "And since you also seem determined not to leave, then I shall." Alex looked down at Katherine. "I want to talk to you, Kate. There's a small ante-chamber just outside. Will you come?"

Katherine nodded and scrambled up, taking Alex's proffered elbow. Father Erkenwald stepped forwards but Alex turned towards him, raised one challenging eyebrow, and walked past.

Elizabeth said, "Father, since you insist on staying, please take the chair by the fire. My cousin will be back shortly I'm sure," and the priest, nodding, accepted.

The ante chamber was chilly and dark. Alex lit two candles with the tinder box lying beside the empty hearth, and stood there, hands behind his back. "Sit down, child," he said.

Katherine shook her head. "Are you really who they said you were?"

Alex frowned. "I'm Alex Quyrril," he said. "Bowyer was a fabrication. But that was the only lie. I'm not Baron Mornington, and never will be. My father was, but he was killed in the battle. So was my elder brother. On past experience, I expect my family to be attainted in the upcoming parliament so I'm nobody, just as I told you I was."

Katherine sat down heavily on the long settle behind her. "You might have told me the truth," she said. "I trusted you."

Alex kept his distance. "Well, you can trust me now," he said. "I certainly didn't poison your damned husband, just in case you're wondering. He died of the Sweats, exactly as you thought. I recognised the symptoms."

"I never believed anything else," said Katherine crossly. "I'm not a fool. And you weren't giving him secret potions. You were just trying to keep him drunk like I asked you to. So it's all my fault. Which is why I came here, just to help. But I thought you were a destitute kitchen boy. So and I came to give you money, and offer to bring you back." She sniffed. "I wanted, I mean I was going to – and all the time you were stealing from me. I meant to offer you a post as my personal secretary. That must sound really silly now, and I didn't even know if you could read and write, but – I felt – responsible. So now you can laugh at me."

He didn't laugh. He leaned over, tilted up her chin with one finger, and kissed the tip of her nose. "A very sweet thought, Kate. But it seems you'd do better to go home and forget about me."

Katherine blew her nose. "But I don't understand. And I suppose I'm not angry, but I ought to be, I mean about the stealing. Did you hate me all the time because of your cousin's title? I didn't mean to take it. That is, I never wanted to marry the beastly earl in the first place and I pleaded with my father not to make me. Edmund was fifty-two for goodness sake."

"And how old are you, anyway?" smiled Alex. "I suppose you're sixteen or seventeen. You look about twelve."

"I'm eighteen," said Katherine with dignity. "You only look about twelve too."

"Good lord," said Alex, startled, "I'm twenty eight. As far as I can remember, anyway. It's November, isn't it? Then I'm nearly twenty nine. Too much has happened for me to keep count. Anyway, I may not be a common soldier or poacher, but I'm nobody of any importance. I'm entirely penniless, and I confess I did steal from you. First to bribe Merevale's way out of the Tower, and then to help finance my own escape to Colchester to join the coming rebellion. Except I ended up giving most of that to London's beggars. I apologise."

"But you haven't denied hating me," she pointed out with a hiccup, "because of the title."

"Silly little love," said Alex. He bent over again, and this time kissed her very firmly on the mouth.

CHAPTER TWENTY-TWO

He had intended reassurance more than passion, and affection more than desire, but then his mouth forced hers open and he tasted the sweet spices on her breath and the heat of her surprise. Her lips were firm beneath his, and moist, and tentatively yielding, and his hands, tempted further, moved from her shoulders to her back and then around her waist, crawling upwards, his fingers discovering the warm valley beneath her breasts.

He pulled back. Her eyes were closed, her lashes dark curved powderings against the white of her cheeks. The breathless shimmer of the little candlelight played amongst the curls peeping beneath her cap. Alex sighed and let her go.

Her eyes snapped open, startled little windows into wide confusion. "Oh," she said.

"You see, Kate," he said, very softly, "I'm not trustworthy at all. I'm not a person you should – encourage."

Katherine had some trouble pronouncing her words. "I never knew it – felt like that," she whispered.

Alex stifled the several questions that came to mind. He shook his head. "I'm a fool. If someone had walked in – besides, I've nothing to offer you except misery, Kate, so I've no right to touch you at all. Perhaps that damned priest's right about my lack of morals." He was sitting close to her now, his arms no longer embracing her, but clasping both her hands in his. "Your hands are cold," he said.

She was staring into her lap at their entwined fingers. Then she raised her eyes. "You don't have to offer me anything, Alex. I don't want anything from you. I don't expect it. But I never had a proper friend before. Oh, dear Sara of course, but it's not the same thing. There are acquaintances, and people you're polite to, and family, and personal servants who are caring and kind. But you Alex, you're – different."

"That's not exactly in my favour at the moment," Alex smiled. "This damned priest intends to take his accusations further, you know. He'll be whispering in the king's ear next, I can see it coming. I have to get away. I always meant to join – well, that's beside the point. It's just easier if I leave."

She shook her head. "It will look as though you're guilty."

"Ruin the proud name of Mornington? Do I care?" He grinned. "The two relevant families know the truth, my dear, and I've no immediate family of my own anymore. Maybe I can do some good, joining the rebels. I'm achieving nothing here, except my own ruin."

"You're helping me," sniffed the lady, "which may seem like nothing to you, but seems like something to me. Besides, what happens if your rebels succeed, and get rid of this horrid new king? You won't come back a hero. You'll come back a – wanted felon."

"Oh, I doubt it's as bad as all that." Alex shrugged. "No one's actually arrested me yet. I intend leaving before they do."

A faint white condensation from their breath on the cold air between them turned ghostly in the candlelight. Katherine said, "Will you at least stay for – the funerals?"

"Yes. I'll be here for that." He began gently rubbing the circulation back into her fingers. "Look, you're frozen, and I need to talk to that young idiot Stephen. Will you come back into the hall, and have dinner with us? I promise not to disappear in the meantime."

He began to rise from the settle, but, hands still entwined, she pulled him back down. She stared very resolutely into his eyes and coughed, a little nervous. "Since there might not be any more opportunities," she whispered. "I just want to ask one thing. One – favour."

"Of course," he frowned, holding her hands tighter. "Anything, little one. Tell me."

"Kiss me again," she said.

Alex climbed the stairs to his young cousin's chambers with a lurch of insistent excitement, which seemed to have somehow weakened his legs and obscured the normal processes of his thinking. It was both illogical and inconvenient. His breathing had become fast and shallow and his head felt unusually light. He sighed and pushed open the door to Stephen's large bright solar. Inspite of his three months of promoted nobility, the new earl still lived in the nursery wing, surrounded by nurses and tutors.

It was sleeting again outside, thrumming against the window casements and turning the thick green glass into opaque silver. Stephen, still in his coronation best, was sitting on the floor staring into the fire. He was alone. He looked up as Alex entered, and scowled. "I told everyone to go away," he said.

"Telling me to go away will do no good at all," said Alex, promptly sitting down on the rug beside him. "You know what you have to tell me."

Stephen glowered. "I won't. And you can't make me." He sniffed, eyes tear blurred. "And anyway, you said you didn't need me."

"I said I didn't need you to lie on my behalf." He put his arm around the boy's shoulders. The small body quivered. "It was brave, little one, and kind," Alex said. "But I didn't kill your uncle Merevale you know, any more than you did. I loved him too. I have no idea what happened – though I think – but I need to know why you confessed, my child. Was it to save me – or for someone else? Did you see something that night?"

Stephen relapsed into Alex's arms. "No. I didn't know anything'd happened at all until this morning. Mother didn't even tell me anything yesterday. But then she said Uncle Mel couldn't be buried in the church, if they said he did it himself. And he couldn't have done it himself. He – he cared about things. He wouldn't have done that – not

194

to mother – not to me. And then I heard them say it was – you – who – killed him. And that was even worse. So I thought - "

Alex held him tightly while he cried. "You're safe now, little one. And so is Merevale. We'll both miss him, but whatever happened, he's at peace."

"My tutor says I shouldn't cry," sniffed Stephen.

"If I wasn't such a fool, I'd cry myself," Alex said. "Now. Trust me, and tell me what inspired this courage."

"Oh well." The Earl of Burton rubbed his eyes dry with his fists. "It was Aunt Mary."

Alex blinked. "In what way, Aunt Mary?"

"She told me this morning," said Stephen. "After mother said about Uncle Merevale. And I was – snivelling. In the corner. And Aunt Mary came over and told me – she said I had more important things to care about - well she said - "

"What the devil did she say?" frowned Alex.

Stephen raised large bloodshot eyes to Alex's. "She said I was your son."

Alex sat in total silence for a moment. The sense of unreality which had whirled into each crevice of his life since discovering his cousin's butchered corpse upon the bed, now became a vortex, and blew through his head like a gale. He could not think at all for a heartbeat. Then he swallowed and looked back down at the boy beside him. He shook his head. "Your Aunt Mary," he said calmly, "is mistaken. I should be proud to call you my son, Stephen. But you are not. I have no child. Your father was the Earl of Burton, who loved you dearly, and must not be denied." He waited a minute, but when Stephen did not answer and seemed perplexed, Alex said, "How much do you know, my dear, about the parenting of children?"

Stephen grimaced. "Men kissing women. Aunt Mary says you kissed mother." He blushed and gazed back at the flames. "She says you kissed mother a lot, just before I was born."

Alex sighed. "Your Aunt Mary is a damned muddle-mouthed interfering cully-headed pillicoot," he said. "I happen to have been very fond of your mother at one time. Which is not to say – that is, naturally I still am. As for kissing – it's not quite that simple. Anyway, whether I kissed your mother or not, that was before she met and married your father. There isn't the slightest possibility that you're my son, and you have my promise on it. Your father was your father, and that's that. I shall have a word with your dear Aunt Mary."

Stephen, seeming initially relieved, now straightened again. "You won't tell mother, will you."

"No," said Alex. "But perhaps you should. Or then again, perhaps you shouldn't. Now, no more strange confessions. It's damned uncomfortable in Newgate you know."

"I was a bit worried about that," Stephen admitted. "That was why I put on my best clothes. I thought maybe – if I looked grand – they wouldn't throw me in the pits with the rats. They'd give me one of the nicer cells upstairs."

"It's a point I shall keep in mind," smiled Alex, "when my own arrest appears imminent."

"Well," said Stephen, "you could do with dressing up a bit you know. You keep wearing that horrid blue stuff. It's all rough and grubby too, and there's red stains on your shoulder. And that boy downstairs who came with the lady, he's got exactly the same sort of clothes on. They don't look good on him either."

Alex returned to the great hall where the long table had been brought forward and spread with bleached linen. The Lady Elizabeth was instructing Jenkins to have the pewter put away, and bring out the silver. The platters and spoons, well-polished, were carried in, and a terrine of crab cooked in saffroned milk, being the principal dish of the main course. Since the young earl was being served in the nursery, the dowager countess took the high chair and she and her guests sat down.

Elizabeth said, "I've brought out the best silver in your honour, Alex." She giggled. "Please don't steal it."

Alex looked around. "Where's our esteemed reverend father?"

Daniel frowned, helping himself to the eels in aspic, which had just been put in front of him. "Damned man thinks you're the devil incarnate, coz. He won't eat at the same table as you. He won't bloody leave either. We've had to serve him in the ante-chamber. Dinner's already damn nigh an hour late, and we had to wait again while the cook made him a special halibut broth. All he ever eats evidently."

The Lady Elizabeth nodded fervently. "He's most peculiar, Alex. I mean, I told him we're not wicked idolaters or something, but he seemed to think our food's far too rich."

"It's the full moon, if you ask me," said Daniel.

Alex smiled, taking a handful of oysters onto his plate. "A lunatic? Yes, but more of a fanatic, I believe. You've seen he carries the marks of the smallpox? He wouldn't be the first man to beg Christ for his life, and then swear it to God's service after salvation. I just don't see why he's decided to cast me in the part of the murderous demon."

Daniel smirked, mouth full of smoked trout and sugared mustard. "Oh well, coz," he said, spitting out a fish bone, "you can be an awkward bugger, apologies to the ladies. You can't expect everyone to like you, you know."

"Indeed," said Alex. "Thank you, and I take your point. But I've never craved universal popularity as it happens, which is not quite the same thing as being suspected of multiple slaughter. And since there's no other motive, presumably simply in the cause of demonic pleasure."

"As for that," Daniel discovered another small fish bone caught between his teeth, "I've no idea what all this poison business is all about. Always did think it damned odd you wanted to work in someone's kitchen. And naturally you don't like Lancastrians. They all ought to be poisoned as far as I'm concerned." He grunted suddenly, remembered the Lady Katherine, and turned with a conciliatory nod. "Begging your pardon, m'lady. Nothing personal." He turned back to Alex. "After all, that damned priest seems to think you were shoving all sorts of terrible things into people's cups. Perhaps you did."

Alex paused, oyster in hand, and raised an eyebrow. "Inspite of an evident desire to rid the country of Lancastrians in general, coz," he said, "just why would I specifically wish to kill the new Earl of Sheffield, do you suppose?"

Daniel smiled. "You know damned well, Alex." He looked to Elizabeth with a friendly wink before turning again to Alex. "One man out of the way, leaving the ground swept clean for the cock to preen his feathers. You always did have a way with the ladies."

The Lady Katherine gulped and quickly raised her napkin to her mouth. The Lady Mary began to giggle and the Lady Elizabeth glared at her brother in fury.

Alex interrupted whatever Elizabeth was about to say. "You have the manners of a swamp pig, Danny," he said softly. "If I wasn't a guest in this house, if we weren't all in mourning and if you weren't my cousin, I might show you just how brutally murderous I can be."

Katherine put down her knife and spoon and looked around at her hosts. "It's hardly a proper discussion for the dinner table," she said, "but I really do think I ought to make one thing clear. Alex, I mean, Mister Quyrril - is that right? – has always treated me with the greatest respect, inspite of what that horrid priest said. And he certainly didn't poison anyone. The earl, my – husband – often asked Alex to mix some, what you might call, intoxicating drinks." She blushed, stumbling into embarrassment. "My husband was a man who liked his liquor. Master Bowyer – I mean Mister Quyrril, did – nothing wrong."

"Well, he's changed then," said Daniel bluntly. "Always used to be getting into trouble. Ran away with my sister once. I was damn nearly obliged to murder him myself."

"I'm beginning to wish you had," sighed Alex.

Elizabeth swallowed her honey cakes and her fury altogether, and turned to her brother and his wife with a sweetened smile. "I think," she said, "that until Merevale's funeral is over, we might try to forget this whole business. After that, well I think perhaps some different arrangements regarding living quarters? But we shall see. In the meantime, I must apologise to the Lady Katherine for the difficulties of the situation, and hope she'll forgive the – unwarranted subjects of conversation – and the uncouth company."

Alex grinned. The Lady Katherine nodded and hiccupped. "Nothing. I mean, of course. I wasn't even invited. And I really ought to be going."

"No you won't," said Alex. "You and I and Lizzie have something to discuss."

After dinner, comprising only the one main course followed by wafers and hypocras, Daniel strode out to the nearby church of St. Olave's to speak to the priest regarding arrangements for the necessary interment, and the Lady Mary, finding herself most pointedly excluded, went to lie down in her chamber and recover from the trials of the day. Father Erkenwald was abandoned to his solitary dinner and Elizabeth quickly led both Katherine and Alex into her own solar, the large upstairs room attached to her bedchamber. The fire had already been lit and although the window was large, the heavy rain obscured the light and Alex quickly took a spill from the fire and lit the many candles.

Elizabeth sat her young guest on the deep cushioned window seat, and then sat beside her. They both looked up questioningly at Alex. "You said you had to speak to us, Alex dear," Elizabeth said. "I can guess what about."

"In part you can Lizzie," Alex said, "but there's a few other points I want to make clear as well." He pulled up a small chair and sat facing them. The reflections from the rain moved across his face, leaving his eyes deep in shadow. "I take it I don't have to assure either of you that I didn't murder anyone? No? Then let me say this. I have a hearty desire to murder this damned priest, but since I can't, I intend leaving, which should give you all some peace. But I owe both of you my apologies. First of all, because Merevale's true killer will probably be left unknown. And secondly, because I have to abandon the woman I'm in love with. She'll be a great deal better off without me, but Lizzie, I want you to look after Kate. She's all alone, and she's quite absurdly innocent. She hated her husband, but his death leaves her in a damned miserable situation. Whether this wretched new king will take up the habit of awarding pensions to widows without heirs as Richard did, I don't know, but the title's bound to be passed on elsewhere. That means the house will be taken."

Katherine bit her lip, inhaled, blushing but silent. Elizabeth took Katherine's hand and squeezed it, but she spoke to Alex. "Is this the young lady, my dear, who you once mentioned to me? Asking me to have a word with her on certain – personal matters? Although of course, there was never time to follow that through."

"Yes, it is," said Alex. "That's not important now. I just want to be sure you're both alright once I'm not around anymore. I know you can't depend on Danny - and Mary is - well – best kept away from Stephen. I'll explain that another day. Just keep Father bloody Erkenwald out of the house if you can. And although I hate to speak of Merevale in such a heartless way, I think I should point out that he didn't die as I stood at his bedside the way the damned priest tried to imply. I've seen enough of death on the battlefield and I'm not an inexperienced fool. The blood on Merevale's body was dried black and he was stiff and very cold, which means he'd been dead for some hours. I believe he was killed sometime in the middle of the night whereas I found him mid-morning. What's more, earlier the previous evening, he hadn't been alone."

Elizabeth sniffed. "Of course not, if someone killed him."

"I don't mean that," said Alex. "Well, never mind. It's probably not important. But he didn't kill himself, Lizzie. Just remember that, after I'm gone."

Elizabeth flung down her kerchief on her lap. "That's just not acceptable, Alex," she said. "I forbid you to go."

The Lady Katherine's fingers were tight clenched, knuckles white. "I forbid it too," she said. "I may have no right, but in view of what you said – and did – I'm forbidding it anyway. You just can't leave."

"Lovel can go and get himself killed without your help," said Elizabeth. "And you know it, Alex. You keep telling me you're not a fool, well stop acting like one. However many loyalists Lovel manages to muster, they're not going to mow down thousands of the king's men. And he's a ruthless man, this Tudor usurper, with all the signs of becoming a tyrant. So it's us that need your help. How dare you consider leaving me alone in a house with a murderous maniac? And how dare you carelessly tell a young lady you love her as you walk out of the door, never to see her again - abandoning her to that hideous priest's accusations while she becomes homeless and destitute. And how dare you run away leaving us to try and defend you in your absence? And how dare you leave the taint of guilt and cowardice on your good name, which reflects not only on your poor Uncle Godfrey but also on us, your cousins. And how dare you leave little Stephen without an honourable man to turn to, after he's already lost his grandfather, his father and his Uncle Merevale?" Elizabeth paused for breath. "And while I think of it," she resumed rather faintly, "how dare you leave Merevale unrevenged!"

Katherine smiled rather sympathetically. "I hate to kick a man already on his knees," she said, "but I really have to add my own capricious little complaints. You can't possibly tell me you love me – not that you actually did, you referred to me as if I was positively deaf – and then run away. As if you're frightened of me."

There was a short silence. The fire spat soot. Alex sighed. "To hell with it," he said eventually. "I suppose I'll have to stay." The sigh turned into a grin. "You're right of course. No doubt I'd have got half way to the South Weald, on a nag I'd have to steal from your stables by the way Lizzie. And then I'd have thought better of it, and turned around and come back. I just hope you're both prepared to visit me in Newgate."

CHAPTER TWENTY-THREE

"I may need to accept that job you offered, Kate," Alex said. He had taken Elizabeth's place on the window seat, and Elizabeth herself had left the room, promising to see Father Erkenwald and again attempt to get rid of him. Although he sat close to her, Alex had not taken Katherine's hands, as if expecting his fingers to run away with him.

The Lady Katherine sat meekly beside him, trying very hard to look unconcerned. "If that's what you want, Alex. But if Shaddle knows about the stolen silver, and that horrid priest is hovering on the doorstep? Especially now he knows exactly who you are. I admit – well, that is - I'd like you to come back to the house. It was what I was hoping. But of course I assumed, with the Lady Elizabeth frightened to be alone – you'd want to stay here."

Alex shook his head. "In light of all the accusations," he said, "I shouldn't stay in either house. I'm sorry to have to leave her to Danny's tender protection, but he's capable enough and Lizzie'll be alright. Besides, I could hardly sleep in the same room, so she'd still be on her own. She can have half a dozen maids and dressers and pages sleeping on truckle beds spread around the chamber instead, so she's safe enough. Anyway, the person I suspect, is hardly going to attack her."

Katherine flinched. "You suspect someone?"

"No. That is, not really. I shouldn't have said it." Alex stood abruptly and began to pace the room. Katherine watched him. "For God's sake, don't repeat that to Lizzie," he said. "Since it seems I'm staying in London after all, I'll start doing my own quiet investigating."

"You're making me dizzy," objected the lady. "I do wish you'd sit down. And I do wish you'd tell me what you meant when you said – what you said to Elizabeth. About me." She paused, blushing faintly. "You did mean me, didn't you?"

So he sat beside her again and took her hands after all, tracing the slim line from the tips of each finger down to the wrist. "Yes, of course I meant you. But that's something else I shouldn't have said." He raised one hand, and then the other, lightly kissing each palm. "And kissing you – before – was unforgivable. You may be as innocent as those kittens you rescued, but I'm not, and I'm supposed to know better." He sighed, leaning back against the window sill, her fingers still imprisoned by his. "While you're in mourning, I can't come anywhere near you. I'd put you under suspicion as well as myself, apart from the natural impropriety. Besides, as I keep telling you, I've no right to offer for any woman's hand, Kate. I'm homeless and penniless and I was already incognito and on the run."

Katherine sniffed. "You could ask the king if you might keep your lands and title. I think he's stopped arresting people."

Alex sighed. "I believed I couldn't ever bring myself to do that. Now perhaps – I don't know. Half the kingdom's swallowed their pride for the sake of their property and families. I could do the same."

"Well, you should," said the lady, "for your own sake. Men have the silliest ideas about pride. But if you think I'm waiting for you to marry me, then you can forget it. I'm not. I told you before Alex, I don't want anything from you. Except friendship of course, which I want very much." She sniffed again, unable to retrieve her hands or seek a kerchief. "Perhaps I ought to tell you – I – that is – I'm never, not ever, getting married again. Never." Her voice faded. She blinked up at the man still tightly attached to her fingers. She had not expected him to be grinning quite so widely.

"Plan on mourning your dear departed husband into your dotage?" he murmured. "Or joining a nunnery perhaps? Or just worried I might not want to stay soused and insensible every evening?"

Katherine wrenched away and blushed scarlet. "That's a horrid thing to say. I don't have to marry anyone if I don't want to. I'm a widow. I don't even have to obey my father anymore. And certainly not you." She struggled for a kerchief and blew her nose. "You can be my personal secretary if you really think that's a good idea. But – nothing else. I don't want anything else."

Alex encircled her immediately into his embrace, pressing her cap askew against his shoulder. He spoke softly to her ear. "Don't cry, little one. I won't tease you." He offered his own clean kerchief. "I intend coming back to look after you and I'll find some way to explain everything to Shaddle." He received the kerchief back, now a little damp. "Do you mind about your purloined silver, by the way?"

She shook her head, further detaching her cap. "I expect you did it for the best."

"Oh well, as to that," he smiled, "I did it for my own ends, and having a marked lack of respect for any Lancastrian's property. I never actually thought about it belonging to you."

She looked up at him. "Does it now, Alex? Can I sell things?"

"You should wait before disposing of anything interesting," he advised. "Without your husband's testament, it'll all revert to the crown and you'll have to petition the damned king for your rights. In the meantime, rushing to pawn the family silver might give a wrong impression." He smiled again, one quick dimple, and reached for her curls. "Now sit still while I fix your cap, or we'll have the good priest jumping to the usual conclusions and screaming iniquity and immorality all over again."

Alex escorted the lady downstairs and thankfully discovered the hall deserted. Arranging his brother's interment was likely to involve Daniel for the remainder of the day and into the evening while the rest of the family seemed to be busy elsewhere. Already the light was sallow, the rain still streaming from a sky deep twilit behind the black leering clouds. The hall, huge within its shadows, was dreary now.

The candle stubs were guttering, the fire hissing low and a damp chill whispered its echoes amongst the draughts. Katherine shivered.

It was Elizabeth that Alex set off to find, but it was Mary who found him. She was escaping Father Erkenwald. The priest's voice followed her. "The work of the devil indeed. Devilry and harlotry."

And Mary's voice, rising shrill from the shadows, "Really father, it's not even your parish. I'm just thankful I never attended your church when we lived in The Strand ourselves. We always went to St. Bartholomew's. Much nicer. Father William was always so calm." She appeared from the antechamber, straightening her apron. She grimaced at Alex. "And don't bother asking," she told him, marching across the boards towards the stairs. "The man's hopelessly excitable. I merely told him celibacy was a waste of God's good intentions." She whisked upstairs as Father Erkenwald's accusations of blasphemy drifted into faded and indiscernible mutterings.

Then Elizabeth was suddenly at Alex's elbow. "Will someone get that blasted priest out of my house? Stephen will hear him and he's already so upset. Alex, Father Erkenwald's only here because of you. Can't you get rid of him?"

"I'm leaving now, Lizzie," Alex nodded. "No doubt he'll follow me. But I'll be back sometime tomorrow – I'm not abandoning you, but you know I can't actually stay here now. In the meantime, keep cosy, fill your bedchamber with the servants you trust, keep Mary away from Stephen, and be brave."

Elizabeth sniffed. "I suppose you have to go, Alex dear. But I think it might snow. Take poor Mel's cloak, but come back, or I shall never speak to you again."

"If I don't come back, you couldn't anyway," Alex pointed out. "No, don't get pissy, coz. I'll escort Kate home, and try to stay there with some semblance of respectability. I've two funerals to attend, and I've every intention of marching in Mel's procession with his bier to my shoulder. After that – well, who knows?"

Tom was sent for, hauled away from pork fritters, ale and gossip in the kitchen, and Alex helped Kate snuggle back into her cloak while she stamped her feet, encouraging warmth into her numbed toes. Alex was swinging his cousin's best beaver lined cape around his shoulders when the priest pattered up behind.

"I see you are leaving, my son," murmured Father Erkenwald. "And you intend escorting the young widow safely to her home? Then perhaps I shall accompany you."

"Quite unnecessary," said Alex. "Since I'm in her ladyship's employ, my escort is perfectly adequate, I assure you. I'm sure you're expected back at All Saints for Compline and pallet, father."

The priest maintained a benign smile. "But London's streets are perilous, my son, and your own reputation is, shall we say, becoming ever more blemished. There is no greater security than our Holy Father's own divine grace diffused through the presence of his humble servant."

Resisting the desire to tell the priest to go to hell, Alex buttoned his cape over the incongruity of his livery. "On the contrary, father, I believe the good Lord quite capable of protecting the lady without your sheltering arm. In fact, I insist. Follow if you must, but I'll offer no invitation to walk beside us. Now – Lizzie, I've explained my intentions, and you know I'll be back. In the meantime, look after yourself. Tom, keep close, it's getting dark." He offered his elbow, the Lady Katherine clasped it warmly, and they left the house in Cripplegate.

They lowered their heads against the wind and rain, Katherine holding her hat in place, Alex tugging his hard down over his brows, and the page scampering behind. The shops had closed, though there were still two hours before curfew. Alex headed for St. Paul's, where they could enjoy some shelter and dry off before the next onslaught. Their velvets and furs streamed out behind them as they scurried down into Cheapside, the wind howled, the sleet turned to hail, and finally Alex pulled Katherine beneath a goldsmith's dark overhung porch.

"Well, I think we've got rid of that horrid little man," said Katherine, gasping for breath. "But I've no pattens and my boots are squelching."

"All very well for you two," objected Tom, hopping around in the rain beyond the narrow jutting shelter. Three tiny balls of iced hail collected in the brim of his hat. "I'm still out in the thunder. Let's get going."

"Quiet, brat," grinned Alex, wiping the rain water from his face where it still dripped from hat and fur. "We slaves are meant to suffer the scourges of natural inclemency. The lady needs a moment's rest."

"You know," shivered Katherine, "I don't want to alarm you, Alex, but it's going to be awfully difficult when we get home. Father Erkenwald's going to keep on and on until something happens. He'll have you for theft if not for murder."

Alex shook his head, which sent raindrops into her face in a cascade. "What they found was still on your premises," he said. "And as far as anyone knows, your husband gave me everything voluntarily."

"Why would he?" Katherine said. "It doesn't sound terribly convincing."

"Doesn't have to," said Alex. "As long as you back me up. Let's say your wretched husband wanted secret distilled liquors."

"He had money," frowned the lady. "He didn't need to sell the family silver. I might have to, but he didn't."

"Not for sale. Gifts, in gratitude," said Alex. "And an autopsy will prove he wasn't poisoned. Now, never mind about that for the moment. Are you ready for another quick burst?"

They put their heads down again, and ran. As they reached the pillars of St. Paul's, the lightning blanched the clouds, ripping through the sky in six silver slashes. The thunder rumbled its instantaneous vibration and the Minster's soaring wooden spire shuddered. On the steps of the cathedral a raven was bathing, flushing the dirt from its feathers in a flurry of busy black quills. The lightning hit again, sudden and startling. Alex grabbed Katherine's hand and pulled her into the dark chill of St. Paul's.

"One day the lightning really will catch, and that damned spire will burn like some poor misbegotten bugger of a heretic," Alex shook his head. "Then it'll be shit for everyone and God help the priests."

"So much for His divine grace," muttered Katherine, huddled and soaked beneath her cape. "But you really must stop swearing, you know. You'll make a very bad secretary. Your language is shocking – and in church too."

Tom wandered off to peer at the wooden trays of the itinerant vendors and Alex led Katherine to a small fire which someone had lit across the sacred tiles of the nave. It smoked and spat in the vaulted draughts but the little pile of faggots flared higher when a woman already crouched there, tossed a bundle of twigs to the flames. A child, half naked, crawled closer and hugged his small body to the warmth.

The cathedral was crowded. The late Mass and a steady chanting behind the pulpit; the crowd shifting their wet boots, gazing up, muttering their responses, the tumult of the rain and thunder louder than the priest. A hundred people or more were sheltering from the storm; a baby crying, a merchant and his wife arguing, two men organising a wrestling match and another taking wagers. Trickles of water snaked the mosaics and the smell of wet felt merged with candle wax, a thousand tall flames shimmering into the soaring shadows.

"I just need to warm up a little," Katherine shivered. "Then I don't mind getting wet again."

"Your hat's turned into a soggy lotus," decided Alex. "No stiffening left in it I'm afraid. And it can't be that close to nine o'clock yet, they haven't finished seven o'clock Mass. Just keep an eye out for that wretched priest."

Katherine leaned against a pillar and pulled her cape tight. "I just want to get home. I hope someone thought to light a big fire in my bedroom." She glanced thoughtfully at her dripping escort. "I suppose you and Tom are even colder. That livery isn't very warm, is it?"

Alex smiled. "Not terribly."

"And I suppose," Katherine said, "you sleep in one of those horrid little servant's rooms where there isn't even a hearth. But now you're going to be my secretary, and you're not going to hide your name anymore, so you'd better have one of the guest chambers."

Alex shook his head. "My dear child, I've every intention of pretending to be your secretarial clerk, which means I certainly shan't be shouting my real name within your walls. Though mind you, don't go expecting me to copy out illuminated manuscripts or manage the household budget, for I won't do it. Anyway, sleeping in one of the main rooms would occasion enough talk to ruin your saintly widow's reputation for years." He had removed his hat and was wiping it dry. "Besides, I've no problem with sleeping, whatever the conditions. I've slept under a tree many times before now, and no doubt could sleep in one if I had to. I've slept slumped on the back of a charger, just a few minutes rest waiting for the call into battle. I haven't yet got to the age of dreaming for feather mattresses."

"You do keep fussing about my reputation," complained the lady. "Which is my business, not yours. And I admit I've never slept under a tree, but I'm sure I could if I had to. I can be most enterprising when I'm allowed, and I wish you'd stop thinking I'm some insipid little rose petal, or an orphaned sparrow or something. I can only imagine the girls you've known in the past must have been a pathetic bunch."

Alex grinned. "They had other attributes," he said. "But let me just point out that your reputation is my business, and if I ever ruin it, I'd certainly be held responsible. Now, how do you feel?"

"Absolutely fine," lied the lady. "Let's get home."

They discovered Tom arguing with a man demonstrating the wooden whistles he sold, and hauled him away. "Alright. Time for the last run," said Alex. "At least let's get as far as Ludgate. There'll be a crush there, so we'll be soaked again anyway."

The hail was thick, the cathedral's outer courtyard frosted white, and the narrow alleys flooded into filth. The gutters had overrun with debris swept down by the rain, and a horse had galloped through, its rider in a hurry for his open hearth and his mulled wine. The hooves had churned mud and muck together into a thick slime impossible to avoid.

With the storm and the last crush before curfew, Alex was right. The gate out of the city was packed. Alex grabbed Kate's hand, shouted at Tom, and began to push through. Kate was soon stuck between a portly woman with a goose under her arm, and an elderly gentleman trying to protect his basket of tripes, pestells and onions from the rain. The goose struggled and hissed. Alex lost Kate's hand and whirled, reaching for her again.

He grabbed Tom's collar. "Look brat, I can hardly drag your mistress through this mangle backwards. Run on ahead, and make sure she's expected. Tell Shaddle. Order every fire lit and a hot broth made ready, with Sara waiting to take her straight to her chamber. She's frozen, soaked and worn out."

Tom refrained from mentioning that he felt much the same himself. He nodded, ducked, pushed through the mire of legs and skirts, running through into the wider civility of Fleet Street.

Alex turned again for Katherine. He grinned. She was looking particularly forlorn. "I've sent your brat on," he said, "to warn the staff you're coming."

The lady wiped the drips of rain from the tip of her nose. "I must confess – I'm dreaming of getting these horrid leaky boots off, and this soggy headdress. And then – oh for a glorious hot bath."

They were through, jostled but escaping the now furious goose, and had crossed the bridge when Tom reappeared full tilt from the shadows, breathless and stuttering. Previously soaked, now shivering, he clutched at Alex's arm.

"There's a band of armed men strung right across the street in front of the house," he croaked. "Ready to take you, they are. There's Shaddle and Prongton the head groom, the Sheriff, and that mean priest from All Saints. He must have got past while we were in St. Paul's. The sheriff has a rolled parchment with a seal; it's a warrant I reckon, and there's six of the sheriff's armed men from the Watch, puffed up and muttering under their breath about wickedness and slaughter." Tom bent over, grasping his knees and gasping for breath. "I ran around behind them," he panted, "and got a word with Prongton. Calling murder of the master they are, stealing treasure and worst of all - " He ran once more out of breath and stood staring and gulping.

Katherine wavered beneath the streaming sleet, waiting speechless. Alex said, "Calm down, little one. I'm not dead yet. Now – the worst is?"

"They say you've abducted the lady," Tom wailed.

CHAPTER TWENTY-FOUR

"Tom, escort the lady back home," said Alex, pulling his cloak tight and brushing hail stones from its shoulders. "Make sure she's well looked after as soon as she gets in, or she'll be collapsing with the palsy." He turned quickly to Katherine. "Kate, you know what to do, but don't go taking my part to the extent of looking guilty yourself." He grinned, squeezing her little cold fingers. "That wouldn't help either of us. Make it clear you visited the Earl of Burton and his family purely of your own volition. The damned priest knows that perfectly well since he saw you there, so if he's claimed seduction, abduction or anything else, it's outright malevolence. Just to insure the warrant I suspect."

Katherine shook her head. "Alex, come back with me. All this is absurd, and I can prove your innocence quite easily."

"Well, it'll be damned useful if you do," Alex said. "But I'm not going to sit in Newgate while you do it. You don't know what that place is like, Kate. Come to think of it, nor do I, but I don't intend finding out. I've heard enough stories and the stench gags anyone just passing outside. I've no money on me so they'd chuck me in the Limbos until someone paid my way into one of the better cells. I could be held there a month before someone managed to get the warrant repealed. Depends who signed the damn thing."

"But it's all horrible. It's completely unjust," exclaimed the lady.

"What's that got to do with the law?" said Alex. "They'll serve the warrant first, and worry about the truth later. There's gaol fever so rife in Newgate, men have died within the week, and then been proved innocent the same day they're buried." He relinquished her hand and began to step backwards. "No, my dear. I can disappear into the Eastcheap slums within an hour, live to prove my own innocence and discover Mel's murderer too."

She hiccupped, reaching out for him. "But how will I find you again?"

"Kate, for the Lord's sake, just hurry and get inside out of this damned rain. Your appearance'll put the lie to the abduction story at least. I promise to stay in London, and once I'm settled I'll get word to you, and Lizzie too."

"Alex - "

He shook his head. "There's no time, my love." And he turned on his heel and strode into the long dark.

In a few minutes Alex was back into the winding sludge of London's alleys, cutting down quickly to the lower streets and the flooding banks of the Thames. The waters had slopped deep through the wine shops and spiceries and was climbing the mossy stones of Baynards. A squall of gulls had found the drowned corpse of a dog, eyeless and half eaten by crabs. They hovered, pecking, flying up again as the tidal surge slapped them against the cranes and little barges by the wharves.

Lightning struck again, crackling through the hiss of rain, broken by thunder rolling away across the far density of the city. Alex ducked up Pudding Lane towards Eastcheap, turning directly into a narrow alley sloping south. It was pitilessly dark. Behind some of the windows a faint smear of candlelight hovered, a timid flame, just enough for supper and then snuffed before huddling into bed; the only bolster against the cold. As a virulent shaft of lightning struck and divided through the black above, Alex recognised the house he had been searching for, squashed narrow between two others larger, and crossing the cobbles with a jump over the sluice of the central gutter, he began to bang on the door.

The woman who answered recognised him immediately and with an open mouthed gulp of surprised satisfaction, wrapped her arms around his drenched body and kissed his frozen cheek. Joan Hambury's bosom, being softly ample, welcomed Alex with a luxurious heave of heart beat and he was immediately dragged into the downstairs room of the little house. Pleased to be recognised since he would not otherwise have recognised her, Alex was bundled into the stuffy darkness, pushed backwards into what he hoped was a chair, and each of his feet promptly raised, one at a time and without requesting permission, as large practical hands removed his sodden boots and wrapped him in the prickle of a woollen blanket.

"Now, my lambkin," said the woman, raising her voice sharply over the sound of a baby crying, "and what is it your faithful Joannie can do for you after all this time?"

Alex heaved off Merevale's fur lined cloak and pressed the wet bundle into Joan's arms. "This," he said. "You can take this, do what you like with it since I imagine it's worth a pound or two, and let me stay here for a few days. To be honest, I should point out it might be more than a few days. It could even be a few weeks, but if that's a problem, I'll find somewhere else."

"Stay here?" The woman frowned. "My pet, you're welcome to my bed, my hearth and every scrap of food I can find for you. But what would a young lord like yourself be doing wanting to stay in the Eastcheap amongst the beggars and whores? I've a room down and a room up, and you can take both, my lambkin. But it's castles you should be staying in, and palaces and manors. So you tell your Joannie what's amiss."

Alex grinned. "The only castle I'm invited to is Newgate, Joan. I'm a criminal on the run a dozen times over, and evidently a desperate villain. But there's a child crying somewhere. Have you a new husband, for I'll go if you have. I won't cause you trouble, and I've nothing to offer for payment except the cape."

Joan shoved the steaming wet material back at him. "And I won't take this. With winter as drear outside as the new king's face, and you wearing nothing but a doublet and shirt? Never, my lambkin. And as for the brat grizzling, it's my grandson, poor mite. I've no husband, nor want one. You might remember I had a daughter. She took to the stewes, and leaves her gettings with me."

Alex shook his head. "I should have given you more when I had it. Looks like you've made do with very little."

"It was enough." She knelt beside his chair, poking a little warmth into a sooty fire. "You bought me this house and that's a blessing I've never forgotten. Nor wasn't your place to do that for me, but you did it all the same."

The rain was seeping under the door, trickling in tiny threads across the beaten earth, catching the firelight in sudden glistening red. There were old grasses and reeds spread in thin patches across the floor, and the water leaked in and was absorbed there amongst the scrabble of beetles and the dust and dirt of a tired year. "Then I'll stay, if you'll have me," said Alex, "and I'll find a way of paying for my board sooner or later. What do you live on at present, if there's no man and you've a baby to rear?"

Joan shrugged. "My Margery brings me what she can, time to time."

Alex smiled. "So if I stay, I'll be living off the proceeds of whoring. Seems a just and fitting destiny."

Joan was brushing off his boots in front of the fire, wiping them dry and clean with the rushes from the floor. "Not only, my pet, though I see no reason to turn down good honest pennies. But I works in the brewery behind the timber wharf some nights as well, and I've a neighbour is a wheryman, though his boat's rented, and when he's too pissed to see what's river and what's land, then I runs it for him. Not proper work for a woman, they says, and I've bin threatened by the guild, but they can spit into the wind. I can rush the starlings like the best of them, when I must."

Alex grinned and stretched his hosed toes to the little fire. There were holes in both heels, and the knitted wool steamed like string beans in a cauldron. "You're a trusting woman, Joan," he said. "You haven't even asked what I've done."

"If you want me to know, you'll tell me." She stuffed more dry straw into the boots and left them in the faint warmth beside the grate. "Besides, I'd guess it had something to do with having the wrong king on our throne, and the wrong man winning the battle where I'd wager you was fighting, and for the right king too."

The child, unattended, continued to cry, screams now becoming despondent whimpers. "See to your grandson," Alex said. "I don't need mothering. And for once you're wrong. Yes, naturally I fought for the right man and the wrong man won, thanks to foreign mercenaries and English traitors. But it's murder, theft and raptus I'm wanted for now."

"Ah," said Joan, marching over, hands on hips, to a small wooden box in the far corner. "Nothing new then." She heaved a writhing four month old from its make-shift crib as it struggled to escape its swaddlings. "So who's the female this time?"

A sharp tap on the door vibrated through the flimsy plaster walls and even the infant's cries were startled into sudden silence. Joan stared at Alex. His eyes, now accustomed to the murky light, stared back. Then he sat forwards and reached for his boots. "Expecting someone, Joan?"

She shook her head and laid the infant quickly back into its wet bedding. "Not this time o'night and not in this weather. Margery's busy at work and if it were Matt from next door, he'd be pissed and roaring and 'd walk right in."

"Then it's for me," Alex nodded. "I've been followed, though that surprises me. No matter. I won't run, not again. Let them in, Joannie."

Joan knelt beside Alex, helping him on with his boots. "Bring the Watch in? You're sure, my pet? There's a way out back where I keeps the goat, and a window casement will open far enough to squeeze by. You'd be gone afore I opens the door."

Alex smiled and stood, grabbing up his cloak. "No. I'll face my gaolers this time, my dear. Let them in."

Someone knocked again, a little more desperately, a little louder. Joan opened the door wide. The rain swept in with a hail splattered gust. Behind the wind stood a young woman and a small boy.

"Good God," said Alex. He leaned forwards over Joan's shoulder, grabbed Katherine's arm and pulled her inside. Joan slammed the door shut. The thunder rolled, the thin walls vibrated. The threshold was keeping neither the thresh in, nor the water out. Alex glared at his unexpected guests. "What the devil do you mean by this?"

Katherine peered around the one small room with faint confusion. "I thought – well, I just thought." Water drained from her hems, her sleeves, the remains of her headdress, and her nose. She stuck her chin out, emerging from the warmth of her fur collar, now sodden. "And don't you dare be cross with me, Alex whatever your name is. I did what I thought was best, which is what you always say you're doing."

"What I do," said Alex coldly, "is never misconceived idiocy."

"No," glared Katherine. "Just criminal lunacy. On a straight road to Bedlam or Newgate."

Joan, having decided that the unexpected visitor was no sheriff and no threat, had again taken up the crying baby. She returned to the hearth, kicked the dying embers into a sudden flare, and dumped herself on the chair which Alex had left. "This is the abducted wench then?" she suggested. "Looks like the same old story over again to me."

Alex immediately grinned, looking from Katherine across to his tolerant hostess. "Not quite, Joannie. Meet Katherine, the recently widowed Countess of Sheffield."

Joan began to unwrap the infant's swaddling. "Well, don't expect me to curtsey," she said. "You're welcome in my home, young lady, but I'd be obliged if you'd tell me what you want from me, apart from shelter. For I've no wine to offer, nor supper, nor spare faggots for a better blaze. I've another chair and a stool, Alex, if you'd fetch them from beneath the window. But I'm a mite unprepared for fashionable visitors."

"Don't be a bloody fool, Joan," said Alex, hauling out a small rickety chair and a three legged stool from the darker corner. He then helped Katherine off with her cloak and sat her on the chair by the fire, sitting himself on the stool. "She hasn't come for the Lord Mayor's feast, and she's not my lover. She's come to help me, though that's just as absurd."

Tom, with a curious eye at the infant on Joan's lap, nodded cheerfully at this statement. "I told her," he declared. "We was just three little steps from a hot supper, a hot fire and a warm bed. And round she turns, like a spinning top on a stick, she does." The baby had fixed its wide blue eyes on the nearest animated object of interest, and with a wet lipped gurgle, beamed at Tom. Tom promptly sat on the floor at Joan's side and stretching out a delighted finger, stroked its cheek. "Besides," he said absently, still enrapt with the child, "it was your fault. What you said to her, before disappearing. You shouldn't have said that. You ought to know what women are like."

Alex blinked, Katherine blushed, Joan stared, and the baby continued to gurgle saliva down its chin. "I stand corrected," said Alex, with a faint twitch at the corner of the mouth. "Unfortunately, I've no memory of saying anything at all. My mind was most definitely on other things."

"Probably the trouble," said Tom, turning around at last. "You called her 'my love.'"

Joan chuckled. Alex grinned. "Undiplomatic brat, to repeat such things," he said. "And I imagine your mistress will beat you senseless for it when she gets you alone again, and well deserved I'm sure. But we'd best be practical. Neither of you can stay here. But it must be gone curfew and the gates'll be closed by now. Getting back to The Strand won't be easy."

Katherine had clasped her hands tight in her lap and was trying not to shiver too noticeably. "If you'd all like to stop making plans on my behalf and talking about me as if I wasn't here, I could explain what I intend to do." She lifted her gaze and glared at Alex through the dark and the smoke haze. "I won't be sent here or there, and I won't have other people telling me what to do. I'm not a child anymore, and even if I was, it wouldn't be you could order me around. I employ you so I should be telling you what to do."

Joan looked interested. Alex kept grinning. "I think I should inform you I've officially left your employ," he said. "A secretarial clerk with a warrant out for his arrest would be a fairly poor servant to trust, especially when he can't even safely enter your premises."

Katherine ignored the interruption. "I'm not going home and I intend staying close by. I'll find accommodation in an inn," she said. "Or rent a room, or whatever people usually do. Tom has to go back, and tell that silly sheriff you haven't abducted me. Now that Tom knows where you're living, he can start delivering things tomorrow, like food and money and clothes and anything useful. I have to stay nearby, because if they find you and try to arrest you, I'm the only person can prove your innocence."

The infant had a grip on Tom's finger. "Had a little sister once," he said. "'Bout this age. Afore I was put into service it was, and she was a lovely little thing." Tom cheerfully waggled his finger, making the baby chuckle.

"I didn't know you had a little sister," said Kate, momentarily diverted.

"She died," said Tom.

The conversation was bending towards subjects more in Joan's scope of interest. "They do that," she remarked, "just as you get attached to them. A weakly babe is a terrible drain on the affections, that's all it is."

Alex firmly interrupted. "Katherine will have to stay here overnight," he said reluctantly. "The Ludgates will be locked for the evening, so there's nothing else for it, and she most certainly can't wander the streets in this storm looking for a tavern. Tom can return to The Strand by river, and I'll find the tavern for myself." He raised an eyebrow to Joan. "Is there an inn you'd recommend?"

"I'd not recommend anything around here," said Joan, still stripping winding cloths from the now half naked baby. "And since not one of you has a breath of sense, I'll tell you what ought to be done. I'll get Matt's wherry and take the lad upriver, if that's where he needs to get. The lady can have my bed upstairs, and you, young man, can sleep down here. May not be considered proper in your circles, but long as you stays in yer own beds, who's asking? Round here, won't be blinked at. I've a bit of spare bedding you can spread on the floor, though there's a few puddles around now. Reckon by the time I gets back, you'll both be asleep and I can creep in beside the lady with no disturbance. In the morning, you can argue it all around again. With luck the storm'll have blowed itself out by then, and someone'll be able to explain to me what all this is about."

"Oh, I can do that now," said Katherine, beginning to thaw out somewhat. "Simply that Alex is ridiculously stubborn and doesn't know what's best for him. We sort of – got to know each other and now he's my only friend in all the world. Then he did some very kind things to help me out when I asked him to, but it got him into trouble. Now he's accused of things he didn't do, and it's all completely my fault so I'm determined to help, even though he keeps trying to stop me." She smiled across the hearth at her bemused hostess and the nakedly kicking plump legs of the infant, now freed from its bindings. "But Alex is only a friend," Katherine insisted. "Nothing else." She frowned through the pallid firelight. "Goodness," she murmured. "Do even boy babies already have those funny little appendages, then?"

CHAPTER TWENTY-FIVE

The small barge rocked and bumped against its quay as Alex saw Joan and Tom into the shallow depths. Moored close to the unconvincing shelter of St. Magnus the Martyr, the taxi boat was already half submerged with tidal slops, relentless rain and melting hail. Tom peered down with doubt.

"Go on lad," the woman encouraged him. "I'll look after your bony little arse. Quite safe, it is." Joan wore a waxed and hooded broadcloth cape which billowed in the wind and covered her so completely she resembled a gently floating rock. "Useful," she explained, "to keep out weather, and prying eyes both. There's nasty nosey officials sometimes, wanting to know what's out on the river. Well, in this they'll not see I'm a woman, nor recognise my face."

"It's the devil of a sacrifice going upriver in this filthy storm," Alex said, shouting over the gale. "I'd prefer to find a boat for hire instead."

"You'd not find one," said Joan, climbing downwards. "Asides, it's eight pence up far as The Strand this time of night, even running with the tide. Where you going to find big money like that?"

"Sell my cloak, my boots or my body," suggested Alex.

Tom cackled on his way down the little steps outside the church wall. "You could try the cloak," he said, "but I don't reckon you'd get much for the rest." He waded into the boat, which tipped, causing him to sit heavily on the front bench. "And didn't my lady tell you?" He called up to Alex, who was leaning over the wall. "That's one of the main reasons she insisted on coming after you. Being worried you'd not a farthing on you, whilst she's got a purse full of silver. Had it all day but didn't think to pass it over."

Alex sighed. "It's something I'll be grateful for, but as for other matters - " He waved as Joan rowed out from shore. "And remember, brat. Do everything exactly as I've told you."

The rain and the distance disguised Tom's answer. Alex turned and strode again through the back streets to Joan's house, and to the lady waiting there.

Katherine was looking after the baby. She was extremely thankful that it slept peacefully and continuously, though broken by the odd dreaming whiffle and a grunt of well-fed satisfaction, until Alex's return and beyond. She looked up as he came in and rearranged her expression.

He had brought back kindling, purloined from the churchyard where it was frequently and illegally stored by the forest workers with no gardens or sheds themselves in which to keep it. Now Alex knelt and began to build up the fire. The hearth was shallow and unmantled so the smoke gusted as the flames scattered and took force, but a renewed warmth swelled out into the room with a roll like waves from the seashore. A fierce red light danced up the chimney and into the cobwebs and the low beams of the chamber. Katherine watched him in a careful silence and Alex did not speak until he had finished. Then he stood, looking down on her. For the first time the small space burst with light and colour and heat. His face though, with his back to the fire, remained in deep shadow and his eyes were black. Finally he said, "I'm sorry. I shouldn't have been ungracious, Kate. You shouldn't have come, but since you chose to, I'm deeply grateful."

She was surprised. "I thought you were going to tell me off again."

"I was." He grinned. "But I realise what a nonsense that would be, and how unkind. You're a courageous brat, Kate. I hope to God you won't be ill after this evening's endless tramping in the cold and wet. I can hardly offer you a hot bath here."

She remembered. "It was what I was looking forward to at home.

And I suppose there wouldn't be any tubs here? No – that's a silly question. It doesn't matter now. And I don't mind going out to look for a hostelry. I didn't come here to steal your bed from you."

He smiled, coming around behind her, careful not to obscure the heat from her small cold body. Then he put both hands on her shoulders and she sighed, and leaned her head back against his legs. "Silly puss," he said softly. "I shall be warmer down here than you will up there, and besides, I never intended to take Joan's bed from her. Nor share it, in case you were wondering." He did not see her blushes as his hands began to smooth the tired muscles of her neck and shoulders, easing the knotted tension, his fingers first strong and then gentle. She continued to lean back against him and closed her eyes. The dazzle of the flames stained the insides of her eyelids cerise and the heat, increasing as the wood pile sank, soothed and caressed her. Then Alex slowly unpinned her sodden headdress, pulling each twisted wire carefully from her curls until the starched white cambric fluttered in its small wet pieces, and he picked them up and laid them aside. He rubbed his thumbs gently up from the hollow of her neck, entwining his fingers into the coiled knots of her hair and unravelling it so that it fell loose down her back.

He continued to work, unwinding the damp ringlets so they warmed and dried as his fingertips pressed, soothing and easing against her head. She began to feel very sleepy.

He spoke softly as he worked. "You're quite safe with me, Kate, though the world won't always see it that way. I'll neither take advantage of you nor lead you into danger. But remember this, and accept it, as I tell you. My advice is never arbitrary, and what I tell you to do is kindly meant, if not always to your liking."

"Mm." She was almost asleep. "You think I'm silly, and young, and ignorant. And I am, all those things. But sitting alone, doing nothing and being quietly ladylike and waiting for other people to decide what's best for me, that's just too hard. Waiting – that's the hardest of all. I have to do something when my world falls apart." She turned, blinking to keep her eyes open, and stared up at him. "How do they do it, Alex? All those women, waiting for their husbands to go to sea and sail off into adventure and then don't come back for years. And waiting at home while their lords ride off to war? And they just sigh and fold linen or sew seams on silly shirts." He was smiling down on her, his hands still in her hair. "Please don't tell me I'm so utterly useless that I can't do anything to help," she pleaded. "Please don't tell me just to go home and be pathetically, respectably, dutifully good, and patient, and wear widow's lavender and fiddle with my embroidery! While I wait."

He had been close to saying exactly that. He sighed. "You think I worry too much about your reputation. So let me tell you something about myself, and explain who Joan is, and how I know her." He cupped his hands around her face, turning her again to face the fire away from him, then bent, and kissed the top of her hair. "When I was almost as young as you, my dear, and even more foolish, I thought I'd fallen passionately in love with my cousin. Lizzie was never stunningly beautiful like Dan's wife Mary, but she had character, and I adored her. I asked her father for her hand but he refused, as I expected him to. I was the younger son of a minor noble and had neither wealth nor the prospect of any. Lizzie's as headstrong as you, little one. She decided I should abduct her. The scandal would force her father's hand and ensure us permission to marry. We enjoyed planning it for weeks, but shamefully we also involved her personal maid, one Joan Hambury. Thanks to Joan, the plan worked beautifully and I took both women riding north through the night, to the empty lodge my family sometimes used for hunting parties. I had Lizzie in my arms and half undressed, when my brother turned up. Coincidence, or providence, whatever you call it. He'd come alone wanting peace to sort out his own problems, poor bugger. Found me about to ruin my cousin's reputation forever, rescued Lizzie, knocked me out, and took the lady back to her father. I've been thankful to him ever since. He saved me from a ridiculous mistake, and Lizzie's father arranged her immediate marriage with a large dowry. Edward was highly patient and respectable, an earl and a rich man, whom she ended up loving. The scandal was well hidden, but a few found out and remember it. Dear Mary even told young Stephen he's my son, knowing he was born so quickly after Lizzie's wedding."

He wondered for a moment whether Katherine was asleep and had heard little of his confession, but now she stirred, cuddling back against him, and murmured, "What did you do then? What happened to Joan?"

"Joan was dismissed." Alex renewed the slow massage of her neck, his hands combing the waves of her hair, his fingers caressingly busy. "I joined Richard of Gloucester, before he was king that is, ready for the expected battle in support of Burgundy against France, but it ended in that miserable truce. Eventually the Scottish skirmishes, and the war to tame the borders and win back Berwick. Easy for me. I intended getting myself killed of course, but Richard was a better leader than that. Not so easy for Joan. She was ruined far more irrevocably than poor Lizzie. No one would employ her after she'd betrayed her master; involved in the ultimate sin and being already a widow, she had no other home. At least I had the decency to realise my responsibility, so I bought her this house and gave her money to settle down. She was grateful, and promised to repay the favour should I ever want it. I hardly expected to take her up on that. Now, she's just what I need, and thank God she remembers me. She'll also serve as your chaperone until I can get you back home."

The remark brought no answer, neither vehement nor conciliatory, and Alex bent over, watching Katherine's expression. Her mouth was open a little, her eyes closed, and her breathing was deep and even. Alex smiled. Balancing her back against him, he swept one hand beneath her knees and lifted her up against his chest. With her nestled in his arms, he climbed the narrow stairs by the far wall and took her to the bed which stood central in the upstairs chamber.

She murmured something as he lay her down, but it was imprecise, dream mutterings, a small complaint as she lost the close warmth of his body. Alex explored the room, found that the window shutters were broken and could not be hung, but discovered a small chest of spare bedding, coarse linen, an eiderdown and a woollen blanket. Then he strode back to the bed.

It was a very old four poster of rough unpolished wood around a palliasse; a lumpy feather mattress supported by knotted ropes slung between the posts. There had once been curtains but only one tattered remnant remained, a dusty fall of blue serge at the head. Alex sat on the edge of the bed, looking at the woman who lay there. There were no candles to light but a starry opalescence slipped through the unshuttered window and the glow of the fire shone faint from downstairs.

Alex smiled. Katherine's face was peaceful and trusting in sleep and her long brown hair lay in damp waves across the bolster. He flicked up the wet hems of her skirt and began to pull off her ankle boots. Her toes were soaked and cold, but deciding it too provocative to remove her stockings, he rubbed her feet between his hands, drying what he could. She wore nothing else he might in all decency remove, but he loosened the stiffened stomacher which held her gown tight from beneath her breasts to the turn of her waist, unhooking each little silken button and laying the material loose in its place. Then he tucked her in, pulling the blankets up to her chin and the swaddling eiderdown over her shoulders.

Then he bent, and kissed her cheek, and sighed, took his own bundle of discovered bedding and plodded back downstairs.

The fire was already guttering for kindling burned quick, and he was not yet asleep when Joan returned with a blast of ice from the opened door. He pretended, studiously snoring, that he was comatose, and lay still until Mistress Hambury had stomped upstairs. Then he rolled over, shook the nightmares from his waking mind, and finally fell into sweeter dreams.

Joan was up well before winter's late reluctant dawn, and it was still very dark. Alex, deep in sleep, woke with a lurch and sat up, head spinning. The ashes still spread across the hearth were cold and smelled of soot. The chamber shivered within its damp draughts. Joan put her hands on her hips and stared down as Alex emerged from his bundles. "Good God, woman," said Alex, blinking away confusion. Remembering where he was and why, had taken a moment. "It's still the middle of the night."

"There's the brat to feed, and the day to get started," Joan smiled. "You stay there if you want, my lambkin, just don't blame me if I fall over you."

Alex grinned and, still fully clothed, scrambled up, quickly folding the bedding and stuffing it into the space under the stairs. "I need more hours than the day has, so the sooner I get going the better. Is Kate awake?"

Joan shook her head. "Poor mite sleeps like a mouselet. Just a twitch of the nose and a grunt every now and again. You'd better go up and rouse her."

Alex stretched, nodded, and pushed the tousled hair back from his eyes. "I doubt she's ever slept in her clothes before, and half wet too. But I can't leave without a word. She can sleep again afterwards." He tugged on his boots. "Will you be out today, Joan?"

"Not till later," she said, "when the brewery starts the second shift."

Alex turned to the stairs. "She can stay here then? You'll look after her?"

Joan smiled. "Much as my mothering ever helped anyone, I can. It's true she's not your mistress then?"

Alex was half way up the stairs. "Not in the way you mean." He paused a moment, looking down with a grin. "Nice to know my friends always think the best of me."

Too early for winter's daylight, the bedchamber remained obscured in draught and shadow. Alex sat gently on the bed and looked at the breathing bundle beneath the covers. Used to warmer bedding, Katherine had immersed herself. Only the top of her curls emerged. Alex leaned down and whispered. "Will you wake, little one? It's close to dawn, and I need to leave shortly. I've no hypocras to offer you, but there's ale warming in the pot downstairs, and there's cheat rolls, though a little stale I believe."

The creaking of the floorboards had disturbed her. Now Katherine blinked, peeping up beyond the blankets. "It's – you," she said, still in the voice of sleep.

Alex resisted the temptation to wipe a damp finger beneath her lashes, cleaning away the last of the dreams. He sat still and smiled instead. "Yes," he said, "and thoroughly improper, an unmarried man at your bedside. But you're fully dressed, my dear, and no one knows except us. Now, will you come down, or shall I bring the ale to you here? There's nothing for you to get up for of course, and you might prefer to sleep longer."

She managed to sit up. Her shift had become twisted during the night and the gauze fichu had detached, revealing considerably more cleavage than normal. She appeared quite unaware of the fact, Alex being inescapably conscious of each curve. He managed to keep his eyes firmly on her face. She said, "You're leaving? But you want me to sleep? So you intend going off without me. I didn't want to sit at home and do nothing and just wait. Now you're telling me to sit here and do nothing and just wait. That would be far, far worse."

Alex shook his head. "I have to try and see Lizzie and Dan, and set up some sort of plan. But Tom's coming later, bringing news and supplies. You have to be here when he comes. I shouldn't be. What if Tom's followed? Dear Father Erkenwald seems mighty adept in the shadows. So stay here my dear, just this one day. I'll be back before curfew, and Tom can keep you company meantime. If you change your mind, leave with him and go back home. I'll catch up with you when I can."

Katherine managed a sleepy eyed glare. Alex waited patiently for her arguments. What she said was not what he had expected. "Where on earth," she whispered, "is the privy?"

Alex grinned. It was far too dark to see her blushes, but he heard them in her voice. "The nearest one? Probably the cubicles half way down London Bridge. Not that there're meant for women of course. I'm afraid you'll have to use the chamber pot – it's presumably under the bed, and then empty it out of the window into the street like everyone else does around here."

Katherine sighed. "And no waterpipe from the conduit either, I suppose?" He shook his head. "Well, I'll come downstairs in just a minute. Promise you won't leave before I come down?" Alex turned the headshake to a nod. His gaze drifted to the swell of her partly uncovered breasts, and instantly rose again. Katherine said, "And I've never eaten cheat in my life, but I suppose one sort of bread's as edible as any other. At least I can give you what money I have. Then you can come back with good bread - and lots of other food - and kindling - and candles."

She had started to climb from the bed so Alex moved back, and stood. "Either give it to Joan or to Tom," he said. "Better still, ask Joan what you should get, then go to market yourself with Tom as escort.

That'll make the day pass quicker. I'll pay you back when I can, if I manage to live long enough."

Joan was feeding the baby. A teat made from pig's intestines was attached to a small earthenware bottle. The goat was tethered behind the house. Joan looked up as Alex came back downstairs. "You've told your lady you're abandoning her with me for the rest of the day? No doubt she was well pleased."

"Delighted."

Joan grunted and heaved the baby over one shoulder. She began to grind her hand into its back. It made no complaint, presumably used to its grandmother's attentions, and dutifully hiccupped. "Kate's a nice little thing," said Alex, "and about as innocent as your grandchild. She's also bored, and miserable, and invariably foolish – so be patient. She has some money, which might make you a little more inclined towards her. When her page turns up she'll take him shopping. Tell her what you need and don't be modest. No need for us all to starve just because of false pride."

"Money," nodded Joan, "is for the spending."

"And don't forget the candles and firewood," said Alex. "The damned house is as dismal as a Scottish crofter's."

"Glad you appreciate my hospitality," she said.

Alex poured the ale he had been heating, and put the rolls of cheat on the small table. "In case I forget my manners later on," he said, "let me tell you I appreciate it very much. And I'll make damned sure you don't suffer for it."

The sun rose fitfully, inching above the church spires and straining through the clouds. The daylight, barely grey, found a narrow passage through the unshuttered window. The steam from the three cups rose like powdered froth on the cold air and caught the sun in a dither of silver.

"And will she suffer for it?" Joan stuffed the bottle back towards the infant's reaching mouth and frowned at Alex. "Don't your lot waste half their lives worrying about the proprieties? Last time t'was the Lady Elizabeth's watchful father kept her safe. I gather this girl's all alone. You'll ruin her sure as shit in the gutters, staying here with you in the same house."

"Certainly would, if anyone ever got to know about it," said Alex, "which is why no one must. But folk around here won't give a damn, and in the meantime, you stand as chaperone." He grinned, kicking the new laid fire into sparks. "Besides, I mean to marry her eventually, once she's prepared to accept me. So I'll dispel the ruin myself."

Joan chuckled. "Thought as much. Does she want you?"

"As it happens," Alex said, "no, she doesn't. But that's a subject I'll save for another time. I've a lot to achieve today, if you'll look after my lady for me. Just don't tell her anything too dreadful on my account."

"Lie, you mean."

"That'll do it," grinned Alex.

He left Eastcheap and aimed North West shortly after the frosty light had fully risen. Wrapped well within his cousin's fur lined cloak, his liveried cap, still damp, pressed unsuitably low on his head, the serviceable broadcloth of the one ill matched with the luxury of the other, Alex dodged through a couple of churchyards and out into the deep shaded smells of the Poultry. The storm had blown and yesterday's puddles had turned icy, trapping the floating excrement into yellowed translucence. There was a gusty sharp wind which caught at his cloak and the worn soles of his boots slipped and slid.

It was still comparatively early when he arrived at Cripplegate and came into the Burton House through the back courtyard and the stables. Striding through to the main hall, he looked around suspiciously for aldermen, constables or sheriffs but the echoes were quiet. The hall was empty. A laundry girl, skipping downstairs with an armful of linen, saw him by the empty hearth.

"The countess," said Alex. "Where the devil is she?"

Lizzie peered over the carved balustrade. "I'm here, Alex. Come up quickly."

Back in front of the large hearth and its blaze, Alex said, "Well? Has anyone been back for me? That damned priest has talked some idiot into putting a warrant out for my arrest so I'm in hiding again, coz."

The Lady Elizabeth gulped slightly. "They're really serious then Alex? They think you murdered Mel? They must be mad."

"Having a healthy desire to keep my head attached to my neck," said Alex, "I didn't wait around to study the warrant, but I'd guess it's for the wilful murder of the Earl of Sheffield. As it happens, interestingly you must admit, it seems I'm also accused of the abduction of his widow."

"Abduction? The young women who came here yesterday, looking for you?" demanded Elizabeth. "How utterly absurd."

"Well, as it happens, the lady in question isn't helping," Alex grinned rather ruefully. "Instead of going home and disproving the charge, she followed me back into London's sweet and cheery slums. She spent the night in my new hostess's bed, while I slept downstairs on the floor." He noted his cousin's raised brows. "Yes, I know my dear, most improper. But note how carefully I've described exactly where we each slept, and how far removed from each other."

"But it's ludicrous of you both Alex," said Elizabeth. "Another scandal attached to your name."

"While you, naturally, would never behave in such a shocking manner." Alex laughed. "Besides, what is going to ruin me more completely? Seduction of the widow – or murdering her husband."

"Oh well," said the lady, "if you're going to be pedantic about things. And I think it's very mean of you to allude to my past. You know quite well how respectable I've been ever since."

"Listen, Lizzie." Alex sat quickly on the settle beside her. "Never mind about the past. I'll give you my new address, so you can contact me in need but I beg you not to give it to anyone else. We've no idea who killed Mel, and that's my next mission, but I've a keen interest in keeping my head while I'm at it. Fact is, I'm staying with Joan."

"Alex!" Elizabeth was shocked. "You mean you've allowed poor Katherine to stay in the house of a trollop?"

"You're positively boring sometimes, Lizzie," he said. "I'm damned glad I never married you. I mean Joan Hambury, and you of all people should remember her."

"My Joannie?" Elizabeth sat up straight and clapped her hands. "How delightful. I'd love to see her again. She isn't – I mean, she doesn't think too badly of us, does she? I suppose we rather ruined her life too. But how do you know where she lives?"

"Because I bought the house for her, nine years ago."

Elizabeth gaped. "You – you never told me. I always felt so guilty about poor Joan."

"I couldn't tell you. I wasn't allowed anywhere near you for years." Alex smiled. "Now, my dear, I intend visiting Mel."

The Lady Elizabeth sighed. "He's been laid out in his bedchamber, Alex," she said. "He's due to be taken to the church this afternoon. The funeral vespers will be held tonight."

Alex nodded, turned abruptly, and strode the corridor to his cousin's room.

The pale cold body was stiff upon the bed. The covers had been stripped to one sheet across the mattress, the corpse's head supported by a clean bolster. Merevale lay naked, his hands crossed upon his chest and a light linen cloth covering his loins. His eyes were closed, their expression of confused pain now hidden. The tiny wound around his nipple had been cleaned and dressed and was now invisible, but the bite on his thigh remained, the teeth marks pale. Alex pulled up a stool and sat beside the bed. He watched his silent cousin and he stared around the room. Several things were already obvious to him. But there was more which was not. It was a long time before he arose and went back downstairs.

CHAPTER TWENTY-SIX

Alex was dressed in dark velvet; his cousin's doublet, shirt and short coat. Merevale had owned no funereal black so the clothes Alex had taken did not put him in mourning, but remained sombre and plain. The fur trimming on collar, sleeves and peplum was marten, and very narrow. His boots clasped high above the ankle and the buckles were soft cloth, the hose not striped nor parti, neither silk nor adorned. Alex had been able to wash and shave and his dark hair now gleamed in the faded sunlight.

He found the Lady Mary sitting beside the window in the small downstairs solar, peering at her crewelwork through the gloomy morning light. She looked up and seeing Alex, frowned. The expression did nothing to spoil her.

Alex closed the door quietly. "Alone, Mary? Unusual for you."

"If you're going to be disagreeable - "

"I probably am, as it happens." He pulled a chair close to her, and sat. "But I'd appreciate the truth for all that."

"No doubt you consider me an inveterate liar?" She giggled suddenly, tossing her embroidery to the floor. "Come on then, Alex. Give me your insults. Though it wasn't insults you offered me once, I remember."

Alex nodded. "Which is why I know you were in his bed the night Merevale died. I want to know what happened."

Mary giggled again. "In detail, Alex? Is life so dull for you now? Well, it should be an edifying conversation."

"I'm unshockable, my dear," Alex said. "But some things hardly need describing and I'm not interested in games. So simply tell me what I need to know. Did anyone interrupt you both? Noises, a maid, even Danny?"

The lady glared and hissed through her teeth. "Vile, vile man. I never liked you, you know Alex. And now you can leave. I don't wish to speak with you again."

"No good, Mary," he said. "And it'll only make me more suspicious. So was it Dan then? Do you know he killed Mel? Or did you do it yourself?"

Mary, sitting very straight, glared at her husband's cousin. "Shifting blame, my dear?" she spat. "Merevale was alive when I left him, limp, happy and too tired for anything else but sleep. When I fuck a man, I leave him neither breath nor spunk, but I don't kill him off entirely. And Dan knew nothing."

"Dan knows," said Alex. "Everyone knew. I'll make no accusations, but jealousy's a good motive for murder."

The lady stood abruptly and her chair toppled with a crash. "It is indeed," she said. "But what if it were you jealous? I've had better men than you at my feet, and once I've had a man, they always come back for more. So you knew about me and Mel? And decided to eliminate the competition?"

Alex stared up at her in wide eyed amazement. "Even you can't be that stupid, Mary. It's more likely you know damn well it was Dan. Shall I be the scapegoat then, to protect your easy living and your guilty husband?"

She left him at once, flouncing from the room with a sweep of taffeta. Alex stayed for some time, gazing into the fire.

The family was seated at dinner when the first interruption brought Jenkins to the doors.

"Alderman Roper is come my lady," Jenkins announced. "Shall I inform him that no one is home, my lady?"

"Oh, bother," said the Lady Elizabeth.

"Damn the man," said Daniel. "Send the fool away."

The Lady Mary tittered. "I expect it's dear Alex he's come to see."

"The gentleman has asked to see the Countess," Jenkins bowed slightly.

Elizabeth stood, flinging down her napkin. "I'll speak to him in the antechamber," she said.

The young earl Stephen having been served in the nursery, Alex remained smiling sedately at his cousin Daniel and the Lady Mary. Both continued with their dinner in silence. The Lady Mary, scooping the centre from a crushed grape tart, offered a slice to Alex.

"Mel's vespers tonight then, coz," Alex said eventually. "I take it you won't object to my attendance?"

Alex watched Daniel's scowl deepen. "Do what you like. None of my business."

"And with bloody murder being obvious so no autopsy necessary, Lizzie says they're taking the body to lay out in the church nave this afternoon." Receiving no reaction, Alex continued, "I've every intention of making my final goodbyes. No objections to that either?"

Daniel looked up briefly. "Not frightened of the corpse bleeding in the presence of its murderer, then Alex? No? Well why should I object? You were closer to my brother than I ever was."

Only one course had been prepared and was nearly consumed, the Lady Elizabeth still absent from the hall, when Jenkins announced the second interruption.

"A boy, claiming to be a page at the House of Sheffield," Jenkins said, addressing Alex, "is waiting on the doorstep, my lord."

"Tom?" Alex raised an eyebrow. "You'd better let him in."

He got up from the table and followed the Steward to the main doorway. Jenkins flung both doors wide, and Alex stared. Jenkins bowed and retreated and Alex was left staring at a small figure wearing pale blue livery similar to that which he had worn himself until two hours previously. The cap, tugged almost to the nose, seemed top heavy, as if concealing far too much hair. The shoulders drooped a little, well wrapped in a short broadcloth cloak. The cape fell mid-calf, and below it, the hose was wrinkled and rather grubby.

"Good God," said Alex.

"Well, that's less vulgar than the things you usually say," said Katherine. "So are you going to let me in or not?"

He stepped aside and led her quickly to the dark passageway beyond the pantries. "You prance around in boy's clothes," he grinned at her, "then object to my swearing. Or are you just hoping to scandalise my cousins?"

She smiled back. "I thought you'd tell me off. You don't mind too much, do you?"

"Of course I mind." He took her hands, rubbing them between his. "You're frozen. Now, how am I going to warm you up without frightening the life out of you?"

Katherine sniffed and retrieved her hands. "You could invite me to sit by the fire."

"Come on." He took her elbow and led her to the back stairs. "Lizzie hopefully won't mind us using her chamber. But she's with that damned officious alderman, and there's Dan and Mary ready to pretend being shocked in the main hall." The servant's stairs divided on the top landing and an upper corridor led through to the countess's private quarters where a bright fire crackled in her solar. Alex sat Katherine beside it and drew up another chair for himself. "And what have you done with poor Tom? Sent him back home stark naked, or dressed him in your clothes? I can just imagine him tripping over your skirts."

"You don't have to hide me," Katherine insisted. "They're not going to recognise me like this. Even you took ages and ages to realise I was a girl the first time."

He laughed. "For one thing I was dizzy, confused, and wounded. For another, it was dark as purgatory." He took her hand again, still laughing. "And come to think of it, I did know. It took me all of a minute."

"Do I really look - that bad?" she demanded. "Would people guess?"

"Well, in a padded doublet, and if you keep your cloak tight and stop your hat falling off, though you shouldn't even be wearing it indoors you know - "

The third interruption amused him far less. An hysterical scream echoed up the stairs, the sound of wild sobbing, and men's voices raised. Alex stood at once and strode to the door. He looked back briefly over his shoulder. "Stay here. Stay quiet. And for God's sake, do what I tell you for once." He closed the door behind him and hurried down the main staircase. It curved and widened directly into the great hall beyond the minstrel's gallery.

Two candelabra lit the huge space but one had toppled, its candles extinguished. Someone was slumped face down across the long dining table, arms flung over the spilled wine and remaining spoons, platters and napkins. Opposite Mary stood wailing, arms crossed tight around her, fingers tugging at her trailing sleeves.

She choked, heaving as though struggling for breath. The lady Elizabeth stared, having rushed from the antechamber, now clinging to the back of a chair and gasping in horror. The alderman had come from the main doors, Jenkins bustling behind.

The Lady Elizabeth stumbled across to her sister-in-law and tried to pull her away. Mary shook her off. Alex strode from the foot of the stairs as Jenkins hurried from across the room. Together they lifted the body and eased it backwards, leaning it against the rise of the high backed chair where it sat. Mary screamed again. Elizabeth turned, and stumbled from the room, her hand to her throat. The alderman stepped forwards, peering down.

Daniel, now slouched heavily in the chair, was still warm though the bleeding had ceased. His neck had been severed with a deep clean cut stretching almost from one ear to the other. The opening gaped a little and, like the frame of a portrait, the golden ruffles of his collar bordered the seepage of oozing gristle and veins from within. The blood was darkening but not yet dry. Across the table and diluted with spilt wine of the same shade, the blood lay in pools, still travelling in its vagrant trickles down the cracks and indentations of the aged oak.

Alex's hand on Daniel's shoulder was trembling a little, as though it had finally found its own limits of endurance. The alderman cleared his throat. "Stand away, sir."

Alex shook his head. "He'll topple, you fool, if I don't hold him." He looked around, and nodded to the Steward. "Send for the sheriff, Jenkins. And get the Lady Mary's maid down to help her to her chamber. Make sure young Stephen doesn't come in here, or anyone else yet. There's no knowing how many heard the screams." As Jenkins left, Alex turned to the alderman. "I intend carrying my cousin up to his bed. Come with me if you wish, but if you've any objections, you can go to hell."

Mister Roper appeared unable to choose the correct words, so Alex hoisted the limp body against his chest, one arm beneath his knees, and carried Daniel slowly up the stairs to the darkened passageway and to the bedchamber. The corpse was heavy and unwieldy. Alex was suddenly aware of deep weariness, but it was not the weight which tired him. He laid his cousin carefully across the curtained bed and stood back. He was aware of the alderman close behind him, and turned. "My lord," said Mister Roper, "I must inform you that when the sheriff arrives, I shall ask him to place you under arrest while investigations proceed and a warrant is drawn up by the coroner."

Alex sighed. "If you do that, sir, you will be made to look extremely foolish. I wasn't even in the room."

"Then who was, my lord?" The alderman frowned. "Someone, obviously. Do you accuse this gentleman's lady wife?"

"I've no idea where anyone was," said Alex. "I was upstairs, speaking to someone else. I heard the Lady Mary scream, as I imagine you did."

"If someone can verify your absence, my lord - "

"We'll leave that for the moment," said Alex, "but someone can, if needs be. In the meantime, I suggest we both return to the hall and wait for the sheriff to arrive."

He looked back once at his cousin's body lying, as Merevale had done, with eyes closed and mouth slack in the shadows of his own bed. Merevale had been naked, Daniel was clothed, but the slice across the throat was the same. Then Alex turned again and went quickly back downstairs. The alderman followed closely.

Neither lady was present in the hall, but Jenkins stood waiting, his hands behind his back and his eyes fixed on the sticky blackening stains across the great dining table. On the other side the hearth blazed with dancing light and warmth. Reflections sped around the hall, and all scarlet. The wine, the fire, and the blood. The candlelight turned menacing.

"Wine, Jenkins," Alex ordered. "And you'd better not call for the table to be cleared until after the sheriff gets here. You've sent for him?"

"I've sent young Francis with a message, my lord."

It was the apothecary who brought the wine on his way up to cleanse the corpse, a special hypocras he had prepared as a bolster to the senses. Alex thanked Mister Psalter, took the solitary cup and pulled a chair across to the hearth, where he sat stretching his legs to the fire. He looked up at the alderman, whom he did not invite to sit and who had not been offered refreshment. "I've no idea where anyone was when this happened," he repeated. "I was upstairs. You were downstairs with the Lady Elizabeth. Tell me what you know."

The alderman, a little shaken still, did not object to being questioned by his main suspect. "But I was not with the lady Elizabeth, my lord. After speaking with the countess, I prepared to leave. Then for some considerable time I stood at the doorway, speaking with the Steward, again attempting to ascertain the circumstances of the first young lord's death. I came back into the hall only when I heard the lady's screams."

"Damn," said Alex softly.

"You came downstairs immediately afterwards, my lord, as I saw. But I cannot accept that you were absent for the entire period, during which time I was absent myself. The only gentleman whose position I can verify throughout, was Mister Jenkins, and I cannot believe him to be under suspicion in any case. That leaves only you, my lord. I see no purpose in your denials."

"Don't you, by God?" Alex stared at him. "What about the women? And probably half the household?"

"A crime of such wicked violence could never be committed by a lady, sir. And servants would have neither the motive nor the courage. Unless you have specific information - "

"I've proof of my own innocence, but that's all," said Alex. "And I've an idea I'm not about to be believed. Especially since I prefer not to say whose company I was in."

"I assume only some member of the staff remains to corroborate your story, my lord. And since the servants would be easily intimidated and are naturally accustomed to obeying their masters, I would place no reliance on anyone of them to speak the truth, except Mister Jenkins who was already in my company."

Alex opened his mouth, began to say something, stopped, and shut his mouth again. "You leave me little allowance, Mister Roper. Are all servants liars by nature then?"

The alderman sniffed. "I am aware that until recently," he eyed Alex's new attire, "you placed yourself in kitchen service at the House of Sheffield. But since you are also, I understand, a gentleman of title and the son of a baron, this is not a reference to your own state. However, I must also inform you that in this instance I cannot at all believe what you tell me. This is the second bloody murder which it seems only you, sir, could have committed."

Alex sighed, gazing back into the flames. "Only me? How – inconvenient." He stood very abruptly, straightening his doublet and draining his cup. "Now, there's someone I need to speak to upstairs. The Lady Elizabeth of course, amongst - others. And I intend speaking with them in private. You will neither accompany nor follow me, and I give my word, which no doubt you'll not believe anyway, that I'll make no attempt to jump from the windows. You can wait for me down here, and I'll be back before the sheriff arrives."

The alderman, unsure, stepped back and Alex once more strode to the great staircase and ran quickly up. He went immediately to the Lady Elizabeth's solar, tapped on the door and entered without waiting. Katherine, her cloak tugged around her, stood cowering back against the window enclosure. The Lady Elizabeth was seated on the edge of a small chair, facing her and glaring furiously. Her gaze switched to the doorway as Alex entered. "You are truly a – horrid, horrid creature." She bit her lip, catching her breath. "And is Danny – really – dead?"

Alex said, "I'm afraid so."

He went towards her but she held up both hands. "Don't come near me, Alex. I'm not a fool, you know."

"Good God, woman, you don't really believe I did it?" Alex demanded.

Elizabeth extended one trembling finger. "Her," she explained.

"Ah." Alex walked over to Katherine, put his arm around her and sat her on the cushioned window seat. He sat protectively beside her, removing his arm from her shoulders and instead taking her hands. "You guessed?"

Elizabeth was very pink in the face. "You've dared bring your – your – and made arrangements to meet here – thinking she'd stay anonymous – even though yesterday you told us – saying she was the widow – and you've lied about everything." She paused a moment, summoning breath before continuing. "So what else have you lied about, Alex? What else have you done?" Flushed with emotion, fear and affront, the lady clasped her hands tight, fingers rigid.

Katherine was also red faced, both from embarrassment and shame. She clung to Alex, which did not make his denials more believable. "As usual, Lizzie, you're behaving like a bloody fool," he said crossly. "This child is exactly who I said she was. The fact that she also happens to be a blithering idiot, is more an indication of feminine brainlessness rather than a slight on her morals. But, banal as it may seem to you, I'm rather more concerned about my own head at present. Apart from a possible threat from the new king, there's a warrant for my arrest posted outside the city boundaries, and now I'm threatened with arrest here too. It's a habit I'm getting a little tired of."

"You have to tell me what's happened," said Kate, wide eyed. 'The screams – arrests, and the Lady Elizabeth won't explain – well – I don't understand anything."

"Neither of you do," said Alex promptly. He continued holding Katherine's hands warm and tight, but it was Elizabeth he addressed. "Just who was in the hall when Danny was killed? Where the devil was Mary?"

Elizabeth shook her head and stared into her lap. On the table at her elbow, a small silver cup sat untouched. She reached for it absently, then sighed and handed the wine to Alex. "I was alone in the antechamber. I was thinking, just trying to make sense of things. And feeling miserable – you know - remembering the sweet things about Merevale. Remembering his face."

"Damned cold in that poky little room for lengthy reminiscences," said Alex, taking the cup and draining it immediately.

The lady frowned. "Wondering if I did it now, my dear?"

"So where was everyone else?" Alex demanded. "I was up here with Kate. The alderman and Jenkins were talking together on the door step, not that either of them is of any interest. So where was Mary? She must have seen who did it."

"Or done it herself," said Elizabeth.

The fourth interruption was less surprising, though came sooner than expected. The alderman accompanied Jenkins to the great doors as they reverberated with summons. The sheriff, his duty constable, and two sergeants at arms entered immediately. The floor boards creaked and vibrated with five determined pairs of boots. The alderman's voice rose, three quick orders followed by Jenkins's complaints. "If you'll wait here," he said, "I shall inform her ladyship. It is in no way proper for common persons to enter these premises without her sanction."

"We've the right to search," objected the sheriff. "The warrant's signed and sealed by his honour the Mayor. I've a right to do my duty."

"Not until I say you do, you don't," said Jenkins. "This property may not constitute as sanctuary, but it's the private abode of an earl and the dowager countess, and it's a nobly born gentleman you intend arresting here. I won't permit anything resembling a common hue and cry under my jurisdiction. You will await me here, my good man, until I officially announce your request to enter."

The alderman, and the four men who in fact had already fully entered and were standing gratefully close to the hall's blazing fire, stared in some indignation at the Steward. "No one said nothing about it being a titled gentleman," said the sheriff.

"Nor is he," the alderman objected. "His father may have been, but there's no one proved he's a title, nor even claims it himself. Until today, he was dressed in simple livery. Worked in the kitchens, and admitted it."

Jenkins had approached the stairs and was about to climb them when the fifth interruption brought him back with a sigh to the main doors. On the step stood the small chilly figure of a robed priest, close beside the sheriff and two sergeants at arms.

Alex, Katherine and Elizabeth, peering over the high shadowed balustrade at the top of the stairs, looked at each other. Alex swore, and shrugged.

CHAPTER TWENTY-SEVEN

Alex pulled the two women back into the small solar. "Seems like my time's up. But they mustn't find Kate dressed like this."

Elizabeth clutched his arm. "You have to get away. Get back to Joan's."

Alex smiled. "I gave our friendly alderman my word not to jump from the window."

"Nor will you," said Elizabeth at once. "You'll take the other stairs to the kitchens, and go out through the stables. There's not time to saddle horses, but you can probably both travel faster on foot if you hurry."

Alex stood. "I'll send a message with Tom. Send him back with news of any developments." He took Katherine's arm and led her quickly away and into the darkness. The back stairs were unlit and threw no shadows. Alex signalled Katherine to silence. They left the house through the empty pantries and ducked into the cobbled courtyard. A horse neighed and kicked its stable door. Two grooms carrying buckets of water did not look up. Within minutes Alex had Katherine back into the side streets of Cripplegate.

Tom was nursing the baby as Joan stirred something in the pot hanging over the hearth. The fire surged high and Joan pushed the pot aside as a small explosion of soot tumbled from the chimney. The pot smelled of onions. Alex pushed Katherine indoors and slammed the door shut against the icy bluster of wind. The door rattled. "You've made the fire smoke," said Joan. "And the candle's blown out."

Katherine went to the hearth, stretching out and rubbing her hands together. The glow reflected across her face. Alex relit the candle. Tom, he noticed, was neither stark naked nor wearing skirts. "Well brat? Have you no control over your mistress? I take it you brought her those clothes simply to ensure more havoc in my life?"

Tom grinned. "She's the lady. I just obeys orders."

"I hope you brought some more useful things too." Alex nodded towards the stacked piles next to the hearth. "A good deal of firewood, I see. And candles."

"The lad brought plenty," said Joan, "and went out and bought more afterwards. All thanks to the good lady's orders as it happens, so no need to be having words with her. Not that I see the point of her wearing them boy's stuffs, skirts being a lot warmer, I'll bet." She was handing Alex a large wooden bowl, having ladled the soup. Alex regarded it with suspicion.

"One day I'll teach you to cook," he said with a faint shudder. "What is this? Cabbage gruel? Even Hewitt managed better than this. Besides, I've already had dinner."

"This is supper," Joan objected. "Dinner's a long time since, though no doubt us degraded ignoble souls eat our supper earlier than some. And thanks to the lad, there's a good deal in it more than cabbage."

"Yes. Onions and leeks," said Alex, peering into the bowl he held. "Soggy stale bread and the occasional knob of floating bacon." He discovered a spoon and sat at the table where Katherine had already retired with her meal.

Joan was sitting, having drawn the stool to the table. Tom packed the complaining infant back into its box and helped himself from the cauldron. "Got to being a good cook, Mister Bowyer did, in our kitchens," he informed Joan proudly.

Joan raised an unplucked eyebrow but Alex interrupted her unspoken query. "Listen," he said, pushing his bowl away after the second spoonful. "My life's getting ever more complicated, so let me explain a few things here. First, my name's not Bowyer, it's Alex

Quyrril. I've no idea whether I've got a home, but if I do it's a long way away. I'll find out more on Saturday I expect, when our gracious king holds his first parliament."

Tom reached for Alex's discarded plate and quickly finished off its contents. Katherine said, "You have estates?" She laid down her own spoon and reached for the ale jug. "Well, they can't put you in Newgate."

Alex grinned. "My status might earn me forgiveness for a common disturbance, but not for two bloody murders," he said. "Even my noble head doesn't merit me pardon for that, nor the dubious comfort of the Tower, not for the ignominious slaughter of my innocent and noble cousins. And certainly not for the poisoning of the even more noble Earl of Sheffield." He leaned back in his chair while Tom served the ale. "Besides, which prison they chain me in, and what block they behead me on, isn't exactly my main concern."

"They've got no proof of anything," said Katherine with a reproving glare. "They won't dare touch you."

"Well of course there's no proof," Alex said, "since I'm damned well innocent. But I don't mind telling you, finding Danny like that nearly finished me off. I wasn't a loving cousin and didn't like him overmuch as it happens, but doesn't mean to say I want to see the insides of his throat close up. Mel's death touched my heart, but Dan's may be more of a serious threat to my freedom."

Alex was still explaining when he realised the small amount of food he'd eaten now tasted like bile in his mouth, and the cobwebbed ceiling had begun to whirl. His voice faded, becoming husky, and he bent suddenly, frowning and gripping his stomach.

Katherine jumped up. "What's the matter?"

Alex shook his head. "Nothing." He straightened, breathing deep. "Damned headache, that's all. Now – no one here was present there, but - " and abruptly stopped speaking.

Joan frowned. "There's not many as gets a headache in the belly. Don't tell me my cooking's as bad as that."

Alex swallowed but managed a smile. "There're more important things to think about. For instance, there's no way I'll get to Mel's funereal vespers tonight, but somehow I mean to get to the procession tomorrow. And Kate – what about your own husband's funeral? Has an autopsy been planned?" His voice faded out again. His face now contorted, he was sweating and hunched over, one hand clutched to the waist. He shook his head, trying to clear it.

"You're ill," said Katherine, gripping Alex's shoulders, one palm to his forehead.

Joan frowned. "Can you stand? I'll help you up to bed."

His eyes stared, oddly dilated, as if shadows grew within. He seemed suddenly confused. "No. Yes - " Alex struggled to his feet, toppled, and crashed to the ground.

Katherine, Joan and Tom were onto him together, crowding around. "Get his feet," Joan shouted, gripping him beneath the arms and hoisting him upwards. "We'll get him to bed." She took most of his weight, stumbling backwards to the foot of the little staircase. One each to a leg, Katherine and Tom grappled forwards and they bumped Alex up to the bedchamber. He was quite unconscious.

The room was lost in a gloom thick as curtains. Joan sent Tom down for candles and a lit spill from the fire. Alex caught his breath as though choking. Katherine, clinging to his cold limp hand, arranged pillows and pulled the covers around him. "He's – freezing," she whispered.

Joan shook her head. "The man's sweating. He's fevered."

"No, it's a cold sweat," Katherine muttered, tucking blankets to his chin. "He's as cold as – as – death."

The sweat glistened in the candlelight that Tom brought to the bedside. Alex slowly opened his eyes. They appeared bloodstained and he squinted in the flickering light, not sure what he saw or believed. He voice was guttural and the words slurred. He said, "What's happening? Am I pissed?"

Katherine still clutched his hand. His fingers came slowly back to life, curling tight around hers. She shook her head. "You can't be. You're – ill."

He tried to open his eyes wider, as if his sight was as tipsy as his voice. "It's the Sweats, then?"

She gulped. "No. I don't believe that."

"If it's true," he said, voice dull, "get away from here. Tom'll take you home."

"It isn't true," Katherine said. "I should know. It's not the same."
Joan was leaning over her shoulder. "But he's sweating."

Alex closed his eyes and relaxed back against the pillows. "Kate, go
home. Get her home Tom." He blinked, peering again through the
gloom. "I'm sorry to die in your house, Joan." He smiled briefly,
though it appeared an effort. "Hardly polite. But I've the devil of a
headache."

Katherine sat straighter. "It's not the sweating sickness and you're
not dying. Are you listening to me? I refuse to allow it."

Tom, unsure what to do, had brought ale, wine and boiled water.
"Give him the water, child, I don't reckon the rest will help," Joan said.

"You're not sweating hot," Katherine continued. "Do you hear me?
It's different. You're cold. In fact you're freezing. And it may have
started just as quickly, but you're not delirious. Your words are just all
blurred. I don't know what that means, but it's not the Sweats."

Alex reluctantly opened his eyes again. "Yes, I'm cold," he said.
"And I'm about to be – bloody sick. I need privacy – and a bowl –
quickly."

Joan grabbed the chamber pot and pushed it onto his lap. "Forget
the privacy. My old man did this every Saturday night. I got used
to it."

Katherine supported Alex as he bent forwards, holding his dark
damp hair back from his forehead with one cool hand. "And I'm not
leaving either," she said softly. "I nursed my husband. Do you think I'd
leave you?"

After a few moments Alex slumped back again with a sigh. Joan
passed the chamber pot to Tom. "Here, boy. Clean this out and bring it
back. Take it out to the gutters first. The conduit tap's just up top of
the street. Hurry. And find another couple of bowls downstairs. Then
collect a bucket of water." Tom, a willing and experienced slave,
scuttled downstairs.

Eyes shut again, Alex said, "Blood – wasn't there?"

Joan nodded. "Blood in the vomit, yes. How do you feel now?"

"Fucking wonderful," said Alex. His voice faded once more, his
head heavy on the pillows.

"He's unconscious again," said Katherine, staring up at Joan.

"Don't look at me, my pet." Joan stood, rolling up her sleeves. "You're the one knows something of the Sweats and I'm no more a nurse than a princess. It's my girl you need; she's good with the herbs. Meantime, let's get this young man undressed."

Katherine blinked. "I suppose we should. Should we?"

"We must," Joan said. She smiled suddenly. "I remember you being a mite confused over seeing my grandson without his towels. Well, a grown man's not much different, though like to be a deal larger. But this poor lamb deserves the comfort of his clothes off. Reckon you can let your lad do it all if you want."

"Certainly not," Katherine said, blushing. "I know just what – men – look like. I'm not – ignorant."

"Course you're not," said Joan. "So come on then, and give me a hand."

Katherine held the candle high while Joan unlaced the soft velvet doublet, winding the golden cord through the metal eyelets. Once fully open, the women eased it back from his shoulders and pulled it from him. As Joan unbuttoned the shirt collar, she said, "So if it's not the Sweats then, what do you reckon it is?"

They lifted the fine linen shirt up and over his head. Then the short padded gipon, loosened from the hosiery laces, slipped easily from his body. Alex remained unconscious and his breathing was guttural. Katherine stared down at him. "My God," she said. "There's a rash."

The rash barely showed in the dance of candlelight, but a flat stain was spreading and the silk dusting of dark hair across the chest, sweat slick, showed black against the red beneath. "That means?" Joan frowned.

"There was a rash with the sweating sickness too," Katherine whispered. Then she shook her head. "But it wasn't the same at all. That was lurid and yellow, with horrible black spots like – like dirt. And it smelled like dirt. This is red and flat and clean. But I don't know what it is."

"Well then," Joan said. "Now for the hose."

His hose gripped snug to the top of the thighs and, in the new style, the points were then laced through the waist of the braies before finally attaching to the gipon, now removed. In the jointure at the groin the codpiece was held within the knitted edges of the crotch, tight and starched. Katherine hiccupped and nodded. "Yes. I suppose so."

"Reckon we'll leave the braies," smiled Joan. "But the hose better go. Uncomfortable, I'd say, all that wool and stiffening. Don't know how men put up with layers of sweaty stuff around the arse."

"Um," muttered Katherine. She inhaled, straightened her shoulders, leaned over and began to unlace the points. Joan stood back and watched a moment, then turned and stomped downstairs to collect the bowls and water. The sound of Tom's return had vibrated below with a clank of earthenware against wood and metal, then a deep sigh of relief. Joan's voice was just as loud. "We'll need two more buckets, lad. And fill the other cauldron with water to boil. Keep the fire up too. I'm off out, for I need to fetch my daughter before starting work."

Tom's voice, "What about the baby?" And the slamming of the door.

Katherine continued to unlace the hose, her fingers careful to unthread the cord without wandering too close to unmentionable places. She was immersed in necessary concentration when Alex murmured, "It's not a bad way to wake up."

Katherine dropped the points and started back, blushing. "I was – I mean – do you feel better?"

"Undressing me, are you?" Alex tried to sit, but grimaced and gave up the effort. "Very kind, but I'll manage it myself."

"You haven't answered my question," said Katherine. "And don't go thinking I'm completely innocent, because I'm not. I don't know why everyone keeps thinking I'm a baby."

"No idea why," said Alex. "But I'll still do it myself."

"Just in case you'd forgotten," continued Katherine with dignity, "I know all about men's hosiery. I'm wearing them myself."

"Yes, and damn well shouldn't be," said Alex. "But there's a considerable difference." He heaved himself up onto one elbow, caught his breath and collapsed, doubling over. "Oh, Lord," he gasped.

Katherine quickly passed the clean chamber pot and Alex was violently sick for some time.

Tom tiptoed back upstairs with a cooling jug of pre-boiled water and another cup. He stood back, waiting at the top of the stairs while watching the bed. Katherine had supported Alex, her arm around him as he retched and was sick again. When he finally lay back gasping for breath, Katherine wiped his mouth with her kerchief, beckoned Tom to come forwards, passed him the chamber pot and took the water. She held the cup to Alex's lips. "Drink if you can," she said.

Alex sipped, coughed, then turned his head away. Tom had disappeared again downstairs. Alex said, "Jesus. I feel foul. Where's Joan?"

"If you need anything done, I'll do it," said Katherine. "I'm not useless. And besides, she's gone to get her daughter."

Alex opened his eyes. They were bloodshot and he saw through a mosaic, scarlet grouted. "That should be interesting."

"Why?" demanded Katherine.

"Oh – nothing," said Alex. "Just – that is, she's the baby's mother."

"Is that so interesting? Anyway, Joan says she's good with herbs."

Alex hoisted the bed cover up again to his waist and managed to smile. "Listen my love, I've no damned idea what's wrong with me. If you're right and it's not the Sweats, and it seems I'm not dead yet though I feel like it, then it could be contagious and there's no point you putting yourself at risk. I doubt it's the pox and it doesn't feel like the pestilence. Joan's daughter may have a guess. In the meantime, since I've taken over the bed and doubt if I could leave it yet, you should go home."

"Alex, it's way past curfew and the gates will be locked," said Katherine at once. "You've lost track of time. It could be past ten. It could be past eleven. Besides, it's freezing outside. "

"Damnation," said Alex and closed his eyes.

Within moments she decided he was asleep. His breathing was even and gentle, his hands limp on the bedcover. With the excuse of not wishing to awaken him, Katherine made no further attempt to remove his hose. Instead she bent over, face in her hands, and began, very softly, to cry.

CHAPTER TWENTY-EIGHT

K atherine was still at the bedside, curled sideways with her head on the damp pillow next to Alex when she heard Joan return. For a long time she had watched Alex sleep. His eyes were closed, hers were tired and tear stained. Around the room were the waiting jugs, cups and buckets of water. Several times Tom had been sent to empty and wash the bowls and chamber pot.

The door downstairs squeaked, the sound of the gusting wind was momentarily louder, then the click of enclosed safety. The floorboards creaked, followed by a good deal of whispering. Katherine stood carefully, wiped her eyes, and tiptoed down the stairs.

A younger woman had swept into the house behind Joan. She was wrapped tight in a hooded cape of matted yellow blod, but tossed this off and hurried to the fire. Tom had kept the blaze high and the young woman huddled there a moment, rubbing her hands together. Tom was cradling the sleeping baby but the woman went to him and took the child, which woke, screwed up its eyes ready to yell, saw its mother, wrenched free of its shawl and swaddling, grabbed a fist of her hair and smiled. The woman's gown was deep cut and no edges of her shift were visible, opening to a sweep of grubby blue Kersey wool merely scraping the swell of her nipples. With her son balanced in one arm, she dipped the other hand into her neckline and drew out one large breast. With an eager slurp, the child and the breast were brought together. The woman then settled herself in the chair next to the fire and stared up at her audience.

Tom, utterly fascinated, sat on the little stool watching the procedure. Joan had set a cauldron of water to boil and passed a torn heel of bread to her daughter. Katherine, hair loose down her back but still dressed in boy's clothes, walked forwards, blushed, and smiled. "You must be Margery," she said.

Joan nodded. "And once she's seen to little Will, she'll have a look at your young man. Good with herbs, she is, 'mongst other things."

The wind was howling, blustering down the chimney and sending the smoke out into a dirty swirl. The candle stub hissed and guttered. Joan lit another. The baby unattached itself and began to cough. Margery wiped its mouth with her skirt and clamped it again to her chest. "You tell me what's wrong with your man, mistress. I'll not be long with the little lad."

Katherine took a deep breath. "It started very suddenly," she explained. "Alex was quite well one minute and staggering the next. His voice was slurred and I don't think he could see properly. He was sweating ice."

Margery shook her head. "Not the Sweats then. Any sign of buboes?"

Katherine gulped. "Oh dear God, no," she said. "It couldn't be that."

"None on neck nor under arms," Joan interrupted, "for I noted it. As for the groin nor cods, we don't know. Never got that far for looking."

"Eyes bloodshot?" Margery said. Katherine nodded. "And vomiting?"

"That's the worst," Katherine whispered, twisting her fingers. "Over and over. He sleeps, or loses consciousness. He'll wake suddenly, heaving and retching. Then in minutes he's asleep again. It pains him too, and the vomit's bloody."

"Examine his crotch," Margery said cheerfully. "But it'll be the pestilence anyways I reckon. Sometimes the buboes don't come for a day or more, and when they do, he's most like dead. That's that, then. It'll be all of us soon no doubt."

"You can't be sure," whispered Katherine.

Joan interrupted again. "You're a fool Margery. It's not the great death," she shook her head. "Don't go frightening the lady. The man's not sick enough, sleeps too much, almost peaceful like, and then wakes with a clear head as if healed."

"He's quite coherent for a moment or two," said Katherine. "He smiles and makes jokes. Then suddenly he passes out, or starts to vomit."

"'Tis something else," insisted Joan. "Go take a look."

The baby, replete and sleepy, was shoved into Tom's waiting arms. Margery smeared away the last leaking droplets of milk and heaved her breast back inside her gown. "Come on then," she said. Joan hurried behind. Both women being considerably larger than Katherine, she was pushed to the back.

The billows of sooty smoke had risen to the upper floor, and since there was no door either at the top or the bottom to keep anything out, the candlelight was hazed in grey. Through the unshuttered window the fat glimmering moon peered in. Alex seemed asleep but as Margery swept the covers from his body, he woke wild eyed and rolled over, heaving. Margery shoved the chamber pot under his nose.

Joan peered over her daughter's shoulder. "'Tis my girl Margery, lad. Knows medicinals and a bit of doctoring. She'll get you well."

Alex leaned back again against the pillows, catching his breath. "I'm best left alone. If it's the Sweats or the pestilence, no one else should be here. If it's something else, it'll clear on its own." He tried to look around. "Where's Kate?"

"I'm here," she said, peeping between the others.

"Well, don't be," said Alex, losing breath again.

"Men," remarked Margery, her hands probing Alex's chest and face, "are a pestilence all on their own." She began deftly undoing the lacing of his hose.

Alex sighed and closed his eyes. His arms were limp and his breathing stertorous. "Joan," he said faintly, "get this woman's sticky fingers out of my codpiece."

"Not this time, lad," smiled Joan. "A necessary examination, I'm afraid."

"And I've seen enough of them not to be impressed," said Margery. "But there's no buboes, which is all I've an interest in – this time anyways. Now, how do you feel?"

Alex struggled to hoist up the bedcover. "Better now," he said, gripping the blankets with some determination. "So what the hell have I got?"

Margery chewed her lip. "Could give a list of what you haven't got," she decided. "Not the Sweats, and not the pestilence neither it seems. No blisters so not the smallpox. Not ague nor cholera nor the palsy. Reckon can't be the influenza and clearly 'tis not gaol fever, nor likely the dysentery since the shit ain't runny, nor bloody cough since there ain't no cough."

Alex sighed. "Nor haemorrhoids nor pregnancy. But I need a bowl – fast."

Katherine presented it. "So, please," she pleaded, "what can it be?"

"Well," said Margery, stepping back with a shrug. "'Tis clear. The lad's been poisoned."

Everyone stared at her. Katherine said, "Good God."

"Bugger," said Joan.

Margery nodded happily. "Reckon so. There's bin the dwayberry, for the lad's eyes is all black bruised inside, and a touch of antimony too no doubt. As for anything else, I wouldn't know, but tis a good recipe. Complicated, I'd say. Bought by one what knows, and brewed by one experienced."

Alex's eyes had snapped open. "What's the end of it then? How toxic? Tell me straight, am I dying?"

Margery shook her head and smiled. "Don't reckon so. Took a small dose p'raps. Or maybe meant just to keep you out of the way a bit. On t'other hand, you coulda been meant to eat more, but stopped too soon."

"You mean," Alex said, "this God awful agony has been the intentional gift from someone I know?"

"Some folks have interesting friends," Margery shrugged. "Not likely to be a stranger, though, is it?"

"It could have been a mistake," whispered Katherine. "And meant for someone else."

"Oh well," Joan said, apparently satisfied with the diagnosis, "since that's been sorted, I'll be off out. Be late for my shift, and I can't afford to lose my job. The rest of you can finish off the supper from the big cauldron."

Margery snorted and nodded towards Alex. "He ate your gruel, did he? Don't reckon I'll eat the same." She stomped downstairs behind her mother. Within minutes Tom clattered back up, in good time to take the chamber pot yet again for cleaning. He muttered something about only being useful for one thing as he disappeared again. Katherine was left alone with Alex.

She sat on the edge of the mattress and held Alex's hand. She smiled, she hoped reassuringly. "Well," she said briskly. "You can stop ordering me away now. At least poison isn't infectious."

"Murder seems to be," said Alex softly, though without removing his hand.

Unhampered by skirts, Katherine curled her legs up, sitting on the bed. "Do you feel absolutely dreadful, dear Alex?" she said.

He looked sideways at her. "If I puke into your lap," he said, "it will be your own fault. I seem to be having a very bad effect on you. You wave your legs in my face, try and strip me of my hose, and now climb into bed with me. You'll be after my virtue next."

Katherine giggled. "According to the story you told me last night, you haven't – well, never mind about that. But it's good. I mean, I suppose," she wrinkled her nose, "you can't be feeling too bad if you want to tease me."

He closed his eyes. "I've a headache fit to flay an ox, I can't stand and half the time can't move even a finger, I can't see anything clearly, and my throat feels burned. And that's not to mention the vomiting." He opened his eyes again and smiled rather weakly. "And I'd give a lot for a cup of cool water."

Katherine filled a cup from the jug of previously boiled water and brought it to him. He tried to take it but could not, so she held it to his lips. "Your eyes look very strange, Alex," she said, kneeling over him on the bed. "The pupils are very, very big and black and the lids are black too. But there's streaks, like blood, and your lips are cracking. Who could have done this, Alex? Do you know?"

Alex swallowed with difficulty and sighed. "Anyone at the Cripplegate house." He shut his eyes, as if remembering. "Not Danny under the circumstances I suppose, and obviously none of the servants. That leaves - "

"Mary and Elizabeth."

"Absurd," Alex muttered. "Why either? I'd suspected Dan, you know, of Mel's murder."

"What if it's all of them?" Katherine lowered her voice. "What if Daniel killed Merevale and then the Lady Mary poisoned you to protect her husband because she knew you were close to the truth? Then the Lady Elizabeth guessed about Daniel killing Merevale, and so she killed him."

Alex kept his eyes closed and spoke to the dark. "Or Danny slipped me poison knowing I was suspicious of him, and then Mary killed him, realising he'd murdered poor Mel in a jealous fit. She'd given up hope of Dan getting the title back you know, and perhaps she'd been more fond of Mel than I'd realised."

"And even the little earl confessed to the murder," murmured Katherine.

"Stephen? He's just eight years old, for goodness sake. No – he said that because - ." Alex's fingers tightened around hers. "What a bloody, damnable mess my wretched family all are, my dear. You'd best not have anything to do with me."

"I," said Katherine with faint contempt, "stand by my friends." But Alex was very suddenly asleep.

She extricated her fingers and crept back downstairs. Tom was curled at Margery's feet, having built the fire back high. The baby slept, grunting complacently from its makeshift crib beneath the window. Margery, fingers tented beneath her chin as if in supplication, was staring into the flames. She looked up as Katherine came down. "Well, he's not dying, your gent," she said quietly. "But might take a few days afore the muck clears from his innards."

Katherine sat, nodding. "I'll nurse him, however long it takes. It's frightening of course, knowing that someone tried – but if you could advise me on what to give him as medicine? And I apologise for my clothes. I suppose I must seem sadly – improper."

Margery stood with a snigger, brushing down her skirts and adjusting her bodice which had a tendency towards uncovering her bosom entirely. "Improper? Well, that's a laugh. Don't you worry about what I think, my dear, for where I comes from I've seen all sorts and couldn't care less. But it's gone midnight and I needs get to work." She discovered her cape and threw it around herself. The coloured wool had run in the rain and the shoulders had faded, the dye collecting in hearty virulence along the hem.

"I'll look after the baby," Katherine offered.

"Oh, the brat'll sleep till gone dawn," Margery assured her. "And I'll be back after that, with herbs for your good gent and what's left of yesterday's bread, since the baker owes me. Me Ma comes back around seven, and then I'll be off again." She indicated the ceiling. "He'll be alright till then. Just get the bowls to his chin in time. That bed's seen plenty, but poisoned puke's a mite hard to clean up."

Once Margery had left and the ice blown wind with her, Tom hauled Alex's bedding from the night before out from under the stairs and began to make up a pallet by the fire. "Well, lady," he said in a hoarse whisper quite as loud as his usual voice, "I reckon it were that maggot faced priest tried to do our Master Bowyer in. Mister Quyrril that is."

Katherine felt suddenly desperately tired. "I don't think so Tom. I don't like Father Erkenwald, but I can't imagine – besides, he wasn't there."

"Priests do things others can't," said Tom knowingly. "Nasty little man. Reckon his ma fed him knotgrass to sell him as a jester, but he was so sour, so she gived him to the church in penitence."

"I think," said Katherine, "father Erkenwald's just naturally very short. Now, thank you for making the bed, and I'm going to lie down on it. You'll sleep with – Alex – and help him if he needs to be sick?"

"I'm getting good and practised with bowls and pots," Tom nodded. "You sleep well lady. Perhaps he'll be better in the morning."

She doubted it. "Can you lock the front door?" she wondered.

"No one locks doors round this sort of place," Tom grinned. "Only the rich locks their doors. Just sleep, lady, and don't go worrying."

Exhausted and drained, Katherine expected to sleep at once, but she did not. Unable to undress, she was troubled by the unaccustomed woollen hose which twisted, catching around her legs. She decided it would have been kinder to undress Alex completely after all, though did not have the courage to do the same with herself. She had removed her padded doublet but kept the shirt and warm gipon, then curled beneath the thin blankets with her knees to her chest and her hands tucked between her legs. She was not cold for the fire still carried warmth and crackled close to her ear, but the little wooden tenement creaked in the wind, draughts crept insidiously from beneath the door and down the chimney, dust and cobwebs swayed from the ceiling beams and everything rattled. More than anything else it was her mind that kept her awake, and her thoughts rambled quickly into nonsense. She recognised nonsense, and yet could not escape from it. When she finally slept, the dreams blazed brighter than the fire and the nonsense became threatening.

She had slept for about an hour when the door flew open, a flurry of wind and rain entered in wild alarm and boot steps vibrated. Grabbing the covers around her, Katherine sat up in panic. The fire had turned to stinking soot. Something else smelled worse and a bristling chin came down to her level. "Li'lle Marge, ish it? Come 'ere, darling."

The open door had swept the soot into every corner, the ashes into her face. The slam of it shutting echoed. Katherine opened her mouth to scream, found it full of coal dust, remembered Alex upstairs, and managed a furious silence. The figure leering over her was little more than a shadowed bulk in the darkness, with a stench of stale beer and garlic. The shadow reeled, top heavy and incapable of keeping its feet.

"Get away from me," Katherine hissed. "I'm not Margery. She's at work. If you come any closer, I'll stick my knife in your gut."

The figure sank to its knees beside her. "Oo'sh you, then?' it complained.

"The Lady Katherine," she whispered, holding the blankets tight to her chin. "Get away from me."

"Gisha cuddle," pleaded the shadow.

Inspite of her words, Katherine had neither knife nor dagger. She wriggled backwards, limited by the cold open hearth behind her. "You smell disgusting," she said. "Get out, or I'll call my – my father."

A large hand appeared in the thin ray of moonlight. "Don' be mean," Katherine's visitor said. "Gisha feel." The hand descended with a surprisingly accurate instinct for anatomy. It clamped with considerable determination on her breast, the other hand tugging away the bed covers.

Katherine squeaked. "You foul pig." She kicked. The man bent towards her, his clasp tightening. Katherine kicked again, made contact, but without shoes the contact made little impression.

The man objected to this unexpected reaction. "You owes me, li'lle slut. Open yer legs."

A slightly weak but clear voice came from the shadows behind him. "Let her go or I'll slit your throat." The moonlight found the knife blade. The attacker, still on his knees, lurched backwards, immediately relinquishing Katherine.

There was the sound of a tinder box and a candle flame appeared suspended in space. Tom's voice, "Can I kill him, mister? Can I?"

"Certainly not," said Alex. "Just hold the candle while I decide whether to kill him myself."

The unexpected visitor was forced over and away from the pallet, Alex's dagger up tight against his throat. With his other hand, Alex grabbed the man's hair and pulled his head back. Unable to speak, the man produced a gurgling sound. Katherine whispered, "You'd better not kill him."

"Quite right," said Alex, voice a little slurred. "Think of the mess." He bent his head closer to the struggling man. "If I let you go, you will leave quickly and at once. Do you understand me?"

The man nodded wildly. Tom, dancing around them so that the light from the candle fluctuated between blazing flame and sudden shadow, said with disgust, "You can't let him go."

"I have to, I'm afraid," said Alex, releasing the man's hair. "A shocking waste of knife practice I know, but he's probably one of our hostess's best customers."

The man staggered to his feet, looked around in utter confusion, toppled towards the door and managed to wrench it open. He left it swinging in the rain as he disappeared into the shimmering moonlight. The wind shut the door for him.

Katherine straightened her clothing. "Thank you – so very much," she stuttered. "But you shouldn't be – I mean – you're sick."

"You should have called me," said Alex weakly. He was losing balance, swerved, bumped into Tom, and promptly collapsed onto the pallet.

Katherine bent over him. Tom peered past her shoulder. "Out cold," he decided.

"Help me get him back to bed," she said quickly, her hands beneath his arms. Alex was still stripped to the waist. Katherine bit her lip, ashamed of her nerves. She had never before touched a man so intimately, but his skin was dry and cool and she was surprised to feel a faint pleasure at the contact. The candlelight gleamed across the smooth rise of his muscles. It showed that Alex had hitched up his hose again, tightening the laces through the waistband of the braies.

Katherine was, however, quite unable to lift him.

Tom shook his head. "He's too big. We'd never make it. Probably kill him trying to bump him up all them stairs. He'll have to sleep down here."

Katherine sat back on her heels and sighed. "We'll make him comfortable then. And you'll have to sleep next to him and look after him if he needs to be sick. And get one of the better pillows from upstairs, and the big eiderdown too. It's cold down here now. Should we make up the fire again? Better not perhaps, it might be dangerous. And bring down one of the jugs of boiled water, and a cup, and the chamber pot just in case. And try not to bump into him in the night. In fact - ," she paused for breath, "have we enough blankets and things to make up a separate pallet?"

"Oh stop fussing," grinned Tom. "And go to bed."

CHAPTER TWENTY-NINE

"Well I wasn't going out in the middle of the night now, was I?" objected Tom. "Besides, it was raining."

"Well, go now," said Katherine firmly. "All this needs cleaning up. And I want another bucket of water for boiling. I think – I really do think - he needs a nice warm wash."

"You'll find no bath tub nowheres 'round here," frowned Margery. "Though I reckon me ma could get an empty barrel from down the brewery. But why bother with immersions since we can't lift him easy anyways? You'll do better to put a cloth under his arse and do it on the floor. I'll get his hose off."

"No need for that," said Kathcrine quickly. "Face – and chest – will do I think. I mean, it's not as if - "

"No, the lad's not got the runs," said Margery. "You fix him up then, and I'll start boiling the yarrow with a touch of betony and rue. Out cold again he is, poor sod, but he'll come round when the medicks start up sweet."

He did. Above the sour smell of vomit and bile which permeated the two small rooms, a drift of sudden concentrated delight cleansed the air. It was a reminder of gardens and growth, spring after winter and sunshine after rain. Margery stirred and the bubbling water absorbed the gums and scattering of fresh flowers, the sap of yarrow and the wild perfume of mint. "Thirsty," muttered Alex, opening his eyes and blinking. His pupils were huge and reflected the firelight in demonic exhaustion.

Katherine, crouched beside his pallet, held the cup to his mouth, one arm cradling him to drink. When she lay him back again on the bolster, he closed his eyes but did not ask for the chamber pot, nor did he retch or heave. She bent low to speak softly to him. "You seem a little more stable Alex," she said. "And Margery's here. She's making medicines."

Alex smiled weakly. "I smell them."

"And afterwards," continued Katherine, "I'm going to give you a bath." His eyes opened again rather suddenly in startled objection. Katherine said, "Oh, not a real bath of course. But you're still cold even in front of the fire, and I think it's because you're shivery and wet with a whole night's icy sweating. Even the blankets are damp. You'll feel a lot better after a nice hot wash."

Alex smiled again. "Very motherly."

Gradually taking strength, he was helped to sit, propped back against Margery's lap. He drank a full cup of her medicine and a spoonful of rue vinegar, then breathed deep and even and did not vomit. Margery shifted him back against the heaped pillows, and stood. "He's doing well. Just rinse him off that sickly sweat," she advised. "That'll sort his mettle."

"I could pay for a barber to come in and bleed him," suggested Katherine.

Margery pulled a face. "Lad needs his blood," she said. "Too weak as it is, not much better'n sheep's piss."

Alex sighed, eyes closed. "When you two have finished discussing my personal inadequacies," he murmured, "I should like to point out that I'm neither deaf nor incapable of speech. I can make my own decisions. And I'm also perfectly able to wash myself."

Margery grinned. "Argue it out, lad, no bother to me. I'm off. Me ma'll be back in a bit, I've fed the babe, your little lad's washing the pots up the street at the tap, there's cheat and salt bacon, having no fish for Friday breakfast though I don't reckon you should be eating ort yet, there's light ale, good beer, boiled water for drinking, and enough medicine brewed for the day and the night to come. I'll be back this afternoon. In the meantime, I doubt you're capable of wiping your own arse, let alone washing your back. But you and the lass can fight over that once I'm gone."

The house was otherwise empty when Katherine cradled Alex back against her body, her arms around his waist, and began to wash him with the softest cloth she had found and the hottest water he could bear. Without further complaint, his head relaxed, his shoulder against her breast and his eyes closed, he allowed her hands to soothe him and the water to cleanse him. There was no soap left, for what she had ordered Tom to buy from the market had all been used on scrubbing out the bowls and chamber pot many times. Instead, she used her fingers.

She had discovered pleasure in the touch of him, and knew already it was an exercise she might at least partially enjoy. She explored the long silk of his body, the dips and valleys, the smooth lines of his ribs and the hard rise of his battle hardened muscles. She felt his nipples stiffen to little buttons beneath her palms and the scattered dark hair on his chest part between her finger tips. A soft arrow of black hair pointed down from his stomach to below the waistband of his braies, and she saw the muscles respond there, but looked away and did not wander. She washed his arms, which lay limp, but saw his fingers grip and clench, as if he dreamed of other things.

She washed his face, gentle around the lids. She tried not to soak his hair, but lifted the thick strands away from his forehead, carefully wiping the cloth across the high hollow planes beneath his cheek bones and down to the curves at the corners of his mouth. Then she discarded the cloth, soothing away the water with her palms. He sighed, but did not open his eyes.

When finally she had finished, she knew he was asleep. She wrapped him in the marten lined coat he had brought from Merevale's garderobe, nestling him in the soft fur cocoon, and pushed another pillow beneath his head. She had taken care not to puddle water on the floor, but found that her own shirt and hose were soaked. When Tom crept back in, she left him to watch the fire and went quietly upstairs. There she changed back into her women's clothes.

It was after Joan returned from work that Katherine took Tom with her and left the house. Joan, smelling strongly of wort and suds, came back from the brewery night shift at seven and though the sun had not yet fully risen, a pale gleam puckered the clouds and spangled the church spires. The bells were silent. Katherine explained Margery's medicines to Joan. "He's to have as much of the brew as he'll take," she whispered, "and a spoon of rue vinegar after each draft. But he's much better already and hasn't vomited once this morning." Then with Tom trotting close, Katherine pulled her cloak tight and set off down Lower Thames Street towards the distant Ludgate.

The streets were quiet and in places deserted, so it was some time before Katherine realised that her thoughts, unfamiliar and mostly unwelcome, had absorbed her so completely that she had listened to nothing Tom was saying.

"Now there's gratitude for you," he raised his voice with a tug at her elbow. "Slog away day and night for you, I do. Cleaning basins, wiping up puke. Do this, do that, and you don't even remember I'm here."

She apologised. "And I appreciate everything too, though I'm sure pages aren't supposed to complain so much. Anyway, back home first and if you're not very good, I'll leave you there. And afterwards the Earl of Burton's house."

The chill was cutting through the mist and the new dawn was pink, shafting into a reflected dazzle along the Thames. Where the streets were empty, the river was crowded, but she did not look back towards the bridge where a low tide had left the pillars tall rimed. There was an east wind cutting up behind her, travelling in from the sea and whipping at the hems of her skirts, chewing into her ankles. A silvery misted drizzle threatened to turn to sleet. She hurried, calling Tom to keep up.

The wharves were sullen in the wind, the cranes neither clanked nor creaked, only wheezed a little in the whine of the cold. Within the great Steelyard and the Vintner's Hall the first preparations for the coming Christmas season were already practised, Mystery plays ready to be staged, mummings discussed and settings for feasts planned. Now all over London the Guildhalls were alight and the church bells had started to peal. The sleet held off until she was through Ludgate where the torches flared in the high wind. As the clouds sprang from mist to lowering black and the wind began to howl, Katherine and Tom made a final dash for the Sheffield House.

Shaddle opened the door in astonishment. His smile became seasonal. "My lady. The blessed Lord has brought you safe, when all the household feared - "

"I am exceedingly wet, Shaddle," interrupted the lady. "Where's Sara? And I hope the fires are all lit in my private chambers?"

"I shall see to it at once, my lady. In the meantime, the fire in the hall was lit some hours past and is already quite hot."

Tom skipped off to the kitchens for hypocras and gossip, while, stripped of her sodden cape, the Lady Katherine sat by her small bedchamber fire, stretched out her toes and sighed. First duty accomplished, as she waited for the comforting embrace of her nurse. Sara Whitstable, at least, would believe every word she was told, truthful or otherwise.

Once dry, comforted, warmed and renewed in confidence, the lady returned downstairs and addressed her staff. "I have not been abducted. I have not been ravished or attacked. I am visiting friends, and intend to return there after dinner. Important messages for me may be delivered to the Lady Elizabeth at Burton House in Muggle Street. I've returned merely to assure everyone of my safety, and to oversee my late husband's funeral."

"His lordship's several young gentlemen friends are already in the house, m'lady," Shaddle bowed. "Having come for the procession, m'lady."

"Damn," said the lady.

Shaddle blinked, straight faced. "Shall I request the young gentlemen to attend you in the main hall, m'lady? They are at present breaking fast in the Western solar upstairs."

"I'll see them here once they've finished," Katherine said. "And please arrange the funeral feast for as early as possible Shaddle. I need to get to Cripplegate before three."

"Of course, my lady."

"I – suppose," she said, "that the funeral service and the interment will be presided over by Father Erkenwald at All Saint's? Yes, I imagined so. Well, naturally I won't be present so I suppose it doesn't matter."

"I fear it would be too late to alter the arrangements now, my lady," said Shaddle with some doubt.

Katherine shook her head. "No. Far too late. I'd just like to point out a few more important – details. Firstly, Master – Bowyer won't be returning here."

"I imagine not, under the circumstances my lady."

She shook her head again. "Your assumptions are quite wrong, Shaddle," she said. "Master Bowyer neither stole anything, nor had the slightest connection to his lordship's death. My husband died of the Sweats as the autopsy report now states, and Master Bowyer was the only person with the courage to help him during his – final turmoil. Father Erkenwald is mistaken. In fact, he's an infernal nuisance."

Shaddle sniffed and lifted an eyebrow. "As your ladyship says."

"Well, it's true," said Katherine. "And naturally the estate will make a generous donation to All Saint's for the funeral service, and for the prayers, but I want no special monetary gifts made to the priest himself." She sighed and clasped her hands tighter. "It's most annoying to have to contribute to my own discomfort. And I'd like to point out that Father Erkenwald isn't welcome in my house once the funeral's over. Not that it will be my house for long, I suppose. I've no idea how the title and the property will be entailed in future, but I shall remove my belongings once I've – settled a few things. Now – about these friends of the earl's?"

"And will your ladyship be wishing an escort to attend the laying out of his lordship in the church this morning, my lady?" Shaddle shifted slightly from one foot to the other. Things had all been much easier in Yorkshire. "The staff all attended early Mass and passed by the coffin in turn, my lady. But I should be happy to return if your ladyship requires an escort."

Katherine sighed again. "Thank you, no. I'll sort it out myself Shaddle."

Shaddle smiled. "Under the circumstances, my lady - "

"Quite," said her ladyship.

With her nursemaid behind her and flanked by two men whom she had first met on her wedding day and never seen since, Katherine stared down at the open coffin and at her departed husband. The late Earl of Sheffield, his eyes closed, appeared to be smiling, which, she thought, was an unwarranted impudence. The coffin, lying on the bier in the candle lit nave of All Saint's church, was of simple oak and thick lined with lead. The earl, inspite of his smile, was quite naked as his corpse had not yet been wrapped, though his loins were respectfully covered with a linen cloth. His legs looked pale and pimpled, the bones crooked and the knees protuberant, the feet cleaner than she remembered them. The church was distinctly chilly and Katherine wondered if he was cold, or if he already enjoyed the cheerful warmth of hellfire. The two hundred church candles, for which the estate had paid, were brightly numerous but they shivered reluctantly in the draught and every time someone walked past, a few snuffed out. The smoke swirled and was making everyone cough. Hymns were already being sung by the small priestly choir; an expensive and charitable tribute from a grateful king who could not, after all, be present. Only one day before his very first parliament, King Henry, the seventh of that name, had no time for the funerals of friends no longer useful.

In front of the large gold cross above the pulpit, a small figure in long robes was bent, chanting softly. Father Erkenwald was also fully occupied. Keeping well back and at the foot of the pulpit, Katherine knelt and genuflected. But she whispered no prayers for the soul of her dead husband. It was for Alex Quyrril's recovery that she prayed.

It was gone three of the afternoon when the Lady Katherine arrived at the Burton House in Cripplegate. It had stopped raining but the wind was still sharp, so she bustled quickly inside immediately as Jenkins opened the doors. With Tom out of breath at her back, she was ushered into the main hall where a large fire was lit as usual. The grand table was already set with silver and dazzling with candles. The funeral feast for Daniel Corby and Merevale Corby, uncles to the Earl of Burton and sons of the original Earl of Sheffield, was to be a far grander affair. The processions had not yet returned from St. Olave's and the ladies Elizabeth and Mary had remained quietly in the church. The Lady Katherine sat and waited.

It was Reginald Psalter who brought her hypocras. The apothecary, always dark dressed and now in mourning, bent like a thin branch in silhouette. Katherine looked up and thanked him. She was aware of his reputation with the careful concoction of spiced and concentrated hypocras. "It's Mister Psalter, I believe?"

"Indeed, my lady."

"You worked for a short time with a Master Bowyer?" Katherine smiled. "He's spoken to me about you, how much he learned from you concerning herbs and spices." The apothecary bowed again. Katherine sipped the drink he had brought her. "Of course, Master Bowyer is rightfully Mister Quyrril. You know about that, I believe?" He did. "And you understand the situation?" He understood. "So I wonder if I might talk to you concerning Mister Quyrril? You see," Katherine paused before continuing, choosing her words carefully, "my friend has been suddenly taken ill. Very ill. I believe he nearly died."

"I'm exceedingly sorry to hear it, my lady."

"He was poisoned," she said.

The apothecary straightened, shocked. His voice sank low. "I pray you are mistaken, my lady. Indeed, this is not one of those wicked states of Italy, and poison is hardly a common business in our great metropolis. Truly, whenever a gentleman of power is suddenly stricken, there are rumours. The Duke of Clarence accused his servants, there were repeated scandals at court, and even murmurs concerning the unexpected death of our dear King Edward. But these were never proved, my lady, and I am sure there is not a word of truth in any of them. Mister Quyrril has been ill no doubt, but with the sweating sickness perhaps, the influenza or the ague."

Katherine stared at the thick concentrated ruby of her hypocras. Its syrupy perfume of cloves and anise began to cloy. She shook her head. "A – physician – diagnosed poison. Thankfully Mister Quyrril appears to be recovering. But you're obviously aware of the two recent murders in this house, Mister Psalter. An attempt at a third would hardly seem so far-fetched."

The apothecary clicked his tongue. "The lord Daniel Corby was my employer, my lady. His death has touched me deeply. His dear widow is much affected. But these were acts of violence. Poison is another matter altogether."

Katherine peered deeper into her cup, as if expecting to see visions there. "They say poison is a woman's weapon, Mister Psalter," she whispered.

"My lady." The apothecary bent his head again, as though cautious of being overheard by some wandering Italian nobleman. "They say in Italy, death by poison is everyman's weapon. I hear that in Florence it's such common practice, it is becoming an accepted pastime, such as a Sunday afternoon stroll. Even the clerics – but I can say no more. Such things do not occur in our civilised country, I assure you, madam. I shall make up a cure for our gentleman friend, a recipe to purge the body of many common ailments. I promise it will be most efficacious. A little chardequince I think, well spiced and peppered. And I doubt the Lady Elizabeth would object if I offered some treacle, recently imported from Genoa and at considerable expense. The Italians, you know, must be experienced at understanding the best antidotes for their own favoured sins, so if poison has indeed been administered – though I cannot conceive - "

She was obliged to stay for the funeral feast. She decided that two three course dinners in one day was excessive, but the second, being more lavish, better cooked and more companionable, was at least enjoyable, though fish was not her favourite dish. She felt no guilt regarding the fact that the Earl of Sheffield was sent off in a modest manner, whereas the two untitled gentleman, more dearly loved, were sent to their heavenly rewards with the procession and observances due them.

So when the Lady Katherine finally left Cripplegate it was almost dark, she was exceedingly well fed and wined, and had concluded everything she had intended and a good deal more. Tom dragged his scuffed heels behind her, supporting a collection of bundles which weighed him down. The smell of the river was close and the sky black when they arrived again at the Eastcheap residence of Mistress Joan Hambury.

Alex could be heard upstairs, retching into the chamber pot.

CHAPTER THIRTY

"I t comes, and goes, and comes again," said Joan. "And the lad's done nothing so much as puke one minute, and complain the next. Missed you, he did."

"But he keeps telling me to go home," objected Katherine.

"Men are like that," nodded Joan. "Best just ignore what they says. Smile, say yes, then do whatever you want."

Tom was unpacking. Katherine had brought a great deal from her own premises, and some more from the Lady Elizabeth. There were sweet smelling beeswax candles, soft Spanish soap and large wrapping towels. She had brought shifts, gloves and boots for herself and more clothes for Alex, and above all she had brought three purses of silver and several small items for sale or barter. She lit two candles and carried them carefully upstairs. Alex was on the bed, lying back against the heaped pillows. His eyes were huge, black and bright. His face was whiter than the bolster. He watched the candlelight float upwards from the stairwell and smiled as Katherine crossed the boards towards him. "You've been busy, Kate." His voice was desperately tired, but the words clear.

She had been so frightened to find him worse. She did not say so. "I've been home, Alex. It was Edmund's funeral, you see. Father Erkenwald was thankfully too busy to make a nuisance of himself, and

I've been able to bring things I thought we needed. I made an official statement too, and wrote it down with Sara as witness. I've no seal of my own, but I think it will suffice. Shaddle will take it to the sheriff's offices tomorrow."

She sat on the edge of the bed, still holding the candles. He smiled a little. "Am I exonerated from raptus then?"

"They know I wasn't abducted. I think I spoiled a month's worth of gossip and scandal. Most of the staff looked quite disappointed." There was a stool beside the bed and she placed one candle there, tall in its silver holder. She stood the other on the chest beneath the window. It flickered in the draught. "Edmund's autopsy confirmed no poison and the funeral's done with now. I'm doomed to a month at least of wearing black and lavender and I've only the one suitable gown, so it'll get sadly creased and shockingly worn."

"Lies and hypocrisy," smiled Alex. "Since no doubt you'll enjoy risking my sanity as usual, cavorting in boy's clothes under my nose."

Katherine came back to the bed and sat, looking down at him with a frown. "I don't know why you object," she said. "I know it's supposed to be terribly shocking and my father would have beaten me for it, but after all, they're very decent clothes. They cover me up from toes to chin, which is more than most lady's dresses do."

"That's hardly an explanation I feel lucid enough to attempt just yet," Alex said. "So what else did you achieve today, brat?"

"I went to your cousin's house afterwards," she nodded. "They held the two funerals together. I explained why you couldn't be there. When I said you were ill, and why you were ill, both Lady Mary and Lady Elizabeth seemed very shocked and surprised. Elizabeth promised to send anything that you need, but she'll keep this address secret of course. I've brought you clothes, and money, and her blessing. Oh, and medicine from the apothecary."

"Come here," said Alex.

She kicked off her shoes, crawled obediently over the mattress, adjusted her skirts, and sat beside him. Immediately he put both arms around her and drew her down, cuddled against his chest. He was once again wearing his shirt and she rested her cheek on the warm pleated linen and curled there, content within his embrace. "I suppose this is shocking too," she murmured.

"Reprehensible," he smiled. "But irresistibly tempting." His hands, firm around her back, did not wander but held her tight, and he kissed the top of her rain spangled hair. She had removed her headdress and the pins holding her hair wrapped in its careful coils were coming loose. "Everything we're doing is wrong, my dear," he said. "You shouldn't be here at all, certainly not in my bed, not in this room, not even in this house. One day, when I can, I shall make it alright by you. In the meantime, since you know you can trust me, I'm simply grateful to have you close."

Her own fingers crept around his waist. "Joan says you missed me."

He nodded. "I have. I wasn't sure if you were coming back and I was worried. But at the moment I'm sick and ridiculously weak, and tomorrow I'll regret admitting it. You'd have done better to stay at home instead of running around town in the cold, busy with tasks just for me."

She wriggled, looking up at him for a moment. "It wasn't just for you, Alex. Some of it was for me too."

"I hope so, my dear. A few clothes, I suppose. At least a good dinner. Your wretched husband's funeral. I trust Lizzie gave Mel a decent commemorative feast."

"There was something else I had to do for myself." Katherine lay her head back down against Alex's breast, and sighed. "I wanted to ask Elizabeth's advice. You see, I was going to ask Joan, or Margery, but I got a little embarrassed. They say things in a certain way, you know. Very blunt, and a bit too loud. So I asked the Lady Elizabeth instead. I thought I'd understand her more - comfortably."

Alex frowned. He hitched himself up a little onto one elbow and peered down at the girl in his arms. His hold on her tightened. "You'd better tell me, Kate. Or are you too embarrassed? I can probably help, if you let me."

She hesitated, then sighed. "I think I'm pregnant," she said.

In the very short pause, Alex's clasp tightened further. Finally he said, "My dear, are you certain? It's so – very soon – I believe too soon to tell. Lizzie surely knows better than I do, but – you were married less than two weeks, Kate. Now only a few days after his death, how can you tell?"

"That's what I wanted to ask Elizabeth," sniffed Katherine. "She said – two things. Both those things – fit."

Alex was silent again. His head pounded, slowing the processes of his brain, disguising both thought and feeling. Then he heard her crying. He bent his head at once to her ear, her hair tickling his mouth. "Marry me, Kate," he said softly. "If you have a son, he'll be heir to the Sheffield earldom. But at least I can look after you. I've nothing to offer except my own determination, but you shouldn't be alone at such a time."

She tried hard to stop crying, but could not. "You can't marry me because you feel sorry for me."

Alex smiled. "At the moment, I feel more sorry for myself. I feel damned sick, Kate, and this is the least romantic proposal I can imagine. The bed's damp and flea ridden, and no doubt I smell of dirt and vomit. But I've intended to marry you ever since I dragged you home with two kittens in your apron. I just meant to put my own affairs in order first."

"Your own affairs have got worse and worse," Katherine pointed out.

He smiled. "Yes. Most unhelpful. I've obviously become increasingly inept. But things will get better my love, and I'll try and make you happy. I must confess I hadn't envisaged becoming a father quite so quickly, but if I manage to live through this damned sickness, I'll have the strength for anything, I promise."

Katherine managed to extricate one hand and discovered her kerchief. She blew her nose and sat up a little. "I've been thinking all day, Alex. Over and over until my head hurts too. I don't want to get married. It's a nice thought – in a way – I mean, being looked after, and having a friend close all the time. But I can't marry you. I told you before, and I haven't changed my mind. And you wouldn't like being married to me." She peeped up at him. "I just want you to understand. And forgive me – and please just go on being - a friend."

"Silly little goose." Alex reached under the pillows and discovered his own clean kerchief. He pulled it out and dried Katherine's tear stained face, which looked small and pinched and very miserable in the flickering candlelight. Then he leaned down and kissed the tip of her nose. "Listen, my love. At the moment I'm as useless as a one armed juggler and as weak as a mouse in a trap. Allow me a couple of days, and I'll propose to you with a little more grace. And I warn you, I'm horribly stubborn and unlikely to take no for an answer. I've a damned good idea why you keep turning me down, and that's something I can cope with, given time. If you ever summon up the courage to let me in on your secrets, I can help a good deal more. In the meantime, you're my little sister, and I'll look after you as a brother should."

Katherine snuggled close again. "That's nice, Alex. That's what I want." Her voice was muffled, buried again in the folds of his shirt.

"Not that this is precisely what a brother should be doing," Alex smiled, and one hand crept upwards, cradling the back of her head, his fingers amongst her curls.

"You don't mind, do you?" Katherine sighed and her breath was warm against his breast. "I'd be a – miserable wife. You wouldn't want me. I know you wouldn't, you wouldn't even be my friend anymore and you'd stop liking me altogether. Especially with someone else's child. I just hope the poor little thing doesn't look like its father."

Alex smiled, twining his fingers through her hair and uncoiling the curls, pulling out and discarding the long pins. "We'll talk about all that another time, my love," he murmured. "I'm still not convinced you're with child. Perhaps – perhaps not. One day I'll get you to talk openly to me, and I'll talk to Lizzie too, if you don't object. For now, you need to sleep."

"You must be exhausted, Alex dear." Katherine pulled away and started to sit. "And I'm tired out too. I'll go down and sleep with Joan."

Alex did not release her. "On one small pallet? And Joan the size of three women? Stay here, my love. I promise not to take advantage."

Surprised, Katherine said, "Would you mind? You usually tell me off for doing improper things. And wouldn't Joan be shocked?"

Alex chuckled. "No, I think you'll find Joan a little difficult to shock. As for me – am I always such a strict guardian? No, stay here with me tonight, my love. No one here cares and no one else need ever know." He tucked her back down, her shoulder beneath his arm and her head to the hollow of his neck. "And I promise not to vomit over you in the night or die in your arms," he added. "But you should sleep in your shift and keep your one widow's gown uncreased."

She shook her head. "That doesn't matter anymore. I'll wear doublet and hose tomorrow anyway. I don't like being a girl. I don't like it at all. I think I'll be a boy from now on."

Alex woke many times in the night. A pearl shimmer crept through the unshuttered window and cut a pale line across the bed, half shadowed, half warm. The headache continued to beat behind his eyes, churning down the neck and into the belly, but he swallowed, resisting disturbance. Katherine remained within his arms, and he held her close, her heartbeat steady beneath his hands. He watched the rhythmic inhalation of her breath across her breasts, the small clutch of her fingers as she dreamed and the occasional twitch of her eyelashes against the gentle rise of her cheeks. His own dreams were sweeter awake than asleep. Although ill, he imagined the things he could not do.

They were both asleep when the church bells of St. Thomas of Acon rang to open the city gates at six of the morning, though too far off in Old Jewry to be heard. But the streets were already bustling. The market was two long hours in business, the stall holders setting up all through Cheapside and Eastcheap, the boys waiting to take out their geese to graze in the open fields beyond the walls, and the respectable citizens doing their duty as Night Watch, thankful to have passed another night without threat or actual bodily harm, returning to the alderman's offices to report that good peace had been maintained and all was well. There were still torches in the streets and it was dark but a paleness, a rose crested promise, flurried the tops of the turrets along the battlements of the Tower.

Within the house it remained quiet until Margery came home with a crash of the door which rattled the walls and disturbed the settled layers of smoke haze and the reek of soot. Katherine sat up with a grunt and Alex nearly rolled out of bed. "Stupid trollop," complained Joan, voice reverberating from downstairs. "Pissed, are you? Feed your brat while I make the porridge."

Margery's voice sounded confused. "Brat don't eat porridge." The clank of pots and ladles interrupted, the scraping of boots and the first whimper of the child.

Katherine was standing now, and trying to brush the creases from her skirts. Alex regarded her. "Slept well enough, little one?"

She smiled and nodded. The room was soft in shadows and her expression was hidden. "I did. But it's strange, and a little – that is, unusual - to wake up with you here watching me."

"Oh well." Alex grinned. "One day, that'll be common practice. For now, - "

The top of Margery's head appeared in the stairwell, with the sound of her own heavy breathing and the baby's slurps. She appeared, swaying slightly, and evidently cheerful. One breast had been hauled, hugely pink, from her bodice and the baby was fiercely attached, precariously supported by Margery's arm. She stomped to the bed and swung herself onto the mattress, back against the end poster and feet facing the head, clogs almost in Alex's lap. The baby appeared undisturbed. Margery said, voice slurred, "Well, lad. How'sha feeling? Med'cin's done the trick?"

Alex was still grinning. "Very well indeed, as it happens," he said. "Though I've had little time yet to feel anything much this morning."

"My medicks dush marvels, ever-time," Margery assured him. "Be up and about shoon, yer will. All thanks ta me."

"I shall remember to be properly grateful," nodded Alex, "as soon as you're in a condition to remember it."

"Great condishion," Margery objected. "Hada busy night, good coin, good bishness. Touch sore in places, but feelin' - " She raised an expansive arm and the other breast fell heavily from her open neckline. "Feelin' exshellent," she finished. She then rolled over, toppled on her side, the baby detached from its food supply and started to roar, and Margery closed her eyes happily, opened her mouth, and began to snore.

Alex removed her wooden clogs, which were under his nose, and threw them onto the floor. Joan's voice echoed from below. "What's bloody going on up there? What's wrong with the child?"

"Lost its breakfast," Alex called back. "Your daughter's asleep."

Katherine approached the bed with evident doubt. Margery, now completely bare breasted, was curled unconscious. The baby lay on its back, red faced and furious. Too tightly swaddled for kicking or waving its fists, it made an extraordinary amount of noise for its size. Katherine patted its head, which enraged it further. "Pick it up," suggested Alex.

"I might drop him," said Katherine. "I've never held a baby before in my life."

Tom, scampering up the stairs, appeared with a smirk. He reached out, unimpressed by the vision of its mother prone and half naked, and took the child into his hearty embrace. The baby stopped crying, opened tear blurred eyes and smiled at its rescuer. Tom kissed young William's minute snubbed and snotty nose and ran back downstairs with him. Katherine sat on the bed beside Margery's feet with a sniff. "I'll be a terrible mother," she sighed. "I don't want to be a mother. Babies - they – frighten me. How on earth are you supposed to know what they want when they can't even speak?"

"Don't ask me," grinned Alex. "I don't want to be a mother either. Don't worry, we'll hire a nurse. Someone experienced, not like your Sara."

"That reminds me," Katherine retrieved her kerchief and blew her nose. From downstairs the sounds of baby chuckles and pots being stirred floated upwards. "I asked Sara to come here today. I do hope you don't mind. She's terribly faithful and she'd never tell a soul. And she's worried about me. So I said she could bring - some shopping."

"Good God," said Alex. "Of course I don't mind but you'd better not tell her how you spent the night. No doubt that's exactly what she's worried about. And I hope you warned her about our hostesses. Margery won't give a fig, but Joan may. Has a good deal of bruised pride already, poor Joan. She never used to live like this, you know, being lady's maid to an earl's daughter. Thoroughly respectable in those days, and misses it I think."

Margery's snores were muffled damp within the billows of the eiderdown. One huge brown nipple oozed a sticky cream, the other was squashed beneath her arm. She looked uncomfortable but sounded happy enough. "Well, I suppose Sara might be a little shocked," Katherine admitted. "And I really don't think you should be quite so complacent either. Are you used to naked women rolling around on your bed?"

Alex avoided answering this question. "I think we might go downstairs," he suggested. "Smells as though breakfast's ready and I think I can manage the steps if I go slow. You go down first. I'll follow you."

Downstairs the fire was bright lit, the cobwebs dancing merrily in the rising smoke, the cauldron of porridge thickening with a gurgle of popping bubbles, and the busy rhythm of the ladle as Joan bent over the pot. Tom, playing with the baby, was on the floor. Katherine flopped into the little chair by the hearth. Nobody seemed in the least censorious or even curious at her having spent the night in the same bed with a man, and the unaccustomed warmth of a small family fireside seemed strangely welcoming. Joan said, "Hungry lass? Here," and passed her a full bowl.

She was eating when Alex came downstairs. He took each step very slowly and clasped tightly to the balustrade, which was rickety and offered little support. Joan went at once to his side and helped him over to the high backed chair. He collapsed onto it and grinned ruefully at his audience. "Don't mention food to me," he said rather faintly. "Ale would be good. Wine would be better."

"We've light ale and strong beer," Joan said, "but first of all, a good dose of medicine's waiting. If you need to puke, there's an empty bowl at your side."

"My puking days are over," said Alex, voice firmer. "But I'm as thirsty as hell. There's only two things I seem able to think about just at the moment. One's wine, and the other I can't mention." Which is when a loud and unusual series of sounds and several repeated curses reverberated from outside and the door was once again thrust open as a large man, a goat and two ducks hurtled into the room.

CHAPTER THIRTY-ONE

T he baby, startled, began to cry. Tom lifted it over his shoulder, patted its back and carried it out of harm's way. Katherine, even more startled, spilled her porridge. Alex grinned and Joan put her hands on her hips and glared. "Matthew Flesher, where's your manners? And me with a household of respectable guests."

The goat, alarmed by the fire which had flared in the wind, bleated and attempted to butt the ducks. The man wiped his nose on the back of his hand and stared around while the ducks flapped, urgently waddling away from the forest of legs, feet, udders and chairs. Alex said, "Good God, man, open the door for the ducks at least."

"Up from the river," nodded the man, hurrying obediently to the door. "Must be flooding again." He kicked the door wide, the ducks scurried outside, an

the door shut again with a gust. "Didn't mean no unwanted interruptions," the man insisted. "Just brought the goat back, begging your pardon. Found her up by Fish Street, bleating fit to bust for the milking, and like to be had for some bastard's dinner if I hadn't grabbed her first."

"Very kind of you I'm sure," said Alex since a silent confusion had consumed everyone else. "Have some porridge."

Joan caught the goat by its loose flying tether and hurried it back outside, while Matt happily helped himself to the contents of the cauldron. "Much obliged," he said. Finding neither spoon nor chair, he stood politely in a corner trying to look small and drank the porridge straight from the bowl. Tom had packed the baby back into its box crib and, mindful of Alex's gaze, began to collect the empty bowls for washing. Katherine watched the newcomer with interest. Built wide with platter sized hands, he was dressed in a waxed cape over a tunic of rough blue wool and Katherine felt faintly ashamed of her fur and velvet. Alex seemed to feel no such compunction.

"You must be the wheryman Joan talks of," Alex said. "Always pleased to meet a man able to offer a hire service in this foul winter's weather."

Matt wiped both his nose and his mouth with the back of the same hand. "I charges no more, nor less than others, your honour," said the man with defensive courtesy and a loud sniff.

"Fool," said Joan marching back indoors. "This is Sir Alex Quyrril. Bought me this house, he did, and whenever he's wanting over the river, you'll take him for nothing or you'll hear about it from me. Now – "

The knock on the door was not at all loud, almost timid in fact, but it silenced everyone. "If it's priests or sheriffs," sighed Alex, "I'm not here."

It was a tall thin woman in a soaked bonnet and a pinched pink nose, carrying two huge baskets. The wind at her back blew her quickly inside, where she bobbed, a little embarrassed, and smiled apologetically around. Recognising first Alex and then her mistress, Sara Whitstable curtseyed in relief. "My goodness," she said. "It is the right house after all. I was just a little worried – not knowing the parish as it were, indeed, not knowing London at all, and I had feared – but seemingly not. It's just a little – blustery outside you see, and then past the Ludgate a whole chimney piece came crashing down behind me. Brick dust everywhere and a piglet caught in the rubble. Most upsetting."

"Sara dear," said Katherine getting up at once, "it's wonderful of you to have got here so early. And all that shopping."

Tom, who had gone out to the conduit tap to wash the dishes, also arrived back and Miss Whitstable was pleased to see another familiar face. The little room was becoming distinctly crowded. Sara handed the baskets over to Tom, who handed them to Joan, who handed one to Matt. The baskets were then unpacked with much intake of breath, small squeaks of pleasure and gasps of admiring appreciation.

"I was able to get everything you asked for," said the nurse. "And some extra bacon and cheese. Mister Hewitt allowed me to bring some small supplies from the spicery cupboard, especially when I mentioned Master Bowyer's name, and even gave me some marchpanes. Being Monday there was little fish to be had but the eel boats had come in, so there is a pair of eels wrapped in linen, but they got rather lively on the way here and I think they may have got into the manchet. I was able to get the bread very fresh so it will last several days, and the pies with sugared mustard too, straight from the cook shop ovens and still nice and hot. Though," she looked around her, "it is possible I didn't get enough of them. I had not expected quite such a crowd."

"I would take you upstairs to speak in private, Sara dear," said Katherine. "But there is someone – sleeping – up there, so I shall have to speak to you here. And I think we are all – friends. I'm very grateful for everything of course. You must have been terribly chilled."

Sara Whitstable shook her veiled bonnet. "It was – quite exciting, my dear. The London markets are so very – large. I had no idea how much one could buy. It seemed as though the whole world was for sale."

Alex was watching the unpacking. "No wine I suppose," he noticed.

"There is a whole tun keg of best burgundy due for delivery this afternoon, sir," smiled Miss Whitstable. "And a half butt of Tuscan Trebbiano coming tomorrow morning. My lady specifically asked for it, and I ordered the supplies not an hour since, direct from the Vintners."

Joan looked over her shoulder, a joint of bacon in each hand. "A keg? And a barrel? And just where do I put them, I'd like to know."

"Stools or tables," suggested Alex. "But they won't stay full for long. Then you've a bath tub and rainwater butt into the bargain."

Gradually the little room warmed, and was transformed. Where the bare boards were worn into grooves and cracks, now new reeds from the threshboats were laid thick and supple. A great stack of faggots skirted the hearth and a new trivet held the pots bubbling with food and clean water from the carrier for the boil. The food was stored in the old chest beneath the window, and the baby's crib brought closer to the dancing flames. The pies, kept warm and flaking in their buttery pastry, made a good midday dinner, together with the manchet rolls and a peas pottage, and Matt the wheryman made only one muttered attempt at a polite refusal and was easily convinced to join in. Alex could not eat, but accepted beer and once the wine arrived, appeared suddenly brighter. He had difficulty standing and it was clear that his head still pained him while he actively disliked the smell of pies and pottage, but he was not sick again and said he preferred the company downstairs rather than staggering back up to bed. Joan bustled, busy with pride in a home newly cosy with affluence, prosperity, and plenty of cooking to do.

Katherine sat close to Alex. When the heat, the dancing light, the smoke and the conversation made her sleepy, she was tempted to put her head on his shoulder, but did not. She said little. She watched the firelight play among the faces, leaping up in black and scarlet shadow-patterns across the rough plaster walls and up into the beams. Tom curled at Katherine's feet and when the baby woke, he fed it with the bottle Joan passed him. Katherine looked down on the top of its small bald head and wondered about the future.

For once Alex was quiet and it was Matt who told stories. He told of the river folk who spoke their own dialect, and how they protected their own, and did their business with dignity, accepting neither insult nor arrogance from anyone, neither rabble nor lord. "'Tis the Thames is heart of this country," Matt said, "and maybe the heart of the world, for our river tides brings the waters from every country to our banks, and when you climbs aboard my small boat, then the water slapping your sides was maybe in France yesterday, splashing the beaches in a foreign tongue and whispering of Agincourt. Tomorrow there'll be a tide from Italy perhaps, telling tales of Venice and the great carracks carrying silks and spices. There'll be waters have once heard cannon shot from the siege of Constantinople, or echoed on past the pyramids through the Middle Sea where folks is heathen and black as polished charcoal."

"Pooh, Matthew Flesher," said Joan, still admiring her new cushions, which as yet only Alex was allowed to sit upon. "You've never even seen the sea, nor bin further east than the Tower."

"That I have," said Matt, now into his fourth cup of ale. "Three days ago I was. Not as far as the sea pr'aps, but at St. Katherine's docks and rowing past them miserable gallows, all sunk in the mud. Three Cornish pirates there is, swinging by their scrawny necks and one not full dead when I went past, kicking his legs and still pissing he was, begging the lady's pardon. They'll be ripe and ready to cut down now I reckon, with three full tidal surges gone over their heads and ebbed again. Crab food for every sailor to see and take warning."

Sara, cuddled tight into a corner politely distant from the fire, sat forward, her elbows on her knees and her chin in her hands. "I have always dreamed of the oceans and far lands," she said, eyes shining, "and the call of the gulls."

Katherine looked up, surprised. "Why Sara, I would never have guessed. You always seemed so - landlocked."

"Well, in Leicestershire my dear, with no likelihood of ever travelling further than market with the pony cart." Sara blushed. "But now living so close to the river, I hear the gulls every day. It is – most invigorating. Quite exciting."

"In winter them gulls scavenge along the banks," Matthew nodded. "There's some as knows us, and will sit up on the prow of an eel boat or a lighter by the wharves bringing fish. Makes too much mess for me, they do, being sloppy shitters, but have character too and will tell when the little shrimp is gathering mid river. When I goes crabbing in the shallows at low tide, they'll know afore I does, and keeps me company if I throws a leg or two."

He told how the wherymen held their own ideas of justice and pride, and how – a few years before his time – when a Lancastrian lord once captured and held in the Tower had escaped, half a dozen boatmen had seen and caught the unpopular prisoner, took him and beat him and left him stripped naked on the church steps.

"And we rescues more than we drowns," he added, "for there's all sorts flung into our waters, by folks as you'd think would know better. More than one boatman's wife has taken in a babe found floating in draff."

It was late in the afternoon when it started to snow. The burgundy, aromatic and twice rubied in the glow of the fire, had already been tapped and only Sara refused a cup. When Katherine shook her head, Alex leaned over, pressing the small pewter mug into her hands. "Try it, my love," he insisted. "Already despising the female state, yet refusing a man's drink? This won't hurt you, and will keep out the cold."

She sat closest to the fire and her face was unfashionably ruddy, sparkling with heat and contentment. Matt was talking and Kate's voice, whispering, was lost beneath it. "I shouldn't. It might – not be good for – might it?"

"Very good," Alex smiled. "Exactly what you need."

"And there's not one of us will charge more than agreed," Matt was saying, "for we'll not cheat each other, even if we've little care for the fools we carry. Begging your pardon, that is."

"No good showing off your trade to me, Matt Flesher," Joan said, pouring out more wine. "When you're pissed fit to panic the trout, then it's me as takes the boat, and none would know the difference. I've shot the bridge and rowed faster and stronger than any of your puny mates. I'm not impressed by your wherymen stick together stories. There's every one of them craps in the river he reckons to love so much – and I'll not be begging your pardon for the saying of it."

Matt nodded cheerfully. "A grand help, is my Joannie. The guild might have a word to say, but none knows, 'cept those as is happy to see her as to see me."

"Why don't you just take the day off, Master Flesher," suggested Sara," when you're a touch – under the weather. It must be hard work, and in all weathers too."

"Lord love you, boat's not mine, mistress," said Matt, emerging from his cup. "'Tis rented and I must work the hours agreed, or be in trouble for it. There's times, since my boat's not a covered tub nor has no awning, when the river's a mite troubled as it were, and I'd as soon not be working and knows I'll not take a penny. But row I must, and don't make no complaint."

"Lies," said Joan at once. "You complain all the bloody time. But it's true about the weather. When it's foul, folk will pay the tuppence extra and take a tilt boat for staying under cover."

"But surely dangerous when it's stormy," said Sara. "Why, I can imagine boatmen might be drowned."

"Happens, but not right often," said Matt, enjoying his appreciative audience. "But by the Bridge, and a high tide flooding back in from the sea, now that's proper dodgy. Can run nigh five hours. Follows the full moon, they does, them nasty swells, and after the last moon we had with this new bastard king's crowning, 'twas a killer with a six hour flooding and deep in mist it was too. There were a gent with his lady, just awalking down Lower Thames, and daylight it were, but the river damp being so thick, they couldn't see nor wharves nor water. Walked right in, they did, and the lady's skirts was sodden heavy and pulled her down. Drowned in a tick. One foot out into the mist, and she were gone with a slurp, for the surge runs beneath and a flat slime above belies a deep current. A bad omen, my mate says, what seen it. Bad omen for the crowning, he says, but then, I says we've no need of omens, for we all knows it's bad."

Alex smiled. "I see that wherymen aren't nervous of the new king's spies either. I believe it's unwise to speak of omens and bad opinions until you're sure of the company."

"Sure as I needs be," frowned Matt. "My Joannie wouldn't have no friends with their loyalties up their arses."

Matthew had moved from describing the dangers of shooting the bridge where the waters up river and down would thunder through a cascade between the pillars, onto a more lyrical description of swans leading their cygnets through the reflections of the flat bottomed showtes, when Margery, having smelled best burgundy, made a loud and comfortably dishevelled appearance downstairs.

"Since when?" she demanded, holding one aloft, her other hand restraining the exuberance of her bosom, "did we have fucking silver candlesticks in this house?

CHAPTER THIRTY-TWO

"Oh, Alex," said Katherine, snuggling up under the eiderdown, "it's like having real friends."

"Poor little puss," he said. "Have you missed friends so much in your life?"

Katherine thought for a moment. "Well, yes," she said. "I was only little when my mother died, and so there were never any ladies in the house anymore. My father didn't entertain, only gentlemen for cards and business, and all the talk was on gaming or farming. There were only servants, and some of them were very nice, like Sara, but they were always careful and polite and worried about upsetting papa. And I suppose I was wilful and naughty and I so very much wanted to run around and climb trees and of course I couldn't, and perhaps a mother would have understood, but my father never did. Papa thought he had to protect me from everyone and everything and he wouldn't let me play with the farmer's daughters or the village children. He was so frightened when I wasn't ladylike. Perhaps he took it as a slight on his parenting." She had a firm but sleepy hold on Alex's thumb. "Today was - magical. And you do feel better, don't you Alex dear?"

"Yes, little one, I feel a great deal better."

There had previously been some argument about who would sleep in what area of the house. Sara had departed well before curfew, not wishing to risk finding the Ludgate locked against her. Matthew had offered his escort. He was due to start back on the river at seven in the evening, but seemed quite unconcerned about the possibility of being late for work. "The wherry's moored out back of Baynard's," he informed the lady, "so right close to The Strand. And needs moving too. We uses the lower buttress of the public latrine there for tying the wherries, but falling down it is. There's some gent will sit there one day adoing of his proper office, and next minute will be deeper in draff than expected. Poor bugger'll fall right in."

Margery had wandered back to her own night's work after fortifying herself against the cold and the customers' demands with the unexpected glory of full rich wine, and Joan was also due on night shift at the brewery. She could, she said, take the infant with her but Tom was more than content to be nursery maid, and volunteered to sleep downstairs by the fire with the box crib at his elbow.

"I'll sleep here with Tom," Alex said. "You go upstairs and take the bed."

"Certainly not," said Katherine, measuring out his evening draft of medicine. "You're sick. You take the bed. I've no objection to sleeping with Tom."

"I'm barely sick anymore," Alex objected. "In fact, I'm perfectly well. And if I do feel sick in the night, there's Reginald Psalter's medicines to try as well. Between him and Margery, I've enough doctoring to have me jumping hoops. I'm certainly not allowing you to sleep on a wretched pallet while I've a full mattress, even if it is flea ridden."

"Oh, what a noise for nothing. Go cuddle up together, do," said Tom, clasping his hands over his ears. "You knows you both want to. Just keeping me awake, you are."

Indeed, having done so once, there seemed little point in being morally outraged on a second occasion. The bed was large enough for four, and though there were fleas in the mattress, there were fleas downstairs as well. Alex stayed in his shirt and hose, but he managed to convince Katherine that she would sleep better in her shift. She undressed first, hopped into bed and then called down for Alex to come up. Alex clipped Tom around the ear and told him to stop smirking, climbed slow and stiff up the stairs, snuffed the candle and toppled into bed. He was feeling considerably less hale than he had claimed, but there was no further desire to vomit and even the headache had faded a little, courtesy of the best burgundy.

Though not drunk, he was slightly looser witted than he might otherwise have been had he not taken six cups of wine and a liberally laced concoction of medicines on an empty stomach. Being light headed, he felt no guilt at all in noticing that his arm, tight around the lady in his bed, was distinctly sensitive to the warmth of her figure. When she had slept beside him in the full barricade of skirts and stiffened stomacher, he had embraced only velvet and the smooth softness beneath his fingers had been fur trimmings. Now having discarded his padded gipon, there was only the fine linen of his own shirt and the even finer linen of Katherine's shift between his body and hers. He kept his hands very still, and sighed. "If you found the company today magical, my love, then you've been short of friends indeed," he said. "A lout of a wheryman, your own nurse, your brat of a page, and two women, both of whom your father would have cast from his house in righteous horror and disgust."

"And you, Alex," she murmured, her arm tight around his waist. "My new big brother."

Alex was becoming acutely conscious of the pressure of her nipples and the rise of her breasts against his chest. "Not sure I should have told you that," he decided. "Let's forget the brother part, and stick to the friend. Daresay I can cope with platonic friendship until – well, at least until we sort out what's best for you."

"And best for the baby, you mean?" She pulled away a little, wedging her shoulder onto the bolster and looking at Alex through the shifting shadows. "Do you mind me talking? I've been thinking, you see. I meant, after Edmund died, to go back home to my father. But I can't do that now. And I don't want to either. He'd treat me like a little girl and tell me off and stop me doing things. Then he'd arrange another horrid marriage."

Alex sighed and rolled over onto his back, staring up at the high threadbare tester and the cobwebs in the beams, visible through the canopy's many holes. The moonlight spun its own fables. "No, you can't go back, not now," he said. "Especially when – not that I believe – but until I'm - " He smiled to the roof. "God, I must be pissed after all." Then he sat up suddenly, leaned over and looked down into Katherine's huge dark eyes. "Listen, my love," he said, "if I'm to stick to the role I've promised and be a friend, at least let me be a friend. So, trust me and tell me why the devil you think you're pregnant after so short a time."

Katherine stared back at him. "I can't talk about things like that with you, Alex," she said at last. "And you may think I'm ignorant and stupid but you can't think Elizabeth's stupid too."

"Yes, I do," said Alex briefly. "And knowing both of you, you spoke to each other in half truths and allusions. So let me tell you, my pet, if your courses have stopped, after everything that's happened to you recently there could be a hundred possible reasons. How late are you?"

Katherine blushed, bit her lip, opened her mouth to speak, changed her mind and hiccupped.

Alex smiled. "Yes, I know, I'm not supposed to know about things like that," he said. "But I do, my love. So, we're talking days, not weeks, and since you just spoke to Lizzie yesterday, I'll guess three days, or four at the most. Am I close?"

Katherine nodded, instinctively tugging the eiderdown up to her chin.

Alex's smile gentled. "And can you tell me, my sweet, how regular you usually are?" he said. "Do three days make so great a change?"

She swallowed and half shook her head. "I can't possibly answer you," she said eventually, "when you're looking at me like that."

He laughed and lay down beside her again, pulling her back firmly into his embrace. He felt her breathing uneven and shallow against him, cornered doe eyes brown and huge. He kissed the top of her hair. "Forgive me, Kate," he said. "Perhaps I'm a bad friend after all. But I can only help if I know what to believe, and I don't trust your inexperience. Now, cuddle up and pretend I'm your sister instead of your brother. If you get into the habit of talking to me about everything, it will help us both."

Katherine nodded obediently, sniffed, muffled her mouth against his shirt and said, "But Elizabeth told me about – other things. Tingling – and tenderness – and – feeling swollen – which is just what happens – and I can't explain any more than that, Alex. Don't ask."

"I don't need to ask." Alex shook his head. "It's too soon for what Lizzie's talking about. She doesn't know when you were married, and unless – well no, you wouldn't. So we still don't know, my sweet. After another week and no change, then perhaps I'll believe it." He held her a little tighter. "Will you have the courage to tell me?"

"Oh, Alex," Katherine sighed. "It's not easy, you know. I only ever had Sara to talk to, and she never knew anything anyway. She just used to get confused and frightened."

"I promise I'm neither confused nor frightened," said Alex firmly. "You just need to get over the embarrassment. I sympathise, but I'm your sister, remember. Not Alex but Alice."

Katherine giggled. "Silly. You don't look like an Alice. Men are so – different. For one thing you don't have to worry about horrid things like this. For another – well – I mean, look, you've even got that funny little bump."

"I beg your pardon," said Alex, somewhat startled.

"Look, there, in your neck," said Katherine, peeping up at him. "I haven't got one of those. What does it do?"

"Tell the truth, I'm not too sure." Alex grinned. "Seems I know more about female anatomy than about my own." He looked down and smoothed the curls back from her eyes, releasing her to lie more comfortably. "I don't pretend to be a doctor my love, as you know very well," he said, "and even doctors seem to have little idea about most of life's mysteries. But I know what's useful, and I've experience of many things, whether I should have or not. And if I'm to suffer the disadvantages of staying platonic, at least you should trust me and learn not to be shy."

"I'll try, Alex dear," she said. "It really is nice to have a special friend. That's another reason I don't want to go back to my father. Just knowing you're here, and close, and safe, is so – reassuring. I look up – and there you are. I smile, and you're there to smile back. But not being shy will be awfully hard. I mean, I don't know much about anything, but I know even less about men."

"So I gather," smiled Alex. "But while I've sworn to be no more than a friend, I can't teach you. In the meantime, I can only offer advice."

"And friendship."

"And certainly friendship."

"You know," said Katherine after a pause, "You're much nicer to sleep with than Sara. She has bony elbows and knees."

Alex chuckled. "I'm flattered, my love. Just don't repeat that remark to anyone else, I beg you." He adjusted his embrace, keeping her snuggled to his side and tucked below the covers. "Though you once told me I snored. Hopefully that doesn't keep you awake."

"Maybe that was only out in the shed when you were cold," said Katherine, remembering. "You don't seem to do it anymore. And if you did, I don't think I'd mind. You have to forgive your friends a few faults, don't you?"

"It seems you do," Alex laughed. "We had better forgive each other."

Her head, nestled comfortably on his shoulder, shifted slightly. "Have you forgiven me, Alex dear, for getting you into all this trouble?"

He stroked her cheek, running his thumb along the soft fullness of her lower lip. "Silly puss, what in the world should I forgive? The trouble between you and your husband is something else we need to talk about one day, but not tonight I think. I imagine I've disturbed you enough. But there's nothing I blame you for, it's that damned priest I blame. I might as well ask your pardon for stealing from you."

"I'd forgotten about that." She sighed. "It wasn't really my silver anyway. And now I'm stealing it too because I suppose everything belongs to the estate, but I brought lots of it here for selling if we need to. If I'm having a baby, I'm sure he won't mind. And if I'm not, and I really, really hope I'm not, then the next Earl of Sheffield will never know any better."

"Quite right," nodded Alex. "I've obviously set you an excellent moral example. I daresay your father would beat us both." He kissed her ear very lightly, resisting the growing temptation to kiss everything else. "I pray you sleep well, my sweet," he murmured, "with golden dreams."

Katherine woke in the middle of the night, the golden dreams having shattered in the dark. The moonlight had drifted beyond the angle of the little window and she could see only the black shape of Alex beside her in the dark. She remembered her dream. She had never dreamed such a thing before and a vague sense of impending shame troubled her. Then she discovered why, perhaps, the dream world had been so vivid and the emotions so strong, for Alex, deeply asleep, held her tightly and one hand was heavy clasped across her breast.

The tenderness and tingling, which Elizabeth had warned her might be an early sign of pregnancy, was aroused so fervently that she could not decide whether it was deliciously pleasurable, or utterly shameful. When her husband, who had the right after all, had touched her there, she had loathed it.

Both Sara and her father, in differing and embarrassingly subtle terms, had warned her before her marriage that wives must, in all things, obey and serve their husbands. From this, Katherine had immediately guessed that something unpleasant was certainly on its way, but she had never imagined the truth. Disliking the truth, once she discovered its reality and its source, then seemed logical enough. The truth in all things had, ever since she was very young, invariably turned into either a hideous disappointment or a ravaging terror. Only Alex, in all her life, had ever promised the reassurance of safe contentment and then given the reality of pleasure beyond expectation. That her body now betrayed her, and that she might be on the point of betraying Alex just when they had discovered a sweet shared friendship, withered the dream and where it had been golden it became dark. Katherine moved his hand, careful not to wake him. The last echoes of the dream disintegrated. She turned, curling away from the warmth of Alex's body, hugging up her knees to calm the arousal and the wanting. It was a long time before she slept again and even then the heat and rhythm of his breathing on her back felt like a reminder of guilt.

When morning came, he was up before her, with the cold like a frosted shimmer on the dark air. His eyes looked bright, smiling into their creases. He was struggling back into his doublet, then sat beside her to pull on his boots, the first day he felt well enough to dress properly. "Respectability again today, my love," he said, and Katherine thought it was a sign.

He leaned over, perhaps to kiss her awake, but she ducked beneath the eiderdown and mumbled something sleepy. He grinned, and his footsteps echoed firm and steady down the stairs. Then she heard him talking to Joan, the sounds of the baby, whimpers turned to suckling, breakfast stirred and the rush of fiery scarlet reflections up the stairwell. Katherine climbed quickly, shivering, from the mountainous swelter of the mattress, and struggled quickly into her doublet and hose.

She eyed the bed for a moment. She had never needed to make one up in her life and no maidservant had ever explained the system to her. She wondered whether she should leave it in its disarray, pull the covers right off in order to air it, or discover the secret of putting it back in order. Since she had no idea how to rid it of fleas, which she was now quite sure were present, she decided that order would be the more practical solution and began to experiment. The entirety being too wide for neatness, she made up one side at a time and realised there was no great mystery after all. The result was less haphazard than she had expected. She gave the eiderdown a proud pat, her first successful attempt at housekeeping, and trotted downstairs.

It had snowed lightly throughout the night and a surface of white velvet lay across the land. Katherine peered through the thick window mullions, wiping a clean circle with one finger. Behind her the fire blazed. The cold thin gleam outside and the busy warmth within seemed deeply reassuring, as was Alex's warming presence. Katherine sighed. She was determined not to spoil it.

Alex, cup of breakfast ale already in hand, was seated, just slightly slumped, on the chair opposite the hearth. He raised an eyebrow at Katherine's clothes. "Hello brat. Plotting disruption?"

"You look better, Alex." She took the porridge Joan gave her. The goat's milk was shiny within its layer of cream. "But you're not eating."

He shook his head. "Not yet, I think. I won't risk anything as threatening as Joan's cooking. But Margery's medicines are soothing and I intend trying Reginald Psalter's glutinous remedies before I risk solid food." He turned to Tom, who was sat on a cushion beside the fire, the baby on his lap and the bottle in its mouth. "I may have an errand for you later, urchin," Alex said. "I'd intended to do it myself, but I've an idea I'm not quite up to striding across the width of London just yet. I need information on yesterday's parliament, and you'll get that at St. Paul's Cross."

Katherine put her spoon down. "I can do that," she said. "I should like to feel useful. Tom and I could go together."

"But you can't go outside dressed like that." Alex frowned slightly.

"I certainly can," Katherine objected. "More proper as an apprentice or a servant than an unchaperoned lady in widow's mourning. No one will give a second glance at two boys out together. I can wear your hat."

Alex shook his head. "Too dangerous and too improper. Someone could recognise you, or involve you in a hue and cry, an accident or a fight. London streets are full of hidden dangers, and that brat of yours couldn't protect a bed bug."

"Now you're talking like my father," Katherine objected. "Strict and old fashioned and stuffy."

"Our relationship seems to be getting thoroughly muddled," grinned Alex. "After last night, and brothers and sisters and now father and daughter. But the fact is, I'm probably not the best person to judge how recognisable you are." He turned to Joan. "Well Joannie? Would you take her for a boy, or know damned well she's a girl in disguise?"

Joan put down her ladle. "I'd take you both for a pair of idiots," she replied. "But the lass looks as convincing as could be expected I reckon, long as she don't lose her hat and show all that hair of hers. I'll go with her, if that solves the problem."

"No, that wouldn't be fair," said Alex. "You worked all night, and had little enough sleep yesterday. Go to bed, Joan. I'll unravel my own knots, given time."

Katherine prepared his medicine as Joan wiped her hands on her apron and trundled upstairs to the newly tidied bed. Katherine held out the cup and spoon from a careful distance. "I want to go, Alex," she said. "I want to feel useful, and I'm not afraid. Isn't that the best thing about being a widow? Not having anyone else tell you what to do?"

Alex swallowed his medicine. "I take your point, brat. And I haven't the slightest business behaving like your father, your husband or even your brother. But I do feel responsible for what happens to you my love, whether you like it or not. So do what you wish, but for God's sake, look after yourself."

"I'll look after her," Tom interrupted.

"That makes me feel so much better," said Alex.

CHAPTER THIRTY-THREE

Joan remained upstairs in bed, sleeping solid as a hibernating hedgehog. Once breakfast was cleared away, Tom entertained the baby by mimicking a piglet, rolling across the floorboards, squeaking and grunting. The child watched this performance with some surprise, finally saw the humour of the situation and began to wheeze. The room swallowed its draughts as the fire reached higher up its chimney, and eventually, cup of wine in hand, Alex began to cook dinner. Katherine watched him in admiration. "How do you know to do these amazing things?"

Alex grinned. "You employed me, remember?"

"And then I suppose you won't even eat it."

"That's why I'm cooking. If I had to eat it, I wouldn't cook it."

"So you've guessed I don't even know how to warm up yesterday's bacon and peas." Katherine passed Alex the ladle. "But I tidied the bed this morning. It looked really nice afterwards." The ladle's handle between them, her fingers twined with his. Suddenly aware of a touch more fire than tingle, she recoiled, snatching her fingers back to her lap. Alex watched her for a moment, then smiled.

"We're clearly becoming a highly domesticated couple," he said. "But just the smell of re-dished bacon and peas pottage would be remarkably bad for my constitution. The bacon wasn't properly desalted and only double soaked, so the peas must have absorbed the rest of the salt. It looked like solid green scum. That infant produces something similar. At least I can serve food fit for you to eat."

"Just as long as you two know I've got the worst job," muttered Tom, who was now skinning the twitching eels that Alex had decapitated. "And not getting no appreciation, neither. Never told to go work in the kitchens before, I weren't. Not my proper place. I'm no scullion."

"You want to eat, whelp, you help cook," said Alex pleasantly.

He reached for the leeks piled in the basket at Katherine's feet. She quickly moved her legs back. His hand brushed her knee. Katherine blushed and moved aside. She said, "Excuse me. I'll get your next dose of medicine."

Alex's eyes narrowed. "The medicine can wait," he said. "Get your brat to go out and wash his hands, and you can throw the fish into the pot."

"Not my fault if I stink," Tom objected. "Them eels is nasty and slimy. And it's freezing outside."

"Nevertheless," said Alex, "you'll go out to the conduit, and just hope the water hasn't frozen in the tap, for you won't be allowed back indoors until you smell sweet and clean." Tom stomped outside and the door slammed shut. Alex turned at once to Katherine, one eyebrow raised. "So what's up, my love?"

She stared back at him. "Pardon? I didn't say anything, Alex. Except I think you should take Margery's medicine."

Alex sliced the leeks in long fronds and tossed them into the pot. "Is there something medically feminine – which you're sensitive about?" he said, frowning. "Or have I offended you in some way?" Katherine tipped the platterful of eels onto the bubbles. She stepped back quickly, removing her hands from his vicinity.

"Of course not. Nothing's the matter. Why should it be?"

Alex had thrown his velvet doublet over the stair balustrade and rolled up his shirt sleeves. As he worked, the long supple muscles flexed, the skin shining moist from the steam and the fine dark hair clinging damp. Katherine sighed and avoided looking in his direction. Alex watched as she stared with determined concentration at her lap.

He nodded. "Very well," Alex said. "As you wish." He turned away and began stirring.

By the time Tom reappeared, Katherine was dutifully chopping a hank of bacon into small pieces. As Alex took each handful to add to the stew, she pulled her hand quickly back, careful not to touch.

"Got bits of finger in there too, I reckon," said Tom, dashing inside with a gust of snow. "You trusting my lady with a big sharp knife? Most unwise. Here, I'll do it."

Katherine smiled, gave up the knife, and sat on the opposite side of the little room at some distance from the fire. Alex watched her choose her chair, shrugged, and returned to the cauldron. He was pinching out his spices. Margery came home just as Alex threw in a handful of ground almonds. "Jesus," she said, huddling by the fire within the matted wool of her large red cape. "Smells like real food."

"Needs to simmer," Alex grinned, heaving up the pot and shortening the chain, increasing the distance between fire and cauldron. "It can look after itself from now on. I've had enough of it and the smell's making me nauseous."

"For a gent with his guts painted out in dwayberry juice, you've come through quick," Margery nodded. "Quicker'n I expected, tell truth. Reckoned you'd be abed a sennight. Moaning for attention as men always does, and filling up on good wine." Having dried and warmed herself, Margery tossed her cape in a bundle to the corner and heaved her sleeping child from its box. She settled herself by the fire, cradling her son, and stretched out her little cracked shoes.

"I'm certainly enjoying the wine, but your medicines were probably my salvation," Alex said, sitting himself back down with some relief. "And I still owe you for my doctoring. At the moment it's only Kate with any coin, but if she's good enough to pay on my behalf, I'll certainly repay everything in time."

Katherine nodded at once. "I'd be delighted, whatever it costs. And I certainly don't want to be paid back."

"Well now," said Margery, "since we's all being so mighty common generous, let's chuck some common sense into the bargain. What'll I ask, d'you reckon, just for helping me ma's friend, being the bloke as bought the house I lives in? And is now paying for food and comforts and firewood, and bloody silver candlesticks too. So bugger your coin, mister." She cackled, which woke the baby. "Smells like you cook a lot better than me ma. So do that instead."

"I'll make no promises. I doubt a daily dose over the cooking pots would be any better for my health than dwayberry juice." Indeed, too long on his feet seemed to have exhausted him and he looked rather sallow in the snow pallid daylight, though where the fire caught one side of his face he was seamed in scarlet. "Your mother's asleep upstairs after her nightshift," he added, "if you need to do the same."

Margery yawned on cue. "After trying your soup, I will," she said. "Fucked out I may be, but I've more appetite than anything. Does that to me, every time. Does the same to the men. No doubt you'll have noticed it."

Alex laughed, with a glance towards Katherine. Since she appeared to have no idea what they were discussing, he said, "Frequently. And since you've the experience to tell, I'd like your advice. Does my lady pass for a boy in those clothes do you think, or not at all?"

Margery shifted her seat and regarded the lady. "With a cape and a hat and keeps to the shadows, she'll pass," Margery said. "Though don't see the fun in the game, meself. And a gent can piss easy in gent's clothes, but for a woman, would be a fuss and a bother not fit the trouble." She shook her head. "But what tickles one'll not tease another, I always says. Pulls you two thighs tight? Then good luck to you and I'll not say a word."

Tom, no longer needed to play nursemaid and now bored with adult conversation, had retreated to a corner and was looking out from the window. Katherine had deciphered half of Margery's remarks and was blushing. Alex laughed again. "Her doublet's more a case of seeking freedom, rather than role playing," he said. "But I appreciate your tolerance."

"Bugger tolerance," remarked Margery. "Should hear of them things the rich gents ask of us girls. Us lot, live around here and has a simple life, well it's a simple fuck they want and easy given. Mind you, it's bloody cold in them alleys, and they needs to be quick or they loses their pricks in a huff, they does, and left with no more than a pimple for play. Bad for business, this winter weather." The child had fully roused and was quickly open mouthed, hoping for milk and attention. Margery obliged with a tug at her neckline. "Used to work in a stewe house, last year," she continued. "But got closed after the battle. Them as put up the coin for backing, killed on the field they both was. Now the place stands shut." She thought a moment, then smiled brightly at Alex. "You seems penny ready. How about starting up a nice new business?"

Alex glanced again at Katherine and watched her awakening comprehension. He turned back to Margery. "Not that I'll be telling you what to say in your own house, my dear," he said, "but perhaps I should warn you that my friend Kate, inspite of her chosen style of dressing, is a good deal more innocent than any widow has a right to be." He grinned. "And much as I hate to turn down the prospect of a good profit, your business deal isn't in my line, I'm afraid. I'll keep it in mind if I meet up with any of my old friends. Before the battle, I certainly knew a few who would've been happy to oblige, but my friends are scattered now, and mostly dead or in hiding. But if you're hungry," he added, "I should think dinner's ready."

With a grab for the new napkins, they helped themselves to the pot, enthused over the taste and quality and took second helpings. Margery then went up to bed, baby in its box under her arm, as Tom trundled back into the cold with the spoons and big wooden platters to wash. Alex turned at once to Katherine. "If it worries you living here my love, and if you refuse to go home to your solitary respectability, I could find somewhere else for you perhaps. With Lizzie, for instance."

Katherine smiled and shook her head. "I think – that's the last place – I mean, I really do like Elizabeth. But well – everyone dies in that house, Alex. Besides, if you think I'm horrid and prudish and cross, well you're wrong. If you're happy here, then so am I."

He was surprised. "You didn't seem so happy with me this morning, Kate. I assumed I'd upset you in some way. But as for prudery, what's no matter for a man is a damned sight different for a lady. I gather you've guessed something of Margery's chosen career?"

"I'm not totally ignorant," said Katherine with pronounced dignity. "I know all about – about – what Margery does. I'm not a baby. If you must know, even Edmund talked to me about – that is, them. So you see, I'm quite - knowledgeable."

"Edmund?" demanded Alex, startled. "You mean your damned little weasel of a husband had the infernal cheek to talk to his wife about whores on his wedding night?"

Katherine blinked. "Shouldn't he have? I didn't actually like it much myself, but I supposed that it had to be normal."

"No, it's not bloody normal," Alex said, "and if I'd known at the time, I'd have done a lot more than just get the fool permanently pissed." He was silent a moment, frowning. "Though come to think of it," he continued, "I'm doing a damned sight worse myself. I'll have to get you out of here Kate. A great deal depends on what you find out at St. Paul's Cross this afternoon."

Katherine glared at him from her shadows. "There you go again, Alex," she said. "Thinking I can only go where you put me, as if I was a – a candlestick. I like it here. Yesterday, with everyone sitting around the fire and talking like that, it was – one of the happiest days of my life. Even though I was worried about – the thing I was worried about. And even though you were sick. It was so cosy. So I'll stay here if I want to. Margery's free to do what she wants with her life, and so am I. I want you to be my friend, not my master."

Alex sighed. "If you can't see why I feel responsible for you, Kate, then you're a pillicoot," he said. "I'll try not to be too demanding, but at least listen to my advice when I give it. You've no notion of the world you're living in, and you must know that."

The snow had banked around the great stone cross, spreading its outstretched arms with ivory crusts like a scarecrow beneath breeze tumbled blossom, but where the crowds had gathered the white had turned to stamped black puddles. The king's new parliament was still sitting, and rumour had already travelled well beyond the London wall. Now the first genuine news, officially published, was announced. To some it mattered, to others it merely gave the clue as to the new king's moods and intentions.

The bitter cold cut sharp, but the snow had stopped and the wind gently unravelled. Katherine pulled her hood over her head, held her cape to her chin and pushed forwards. Tom shoved from behind.

The Recorder was reading out the first business of Parliament; the attainders and rewards. A list was already pinned to the church doors. Katherine peered at the parchment, soiled already from a hundred trembling fingers. "Tell us," insisted Tom, staring with dislike at the dark inky squiggles which meant nothing to him at all.

"You just listen to the announcements," Katherine whispered. "And between us, we'll get all the news."

The exclamations of the crowd, the shuffling and bustling, the ravens croaking from the steeple, the intermittent summoning of bells, a man selling hot pies from the tray around his neck, the shouting of wares, prices, indignation and bargaining, and the furious reaction at much of the news, all made listening a challenge. Tom used his small size, elbowing his way to the front. The attainders were read out in order of precedence and most of the names meant nothing to him, but he had orders to listen out for Quyrril and Mornington. He heard neither.

Many of the great lords of England had fought in the battle for the king they had loved, and now the new king sought a reckoning. Northumberland, inspite of the confusion of the battle lines and his own doubts or inexperience having kept him apart from the fighting, was now held in the Tower. Several more were still imprisoned, and others killed either on the battlefield, or executed afterwards.

Of the loyal men remaining, a full thirty prominent leaders were attainted, deprived of all authority and position, of title, lands and wealth. The original rumour, already widely circulated, was now proved true: King Henry intended dating his rule from the day preceding the battle in order to count as disloyalty to himself what had been loyalty to the previous consecrated king. Thus he could punish accordingly those who had fought against him. This was a ruthlessness never before known since the time of the barbarians; a revenge without precedent and outside law. But it was done. And because it was done, it included, to the amazement of the crowd, the attainder of King Richard himself, third of that name, now called usurper and criminal.

But although the list was considerable, including sentence of death, of imprisonment and of attainder, there was no mention of the house of Quyrril, nor of the Barons Mornington.

Depressed by the news, the dissolution of years of knighthood, heroism and loyal effort, the Lady Katherine slipped away from the courtyard and signalled for Tom to follow her. "Well, my father never went to war," sighed Katherine. "He thought they would all get on very well without him so he wasn't needed. He stayed home and oversaw the harvest instead. Perhaps he was right after all."

Tom hesitated. "Is that where we're going then, lady? After this? Just back home again?"

Katherine sighed and shook her head. "I don't think so, Tom." Her own dreams presented her endlessly with the same question. "I don't want to go back to being boring. And trapped staring out of the window at other people living their lives. Something will come along, somehow, one day, and I'll suddenly know what I ought to do. In the meantime, well, aren't you having fun?"

"When I'm not washing puke out of pots and skinning eels," said Tom. "But you and Master Bowyer, whatever his name is, don't you like each other? I thought you was busy getting together. Already bedding together, and cuddling and whatnot. Shouldn't a man ask his girl to wed, after all that? Isn't it expected?"

They had started walking back through the side alleys, and were now suddenly out in the windy open of Watling Street. "If," said the Lady Katherine briskly, "you start lecturing me on the proprieties as well, Thomas Budd, I shall send you back to Leicestershire, and probably alone. You can walk."

Tom sniffed and wiped his nose on his sleeve. "Just trying to help. My da always told me, when I grew up, not to ever kiss a lady if'n I didn't want - "

"Oh, good heavens," exclaimed the lady. "You're nine. Or ten. Or something of the sort. What do you know about kissing?"

He shook his head. "Good way of getting the pox or the pestilence, if you ask me," he said sorrowfully. "But they do it, all sorts of folks, and all over the place too. I'm not blind. Now, your father and the laundry girls - "

"Well, I don't do things like that," said Katherine with dignity. "And

Mister Quyrril is very nice and respectable, so he doesn't either. And stop smirking, or I shall cast you off. In fact, I ought to cast you off anyway, since you're a horrid little boy and have no respect whatsoever. You're supposed to say, yes my lady, or no my lady, and nothing else."

"I'll keep it in mind," said Tom, relapsing into the sulks.

She was bubbling with the anticipation of informing Alex, once back by the fire within the cosy perfumes of placid affection, that his family had been neither accused of treachery nor condemned to penury and humiliation. No attainder had yet been put upon his name, and consequently, his father's title still stood. Humorous as it might seem, evidently her clerk of the spicery, the man in hiding from a warrant for theft and murder, was a baron with estates, property, wealth and influence. She thought he might need them.

They walked the Lower Thames, bustling along to keep warm and hurry home, far easier achieved in hose than with the hampering bulk of skirts and the drag of a train, but watching the river's grey tumble for Mathew's wherry and the hope of a companionable water's hop down past the Bridge. Amongst the waddle and slap of a hundred little boats, few were recognisable one from the other at any distance. Through the rising river's mist no face gave expression, and only the blur of beard and concentrated frown was visible. Matt was evidently busy somewhere. It was a long trudge along the river bank, and colder than within the cramped hustle of the crowded city. When Katherine finally arrived back at Joan Hambury's little house, she was disappointed to hear from the voices that Alex was not alone. Tom pushed open the door. The pulse of heat swept outwards from its haven within. Katherine pushed the door hard shut behind her, and the heat was enclosed again. At first she did not recognise the man with whom Alex was speaking. He reminded her of an elevated raven and his legs, being so long, seemed jointed twice over as he sat on the low stool, knees drawn up almost to his chin. Dressed in mahogany broadcloth with a slight trimming of beaver, the apothecary was an echo of shadows. He stood at once as Katherine entered, unwinding politely from his place until he loomed above her. "My lady. Please don't be alarmed. I am aware of the secrecy of your domicile, but have been entrusted with messages from the Ladies Mary and Elizabeth, and have brought further gifts from myself."

"We've become a charitable organisation," grinned Alex.

Mister Psalter bobbed. "Oh, please do sit down," Katherine told him. "We hardly stand on ceremony here. It would be – a little absurd." She was suddenly conscious of her boy's clothes, and blushed. "But you knew at once who I am, Mister Psalter? I thought – that is, I hoped - "

"Mister Quyrril warned me, my lady," said the apothecary. "Meaning to forestall embarrassment, I am sure." He sat again, squashing himself and his small stool back against the wall. "Unnecessary I believe, since with my particular knowledge and understanding of the medicinal and anatomical specifics of humanity in all its guises, I could be considered to be somewhat of a master of form, but there again, of a politeness which I can but appreciate, and am glad to have brought my own small recompense for the interruption."

"He's brought hypocras," explained Alex.

"Well, that's most kind," said Katherine, pulling off her hat but keeping herself wrapped within the cape. It was slightly damp but without it, she felt more than usually shy.

"And I've told him he should take his medicines back since they're damned expensive," Alex said. "But he says I should still take them. As an extra measure."

"The herbal brews of the young lady you mention," said Mr. Psalter with a frown, "would seem to have been most efficacious, but hardly in the realm of alchemy, as far as they have been explained to me. Such country mixtures are a natural aid to the strength of the human spirit of course, but cannot be likened to the great science of healing in which I experiment." Both Katherine and Alex nodded appreciatively. "It shows, I believe," the apothecary continued, "that your ailment was one of the natural system, sir, and not the result of toxins and intentionally harmful fluids."

"You mean I wasn't poisoned at all?" Alex smiled. "I believe I was, Mister Psalter. But naturally I should prefer to believe that I wasn't."

"It is perhaps a fault in me," said the apothecary, "that I wish to believe the best of humankind. Our sweet England, being a country of civilised humours, is a land where man, set upon the earth by the great Lord of all mercy, struggles to be the best he can, and will not wilfully harm another unless forced by that other's wickedness."

"Such as cutting the throats of his fellows, and leaving them to die in their own blood?" suggested Alex. "I've left a battlefield strewn with them, only to come back and find the same in my own family. But I take your point, Mister Psalter, and at the very least, will certainly enjoy the hypocras."

CHAPTER THIRTY-FOUR

Alex lit the candles, reaching each into the hearth to take its flame, and then fixing them around the room so that the small space danced and was alive. The fire continued to blaze as the night outside sank into its deepest black, the moon having shrunk to less than its half, and thickly clouded. Then he poured the hypocras into two fine new pewter cups and handed one to Katherine. His hand touched hers as she took it, and she felt scalded, and pulled her fingers away.

Tom curled beside the baby's crib, making faces at the big watchful blue eyes within.

Joan was out. "Got up and left the house some hours ago," Alex said. "Gone to see Matt, I fancy. But she's not working tonight, so she'll be sleeping here." He frowned, watching Katherine's expression. "So it's back to respectability for us, my love. The two women in the bed upstairs, myself and your brat down here on the warm pallet."

Katherine nodded. "That's – just as well, Alex. I mean – respectability. Since you keep telling me how I ought to behave more - properly."

"Now that's just what I don't mean to do," said Alex, raising an eyebrow. "And if I do, then it's clear you take not one jot of notice." She was curled in the high backed chair, her arms on its arms, her feet tucked beneath her. The worn blue knitting of her hose hugged her calves but had grown baggy around her knees and ankles, relapsing into small threadbare folds. Above the knee the stocking, thin cut for a young boy, was stretched a little around the lady's thigh, then disappeared beneath the doublet's pleated skirts. She had kicked off her wet shoes and there were small grubby holes in both her stockinged heels. "But I've got very fond of my scamp of a girl in her unsuitable clothes, my love," he continued. "The studious Mister Psalter was too diplomatic to appear shocked, though I imagine he was. I suppose if I say you should limit the number of people who see you like that, you'd be even more cross with me than you are at the moment."

"You keep hinting about me being cross," said Katherine, crossly. "It makes me sound thoroughly mean and ungrateful, and I'm not cross at all. I'm enjoying myself. And it was a bit unfortunate walking in on that stuffy man unexpectedly, but he doesn't matter, does he? I mean, he's nobody after all. And out in the streets no one knows who I am." She paused, and stared into the fire. "And – you – that is, you don't mind. Do you?"

"It's how I first met you," Alex grinned. "I suppose, truth told, I like it. But you don't seem to realise, my love, how inappropriate it's considered for a woman to show that much of her legs."

"But I'm not showing anything," Katherine objected. "I've a shirt to my chin, and my legs are all wrapped up in wool. All the way. And it's a tunic skirted doublet which is longer than most, and – I can't see the problem."

"Your legs may be covered in wool," Alex grinned, "but the outline's as clear as running naked. And very nice legs you have too, my love. But our friendly priest would have you thrown in the stocks or worse, and if you think it's no more provocative than a billow of long skirts, then you've your head in the clouds. I find it more damned alluring than any intentional seduction, and I'm only your brother."

"You make me sound like a good dinner, or a sugar loaf," said Katherine, blushing furiously. "Men show their legs off in much tighter hose than I'm wearing, and no one cares. And most of them look thoroughly horrid too. Edmund would have looked much nicer in a long skirt. His legs didn't even meet up."

"Gracious," said Alex. "I hope I don't fall too far below your standards. I'd never thought about it."

Tom, who had not been addressed, interrupted from his corner. "Grown-ups," he said, "talk 'bout rubbish most of the time if you ask me, but you two – even worser. Legs! Who cares about legs! I got two, you got two, she's got two. That's all that matters. And what about this politics game, and what we found out today? Did we walk all that way in the rotten cold for nothing?"

Katherine smiled. "Yes, that's the good news, Alex. The attainders were all announced first and not a mention of the Barons Mornington. It was a fairly long list I'm afraid, and I expect you'd have recognised lots of the names, but luckily I didn't. Of course, the Earls of Sheffield had already been dealt with, and no further mention was made now he's dead. But Sir Alexander Quyrril, Baron Mornington, was not on the list."

Alex leaned deep back into his chair, stretching his legs to the fire, and sighed deeply. "Strange," he said softly, "to hear that spoken, my love, for the first time ever. I thought I didn't give a damn, but now – it will help us, I believe." He closed his eyes a moment, then opened them again, smiling. "I'd better contact poor old Uncle Godfrey."

"What? You rich now?" demanded Tom.

"I'll still be sleeping on a straw pallet tonight," Alex grinned. "And so will you, brat. The rest can be sorted once I've solved the murder and mayhem. But it gives me a position from which to exercise some influence, and it gives me rights and a small amount of power. As long as this bastard new king doesn't suddenly discover he's another old enemy unexpectedly alive, and shove the attainder on in retrospect."

"Best keep a low profile for the time being then," said Katherine, remembering her father's preferred attitude to life.

"Oh yes," grinned Alex. "With two warrants out for my arrest, I can be as circumspect as a castrated ram waiting placidly to be shorn. Have some more hypocras, my love, and forget my problems. I've just got a very good idea what to do about it all, both for myself and for you too. And no, I won't explain what that is, for you'll just tell me you won't. And I intend that you will, so we'll save the arguments for another day. Especially a day when your brat isn't around listening and not minding his own business."

Reginald Psalter made a good hypocras and Katherine accepted two more cups of it before retiring finally to bed. But when passed each cupful, she was more than ever careful not to touch Alex's hand, or look directly into the query of his endless dark eyes.

Sleeping with Joan reminded Katherine of why she had never been comfortable with low necked gowns, and generally felt far more suitably covered in shirt, doublet and hose. Certainly the codpiece was a horrible embarrassment, but her apprentice's livery kept that well hidden and it could not be seen, even when she sat. This was not true of any fashionable man's attire, which favoured doublets barely flounced below waist level, exposing not only codpiece and thighs but buttocks as well, even though well clothed in bright coloured hose of silk or wool. Her remarks on her late husband's legs had taken her perilously close to a conversation she had not the slightest intention of entering, but she could admit, silently to herself in the night wanderings of her dream quiet mind, that the shape of Alex's legs was very different indeed, and something she had most certainly, albeit unwillingly, noticed. Dressed in his livery, only a small curve of calf had been visible. Now wearing the rich velvets from his cousin's wardrobe, Alex was exposed as a different man altogether. in fact he was, in some regards, literally exposed. Katherine sighed.

Joan, hopping naked and unworried into bed after Katherine was already curled within it, showed a weight of breast which Katherine believed must surely be dreadfully uncomfortable. She turned her back, cuddled her knees, and tried to sleep. The excess of concentrated hypocras had made her drowsy, but her thoughts kept her awake.

Alex, still very weak, had slept almost at once. She could hear him snoring below stairs. She would not, she decided, inform him that he did snore after all. There was a reassuring and companionable sound to it, and she found that it lulled her, like the distant tidal pound of the river.

When she woke the next morning she realised how well she had slept. A sickly lemon sunshine was already hovering outside the window, and Joan was up. The bedchamber smelled of dust and grime, the accumulated sweat of the bed and an old sullen sourness still hanging undisturbed from the first two days of Alex's violent illness. Katherine shook her head, dislodging the faint displeasure and replacing it with familiar affection and a semblance of home. She hurried into her boy's clothes and shuffled downstairs.

There was only Alex, which surprised her. Even the baby's crib was empty. The fire was built up, and a pot bubbling over it. Alex was slumped in the large chair, staring into the hearth. He blinked, hearing Katherine, and looked up.

"You look unusually morose," said Katherine, a little hesitant. "Don't you feel well? Where's everyone else?"

"Been gone an hour or more," nodded Alex. "And I'm well enough, just the remainder of the damned headache I've had since the poisoning. Slept well, little one?"

Katherine helped herself to the porridge. Porridge had never before been her favourite breakfast and she had considered it bland. She now thought of it as the most comforting meal she could imagine, with connotations of friendship, protection and inner warmth. Indeed, she guessed this morning's porridge owed something to Alex's skills, since it was sprinkled with cinnamon and tasted of ground almonds. "I must have slept very well indeed," she said, bowl in hand. "Look how late it is, with the sun already up and everyone gone out. Has Tom gone to market with Joan?"

"No market necessary, we've a house bursting its laths with food from all quarters," Alex smiled. "No. It's for me they've gone, and thank God Joan didn't trust me with the infant and has taken it with her. She knows someone who can carry a message out west for me and has gone to find him. Evidently there's a company of carriers leaving tomorrow or the next day, though she's no idea if they'll be heading in the right direction. If they are, I'll have to plead poverty again my love, and beg the necessary coin from you. I need to write to my uncle."

Katherine sat and ate her porridge. She kept her eyes lowered to the bowl in her lap. "Will you need to – go back then, Alex? To your own home, I mean. I suppose, put things in order, and – be the new lord?" It was an aspect of the situation she had not previously considered and she felt suddenly bereft and exceedingly forlorn. She kept her expression hidden.

"Eventually," said Alex, watching her carefully. "But not while Mel's murderer is still unknown." Katherine had set her chair at an angle, taking advantage of the shadows. The daylight was not bright and only a pretence at sunshine smeared through the small window, but the firelight was vivid and high and left only small corners in shade. Now Alex shifted his chair around to face her, frowning. "Have you any interest, my love," he said softly, "in the extent, or the position of my family estates?"

"Well yes, in a way," said Katherine carefully, wiping out her bowl with stale manchet. "I mean, I wish you well of course. As a friend. And I don't want to – lose our friendship, Alex. Perhaps I could visit you one day. Though I suppose women aren't supposed to go traipsing across country visiting men."

"I doubt if that would stop you," said Alex.

Aware of his scrutiny, Katherine did not look up. "I know you don't approve of me, Alex," she said. "But I don't do anything really shocking, do I?"

Alex snorted. "Of course I approve of you, foolish brat," he said. "I just want to look after you, that's all. And once I've done what I can for Lizzie and Stephen, and got some solution for Mel - "

"And have you new suspicions?" she interrupted him, pleased to initiate a less personal discussion.

He sighed. "Yes, I suppose so," he said. "But nothing particularly intelligent. Since it's all just guess work, I shouldn't be telling you, but to hell with it. You're as near as be damned – well, anyway, as I see it there's only Lizzie or Mary who could have killed Dan. Assuming Dan and Mel to have been killed by the same person, which isn't definite of course, I see more motive for Mary. Lizzie had no damned reason to be rid of Mel, and besides, I just don't want to think it of her. Which is hardly an intelligent reason, but I happen to know that Mary was with Mel late the night before he died. I know something of Mary's – predilections, let's say – and there were signs on Mel's body that meant something to me. But then, that's no proof of murder, only of cohabitation."

"But then poisoning you, Alex?"

"Well," he nodded, "again, I'd like to think Lizzie wouldn't. Sentimental memories perhaps, which is absurd. She wouldn't even speak to me for years when her husband was still alive. I treated her badly enough and risked her reputation for life, so perhaps she's more reason to get rid of me than Mary could possibly have." He stood up slowly, easing his back, then leaned over the hearth with one elbow to the narrow mantle, staring down. "But the same day I came home sick, I'd eaten in company with Mary and Dan. Lizzie had left the table well beforehand. It was Mary passing my platter, and dishing out helpings from each course."

He kicked a log back into the grate, sending sparks up into his face. Katherine, having finished her porridge, stood and carried the bowl to the small pile of used platters beside the cauldron. As she crossed, skirting well behind Alex, he stepped back to avoid the sparks. He bumped directly into her, and whirled around.

For one moment, both flushed scarlet by flame, they stared at each other. Katherine was wide eyed in sudden alarm. Alex's eyes narrowed. He pushed himself against her and imprisoned her instantly, gripping each of her arms, thrusting her away from the fire and against the wall. She felt the warmth of the solid plaster behind her as her head cracked back, eyes still wide. He was so close she felt the pressure of his chest against her breasts, the bruising clasp of each of his fingers on her arms, the rise of codpiece hard above her own groin. His head bent directly over her, the glitter of his eyes slightly open. Then he kissed her so hard that she lost her breath, and when he released her arms, without conscious intention, she put both hands immediately up to his neck, and clung to him.

He had kissed her before but that had been tentative and gentle. This time was calculated. His own hands moved quickly behind her, one to the back of her head amongst her curls where he cradled her and held her steady. The other pressed to the small of her back, keeping her tight against him, fingers between the coarse broadcloth folds of her doublet. She had closed her eyes. He watched the sweeping curl of her dark lashes. He pulled her closer. His mouth forced hers open, his tongue pushing against hers, exploring. Her doublet was thin quilted, he wore only a shirt, and the swell of her breasts was a conscious enticement. She moved a little against him, breathing shallow and fast. He discovered the inside of her lips and the heat of her tongue against his own. His fingers wandered down her back, clasping the dip of her pelvis, his forearm around her hips. He felt the tug of her hands at his neck. He watched her expression as he held her, forcing himself tight on her. He sensed her relinquish all opposition, accepting him utterly.

Reluctantly, half a step, he moved back and let her breathe. His arms still hard around her body, he looked closely at her, the smile growing. "So," he said, just a breath across her eyes, "you're not angry with me after all."

She had barely breath enough to speak. "I – I never said I was."

"Then why," Alex demanded, "in the name of all that's holy, have you driven me insane doing your damned best to avoid every look and touch of me for the past day and a half?"

She was still squashed between the heat of him and the wall. She felt wonderfully crushed, as if that exact discomfort was what she had always wanted. She managed to smile back and her voice was only a whisper. "Have I? Well, yes, I suppose I have. I can't explain some things. It's – it's – complicated. But I wasn't ever angry. It was myself I was cross with. I don't think I ever could be truly angry with you."

It was as near as he was likely to get to an invitation. He pressed against her again and lowered his face to hers. "Little love. No more escaping then?" He kissed the fluttering of her lashes and the rise of her cheek, following down to the tuck at the corner of her lips. As he kissed her full on the mouth, his hands, no longer resisting temptation, slipped lower down her back to her buttocks beneath the skirts of her doublet, and pulled her hard against his groin. Again his tongue pushed into her mouth. Struggling once more for breath, her own hands gripped the collar of his shirt, tugging his head further down towards her.

Neither of them heard the door. Four pairs of hands grasped Alex from behind, heaving him from her and hurling him backwards with such force that he was flung to the ground. Two chairs crashed, spinning beneath his fall. The cauldron of remaining porridge was knocked from its hook, the chain swung and the pot tipped, dousing the flames like a candle snuffed. His shirt tore, ripping from collar to breast. His head caught the corner of the grate, and fell heavily sideways. Katherine screamed.

CHAPTER THIRTY-FIVE

F ather Erkenwald hopped from one sandaled foot to another, one fevered hand frantic around the staff of his wooden cross, the other trembling and pointing. "Evil, personified," he gibbered. "Now we see the true wickedness of this fiend of foul lusts and blasphemies, three times a murderer, a thief, abductor and seducer. Now sodomy is manifest, that most evil of crimes against the Lord, and he is proved guilty by his own hand upon the innocence of youth."

"'aul 'im up," said the sheriff, reaching down for the scruff of Alex's neck. "Caught in the act of buggery. Lucky we turns up at the right moment."

"'e's out cold," announced another.

"We don't want 'im dead," objected the sheriff.

"Resisting arrest," suggested the second quickly. "Is 'e armed?"

The sheriff ran his hands quickly over Alex's chest and up beneath the fine linen shirt, poking down into the lacing of his hose. "Not armed," he said. "Nor not dead neither. Get the bugger to 'is feet."

Katherine was yelling and threatening everyone with everything she could think of, thumping the sheriff on the back. "Get off him. He's done nothing. Leave him alone. Oh, you've hurt him."

Alex was white faced and his head was bleeding heavily above the ear where he had fallen. Still unconscious and quite limp, he was dragged towards the door. "We can't carry 'im all the way to bloody Newgate," the sergeant at arms pointed out. "We needs to get 'im round. Give 'im a couple o' slaps and wake 'im up."

Katherine, now frantic, turned to the priest. "Father – I beg you - "

Father Erkenwald glared at her in terrified disgust. "Get this heathen – child of the devil from me," he stuttered as the sheriff grabbed her, pulling her away.

"Just a molly-boy," said the sheriff. "Better looking than most."

"I am not a boy, and my name isn't Molly," squeaked Katherine. "I'm just in these clothes – because – while – my gown is being brushed out. I'm a lady."

The door was still swinging, the wind blustered in, the fire had gone out. It was suddenly bitterly cold. A grey mist swept up from the Thames and hung in the echoes. The soot, porridge clammy, was spread across the floor, seeping amongst the proud new rushes, now ruined. Katherine staggered back, sobbing. The priest raised his cross to her face. "Behind me, son of the devil. Do not dare look me in the eye."

"But you know me," cried Katherine. "Don't you recognise me?"

"I will not look into the face of evil," Father Erkenwald spat, turning away his head.

Alex, grey faced and white around the mouth, was partially on his feet. Dizzy and utterly confused, he blinked, stumbling forwards. "Kate?"

She whirled around and reached for him. They held her back.

The sheriff said, "But I thought you said the sinner was a servant boy, father? Wearing a right costly shirt for a scullion 'e is, and them hose is worth a fair penny too I reckon."

"He's the Baron Mornington," sobbed Katherine. "And he's guilty of nothing at all. You have to let him go. He needs a doctor."

"Ah, well, he'll get one of them in Newgate, if 'e's lucky and has thruppence to spare," said the sheriff's assistant. "As for baron whatsit, they all say that."

Alex was gradually making sense of what had happened. He steadied his feet, blinking back full consciousness. His frown was concentrated, his head hurting too much for clarity. "Kate?" he said again.

She managed to push to his side. "Alex, it's a mistake. I'll get to Elizabeth. I'll find someone who can help. I won't leave you."

He managed a small rueful smile. "I think you'll have to, my love. And forgive me, little one, but I won't be able to protect you for a day or two. Get to Lizzie and have her write to my uncle. She knows him and he can help, if he will. But Kate, mind who you trust. Only Lizzie knew where I was staying. Someone has to have sent that damned priest here." He turned back to the sheriff. "I need my boots and my coat," he said. "Once I'm suitably dressed, then I'll come with you quietly. But you won't touch the girl, do you hear? Or I'll set up a fight fit to panic the neighbourhood, and the neighbourhood isn't too keen on sheriffs around here."

"Girl? Boy?" the sheriff's assistant stared at Katherine and at her hair, shimmering in long hazel brown curls down her back. "What's this then? What's going on?"

"Wickedness, in all its guises," Father Erkenwald crossed himself. Smaller than every other person in the room, he glared up at Alex, red eyed and furious. "You are the corruptor of innocence and the bringer of death most foul," he stuttered. "Never before have I met a felon so steeped in crime, so lost to the wrath of the Lord."

Alex sat down abruptly and began to pull on his boots. He eyed the priest with contempt. "You're a fool, father, and don't deserve your cloth," he said softly. "But I won't waste breath arguing with lunatics. I'll prove my case with the courts." He stood again and crossed to the balustrade where his doublet and surcoat hung. He began to dress himself.

The under sheriff dug the sheriff in the ribs. The sheriff watched Alex with growing doubt. "Or you've stoled them stuffs, lad," he said, "or you're the richest scullion I ever come across."

Alex found his hat and pulled it down over the dried blood streaked across the side of his head. "May I present myself?" he said calmly. "I am Sir Alexander Quyrril, the ninth Baron Mornington. At your service, master sheriff. And I'm sorry to have to point out that if we need walk all the way across the city to Newgate, you'll have to be a little patient. I've been ill and am not entirely recovered, apart from the dent you now seem to have made in my head. We may just arrive by tomorrow's curfew."

"Well, I've no horse, lad," said the sheriff. "And no cart. So walk it is." He turned to the priest. "Not that you needs come along, father. I've got the matter in hand."

"I shall come," said the priest. "It is my duty, my son, and I shall see justice done."

"Suit yersell," said the sheriff. "Seems like we'll be a mighty slow parade, n' more like a herd o' geese than a proud march of the law."

Katherine clutched at Alex, taking desperate hold of his hands. "It'll be alright, I promise," she said. "I won't let anyone hurt you again." Something cold and hard pressed against her palm, and she realised that Alex, for the first time, was wearing his father's thumb ring. She nodded. "Don't sell that, will you, Alex dear. I'll get money and bring it to you."

He smiled, and leaning forward, kissed her lightly on the cheek. The priest and the two men at arms sighed with the outrage of moral disgust, Father Erkenwald muttering and again raising his cross. But the sheriff was uncomfortable, looking from the velvet clad lord to the boy with a girl's face and hair. "See Lizzie, my love," Alex said softly, "and I shall be alright, I promise. No need to worry for me. And a word with Joan, and perhaps with her neighbour Matt might bring results as well. If you'd care to come back here after Cripplegate, or send one of Lizzie's staff back for you, no doubt you'll find one or the other."

The sheriff's assistant gave him a sharp push from behind. "Walking slow or not, we'd best make a start, I reckon," he said.

Taller than the others, Alex strode central, avoiding the gutters and refusing the restraint of the men at arms, but his stride was hesitant and it seemed he limped. Before them all marched the priest, exultant, with his cross raised as though leading an ecclesiastical procession, but he was small and his shadow diminished first. Then every shadow merged into the river mist and as the alley narrowed towards its end, they disappeared entirely, as if overtaken by damp despondency. Katherine watched them leave, shivered against the door jamb and burst into furious and helpless tears.

Although she hated losing time, she first scurried upstairs and changed quickly into her woman's clothes. She counted out her last few coins, found them too little, and wiped her eyes for the tenth time, rummaged for her tiny sapphire earrings being the only jewellery of her mother's she still had, and, with a slam of the door, ran out into the street.

Newgate's stone was darkened by three centuries permeated with misery and violence, arbitrary torture, systematic pain, utter hopelessness and absolute filth. The stench of the open sewer running through the dungeon pit, reeked out into the streets beyond. This underground limbo was the gaol's bleeding heart and the sewer its artery, bearing the piss and shit and spittle of three hundred prisoners, drunken vomit, the blood of endless violence, the bloated floating remains of dogs and cats and the carcasses of vermin.

Alex stood one moment in the sleeting cold and looked up past the portcullis to the turrets, then bowed his head, said a silent goodbye to air and sky, and followed his gaolers inside.

The darkness was immediate and the stink formed its own walls. Father Erkenwald, choking, turned towards the sheriff. "He must be manacled. He must be cast into the pit and shackled in irons."

"Not for you to say, father," said the sheriff. "And you'd best not enter here. I hands 'im over to the prison guard for now 'til 'e comes up at court. In four days or so you'll be wanted for making accusations at the trial. 'Til then, father, your part is done."

"Even the wickedest prisoner, most sunk in evil, must have recourse to the word of God," Father Erkenwald insisted. "None better than myself - I am indeed prepared to sacrifice my own well-being - to give succour and hope to the heretic, to the slayer of the innocents, to the - "

"We've a prison chaplain, father, thanks all the same," frowned the sheriff, "and 'tis not your place. You come back for the trial now, and God be with you."

Alex saw only the guard's hand and not the face, a fist of eager fingers reaching for him from the blackness. Close to fainting, he bit his lip and tasted blood, keeping himself conscious and on his feet. His head reeled, his eyes could not adapt to the depth of dark. He could not breathe. But above all, the weakness from the poisoning still remaining felt like reeking soot eating from his belly up into his throat, and the strength he'd summoned to trudge almost the full length of the city was now gone.

The guard said, "Warrant?"

The sheriff handed over the rolled parchments. "Theft and abduction, and three murders, two within the jurisdiction. Now accused of sodomy, though there's no warrant for that. 'E's a desperate case."

"Alex Bowyer, pot boy and spicer," read the guard, peering through the gloom. "Alias Alex Quyrril, soldier."

"There appears to be some mistake," said Alex. He heard his own voice echo. The great stone walls were damp and chill with condensation, the passage high roofed and sloping. He felt for a moment that he was falling, and steadied himself, boots stamped wide.

The guard, long haired and dirty, shook his head like the waving of a small banner. He spread a pair of toothless gums. "Always a mistake there is. Not a guilty man, there ain't, not one, in all the place. Fraudsters what ain't committed no fraud, bawds as pure as the snow and debtors what owes nuffink at all to nobody. But for murderers like you, we've a special place, a good deep pit below, where you'll be chained alongside the rest of them poor innocent citizens."

"The warrants," Alex said patiently, "do not relate to me. I am not called Bowyer and I am no man's servant. Nor am I a common soldier, though I fought in the late battle as Commander of a company. I am the Baron Mornington, and I can prove it."

The guard grabbed his arm. "Less of yer piffle and whining, lad. 'Tis all over for you." But the sheriff was discomforted, and signalled the guard to wait.

"Hold it, Lumbunt," he said. "There's questions – but it's time I'll need for the answering of them. Summit don't hold together, nor this gent's clothes nor his manner." He glared at Alex, resenting the problem. "Better not chuck 'im in the Limbos, nor put 'im in irons.

321

Not yet nohow." He peered closer at Alex, who gazed disdainfully back. "Can pay for your board, can you lad?" Alex nodded. "Right then," the sheriff turned back to the guard. "I'd recommend the Master's Side, and take some care 'till I've finished my investigations. We don't want trouble, do we now?"

It was a tiny room, more cupboard than cell, high up above the gatehouse and appeared hollowed into the stone. There was no window and no sight beyond stone, the slick of sliding damp, and the iron barred wood of the door. There were rings hammered into the walls, but Alex was not chained. He was pushed inside, and payment demanded.

He threw off his fur lined surcoat and shrugged out of the velvet doublet he wore below. "Here," he said, "take this. It's worth a pound or two and should buy me what I need. But don't take the coat, I'll need that as a bed. It's as cold in here as high tide on the river bank."

"'Tis three shillings and sixpence a week's board," said the guard doubtfully. "Nor don't take fancy clothes 'n such. Coin's what I need."

Alex frowned, busily back into the warmth of his surcoat. "Don't be a fool, man," he said. "Sell it and make a profit since it's worth more than simple coin. But I need food and drink as soon as possible, and a chair and blankets. Then parchment, quill and ink."

The guard blinked, intimidated. "If'n yer honour wants, can order yer own bed brought in. We make allowances for that and 'tis normal in these rooms, but costs a shilling and must be brought by yer honour's own servants, and not too big for the space we's got fer accommodating."

Alex regarded the space. "How would I fit my bed in here?" he demanded. "This is a kennel, not a chamber. What other rooms have you?"

"'Tis Newgate Gaol, not no wayside tavern," mumbled the gaoler. "And we's stretched out, we is. What with this new king, his new taxes and gangs o'spies reporting slander across all the city, a glutton of business we has and every prison fulled to burst. I've not got no other room to offer."

"Then I'll take this one," said Alex with faint amusement. "But if I can't fit in a bed, then at least some sort of proper mattress could be brought, with an eiderdown."

Gaoler Lumbunt chewed his lower lip, nodded reluctantly, and lumbered out. Alex collapsed onto the low pallet and closed his eyes. He felt wretchedly sick but did not reach for the chamber pot. It did not look, or smell, as though it had been much cleaned after the regular use of the previous tenant.

The pallet was thin damp straw beneath him, there was a threadbare square of woollen blanket and no pillow, and his head pounded but found no relief. Alex deepened his breathing, attempting calm. He wondered what Katherine was doing, and then deciding it futile to wonder, wondered what he would do himself.

His boots had crunched, crossing the boards to the bed, as if walking on sandy pebbles. He lifted one foot and bent his knee, examining the sole of his boot. It was encrusted with squashed lice. He closed his eyes again, and let his mind drift. Eventually, because of weakness and exhaustion, he slept.

It was the smell which woke him. Alex had no way of counting time, though it seemed to float eternal, but he judged it very late when the gaoler came again, bowing low and bustling. Lumbunt was struggling with a billowing armful of linen, and he was followed by two visitors.

Without regard to his usual manners and ignoring both the gaoler and Elizabeth, Alex blinked in greatly surprised delight, swung his legs from the little straw pad, managed to stand, and immediately took Katherine in his arms, kissing her briefly but firmly on the mouth. "In this foul place my love? I hate to think of you entering here." He smiled. "And your hands are frozen. But I'm truly happy to see you."

"So nice to be appreciated, Alex," said the Lady Elizabeth from the shadows behind, her kerchief to her nose. "And yes it's late but not quite curfew yet, and there are two of my men waiting downstairs to escort us back when we're ready. And when the others arrive with the rest of the furniture, we can all sit down and pretend to be civilized."

"Furniture?" grinned Alex, turning to her. "Where will I put furniture in this hole?"

"Sell anything that doesn't fit," said the lady airily. "But you look quite ghastly Alex. What's this I hear about poison, and you being near to death?"

"Not sure I was near to death," Alex told her, still holding tightly to the Lady Katherine. "But poison seems to be accurate enough. Easier to recover from at least, than a slash across the throat."

Elizabeth shuddered. Behind her, the gaoler and his assistant were bringing in various items. A small cushioned chair was placed behind Elizabeth and she promptly sat on it. She gagged a little and again raised her kerchief. "I've written to Godfrey Quyrril, and I've delivered papers concerning your identity to the sheriff's office," she said. "Then I've an appointment with the alderman tomorrow morning. While I was arranging all that, and money for permitting the furnishings of course, Katherine was speaking to the Constable of this dreadful place. She was most enterprising, Alex. You should ask her."

Other chairs had been brought, a narrow feather mattress without a base, a heap of bedding, and a bundle of clean rushes for the floor. "Sweep it first," suggested Alex, looking up at the guard as he sat on another chair, pulling Katherine down beside him. He thought she looked flushed, though she resisted the urge to bury her nose in her kerchief. "I apologise for the stench, my love," he said, "and for every other foul detail of this whole situation. I shall make it up to you, I promise. Was Newgate's Constable as ill humoured as I imagine he must be?"

Katherine tried to smile. She nodded. "Yes, a very stupid man, Alex, with warts on his nose and terrible breath." As Alex frowned over her heightened colour, she thought Alex looked ill and grey as old parchment, his eyes sore and red rimmed, and white shadows stretched around his mouth. She looked down, hiding her pity. "I explained that all this is a horrible injustice. He didn't seem accustomed to talking to ladies of quality, so I made the most of that. I was very ladylike. You'd have been proud of me, Alex."

He had captured her fingers, clasping them tight in her lap. Her hands were still cold for the room was damp and chill. He smoothed her fingers, warming them and rubbing across the nervous, rigid knuckles. "I'm always proud of you, little one."

"Well, I said Father Erkenwald is being very spiteful," she continued, a little breathless. "I hope you don't mind but I said he has a personal grudge against you specifically because he disapproves of our becoming – that is, not hand-fast of course – but - promised in marriage - " Katherine saw the expression on Alex's face, and hurried quickly on. "Being so soon after my husband's death, since he was the priest who married us, he doesn't approve of a widow cutting short her mourning." She was aware that the clasp of Alex's fingers had become distinctly harder and that she could not extricate her hands at all. She sniffed and continued. "I went back home after meeting with Elizabeth and changed into my very best clothes to try and look more impressive. I told the Constable you were never a servant, but an important friend of the family with knowledge of medicines and spices. And I have a copy of the autopsy report with a sealed paper witnessed by sixteen of the Earl of Sheffield's staff, stating that my husband died of the Sweats and that the priest knew this perfectly well and chose to ignore it."

Alex, with barely the energy to sit straight, still gripped her fingers. "My love," he said softly, "you're an angel, and I adore you. Now tell me about us being promised in marriage."

She blushed. "I know it was very improper, Alex, but I needed something to give me authority to speak on your behalf, you see. And since Father Erkenwald keeps muttering about seduction and immorality, I knew he'd tell the court he saw us – kissing. But if we're promised – he can't – so you don't mind, do you?"

"Mind? Can you conceivably think I might?" He lifted one of her hands and kissed her fingers. His voice sounded increasingly faint, but his eyes were bright in the candlelight. "A sad lowering of status for you I'm afraid, married to a lowly baron after accustoming yourself to an earl, but I've every intention of marrying you as soon as you'll have me, my love. I can think of no more hideous place to attempt a proposal, so I'll keep my peace until I'm free. But it seems, with your help, that may happen soon enough."

Katherine looked back into her lap where their hands were

entwined. "I'm afraid I told another lie, Alex. I told the Governor I was a trusted confidant of the new king. I said I'd be pleased to tell his majesty that at least you were being well treated during your unfortunate – and thoroughly unjust – incarceration."

"Trusted friend –– of Henry Tudor?"

"Well Edmund was," nodded Katherine. "I've never met this horrid king, but he sent us a wedding gift. An arras with something about his favourite saint I think, St. Armel, who I've never heard of. And very badly painted too. Anyway, I did go to the coronation so it was only half a lie."

Alex looked around the cell where the great stone slabs of the walls still oozed their damp, things still scampered in the corners and rustled in the reeds on the floor, and the stench still layered the air thick as grease, but now the small space was furnished with a semblance of comfort. There were cushioned chairs, a tiny writing table and three candles, their hesitant flames sullen and pale through the gloom. Best, because it would bring sleep and the escape into unconsciousness, was the bed. Without space for the great frame of a four poster, the mattress lay upon the ground, but it was thick with feathers and bound in clean linen. Over it lay a fine sheet and a soft blanket, then a heaped eiderdown soft as whispers, and above all a counterpane of heavy quilted wool trimmed in fur. Alex smiled, and sighed. "You're a marvel, my love, though I hate to think of you coming to a place such as this, and having to lie on my behalf. But if it's true and they repeal one warrant against me and ignore the claims of abduction, then it's just the two accusations left for me to deal with. Though they're two most damaging. I could try and buy a royal pardon perhaps, but I'm hardly likely to merit Tudor's favour."

Katherine nodded with a sniff. "They'll never convict you, Alex. I won't let them."

"This is all very affecting, Alex," interrupted Elizabeth, "but as you pointed out yourself, it's terribly late and we ought to be going. At least I've a full purse here for you, which ought to cover anything else you need."

Alex frowned at her over Katherine's shoulder. "Thank you. You're a good girl, Lizzie," he said. "But I'm not sure I should take it, nor do I think I'll need it." He paused, and shook his head. "There's something I need to ask you, my dear, which will sound both ungrateful, and probably damned rude. But you were the only other person I told Joan's address. Who did you pass it on to?"

She had sat patiently quiet for some time, trying very hard to breathe normally and not be sick. Now she stared back at him in outrage. "No one. What are you saying, Alex?"

"That our esteemed priest shouldn't have known where to find me, my dear. That's all."

Elizabeth straightened her back and stood rather abruptly. She clutched her cloak around her, slapping the purse she'd brought down on the chair she'd left. "Yes, it is rude, coz," she said. "Perhaps you'd like to swap places with me, and have me chained in Newgate instead?"

Alex sighed. "Objecting rather too strongly I think, my dear. Don't be cross. It's my life I'm trying to salvage here, and I've accused you of a loose tongue, nothing else."

"To the best of my memory," Elizabeth said, very prim, "I told Mary, who asked, and two or three of the staff, which certainly seemed safe enough. I did not rush straight down to All Saints Church to inform Father Erkenwald, nor to the local sheriffs or the Lord Mayor. And now I think I'll leave. I'll wish you a good night, Alex, and hope you enjoy the mattress I paid for."

Alex sighed, and turned back to Katherine. "You'd better go, my love," he said quietly, squeezing her fingers. "I shall be alright I think, even if I have to stand my trial. In the meantime – may I know where you'll be staying? Have you decided? Will you stay with Lizzie, or go back home?"

"Since she has asked it, I shall go back with Elizabeth tonight because it's so late already," she said. "But then – tomorrow, I thought I'd go back to Joan's." She looked up at Alex and smiled. "No need to look so shocked, my dear," she said. "At least I'm glad you don't find me sadly predictable."

"Predictably idiotic," said Alex with complete disregard for where he was himself. "I should never have taken you to that house in the first place, not that I did, come to think of it, but at least I was there too, to look after you."

"You're hardly a respectable chaperone, Alex," Katherine pointed out. "And I was happy there. I'd like to go back. I shall keep Tom with me, of course, in fact, he's back there already, telling everyone what's happened. He's coming to collect me at Cripplegate tomorrow."

Alex smiled, leaned forwards and kissed her cheek. "I won't quarrel with you my love, and I'll try to stop telling you what to do. Just look after yourself for pity's sake, and – bless you for everything."

He watched her leave, not the loose stride of long slim legs in matted blue woollen hose, calves flexed at each step, but simply a swish of deep red satin and taffeta, a kick of little red leather boots, and a tight waist tucked within a fur trimmed coat.

She turned suddenly at the doorway. The guard was already holding the heavy door open, ready to lock behind her, and Elizabeth was already out of sight. "Oh, and one more thing, Alex dear," Katherine whispered, already half obscured in the cold corridor shadows. "Just that – and I do have the courage to tell you - there isn't going to be a new little Earl of Sheffield after all."

CHAPTER THIRTY-SIX

The nights were stitched in moaning. From outside the wind howled through the winter's dark and seeped in through the old stones. Inside, the misery found its own level, oozing like chilled water through the seams and gaps in walls and doors. A wailing of distant cries shuddered up from the dungeons with the draughts through the floor boards.

The days were utterly blank. There was no brazier, and still weak, Alex remained constantly cold. The room was too small for anymore smoke than the candles sent up and a charcoal burner would have suffocated even the lice, so the damp continued to slither down the walls and icy currents whistled beneath the door. Alex had no further access to his medicines, but he was able to buy sufficient food and good wine. With a considerable distrust in Newgate's doctors, he asked for no surgeon, but passed every hour writing. He wrote in order to keep his mind alive and himself sane, and he wrote to try and understand the unexpected direction of his recent life, winding like the freezing tides of the Styx through his thoughts.

On the fourth day he had another visitor. Lumbunt unlocked the cell door and a tall man entered, walking with a thump and a heavy limp. He swept off his plumed hat and looked down at the bundled figure on the bed with an affectionate smile. Although just a little after midday, Alex had been asleep, and now sat abruptly, brushing his hair back from his forehead. "Good God," he said with a grin. "Uncle Godfrey."

The older man, swinging the wooden stump of his false leg straight out beside him, sat down on the larger chair. "Not been doing too well then, my boy, since I last saw you?" he said. "Not a place where I'd have expected to come visiting, but then, you always did have your own damned stubborn ideas."

Alex stood and lit two candles, wedging them into their holders. Then he returned to the low bed, stretched out his legs and clasped his hands behind his head, propped against the wall. "I didn't choose to come and live in this filthy place, you know uncle," he said. "And I'm planning on a fairly brief stay, if possible."

Godfrey Quyrril shook his head. "Looks like a chamber some families would envy, my boy. Now in the past, Newgate was said to be hell on earth. Starvation, you know, leading to cannibalism in the communal dungeons. Women didn't live too long."

"No doubt a few of those problems still continue down in the pit," Alex sighed. "I'm accused of murder, and that doesn't normally warrant special benefits. So I shouted rank, and got myself a better room. God only knows how I'd have survived if they'd thrown me in the Limbos, as they originally intended. I can smell it from here, but I'm not chained into it. I lie awake here sometimes, pitying the poor buggers trapped down there, whatever they've done."

"You should have come to me after the battle, lad," said his uncle. "For those first few wretched days, I believed my entire family slaughtered. Then I heard something from Lovel, and word that you'd gone to join the rebels. So I left you alone to make your own choices." He rubbed his left knee, tight strapped to the polished wooden leg, then looked over and smiled at his nephew. "But I thought I should come up while parliament was sitting and see if I could sort out the family title, knowing you'd do nothing of the sort yourself as a matter of pride. Got to London yesterday. Called on your cousin Elizabeth, and learned what'd happened."

"A pleasant surprise, no doubt," said Alex.

"Oh well." Godfrey Quyrril scratched his beard. "Never was a quiet day, ever since you grew out of your swaddlings," he said. "John now, bless his soul, was always studious."

"The best of us," nodded Alex. "He'd have made a great baron."

"Then hopefully you'll make a fair one too, my boy, in his honour," said his uncle. "Unless you still mean to join Lovel. For that'll lead straight to death, either in battle or on the block. Not a forgiving man, this new king. No long lists of pardons, as good King Richard gave us."

Alex frowned, and stood quietly. He went to the little escritoire and poured two cups of dark wine from the jug that stood there beside the candles. He handed one to his uncle, pulled up a chair, sat beside him and drank deeply. "Things have changed," he said at last. "My mind, most of all. I still wish Lovel victory, but he'll have to do it without me." He looked up with a sudden smile. "First I need to get out of here," he continued. "Then I'm getting married."

"Best avoid the block then," nodded Godfrey Quyrril. "Marriage needs a strong head on a firm neck. And will this female be a respectable affair, my boy, or are you still into rape and raptus?"

Alex grinned. "I'm attempting respectability, uncle, though you'd never guess it," he said. "Newgate is something of a diversion. How's the wine?"

"Better than I'd have expected." The elder man stretched his one good leg, scratched his beard again, and drained his cup. "Though you've lice on the floor, and fleas in the cushions. Meantime, having little desire to come watch your hanging, boy, since standing too long in the cold makes my bad leg ache, I've arranged to meet a good lawyer in the morning. Young Elizabeth spoke to the Lord Mayor yesterday I gather, and it seems the warrant's shaky."

"Shaky? It's positively ludicrous." Alex refilled both cups. "A decent lawyer should get me out before trial, if you'll stand me the fee uncle. If not, I can always sing the Neck Verse."

"What, recite your Latin for the ecclesiastical authorities?" Godfrey Quyrril had begun to scratch under his doublet, and being muffled up against the cold, it was hard to get into. "From what I hear of your friendly priest, lad, you'd do better to stick to the secular commons. Or should I suggest your title merits the Star Chamber? Or simply the block instead of the gallows?"

"Cheerful bugger," grinned Alex. "And I think I'd sooner keep to the rope thank you, as long as they don't decide on gutting and castrating to spice the public spectacle. I've rarely heard of an executioner taking less than three strokes to do the job. If there's one thing likely to be worse than losing your head, it's probably losing it slowly."

Uncle Godfrey shook his own. "Your trial's due Tuesday, two days after tomorrow they tell me, but I intend getting the warrants repealed before that. Once I've seen the lawyer, I intend finding Thomas Bourchier, if the poor old man's still alive by the afternoon."

Alex frowned. "What, the Archbishop of Canterbury? What the devil has it to do with him?"

"Tell him to keep his bloody priests in order," explained his uncle. "I've heard about this crazed religious zealot of yours, my boy. Not all the factions take much notice of each other, but Bourchier still carries the respect of most. On his last legs of course. Damned Morton took over the coronation, I gather."

Alex, who had little desire to discuss the coronation, and even less the loathed Bishop of Ely John Morton, was on his third cup of wine. "Seems I've a hell of a lot to thank a lot of people for, after this," he said, almost to himself. "I'm surprised I've any friends left, but it seems I have." He smiled at his uncle again. "Forgive me if I get maudlin. I've had nothing to do but think, and that's a dreary and solitary business. First I was stuck in bed for days being sick as a salted salmon, and now since I've been in here, the only exercise I've had was chasing a damned rat around the floor last night."

"That hungry, eh?" suggested his uncle, scratching his crotch. "Never mind, my boy. Give me two days at most, and I'll be raising my cup to you over the dining table, with the feast spread between us."

Joan sat by the fireside nursing her grandson and watching the young woman opposite her, half her age and half her size. She was not used to being gazed at with such prolonged innocence, trust and respect. She felt vaguely uncomfortable. "He'll look after you, lass, once we get him out, that is," she said. "Not as bad as been painted, is young Alex."

"But I never thought - " Katherine blinked. "He's been – ill painted? I know about the trouble with the Lady Elizabeth. But surely nothing else, - oh - not counting this of course."

"Oh, this." Joan was scathing. "There's those'll always hold it agin him no doubt, for a good scandal is better than a dreary truth any day. But I'm not counting this. It's the past I'm thinking of. The lad's reputation's long ruined. Plenty was lies and plenty was true and after my Lady Elizabeth there was other women enough. He were wild, both afore I knew him, during and after. But he's not a bad lad."

Katherine shook her head. "Doesn't Alex have any respectable friends, then? I was wondering about his family, just hoping they'd help, and whether he has friends I should go to. Or would they disapprove because I was married to a Lancastrian loyalist? I'm nobody myself, though my father was knighted when he was young. But he's just a country farmer really, with a few tenants and a small manor, and he couldn't even rustle up a dowry to give me security in that horrid marriage he arranged. So I've no one to turn to." She sighed, clasping and unclasping her fingers. "But Alex must have so many friends, people who know he must be innocent. There's the ladies Elizabeth and Mary, but that's difficult because it was there that everything happened – and Mary wouldn't even speak to me yesterday. She's deep in mourning for her husband of course."

"Mary's more of a trollop than my own daughter is," nodded Joan, "but I don't hold that against her. Life's not worth the living of, lest there's a cuddle in it now and then. And Mary misses her husband no doubt, since he gave her everything and put up with her struts and cocking games for the sake of the bedchamber."

"So I just thought," persisted Katherine, "that you'd know someone helpful, from Alex's past perhaps, who I should go to."

Joan laughed. "I weren't his crony, lass, didn't go to no taverns with him, nor off chatting with his friends. I were his lady friend's maid, that's all." She hoisted the baby over her shoulder and began to pat its back with a heavy hand. "But what rattles me," she continued, "is why you reckon on finding strangers to do our work for us? There's you and there's me. There's my lass Margery, and there's Matt next door. Who else do we need? We'll get the lad out and free, never you fear."

Katherine smiled as Joan tucked the infant back into its box. "That's such an encouraging thing to say," she said gratefully. "But I've been to see the prison Constable, and Elizabeth went to the Lord Mayor. I already have one warrant repealed, and maybe that'll make it easier, but the worst two still stand. So who should I go to next? Do you think I really should try and get an interview with the king?"

"Trouble with you, my girl," said Joan coming back to the fire with a puff, "is thinking them high and mighty folks is the ones as holds the power in London, like kings and mayors, the rich and the pompous, and especially all them ecclesiasticals as gets all riled up and shouts doom and death to the sinners from their pulpits. But in the end, it's not them at all. It's us. It's mob rule as runs this city, lass, and that I promise. Heard of Jack Cade? And there's been plenty others, fighting our own causes. So, we starts our own wars when we wants to, and we're about to start one now."

Katherine blinked. "You want to make war on Newgate?"

"Now, that's something wouldn't do no good at all," Joan shook her head. "No, it's Father Fucking Erkenwald I'm after, lass."

Bemused, Katherine stared back at her hostess. "The priest? You're going to make war on the church?"

"Just that one weasely little bugger," Joan said. "You gentry folks, you thinks it's the holy pope as rules Christendom. Well, I'll grant you, if he was here now I'd bend my knee and I'd kiss his ring and I'll feel myself proper honoured. But it's us as manages the day to day, and make no mistake." She raised her skirts, pushing both swollen ankles towards the flames behind the grate. Outside the wind was rattling the chimney pots. "Go to church every Sunday and feast day, says the law. Or plead some excuse and pay a fine. But who pays the fines?" continued Joan, grabbing up her cup of ale. "Not us, we don't. Them country folks go traipsing off on pilgrimage to cure every sin and ailment, but all they comes back with is blisters, whereas my

Margery's herbals will have you fixed to rights in a week. Them churches got more thieves and murderers cowering inside claiming sanctuary than all of Newgate."

Katherine nodded and smiled, stretching her own little toes to the warmth of the fire. "I suppose I seem terribly ignorant to you. I'm a country yokel, I suppose, with no understanding of the city, or much else either. I was so protected by my father, I'd probably seem like a yokel to the yokels. But I'll do anything to help Alex."

"Well remember this, lass," Joan said. "We're not awed by monks and priests in this city, for they just be folks like us, and some a lot worser. The Lord Almighty knows His own business best no doubt, but we've had priests sued for forgery and slander and a year past one priest was done for murder, and another for inciting others to it too. Screeching and hollering he was, telling his whole congregation to grab some poor rakyer's lad he reckoned had dumped his load o' shit in the churchyard. Well, it were agin the priest the congregation turned, and flung him outta the city, fifty strong and all swearing for his bastard sanctimonious blood. There's been husbands taken a shovel to priests caught with their hands up the poor wife's skirts after Mass, and fathers accusing priests of seducing their daughters behind the pulpit, and giving both a good wallop. There's been clergy chased down the street, and folks have dragged monks off to the pillory for theft and worse. Abbots and priests been clamped in them stocks by the hands of the folks as is fed up with no justice done, locked them in we have, and thrown rotten eggs afterwards. With monasteries cheating honest citizens of more taxes than is just, and more harlots in the convents than in the stewe house down the road, nuns drunk in their own chapels and priests forgetting their Latin for too much wine taken, well, it's no wonder we don't scare of taking some priests by their grimy little necks, and chucking them out their fancy coloured windows, and into the Thames along with the rest of the city's shit."

"I thought," Katherine gulped, "that the clergy were always protected by the church. Isn't Papal permission required just to punish a member of the church?"

"Law? There's laws agin making dams in the rivers, yet well nigh every monastery with a stream has one built. There's laws agin the length of a lady's sleeve if it trails on the ground, and laws agin common folk wearing the silk and the velvet. And who is it obeys laws like that, I ask you? When the law's a fool, then there's only fools as obeys it. That pope lives a mighty long way away. In this country, it's us as rules."

"It wasn't the pope I was thinking of, but the bishops," said Katherine. "Half of them have their own private armies."

"Oh, they likes to keep us pious, by threat and by sword." Joan chuckled. "And we're all scared shitless of hellfire and purgatory when we gets to our deathbeds no doubt. But it's only the rich as can pay for ten years of prayers for the soul departed, and month mind and year's mind, and on into some distant time as even the good Lord will have forgot. And bishops, with their ambition and spite, well, they're the most corrupt of the lot."

"It is," sighed Katherine, "an easier way to think of the world. Not to be frightened all the time about doing the right thing and respecting the proprieties. Not to imagine a vengeful God hearing and judging each word. Not to imagine an eternity of punishment after death."

"So never mind about eternity," Joan said, "for it's the here and now we needs sort out for ourselves. Plans, is what we wants, and I've been making them these few days past. Matt'll be here soon as he ties up the wherry, and Margery'll come once she's made enough coin to warrant a night in the cold. We've all an interest. But in the meantime, I'd like to hear what you reckon is best, for it's your lad we're talking about, after all."

"I'd like to see that horrid little priest forced to give up his accusations. I'm frightened he'll go on hounding Alex even once the warrants have been repealed, so it would be nice to see him stopped. But not hurt, of course, or frightened too much." Katherine watched Joan's expression, and laughed. "You think I'm a coward," she said. "But I truly wouldn't want anyone made to suffer on my account."

"'Tis your devoted gentleman at risk, lass." Joan shook her head with a sigh. "I'm not reckoning on stringing this priest up from the church beams by his balls, but something more than a polite please desist, don't you think?"

Katherine blushed slightly. "And Alex isn't my – devoted anything," she said quickly. "We are – definitely – only just friends."

"Oh yes," grinned Joan. "I'll remember that, I will. 'Tis clear as the nose on my arse."

CHAPTER THIRTY-SEVEN

I t was the first time Katherine had ever entered into a boat. Matthew Flesher took her hand, she stretched out her foot, and the world tipped.

"You'll be alright with me, lady," Matt said. "'Tis nigh twenty year I've made my living on this river. We won't even be shooting up under the bridge, for 'tis low tide, and the water's more sluggish than sprightly."

Katherine tried to say thank you and found she had bitten her tongue, her heart was beating like raven's wings, and she could not speak at all. Joan, peering at her from the wet slosh of the steps, said, "Sit down afore you falls, lass. I'm off to speak to my neighbours one moment."

Sitting heavy and suddenly on the low bench, Katherine stared up. The little wooden stair from the pier seemed to be swinging and Joan appeared a long way off. "You won't be long?" she begged.

Matt grinned. "Still tied up, we are, lady. You'd have to be half crazed and half blind to fall out just yet. Sit still, and get your eyes accustomed to the pitch."

Joan had climbed back to the bank where the muddy river's line joined the low stone walls of the two adjacent taverns. A crowd had gathered, and it appeared that she knew them all.

Katherine dared to look back towards the water, and realised that other small boats had clustered round as the wherymen pointed and called. The discussion became louder, the boats bumped and bobbed. Someone said, "But All Saint's is outside the Ludgate. Not in the city, then, and nort to do with us."

Matt's answer was loud and meant for everyone. "But the gent and his lady is city folk. Besides, they's friends of mine, and friends of Joannie's and that makes it city business. You don't want to know, Ned, then you leave be. There's others as'll come. I know who my mates are."

"Oh, I'll come," said the other. "For the fun of it, I reckon, if nuttin else."

With the weather now mild for mid-November, a faint yellow glitter shone between the floating draff and slap, bringing a sparkle to the water's surface and small leaps of life up from the depths. The fish were jumping, as if mistaking sunglow for flies on the wing. There were twenty or thirty wherries and their wherymen, wind leathered faces and crinkled eyes avid with curiosity, slow paddling to keep their boats in balance with a lazy slop and slurp of the dirty water. On the bank were clustered forty, maybe fifty friends and neighbours. Women under their white cambric or little blue bonnets, men holding to their feathered caps as the wind shifted up from the sea in the east. The chugging clouds held on to their rain and the sun persisted.

"Tomorrow then, or tonight?

"So, tonight it is, and well before curfew."

"Any delay, and the gates closed, 'tis no matter - for we'll take the boats back into the city."

"A small priest? A dwarf is he?'

"And his skin as pocked as Kensington's gravel pits."

"Pocked, is he? Well, it's a sign then, and a punishment from God."

"Father Erkenwald, and doesn't deserve the name of the good saint. So we'll give the bugger something else to remember London for."

She thought her voice too insignificant to be heard below the urgency of discussion, but when she said, "But please, be careful. He mustn't be – killed," – they heard her, and most smiled.

"When we does someone as deserves to be done," a complete stranger replied, "we don't do 'im in altogether, lady. Not dead, that is. Just when we's finished with 'im, the bugger wishes 'e were dead."

Katherine wondered what she had started, and then remembered that she had started nothing at all. It had been Joan's initiative, but she hadn't started it either. Father Erkenwald had started the whole thing.

Once Joan climbed into the boat beside her, the increased weight sinking it considerably lower into the river waters, Matt rowed off westwards, keeping close to the bank. All along the way he called to his friends, both onshore and in the boats.

"For a hue and cry agin' a bugger of a priest bin causing more trouble than a high tide in a high wind. And I promises free ale for those as joins in," Matthew cried over and over. "Meeting at the Bridge once dark, right after supper. Bring sticks and torches and shovels. It's a night of fun and riots we're planning."

And Joan, shouting as loud, "We'll have a right early Mystery play for Christmas, my friends, and all set in a church as is proper. But it's the priest we'll have howling, and he'll play the devil, as has bin this month past, and we'll be the saints and get all the rewards."

An early afternoon with no more than a shuffle of wind and a faint warmth, the city was busy and the river too. The Thames buzzed from the north bank to the south, where the Southwalk started its meander towards Canterbury along the pilgrim's route, and so the streets were lined with taverns, stewes and tenements squashed within the slum tips of poverty and violence – tenants of the Bishop of Winchester – and therefore heartily despised by London's citizens, and avoided too, until wanting the bear baiting, the cock pits, the stewes, the hostelries, and a haven from the city's sheriffs and the law.

London's northern bank encroached on the waters with wharves and warehouses extending their frontage, floating piers, landings and rickety wooden steps. The great stone walls and turrets of the Steelyard and Baynards, the wheeze and creak of the cranes and the endless noise of the wharfside business, split by the whine and whistle of the thin wind through the ship's masts and the thud of their gunwales against the banks. A hundred lighters carrying goods from the great foreign vessels downstream, a hundred busy taxi boats touting for hire, a hundred little showtes weighed down by their cargoes, a hundred wherries which all called the river their own. The Thames had its own smell, brackish and salty with the wafted stench of muck in all its endless variety, and a man who fell overboard would die whether he could swim or not, but simply for the poison he'd be bound to swallow in that first gasping shock of cold. Some of the boats were bright painted, other gilt, some carried banners at the prow, others with proud striped awnings. Colour streamed across the surface, as beneath danced the glittering life of reflections, but the river remained as slug mud and brown as the draff that fed the fishes.

Matthew took Joan and Katherine to the pier just before Baynards, and there they climbed back onto solid stone, with Katherine feeling her legs had turned to aspic. It was still a long walk to Cripplegate but going by river they had saved more than half of it.

Jenkins frowned and stared at Joan, vaguely aware of recognition, but the women hurried inside and the Lady Elizabeth, coming down the stairs to the main hall, shrieked in delight, and rushed upon them. There was a rigmarole of memories and stories to relate, news from the intervening years and talk of family, husbands dead, children born and fortunes made and lost. Katherine sat quietly, always interested throughout the tales, made cosily comfortable in Elizabeth's private solar upstairs, with ginger wafers and Reginald Psalter's famous hypocras served. Alex's shadow frequently coloured the reminiscences, sometimes as hero and sometimes as villain, and although deference was made for Katherine's presence, he continued to romp through the stories as does the passing of the inevitable weather, changing everything and every life, according to sunshine or rain.

"But it's getting late, m'lady," Joan said, stretching back her shoulders, and her face muscles which had become stiff from laughing. "I've a mighty important appointment a touch later, which won't wait, not even for a pleasure such as this."

"And I must get to Newgate," Katherine said with a slight shudder. "I have to tell him everything that's happening. "

"Not much to relate there," said Elizabeth. "But I told you Alex's uncle is in town. Godfrey went to hire a lawyer this morning, and see the Archbishop of Canterbury too I believe. He's even prepared to see the king. There'll be news from that of course, but I've no idea what came of the meetings. He'll be visiting Alex himself, to tell of it."

"I might meet him," said Katherine doubtfully. "Though I rather hope I don't."

"Oh, he'll like you," said Elizabeth. "Godfrey likes everybody. He even liked me before I ran off with his nephew." She stood suddenly, and went to a small chest standing beside the window alcove. "And you must take these, my dear. They're those horrid things Alex wore while he was pretending to work in your kitchens. Dirty old livery, and hardly anymore use to anyone I suppose. He left them here when he changed into Merevale's clothes and dressed properly again. But they belong to you, so I kept them for you, to pass back to your staff."

Katherine looked doubtfully at the little heap of pale blue broadcloth. There was a slight smell of cooking grease, of distant spices, and of sweat – a not entirely pleasant perfume which she had once associated with Alex, and which now, quite suddenly, seemed very pleasant indeed. "I suppose I'll take them," she said, clutching the little bundle. She spread the doublet, holding it up to the pale light against the diamond framed mullions. There was a dark red stain on one shoulder. Katherine shook her head. "I'll pass it on to the laundry girls at Sheffield House I suppose."

Elizabeth blinked, lowering her gaze. "Put it away, Katherine dear," she said. "That – that mark on the shoulder – from my brother – and brings back such terrible memories. Alex cradled Mel when he found him after - and his blood stained Alex's shoulder. That's not something I want to keep around."

Katherine stared more closely for a moment, then obediently bundled the clothes away, tying the arms in a knot around the rest. "I'll take it for you, lass," said Joan as Katherine stood.

She shook her head. "That's alright," she said as they left the solar and trudged back down the stairs. "There's something – so I think I'll keep it with me."

"And tell Alex I've forgiven him," Elizabeth said, shivering a moment in the doorway. "For being horribly rude the other day. I understand, I suppose, and it must be ghastly for him – in there. So tell him I love him – as a cousin should - and I wish him luck. If I think of anything else to do that might help him, well, I'll do it of course."

Joan walked with Katherine as far as the huge shadows of the Newgate fortress. She left her there, staring with loathing at the black iron portcullis and the crush of people hurrying to get though the gateway, past the pervading smell and its hanging cloud of misery. "I'm off, and must hurry. It's Tom as'll be waiting for you, lass, when you've finished in there," Joan said. "He'll walk you back to my place, and you'll both wait there if you please, for what Matt and I've planned for tonight, we'll do better without you. You'll understand, I reckon."

Katherine nodded, pulling her coat tight around her, the fur collar half covering her mouth. As the early winter twilight enclosed the city, the evening's chill was rising colder and the women's breath condensed into damp white mists as they spoke. "I understand," said Katherine. "I'm sorry in a way, because I'd like to see that nasty little man made to pay for his spite. But I'd be very much in the way, and I'd stand out and be noticed if the Night Watch comes running."

Joan grinned. "But you can tell the lad, from Matt and me, as to what'll be going on outside once he crawls into his bed tonight. And when he wakes to the usual reek in the morning, he'll know it's been done, - and there's a priest as'll not be worrying him nor no one again."

"It's so kind of you both," Katherine said, clasping her hand. "Putting yourselves at risk, and going to all this trouble."

"'Tis for Alex I do it, lass," Joan said, lowering her voice slightly. "What my lambkin did for me – well, no soul else ever has, nor charity, nor church, nor husbands. That lad saw me cast off from my work, with a girl child to bring up and no man to look after me, as a result of what him and the lady Elizabeth asked me to do, with me helping him get to his lady love. Though none of it worked to his liking in the end and him thinking his poor heart was broke and with little enough money to start a new life of his own, he bought me a house, and gave me his purse too for what little it were worth, and him a younger son with naught to his name. I'll not forget that. And

Matthew Flesher knows my story and cares just the same, for Matt's wishing to marry me and knows he must prove his own worth before I'll take him."

Katherine watched her new friend's large wadded figure hurrying off, blurring into the dull light and the bustling crowds. Then she turned back to the soaring cold blackness and scurried into the open doorway of the first tower.

As the visitor was announced, Alex leapt from his chair and clasped her hands, grinning, amused by his own enthusiasm. "I should be telling you not to come, my love," he told her. "It troubles me, knowing what you must feel coming to this place. But seeing you's a far greater tonic than anything else I could think of."

"Except being let free," smiled Katherine.

"Which is exactly the news I have for you," he said. He had taken her fully into his embrace, his chin nudging her forehead as he looked down, smiling. "My uncle's been busy. He's a loyal Yorkist, lost his leg back at Towton in the Yorkist cause, but knows how to deal with all sides and still has some influence. He seems to think I'll be out before my trial."

"But the warrants?" she said, voice muffled against his shirt.

"One's already dropped, thanks to you, my love," he said. "Not that abduction's a criminal offence of course unless the family cries raptus, but it went against my moral standing and would have given a motive for my murdering your husband. Now all that's gone. According to my uncle's lawyer, having one murder thrown off the charge immediately makes the others suspect. It shows malice of accusation, without the backing of proof, or evidence of any kind."

She smiled into his heartbeat. "I've some news too, Alex." And she told him, very quietly in case the guards were listening outside, about Joan and Matt and what they intended to do. "Not that it'll help with getting you out, I suppose, Alex dear. But Joan thinks if Father Erkenwald's frightened away, there'll be no more aggravation or accusations, leaving us free to disprove the warrants."

He laughed, delighted with her news. "Wonderful. I shall smile all night, imagining what's happening. I just wish I could join them."

"I don't know how you manage to keep cheerful," she sighed. "I would be – utterly crushed."

He leaned down as if to kiss her, then changed his mind, frowned, and turned his head away. "Crushed? No, I'm not crushed, my sweet. I'm furious, both with others and with myself. The air here isn't fit to breathe, and the filthy smell and the damp and the wretchedness are all soaking into my skin and my clothes. I'll have to burn poor Mel's fine velvets when I get out, and soak myself in a butt of Malmsey like poor old George Clarence. And I shouldn't allow you anywhere near me until then."

"Well, the smell here is particularly – horrid," she admitted. "But I'm getting used to it."

He smiled down at her. "That's even worse. I hardly notice it anymore myself, which worries me. It means I've become part of it. I don't even dare kiss you, since my tongue's more thickly furred than my coat."

Katherine peeped up at him. "It might be – embarrassing anyway, Alex, and just suppose one of the guards walked in? I mean, I know they lock the door behind me, but they must be waiting outside. They might decide to take a look."

"Not likely," Alex grinned. He refrained from telling her what most prisoners did with their female visitors while locked in together, or that the guards, especially when bribed, would no more interfere than serve refreshments. "But don't worry, my love, I'll not attempt romance in a place like this. I'll content myself with dreams."

"You – you dream of me, Alex?"

"I do indeed." He laughed. "I kiss you every night." He refrained from telling her all the other things he was busy doing to her in his dreams every night. "But in those dreams," he said, "I'm home and free and back on the Mornington estates, with King Richard back on the throne and Merevale alive again."

"That reminds me, Alex," she said, pulling a little away from him and pointing to the bundle of his old livery, which she had laid on a chair. "There's something I need to ask, and something I need to understand. And it might – just might be important."

He released her, raising an eyebrow. "About those old clothes? Burn them, my dear. Or pass them on to your staff."

She shook her head. "No, not that." She pulled out the doublet, and held it up to him. "The stain on the shoulder, Alex. Elizabeth says it's – blood."

"It is," he said bluntly. "Mel's blood. I found him naked on his bed, sprawled out with his head at the foot. I picked him up to make him more comfortable, absurd as it probably sounds now. Afterwards I saw the marks on my shoulder."

"I just thought," she sighed, trying to find the right words. "You see, I remember you telling me yourself. You said Merevale had been – dead – some hours. He was cold and – stiff. And another time you said that – after dying – there's no bleeding. Corpses don't – bleed - you said. So, you see - I just wondered."

Alex frowned, gazing down at her and the little heap of stained broadcloth in her hands. He took the doublet and held it to the candlelight. "Yes, the mark's still there." He stared more closely. "But you're right. I've seen enough bodies on the battlefield. I know how quickly blood dries, and it doesn't start again. But there's a superstition you know, that a corpse bleeds afresh in the presence of its murderer. Had you thought of that?"

"Don't be silly, Alex," she said. "It was actually something quite different, and quite important, that I was thinking of."

CHAPTER THIRTY-EIGHT

The crowd gathered, as arranged, by the Bridge. It was winter dark and the shops closed, but being only a little after suppertime, the streets were still busy and Joan's whispering, gossiping friends, amongst the bustle, did not seem at all notable. The city gates remained open, the first stars were out, the wind gusted and fell, and Joan Hambury explained her business.

A faint smell of stale fish; heads, gills, and scales, emanated from the shadows of Fish Hall, scrubbed within but the remnants swept outside and mostly remaining. A little beyond the shadows, the level of the Thames was sliding silently past high tide and into evening stealth. The gentle slurp of the waters from the little boats' bow waves slapped against the banks. The wherries were sliding from the darkness, and joining in a quiet caravan of watchful anticipation.

Over their heads; the Bridge. The first mighty stone pillar enclosed them all in darkness, though high above were the little dancing candle lights from the rows of glittering windows, cosy and thick behind the mullions, with folk at supper, preparing for early sleep, finishing their sewing or their cooking by the fire, heating bricks to warm the beds. All along the Bridge on both sides the little shops clustered, rooms above for the families, gables bending outwards as if to watch the river running underneath. Others, extended to four stories above the shop, tapped roof to roof, cockscomb tile to tile, leaning to meet in a creaking wooden kiss high above the walkway. Whittington's latrine cubicles sat further long, with their small march of openings dropping directly into the water below. The chapel of Thomas Becket stood central, and the small bell rang six. Hearing the hour, some of the candle flicker was snuffed but with the portcullis still up, the crossing remained open and noisy. Although the narrow roadway was pock marked and dangerous so that iron wheeled carts were now forbidden, the Bridge was the busiest street in and out of London, and a place of civic pride. The five traitor's heads staked high over the gate at the Southwark end, five loyal Yorkist leaders executed after the battle including poor Catesby, were now only skulls, their bloody flesh scavenged by birds and leathered by weather, the stench of decay frozen by winter and their misery gone with their sightless eyes, taken by ravens and kites. Only Catesby still wore hair, a few blackened tuffs waving forlorn in the winds.

Hidden by rising fog and the depth of shadow, Joan nodded to Matt. Too many to all travel easily by boat, she would lead her friends on land and meet up outside the Ludgate. Matt nodded back, and smiled. "If folks want a taxi tonight," he said, "they'll be calling a mighty long time." Ignoring the illegality of taking more than three passengers on a wherry, his boat was squashed and six friends sat huddled against the river mists, laughing into their tankards. Matt had kept his promise of free beer. It was Katherine's earrings which had paid for it.

The boats rowed out mid river, sending back the slosh of waves to the banks. Joan wrapped her cape's hood around her bonnet, tucked her hand through her daughter's arm, and strode off down Lower Thames Street with her friends following. Sticks and shovels hidden under cloaks, knives shoved into belts or down bosoms, seeming ordinary folk out for an evening stroll. Margery giggled, part tipsy, happy to have left work behind for a night, but promised a few coins by her mother all the same. The moon came out, little more than a pearly wedge on its journey back to the dark. The stars were increasingly cloud blurred, and the wind began to whistle.

Alex undressed and climbed quickly into bed. The warmth of his good eiderdown now permitted naked sleeping, with the careful folding of his clothes to keep them serviceable for the following day. He had no others to change into, and refused to ask for more to be brought. One good suit ruined by Newgate's noxious humours was sufficient to lose.

He stretched, clasping his hands behind his head. The pillow, though once soft feathers, was now dampened into cold lumps by the low draughts. It would be left to the guards or destroyed as well after his release. After his release, whenever that would be.

He thought of what his uncle had told him, assuring him of the Lord Mayor's sympathy and interest, of the Archbishop's concern, and the lawyer's determination. He thought of what Kate had told him about Merevale's blood on his livery doublet. And he thought of what Joan, and Matt, and their crowd of friends might already be doing down by All Saint's church in The Strand.

They had brought him gruel that evening, and two pestells from the nearby Cookhouse, but he had eaten nothing. He had paid, then given the food to his guard. Lumbunt was eating well these days. Alex found the smell of food made him retch. The effects of the poisoning had now quite left him and the sickness he felt was from the place where he was, and the fear, though ignored and denied, which still slept deep in groin and belly, of what might happen and of what dreams might be lost.

Instead of eating, he drank. It helped him sleep. He dreamed both awake and asleep, always with Kate in his arms and his bed. Sometimes, during the eternal emptiness of the days, he had written to her. But then he had held the corner of the little paper to the candle flame, and burned all the words, letting them float up in ashes, like prayers to some heathen god. Ink was expensive and paper too, but he had used a great deal of it and three nibs to his quill, burning everything before snuffing the candle at bedtime.

Katherine sat in the house in Draff Alley off Pudding Lane, in front of the fire that Tom had lit, and refused to go to bed. They used no candles but gazed into the flames, seeing stories, and threats. "What do you think they'll actually do?" Katherine said, and not for the first time. "And if they're caught by the Watch, will they go to Newgate too, do you think?"

Tom sniggered. "Reckon we'll be spending the next year visiting friends in gaol?" He shook his head. "I don't know London no better than you, lady, but in Leicester, there's not one sheriff with his head in the right place would put hisself up against a crowd the likes of that tonight. And not even paid, they aren't, the Night Watch. With Matt's friends fifty strong and big as they come? And Joan's not much smaller. But I'd like to see that nasty like sneak priest's face, when they catch him away from his pulpit."

"You can go to bed, you know," Katherine told him. "But I must sit up and wait for them to come back, even if it takes all night."

"Won't catch me going to bed," Tom said. "When I thinks what a dull life I had afore coming to London, well, it's not to be credited. Best day I ever had afore this, were going to a cock fight in Leicester, and lost me new shoes on the wrong rooster."

Katherine frowned. "You shouldn't have been going to cock fights at your age. Horrid things they are, with blood and violence and terrible language in the crowd. How old were you anyway?"

"Gawd, I dunno," said Tom with a far off look of remembered delight. "Seven, maybe eight. I reckon I'm near on ten now. But since you met Master Bowyer, Alex that is, well, there's more fun to be had every hour than in all my ten years aforehand. You ought to marry him, lady, whether he asks you or not. What a great life you'd have, with one adventure after another. Mind you, you'll have to keep me on as page."

"It sounds exhausting," the lady smiled. "Besides, I'm not marrying him. I'm not ever marrying anyone, ever again. Though if you must know – he has asked me."

Tom grinned. "In that case, lady, I reckon you've less sense than that goat of Mistress Joan's tied out back. Keeps trying to run away, it does, 'stead of knowing where it's bloody well off. I'd marry him, if he asked me."

Father Erkenwald had finished late Mass, and was alone in his church. Monday evening was never busy, though the winter's cold brought in a few stragglers sheltering from the wind, and he had needed to put out a smoky fire in the nave an hour ago, started by some wretched woman and her six small and filthy children. He had shooed them all away and was pleased to see that no one else had entered afterwards. He was expecting a visit from the abbot of his old monastery, and intended on making a suitably pious impression. Infants coughing and trollops begging would certainly ruin the sanctimony and peace of his own special haven.

The father had not left the monastery under entirely placid circumstances, and the abbot, suffering a sense of irritated responsibility, now felt himself obliged to visit his erstwhile protégé and to make sure that he and his parish were prospering. Although Father Erkenwald had no intention of returning to the powerlessness of the isolated old monastery and its dismal little hospital, he was nevertheless interested in proving his superior understanding, his success with his church and his congregation, and his extreme religious piety. His special talents not having been appreciated by his abbot in the past, he would now, he was determined, be missed, and his departure regretted. The abbot would see, at last how he had been misjudged. He would ask him back. But Father Erkenwald, smiling magnanimously, would not oblige.

The chapel's inner sanctum was blazing with candle light. A wealthy diocese but neither a favoured nor a wealthy church, All Saint's brought in too little for such extravagant luxuries as candles. Recent payment for the funeral of the late Earl of Sheffield and the gold given for the choir - hymns and prayers for the departed soul - had helped however, and Father Erkenwald had been able to buy tall wax candles in considerable number. He had lit almost half. The huge cross hanging before the rose window glowed rich in the light.

He heard the far doors creak open, and turned, sweeping, small but magnificent, down the nave to greet his abbot.

They entered not singly or in pairs, but so many together, squashing and pushing, that it seemed more a throng than a congregation, and then a mass, as if in expectation of loaves and fishes, and Father Erkenwald recognised not one single face, knowing that his abbot was not among them. He stared in growing dislike, and then growing apprehension. He held up his cross and began to chant the first Latin prayer which came into his mind. Then realising it was remarkably inapt, being the blessing of all which was about to be served at the monastery table, he lapsed into a hesitant silence.

The crowd was hushed by the first intimidation of echoes, soaring arches, the golden murals threatening hellfire and the decoration of gilt, silver and ruby. Saint's faces frowned, two stone angels and a fascinated gargoyle watched with interest.

There was one small bench for the seating of nobility, the rest was open space. It was not a large church, but space enough to tread mosaic tiles and ponder on God's certain wrath. Now the people had filled all the nave, puffing up towards the high wooden pulpit. Joan said, "Father Erkenwald?"

Matt pushed forwards. "We holds you accountable, father," he said. "For you've proved malice and spite. I've never heard no sermon of yours, so tell us, d'you preach mercy? D'you preach God's love? Let's hear it."

Utterly bewildered, Father Erkenwald had been forced continually backwards, and was now trapped by the base of his own pulpit. He stopped and glared. "How dare you ignorant commoners come here to question me? You're not even of my own congregation and I don't recognise a single face. Church services are over for today. Come back tomorrow for early Mass, if you dare."

Matt shook his head. "We've a special cause, father, and mean to see it done. But I reckon you've a right to answer for yourself first, if you can."

Joan stood beside Matthew Flesher. "I've a friend called Alex Quyrril, father," she said loudly, liking the sound of her voice spiralling up into the vaulted arches. "An ordinary man, a kind man, a generous man. Never did no special wrong. He's in Newgate now, father, which is no place for an innocent gent. You could tell me why he's there, I reckon."

Father Erkenwald suddenly understood. The fury raged up from his small bare toes to his face. He felt unusually hot as his blood vessels converged and expanded, staining the small circular pock marks across his skin. He seethed.

"That creature you mention," he squeaked, "must never be named within these sacred walls. A monster of demonic evil, a filth of the devil, lost to righteousness - " but he also heard his voice spiral, uncontrolled into the echoes of madness. The priest grappled with his temper and returned to sorrowful dignity. "You are poor lost souls, all of you, turned aside from the paths of propriety by the words of a foul sinner, and I will lead you back to Grace." Father Erkenwald tucked his hands into the sleeves of his robes, hiding the clenched fists, and spoke quietly. "I will preach to you now as you ask me, if you will all kneel before me, my children. I will bless you, and show you the path to purity and truth."

"Yes, it's the truth we wants, father," said Joan. "Then we'll decide on what punishment we reckon suits the crime. So tell us. Go on. What's the truth about Alex Quyrril?"

The faces glaring at him had become a tide. The candle light illuminated the people in a strange dance of black and gold, disguising and distorting. There was no dean or cleric to help him, for, expecting the abbot, he had sent everyone away. He took a deep breath. "I will not discuss this with a mob," he said with considered calm. "I am a man of God. Go back to your homes, my children, and I shall beg our Holy Father on your behalf, to forgive you all for this evening's rash wickedness."

"Wot wickedness, father?" demanded another voice. "Wot you reckon we done, then? Ast fer the truth? That's wicked, then? To come into a church and talk to the priest. That's wicked then?"

"You are poor simple souls," Father Erkenwald persisted, raising his voice again. "You do not know what you do. Go home now, my children. Before it is too late."

"Too fucking late already, it is," said another. "Bloody priests telling us this and telling us that. Us poor simple souls, you says. Well, it's us as pays for this and pays for that. Not a fucking prayer we gets for free, we don't, and not a bloody tune for nuffing. Wot you got for supper, then? I got a crust of cheat, and a smell of cabbage, and won't get no more for a day at least." The man turned loudly to his neighbour. "I say, chuck him in the stocks and let him stay out cold tonight, and no supper neither."

His neighbour grinned. "And you'd better come over to my place for supper afterwards, lad."

"Free beer, it is," shouted someone else. "I'll string this little bugger up and watch him kick for free beer."

"Was a monk like him beat me every night till I bled fit to die," muttered an older man. "After thirty year, I still got them scars."

"Was a friar buggered me when I were a little lad," snarled a tall man, striding out from the crowd. He poked Father Erkenwald hard in the chest and the small priest stumbled back. "Wanted to join the brethren meself, I did, but not after that. Ran away, was caught and beaten, and ran away again. Wot you got to say about that, little bugger?"

The priest was confused and increasingly frightened. "What has this nonsense to do with the sinner Alex Quyrril?" he demanded. "Be gone from my church, all of you, before God Himself strikes you down."

The people swayed, moving forwards, then back. The decorated beauty of the church worried them, the threat of the Lord's anger and the sullying of sanctuary. Some whispered, some had already left, hurrying out onto the cold porch.

"Drag him outside," ordered Matthew Flesher, seeing their hesitancy. "Get the little bugger into the churchyard."

"If you lay one finger on me - " squeaked the priest. "If you dare violate the holy sanctuary - "

"This ain't no authorised sanctuary," objected Joan.

"We've no need to do nothing sinful," smiled Matt. "For we've nothing agin the Church, nor agin the Lord, and never will have. Just agin you nasty little buggers what abuse your power, and gets our friends in trouble without no cause. So I reckon you'll come with us peaceable like, ain't that true, father?"

Having no intention of compliance, Father Erkenwald yet found himself moving, step by small step, towards the church doors. The mass had surrounded him, silently coercing, shifting and nudging down the nave, so that the priest, exceedingly squashed and with his head below the level of everyone else's making him inevitably blind, was slowly carried outside. No hand was laid on him, no force as such, but the freeze suddenly blew directly over his head, and he heard the huge wooden doors slam shut behind him. His sandals touched the porch steps and then grass. The crowd moved aside and he was left standing alone and shivering. The wind gusted up his skirts.

The murmuring and muttering became louder. Away from the echoes, the crucifix and the watching saints, the crowd drew courage. "Tell us now, father. What's a spiteful little bugger like you doing, putting yourself between us and our merciful God?"

Joan stood directly in front of him, peering down balefully. His chin was alarmingly close to wedging between Joan's enormous and quivering breasts. Behind Joan stood Margery, giggling. Beside Joan stood Matthew. Joan said, "Well, little turd. Makes you feel powerful, do it? Making up stuff about folks what done nothing, nor agin you, nor agin no one else?"

The fear was now greater than the pride. "Done nothing?" he blubbered. "That creature's sin was evident and noxious in the sight of the Lord. I caught the wretch, saw him with my own eyes, his foul hands around the widow, clutching at her - bosom. I caught him in the act of filthy seduction, and the blessed earl barely cold on his deathbed. I will not suffer such foul wickedness to go unpunished."

Joan grinned. "Did he now? Well, good luck to him. Wants to marry the wench he does, and that's naught to do with you. Jealous, was you? Got a prick you don't know what to do with – or know damn well, and got no chance? So! One little kiss, and you get the lad done for murder? Jealousy and spite. I knows how to deal with that." She turned around, yelling to all the people now spread across the little walled churchyard. "We knows how to fix up scrawny little buggers like this, don't we? I reckons we deal a quick dunking, and then get back to our warm fires and free beer at home. Agreed?"

A roar of assent ruffled the grasses around the grave stones. The crowd surged forwards again.

Matthew grabbed Father Erkenwald first, pinning both his arms back. Margery stepped up close to him and grabbed the collar of his robes. She tugged. The reverend gagged, toppling forwards, then struggled back. Margery pulled out a small dagger. The priest went quite white. Three men clustered around, holding the tall honey perfumed candles they had brought from the church. The flames blew and buffeted in the wind, but stayed alight. Margery's blade glittered. She shoved it against Father Erkenwald's neck. He screamed and began to gibber his prayers. But the knife sliced only into the coarse woven flax, cutting a deep tear into both thick layers of habit from collar to breast. Margery sheathed her knife, grabbed the torn stuff with both hands. It ripped. The robes fell apart. Beneath he wore not a hair shirt, but a warm woolly petticoat from chest to knees. Margery cut again. She pulled the pieces, tugging them away until Father Erkenwald stood entirely naked.

Matthew laughed. "Ah, jealousy was right," he said to Joan. "Since he's got fuck all there to play with."

"But I reckons he does play with himself," nodded Joan. "There's only a little weasel like that would try and ruin the life of a man with more."

Margery pushed up again, and grabbed. The priest squawked and tumbled backwards as Margery missed, giggling, and tried again. Some of the other women had elbowed a closer position, others were shocked or discomforted and had pushed away. "Wearing naught but his cross?" one woman said. "Now, we don't want the good Lord angry, do we, with the holy cross bumping on that little bare fat belly."

"Take his cross off him and stuff it up his arse," suggested Margery.

"That wouldn't be proper," shouted someone else. "Shove sumitt else up his arse."

A cheerful discussion began as to what was suitable for the shoving, what girth of object Father Erkenwald's aperture was likely to accommodate, and what should be done with him afterwards.

The priest was now crouched on the ground. Wet grass was oozing around him, a hundred furious faces glaring down at him. Several men grabbed his arms and hauled him to his feet. Once released, he sank back down, one hand clutching the cross which still hung around his neck, the other his genitals, which, still being under discussion, were suffering greatly both from shame and the cold.

"Not putting my fingers anyway near that," Joan objected. "But I'll deal the little bugger a spanking, if someone's got a shovel?"

Now sobbing, Father Erkenwald was bent naked over the square rise of a grave stone. Bitterly cold, his skin was turning grey and pimpled, the scattering of pock marks visible between. Joan raised the shovel, and brought it down, the flat wood hard on the priest's buttocks. He squealed and roared. Joan dealt a second blow, a little harder "That'll do," she said. "I'm bloody cold and I want my fire back home. Chuck him in the river, and let's be done."

"I don't want his dirty little corpse floating in my nice river," Matt objected. "Drag him down to the stocks and chain him in for the folks to find bare bollocked and blue in the morning."

"Sunday morning, as is proper," grinned Joan. "When the folks come for Mass, they'll find a mass as they didn't rightly expect."

Father Erkenwald's hysteria had faded to a gibbering through numbed lips. Margery looked at him with faint sorrow. "I reckon I could warm him up," she said.

"We're here to frighten the little bastard," frowned Joan, "not give him rewards."

Which is when the crowd was pushed aside, parting to let through someone with authority, who marched up from the end of the sloping green and stood staring in amazement at the scene spread before the closed church doors. Abbot Pugwald stood open mouthed, shut his mouth with a snap of revulsion, and turned to Matthew, being the largest, tallest and most officious looking male in the closest vicinity. Matt had one hand on the back of Father Erkenwald's neck, holding him in position, buttocks up, over the grave stone. He removed his hand with a grin. Father Erkenwald remained slumped, sobbing quietly. With a joyful disregard for the truth, Matt said, "Hello father. We found your priest playing with hisself behind the pulpit. Disgusting, it were, and frightening the little children. I reckoned a lesson needed learning."

The abbot glared both at Matthew and at Father Erkenwald, who had now tumbled to the grass, and, twisting around, was gazing up at the man he had intended to humiliate and impress. Abbot Pugwald said, "What is the meaning of this, my son? Have you taken leave of your senses?"

Father Erkenwald, being unable to answer, the abbot turned to Matt and to the crowd now quickly dispersing around them. "This is shocking behaviour, sir," he said. "I must protest most vehemently. If wrong has been done, then a complaint should have been raised with Holy Mother Church. For mob rule to take matters into its own hands is utterly reprehensible. It is wicked, sir."

Matthew, seemingly unrepentant, grinned. "No doubt, father. But we likes to protect our own in this part of the country. London looks after Londoners, and always will."

The abbot turned back to the priest, who remained huddled on the ground. "I am sorry to tell you, my son," he said with a gleam in his eye accentuated by the candle light, "I have received complaints about your behaviour by no lesser person than his holiness the Archbishop of Canterbury. I came here to reprimand you, and then consider whether I should replace you in this parish, and bring you back to the monastery with me. And now I find this. It is beyond – all precedent." He looked across again at Matthew. "Not that anything exonerates the crowd's behaviour but – and I repeat, the circumstances are unimportant considering what I have heard from the Archbishop – once your replacement arrives, you'll accompany me back to Gloucestershire. Tomorrow I shall take Mass here myself and preach a short sermon. For the moment, at least cover your shame, my son."

They had already left, wandering back into the shadows, down to the little boats, crowding in for the journey back downriver. Past curfew and the gates locked, only the river offered the way home. There was more whispering than shouting now, a little giggling and some muffled cheers, and the howling wind made more noise than the crowd. But Joan was pleased and hugged her delight to herself.

CHAPTER THIRTY-NINE

"Come on, my boy. It's a fine bright Tuesday outside, and no doubt your lady friend's waiting." Godfrey Quyrril hauled the billowed eiderdown away from his nephew's naked shoulders, and stepped back quickly from any possible retaliation.

Alex woke, blinked, grinned, pushed his hair back from his eyes, and sat up. "The day of my trial, uncle?"

"The day of your release, my boy."

Alex raised an eyebrow. "Are you serious uncle? From what cause? From being proved innocent?"

"Good God, Alex my boy," said Godfrey Quyrril, sitting down heavily on the small chair. "Are you always this disbelieving? Let me tell you the warrants are repealed, investigations pending, the door's unlocked, and I'm here to escort you home. Get dressed, look lively, or are you grown so fond of this place you plan on staying longer?"

Alex was out of bed and hopping into his hose and gipon, fumbling with the laces, all thumbs. His shirt was filthy, his coat was stained, but he was fully dressed in an instant and tugging on his boots. "I don't know how you did it," he muttered, shirt collar askew around his chin, "but I bless you for it. Indeed, I'd kiss you except for knowing how rank my breath must smell."

His uncle smiled gently. "Really, my boy. You almost make me weep."

Alex stood, straightening his shoulders and his clothes. "An interesting prospect, uncle." He grinned, tucking a few small items into the empty purse at his belt, then striding forwards towards the door. "I'd offer you my kerchief, but remembering what it looked like when I last used it, I doubt you'd want to touch it."

"My dear nephew, I don't want to touch you." Godfrey Quyrril pushed open the door, which swung into the shadows beyond. "You must have climbed from the battlefield looking more civilized than that – but we'll soon have you ends to rights. Now, where's that wretched guard?"

"Lumbunt'll be sorry to see me go," said Alex, standing in the corridor, breathing deep. The stench was worse outside his own cell, but freedom always smelled sweet. "He's no doubt a violent bugger like everyone else who works here, but he was good enough to me."

At the tower house above the gateway entrance, Alex Quyrril ninth Baron Mornington, used his father's seal ring for the first time, pressing it into the soft wax melted beside his signature, then witnessed by his uncle and the Constable of Newgate. The doors were unlocked, he ran the narrow stone steps to the ground floor, looked up, and saw the sky.

The mounted groom and two waiting horses were snorting in the cold. Within minutes the party arrived at Cripplegate and pulled up in the Burton House stables. They were expected. Through the back courtyard, they entered the main hall where Elizabeth, giggling, took Alex into a hearty and breathless hug. Jenkins was smiling wide, others of the staff were peeping around doorways. The Lady Mary stood at a distance, smiling absently, hands clasped meekly before her. Stephen, Earl of Burton, was tugging at Alex's coat sleeves.

Alex, looking over Stephen's head, gazed at Elizabeth a moment. "Did you send word, Lizzie? To Kate, I mean. Does she know?"

Elizabeth nodded. "I sent a page very early this morning. The message should be delivered by now. I invited Katherine to come here as soon as convenient."

"Was it terrible?" insisted Stephen. "Do they torture people in Newgate? You don't smell very good, Alex. I wanted to go to your trial, but they said I couldn't. I mean, what use is it being an earl and they still won't let you do what you want? And now there isn't even going to be a trial."

Alex ruffled the small earl's carefully combed curls. "Wretched brat. I do apologise for there being no trial, I'll make it up to you some other way." A cup of hypocras was thrust into his hands, manchet, cheese and more wine was spread ready upon the table, and a huge fire crackled across the hearth. Alex went to stand close to the flames. It was the first time he had been truly warm for some days. His bones had felt deeply chilled, as if Newgate's freeze had entered his heart and lungs. "Six wretched days, seven foul nights and a few dismal hours," he said softly. "So little! It seemed a death sentence, and a year or more locked in that place."

"It was a death sentence," said Stephen with persistent logic. "Wasn't it?"

"I suppose you're regretting not witnessing my execution as much as you miss my trial."

Alex had eaten well and then bathed at considerable length, finally taking another suit of Merevale's clothes for dressing warm and clean, and was now alone, back in front of the fire with elbow to the mantle and foot to the grate, when he heard a small cough behind him and turned in a hurry.

Katherine ran into his embrace and he wrapped his arms tight around her and kissed the top of her hair.

She put her own arms around him too, snuggling to the cedar scented velvet of his doublet. "I've missed you so much, Alex," she said, voice muffled against him. "Nothing's the same without you beside me and – but well, never mind about that." She peeped up. "Have you told them? Have you asked?"

He shook his head, still holding her, still smiling possessively down at her in his arms. He tilted up her chin with one finger and leaning down, kissed her tentatively and very lightly on the lips. "No. I waited for you."

"You smell nice again, Alex," she said. "I probably don't. I ran all the way here, and got very – damp."

He chuckled and released her. "Then you'd better sit down before I squash you." He looked around and saw Tom grinning wide in the doorway and Joan beside him, patiently waiting. He strode over and took Joan's hands, thanking her for everything, insulted Tom, and turned back to Kate. "Then it's time to get started," he said.

It was over dinner, a feast to welcome Alex home and to impress the visitors, that the discussion began. Two courses and twelve dishes in each, then wafers, subtleties and hypocras, Reginald Psalter's best. Godfrey was set at the centre of the table and Alex to his side with Katherine beside him. Mary was quiet, Elizabeth loquacious. Stephen, allowed out from the nursery for the occasion, had two cushions placed on his chair and had to sit very still and not wriggle, although quite against his usual habit, in case they dislodged and toppled him off. Jenkins served but Godfrey carved the swan stuffed with raisins, pig's testicles minced with cinnamon, and crushed mustard grains, sage leaves and honey. Joan and Tom were also feasted, but in the kitchens, where the cook carved the smoked trout stuffed with herbed breadcrumbs, and ladled out the pottage.

"I should point out," Alex pointed out, though not pausing his eating for speech, "I've not been proved innocent of anything, except perhaps the murder of the Earl of Sheffield and the wilful abduction of his widow." He swallowed, and smiled at Katherine. "Fact is, my two cousins were slaughtered, and the murderer remains unknown. The Lord Mayor says he'll order another investigation, and we'll probably get that damned alderman back again soon, poking his nose under the stairs. But I'd sooner find out the truth myself first, and I'm in a better position to do so."

Mary looked up from her plate. She was dressed in black, and looked beautifully wan. "You must have done a lot of thinking in that dreadful place, Alex. So tell us. Who killed my dearest Danny?"

Alex refrained from mentioning that she was his principal suspect. "I thought a fair bit, yes," he said. "But it's amazing what lack of constructive sense a mind conjures up under those circumstances. I seemed to have spent more time in wishful thinking and childhood memories than in helpful insight." He smiled and remained carefully tactful. "But when I came downstairs and discovered Dan slumped over this table," he tapped the linen tablecloth where he sat, "the only other person present was you, my dear. You'd been sitting with him at dinner. How is it you saw nothing?"

Mary seemed unoffended, though she lowered her eyes and blushed a little. "I'll never forget – what was said. I was – angry, you see. I'll never forgive myself. The last words I said to him, the last words he ever heard from me - "

"Which were?" said Alex into the subsequent silence.

"Oh dear." Mary shook her head. "I told him – I told my dearest – to go to hell. I will never, never forgive myself." Alex sighed, and waited. Finally Mary spoke again. "We'd quarrelled, of course," she said. "Indeed, we quarrelled over you, Alex. You'd told us you wanted to attend Mel's funeral, and I told Danny you should not. I was cross with you, wondering - just perhaps – if you'd been responsible for Mel's death. I knew you hadn't really – but I guessed you blamed Danny, so I blamed you. It was all so silly. But Danny and I quarrelled about the funeral. He was a little resentful about Mel I believe, wondering – well – never mind about that. I don't need to tell you everything, and it's really nobody's business."

"So you'd quarrelled," nodded Alex. "And afterwards? You flounced out I suppose, and left Dan alone at the table."

"Until I was sorry about what I'd said, and came back, just a little while afterwards," Mary said, her voice now a whisper. "And found him – like that."

"But just only a few minutes later?" It was hard, even for himself, to remember how time might have passed in any particular place that day.

"I don't think it was long," Mary murmured. "I can't be sure. I went up to my chamber, washed my hands in the basin, checked my hair pins, and sat down a moment. Then I came back down. I heard nothing at all."

"And I was in the antechamber," Elizabeth said, sitting forwards. "Firstly with Alderman Roper, and then after he left I was there a moment or two on my own, thinking about all the wretchedness. I was sitting there when I heard poor Mary scream."

"It was sometime during those hours in this house, that I was poisoned," Alex said, looking around. Only Stephen stared back at him, eyes huge and startled. Alex, deciding not to complicate the discussion, continued. "But I'll leave my own problems, and Danny's death for a moment," he said. "There's something else, about Mel this time. It's something which my Lady Katherine discovered, and not me at all. About Mel, the night he died."

The Lady Katherine looked up. "Just that everyone assumed, when Alex carried his cousin's body, he got – forgive me – blood stains on the shoulder," she said with a hiccup. "Even Alex didn't realise, but then of course he was terribly upset, even if he was a clerk of the spicery."

This remark having confused the entire company, Alex said, "Dragon's blood, not Mel's blood." His uncle Godfrey nodded, reached for the custard tarts and then passed them on to Alex. The other faces around the table stared at Alex in frustrated surprise. "Cinnabar," he explained, mouth full of custard. "It's a mineral, comes from sulphur. Bought as a thick liquid, and has to be mixed with something else like water or wine. Very useful stuff, cinnabar. Used sparingly in food as a spice and for decorative colour, or in greater quantities as a poison. Quite efficient, I've heard. But most common of all, it's a fabric dye. A rich red, the colour of blood."

The stares around the table became fixed. Elizabeth whispered, "But you said Mel was found naked. How could such a strange thing be - ?"

Alex shook his head. "I can't be sure how," he said, wiping his mouth and fingers on the napkin over his shoulder. "I picked Mel up. His neck – well, the blood was crusted and dried. He must have been dead many hours, as I realised. But when I found the red stain afterwards, and it looked like blood, I didn't question it. Katherine did."

"I have a gown," Katherine said. "I wore it often, I thought it suited me you see, and I liked the colour. Red satin sleeves and skirts, and a train that I needed to hold up when I walked. But afterwards, I found my fingers all coloured red. The dye never set very well, and still wiped off after days, especially when it rained. The stain on Alex's livery was exactly the same."

Mary snorted, breaking the hush. "So, Alex got it from you. Or from some other female's gown. It has nothing to do with poor dear Merevale at all."

Alex frowned. "Whatever it was, it came from Mel that morning," he said. "I've no proof of that, but I'm telling you what I know. So what was Mel doing, stark naked, with dragon's blood on his neck?" He looked at his cousin. "Got any gowns dyed in cinnabar, have you coz? Then you'll know what I'm talking about."

"I daresay I have," the Lady Elizabeth sniffed, pushing her plate away. "I don't ask how my clothes are made. I haven't the slightest interest in tailoring and smelly dyes, and I certainly don't visit stinking vats. I've never heard of anything as bizarre as dragon's blood. It sounds perfectly horrid."

Godfrey Quyrril had leaned back in his large chair, wooden leg stretched before him, chin sunk in his collar. Now he sat forwards. "Most interesting," he said. "I've a doublet dyed in cinnabar myself," and he nodded apologetically to Katherine, "though dye set with alum so better preserved I believe madam, since it's not yet suffered from any particular discolouration." He looked up sharply, gazing over the table at the Lady Mary. "How about you, my dear?"

"As it happens, I do know," Mary said with a faint blush. "And I can tell you that my only good red gown is dyed with Kermes, not cinnabar. It's a far more beautiful colour. Shockingly expensive of course, but positively the best. You've heard of Kermes, I hope? I've no use for cinnabar satins, which are certainly inferior."

"This is nonsense," Elizabeth interrupted. "I won't be frowned at because I own a red dress! Besides, it's quite clear he was stained with his own doublet collar. Mel himself must have worn something dyed with the stuff the day before."

"He didn't," said Alex at once. "His clothes were strewn on the floor – as if," and he smiled at Mary, "he'd undressed in a hurry, and not cared about where they landed. They were green, his best, collar in sable, and a plain white linen shirt. But even if he had worn something dyed in cinnabar, I doubt a trace of the dye could have remained wet on his skin without being wiped off after all those hours. Certainly not enough to transfer to my shoulder."

"Well, we don't know, do we?" insisted Elizabeth. "I hope I'm no expert in spices and poisons, Alex. The whole thing's absurd."

"I've got cinnabar whatsits too," said Stephen suddenly from his place opposite Alex. "Nobody ever asks me anything, but I'm not stupid. I've heard of dragon's blood. My tutor told me, because I wanted to know if dragons were real. He says they're not, even though lions and elephants and unicorns are. He told me about volcanoes and sulphur and how you find dragon's blood. And my silk hose are dyed with cinnabar, and I know that too, because they used to be pink, and I didn't like pink, so mother got them dyed red for me after Nurse Cisssy darned them. They're red now, and it keeps coming off on my knees." He sank back a little on his cushions, the last custard tart crumbling between his fingers. "Nurse Cissy told me off for having red knees, but it isn't my fault. It's the dragons." He crammed the custard and remaining pastry into his mouth, and spoke through it. "But I can't see why Uncle Mel wanted red stuff on his neck."

"Nor do I, brat," smiled Alex, though looking directly at Elizabeth. "Nor do I, my dear."

Elizabeth was blushing the colour of cinnabar. "I cannot see it as being relevant," she insisted. "It's not even interesting. Gracious Alex, ever since you started kitchen duties, you've been fixated with spices. You're becoming positively eccentric."

"We need to concentrate on the facts," frowned the Lady Mary, putting down her spoon with emphasis. "There's too much conjecture and supposition. My husband was murdered. We need to find out where everyone was at that one terrible moment."

Alex shook his head. "We all have excuses. We were all somewhere else, though few of us can prove it. And where was the knife? It wasn't on the table when we discovered Danny. There should have been a bloody knife, and the murderer covered in blood too. His hands, his clothes. A trail of it perhaps. Did any of us look for that? Have the staff been asked about blood spots on the floor, leading somewhere in particular?" He sighed and looked around again. Only Stephen appeared animated. A dreary greyish daylight slunk from the long windows, giving a pallid blank expression to each face.

"And why the devil," said Alex, finally throwing down his napkin onto his empty platter, "was I poisoned?"

CHAPTER FORTY

"I've carried a lot more in this boat afore now," Matt said, "but it were dark. Last night fer instance. Nobody couldn't be seen. 'Tis still afternoon now and I'll be fined if they catches me. So keep the little lad's head down, if you will."

"If you get fined, Mister Flesher," said Katherine, looking with considerable doubt into the bottom of the small boat and its dirty trickle of slops, "I shall be glad to pay it."

"Don't worry," said Alex. "I'll sit on the urchin. He'll remain invisible."

Tom sniggered and crouched obediently low behind the painted gunwales. Joan sat on the bench beside Matt, taking the second oar. "Stop moaning," she objected, "and let's get going. Already gone three, it is, and I wants home to sort out everything with my Margery afore dark, and afore heading back to Cripplegate."

Katherine smiled. "I'm delighted you're going back to work for Elizabeth, Joan. I had thought you know, that if you wanted, you could come and live with me. Once I actually know where I'm going to live, of course."

"Good of you, lass," Joan nodded. "But I'm used to my Lady Elizabeth's ways, and it'll suit me, going back there. And her young lad, he's a fine little gentleman. I shall enjoy it there, never you mind, what with regular meals and good company. It were her father cast me off afore and never the lady herself, so we're right and ready for a new understanding. She wants me and needs me, she says. Well, that's always good to hear."

Matthew snorted. He had wrenched the second oar from Joan's grasp, and was now heaving them out midstream. "Wants and needs, eh?" he muttered into the wind. "And wot if there be others as wants and needs, just the same and more?"

"Well, they should hurry up and bloody say it then," Joan said. "Declare themselves perhaps, 'stead of hinting and poking around. Foolery it is, this scared to say ort, and I've no patience with it."

Alex grinned. "You may not be referring to me," he said. "But I'll keep that thought in mind." He sat close to Katherine, his arm around her waist, keeping her warm. She felt considerably safer than she had during her first boat trip. The strength of his body against hers was a reassurance which she knew she had missed, and would miss again, if it were taken away. He looked down at her, one hand holding her tight, the other pulling up her hood over her bonnet and tucking the little veil inside the wool so it wouldn't take the wind. She smiled, and put her head on his shoulder.

Tom sat at the prow, keeping low, and Joan, clambering over heads and hands, had settled herself beside him. Alex and Katherine sat amidships, cuddled on the wide passenger's bench. At the back Matt rowed with a steady rhythm, his breathing deep and loud. The waters, thrust back by the oars, swelled up around the boat. The tide was rising.

They had stopped talking, for the wind took their words. The beat of wood on water and the passage of the river muffled their voices, but the wind hurling straight up from the distant sea and wail of the great white birds were louder still. Rushing past them on either bank was the low sprawl of houses and the high stone of the wharves and guild halls, the wooden cranes now standing silent and idle, and the bobbing wooden piers, busy with folk waiting on taxi boats and hurrying to be first in the queue. The shops were closing, the markets long emptied, but the rising river was crowded.

"Tide's up. Reckon we'll be shooting the Bridge," Matt yelled over the wind's whistle and whine. "Heads down, and hang on."

London Bridge came huge across the horizon, diminishing the quays either side and the boats below. Only The Tower could be seen beyond, its massive stone and spreading turrets looming even higher into the threatening shadows of the clouds.

Around the base of each of the twenty pillars supporting the bridge, a wooden platform protected them from the water's aggressive tumble. Between these floating starlings the river swirled and raged, a high tide's fury at enclosure. Untamed, it rushed in thundering waves between the narrowed archways, creating surges of water the height of a man. The boat headed straight towards it.

Katherine stared ahead, unblinking and horrified. Now the river was louder than the wind and the wheeling wings above were silenced. Only the roaring waters thundered around them. Alex grabbed Katherine, shouting in her ear. "You're safe my love. Trust me. Trust Matt."

Joan was laughing. Tom peeped over the side, unsure whether to embrace fear or excitement. The boat tipped directly into the swelling rush. In seconds they were forced into blackness, the sudden freezing shadow between two pillars with the enormity of the Bridge over their heads blocking out light. In one great surge the waters swamped over the gunwales and soaked them all.

Then almost immediately the boat was through. Not crushed against the bridge supports, not hurled downstream, not dashed upon the banks or thrown upon the starlings. They were under and safely passed, and blinked into the sudden light, smiling as if the sun had come out.

Alex had been holding his hat and now shook it out, drops of water sparkling. Katherine hugged him with a huge release of breath. He brushed the water from her hood and her nose and leaned down and kissed her lightly on the mouth. "Not drowned, my sweet?"

"I thought I should be," she said, snuggling again against him.

Matthew twisted the boat to the left and pulled up at the little pier below the church wall, between the Galley Quay and the Bridge. Here unchallenged, the tide ran swift and strong. Matt tossed his rope, Joan leapt the side and looped the mooring over the bollard. The wooden steps above were part under water and slippery wet. Joan was quickly half up them and leaning down, holding out her hand. Tom hopped out and scampered up.

Alex helped Katherine to stand. "Can you do it, puss?" he asked her softly. "I'll carry you easily enough."

She shook her head. "I can do everything," she said, straightened her back, lifted her chin and lurched from the tipping boat onto the floating pier. Her legs were less steady than she had hoped and it seemed as though her knees had disappeared. Shooting the rapids beneath the Bridge had destroyed her bones entirely. She shook her head, took a deep breath, and climbed the wet steps. There was nothing to hang onto except the step above but she felt the warmth of Alex's body very close and steady behind her. He resisted the urge to hold her up, or even to look up her skirts though for a moment her hems were almost onto his nose. Then when they were finally up, he took her hand and grinned. "Well done, my love. Here we are nigh home, I'm free, we're together - and now life truly begins."

Margery had already lit the fire and the baby was asleep. Tom was sent to collect water for boiling and Joan sat downstairs to explain to her daughter what had happened. After the initial discussion, as Joan explained that she now intended living at the Burton House and working again as the Lady Elizabeth's personal waiting woman and maid, Matt stomped back home next door, with a promise to return shortly.

Alex poured the wine. Then he took his own cup and Katherine's hand, and led her upstairs. "We should leave them to their business," he said. "They've plenty to argue over, for now Joan'll leave the house to Margery, and Margery'll wonder whether it's large enough to start her own stewe, and I shall be left knowing the house I once bought is becoming a brothel. Hopefully that doesn't automatically make me a brothel keeper, since my reputation's already sadly diminished. Then Matt will come back after a suitable amount of ale taken for courage, and will ask Joan to marry him, and she will naturally accept, as long as it doesn't interfere with her working for Lizzie. Matt will agree, since he has no choice, and there'll be a suitable amount of rejoicing as they finish the last keg of wine. None of this is our business, and we'll leave them to it. Meanwhile, we, my sweet, should have our own private conversation upstairs."

"In the bedchamber, Alex?"

"I shall light lots of candles," he grinned, "and try and make it seem thoroughly respectable, as if every young man and his lady friend, and even brothers and sisters, might have an average and unremarkable conversation in the privacy of the only other room in the house. I can hardly invent a new chamber, my love. We will try and ignore the presence of the bed."

"It takes up the whole room," Katherine pointed out.

"We'll look right through it," Alex told her, "as if it had never been there."

Katherine giggled. "Proprieties again, Alex? Even though we've spent two nights together in that very bed?"

Alex raised an eyebrow. "So those aren't embarrassing memories you'd be glad to forget after all, my sweet?" She turned her head away then and did not answer.

Being impossible to ignore, it was the bed that Katherine sat on, having thrown off her soaked cloak and tugged off her boots. Alex, his wet coat across the balustrade and his own boots tumbled on the floor where he had kicked them, stood leaning against the window alcove. Three candles were lit and the small chamber flickered bright, while outside it had begun to rain. The rain pattered against the window, as if tapping for entrance. The room became cheerful though the corners remained in their dust shrouded shadows, and the grimy smears over the little glass panes glowed strangely as the raindrops smothered their translucence and closed them in.

"I've things to tell you, my love," Alex said. "To tell you, but more importantly, to ask you." He watched her, sitting neat on the edge of the bed with her hands clasped in her lap. She had removed her damp headdress, and her brown curls were pinned only loosely, the ends of the ringlets uncoiling onto her shoulders. Her eyes looked dark and big in the candlelight. Alex smiled, inhaling deeply.

. "I know. You're going to ask me to marry you again." Katherine sighed and looked again at her lap. "I care – so much – and you –

you're so special somehow, Alex. My very special friend. I'd really like to say yes. You make me feel happy, and safe, and somehow more alive than I ever used to be. You know that already, I think. You've taught me about hope, and fun, and not having to be frightened, and looking forward to things. So I can't spoil it. If I married you, I'd spoil it. For both of us."

Alex stayed where he was, watching her, keeping his distance. "Nice words, my love. But you know, don't you, that if you keep refusing to marry me, I'll have to go away. I can't stay here. I won't live with Margery, and I won't let you live with her either." He saw her open her mouth to object, and interrupted. "For God's sake, Kate, she'll start her own stewe. Within a week of Joan leaving, she'll have three trollops working shifts in this very bed. How could I leave you here?"

Katherine shook her head. "I've got my own house. For the moment, anyway."

"And so have I." He frowned. "You'd like my place, Kate. It's no castle but it's grand, and large enough for half an army of servants. Not too many draughts and plenty of fireplaces. There's a forest, and a few farms, fish, deer, a river and views to the hills – and, oh, damnation Kate, at least I'm a baron now and for the first time in my entire life I've something to offer a woman."

She gulped. "As if that makes any difference, Alex. I'm pleased – so terribly pleased – for you. For how it's turned out." She stared resolutely at her fingers, tightly entwined. "I just hope you find out who killed your cousins – and then you can ride off – back to your estates – and live happily – and successfully for evermore – and all the local girls will want to marry you."

He gazed at her in silence for a moment. Finally he said, "Before Newgate, I was sure I'd talk you round. I believed I knew why you turned me down, and thought I could prove – but I'm not sure anymore. Perhaps Newgate's still inside me somewhere. It's broken some of my confidence. So I'll say this, Kate. Marry me. I promise not to be autocratic. I won't order you around anymore, or tell you what you shouldn't do. Damnation, I'll even have a suit of boy's clothes tailored for you, in decent fabrics, so you don't have to steal Tom's. I'll take you hunting in the forests. Teach you falconry. Whatever you want." He paused, trying to watch her expressions. She blinked but did not answer, so he said, "I'll try and stop swearing, if it helps. Good intentions sometimes get forgotten, and I can't promise to keep it up forever, but I'll try." He paused again, then said, very softly, "And I'd not force myself on you, Kate, if that's what's worrying you."

She looked up at him then and her eyes seemed suspiciously moist. "I so very much wanted us to be happy, Alex, with you coming home and everything wonderful again. I thought I was getting my special friend back, and I was going to try so hard to make it lovely for you." She sniffed. "But now you're saying, if I don't marry you, you'll go away. I'll never see you again. It's like a – a threat."

He came over abruptly and sat beside her on the bed, clasping her hands in his. He smiled down at her, rubbing her fingers, speaking softly. "I have to go, my love. I've no choice. If I take the title, then I must do it service. It's my duty, and a responsibility to the people on the estates, and the staff, and my uncle and his family. I have to go home, for the first year at the very least. So come with me." She stayed silent, still staring down, so he put one finger under her chin and tilted her face up to look at him. He kissed her, very lightly, on the tip of her nose. "Silly little love," he said. "Whether or not you agree to marry me, I'll try very hard to look after you. I'll make sure nothing hurts you. But if you insist on staying single, it might be a lot harder." He sighed. "You've been too much in my company, Kate, and too many people know of it. There's even the original warrant accusing me of abduction. That means only one thing in most people's minds, and with the warrant repealed, the suspicion doesn't die. In fact, your presumed agreement to abduction just makes it worse. If you don't want to live with me, then I'll have to think of something else to protect your reputation."

She stared at him. "Alex, you're mad. I refuse to start worrying about silly reputations, and anyway, I'm a widow. Widows don't need reputations. I'm never getting married again, not to anyone, so I don't care if lots of horrid men think I'm virtuous or not. They can think what they like. And if you ever mention my wretched reputation again, I shall kick you."

He laughed. "But I can't promise to stop asking you to marry me," he said, "so kick away. When I first met you, you did your best to ruin my marriage prospects with a well-aimed kick if I remember rightly. And I do remember, my love. I remember every moment."

"It was easier then, when I just thought you were a poacher. Now life's got so horribly – complicated." She shook her head with a small sniff. "You worked in my kitchens before, Alex. Perhaps – just perhaps – I could come and work in yours. Then you could go on being my friend, and I wouldn't have to marry you, but we'd be able to be - "

He interrupted her. "Even you aren't that much of a pillicoot, my love. Either you marry me, or I'll find some other solution, though God knows what. But not on my estates, my sweet. That would be impossible and you know it." He lifted her face again, gazing into her eyes. "You want me as a friend. You want me close. Won't you risk marrying me? I'd never hurt you, Kate, I swear."

From downstairs the noise accelerated. Matt had returned, and was roaring out his good luck. Margery was drinking to the newly promised couple, and Matt began singing what words he could remember from a song becoming every minute more bawdy. Alex was fairly sure that quite soon his hostess would be hoping to make use of her own bed.

He sighed, gazing at Katherine. Although he had hold of her hands, she was sitting very rigid and straight and avoided looking into his eyes. Then he leaned closer and pulled her bodily into his embrace. He felt her spine relax a little as she put her head willingly on his shoulder, but she kept her fingers in her lap as he wrapped his own arms around her. He spoke very softly to her ear, where her curls tickled his cheek. "I'm so blazingly in love with you it's sending me mad," he said. "Not touching you, and wondering how the devil I'm going to convince you marriage needn't be so bad. That I'm not so bad." He took a deep breath. "I don't want to try and seduce you, Kate. I was hoping you might take me as I am. Trusting me. Maybe even – after that day when I kissed you – and got myself damned well arrested – I was hoping you might want me too. I know you don't like the idea of intimacy, but you like being kissed, which is part way there." He combed his fingers up through the back of her hair, clasping her head against him. He could hear her sniffing into his velvets, and held her closer. "Can you at least tell me why, my sweet? Is it me? Or what Edmund did or said? Or something else entirely?"

She pulled away suddenly and reached for her wine cup, still full. "It's something I'll never talk about, Alex," she said. "Even to you. Especially to you. You'll just have to go on thinking I'm stupid, and I suppose I am, but I'm not being stupid about this. As for trying to convince me, you don't seem to realise you wouldn't want me, and if I said yes, it'd spoil everything and we couldn't even be friends anymore. Saying no is right for both of us, Alex. Please don't ask me again."

There were heavy footsteps on the stairs, the creaking of the first two steps, the sound of the baby crying, then muffled, Tom laughing, a bump as if someone fell over, then Joan calling, "Are you folks decent up there, lass? For it's warmer down here, and I've right good news to share, and a cup to offer in celebration."

Alex stood with a shrug, tugging on his wet boots again and passing Katherine hers. She had started to answer when there was another bang vibrating from the floorboards up through the walls, and a rattle of the wind and rain at the door. Tom's voice shouted in sudden alarm, Matt, drunken and confused, "What the fuck's that?" and then Margery shrieking. Katherine spilled her wine all over her lap, and Alex grabbed her and dragged her up, his arm tight around her. He had smelled fire. ·

He pulled her towards the stairs and a sudden billow of flame surged up scarlet into their faces. Katherine lurched backwards. Alex grabbed his wet coat from the balustrade and threw it over her head. He lifted her, hauling her up into one squirming parcel over his shoulder and ran with her down the stairs. Without stopping to look at anything else, he strode quickly to the door, kicked it open, and almost threw her out. She pulled off the wet fur from her head and stood shaky and gasping in the dancing puddles, soaked and frightened. "Stay here," he ordered, ducked his head and ran back inside. Biting her lip and blinking, she tried to follow him. Then, shoved back out again, Joan, holding the baby, rushed past her, then Tom with his hair sooty and scorched, then Alex again, with Margery

375

half unconscious tucked tight under his arm. Finally Matt emerged, staggering and bewildered. The flames stormed behind, shooting from the lower to the upper floor, swirling in huge circles, discovering their own path through the limited space, forcing their way beyond. The heat ate across the wooden beams like little blistered crackling teeth, until the wood crumbled and splintered, giving way. There was the sound of cracking windows and a huge roar as the fire found air up through the roof.

The rain pelted downwards, slanting silver against the deep twilit sky. Rain and fire met, sizzled, and the fire moved on. The roof was part tile, part thatch, and the thatch exploded into bursting, spiralling scarlet and gold.

People running, calling, screaming. Alex pushing Katherine back further away, then racing up the lane towards the conduit tap where the local fire bucket hung, Tom behind, Matt finding his feet and coming last. Joan was slapping Margery's face, trying to keep her conscious, only moving her deeper into hysteria. The baby was squalling. Katherine leaned back panting against the house opposite, then ran forward and took the baby. It wriggled, big and fat and furiously terrified and never having held a baby before, Katherine gripped it too tightly, frightened to drop it. Alex came back, a stream of men with buckets sloshing water, someone with a grappling hook, and the whole alleyway was rolling, rushing, screeching, and all ablaze.

A hazy twilight slunk shamed to night and the rain turned to sleet.

CHAPTER FORTY-ONE

U p Draff Alley into Pudding Lane, across to Lovat Lane and into the first shadows of Eastcheap, the fire left its stench and its debris. Twelve houses were destroyed as the flames leapt, quickly catching wood and plaster and lathe. Some would be restored in time. Others were only smoking holes with a crumble of falling blackened beams. Joan Hambury's home no longer existed.

Once Margery had recovered sufficiently to sit forlorn and barely coherent in the adjacent gutter, Katherine had passed the baby into her lap and run after Alex, collecting water and tossing it into the tumult. Joan, having quickly abandoned her daughter, fought alongside the men, trying to save her belongings. Matthew, just half a blink to sober, was immediately able bodied and struggling into the midst of the chaos. His own home, next door to Joan's, fell in the same devastation. To him it mattered less, for he had occupied just one room, already sublet by the couple who occupied two others. The four storey structure had towered over Joan's two storey tenement, its shingled roof shading hers, and had housed twelve separate working men and two families. Its desolation left nineteen people homeless.

Alex had been barely visible throughout, first leading the lines from conduit to alley, then taking one of the grappling hooks, pulling down burning thatch, smashing into walls, creating an opening wide enough to force the fire's pause and slow its passage.

The cries of 'Fire' echoed through the alleys and the crowds had come. Every nearby street was in danger from any furnace uncontrolled. To save their own homes, a hundred jumped up from their own cosy firesides, left their suppers and came running. A conduit tap within reach and the river as close, a hundred buckets, water butts and a heave of panic and urgency.

But it was the rain which had finally doused the flames. A freeze of pouring ice filled the sky, pelting relentlessly down against the heat below. Nature won. The fire became damp smoke, a spit of fizzling scarlet slumped below embers and covered in soot. The wet smoke stank. The people heaved relief and, with advice and offers of help to those now homeless and ruined, returned content to their standing, solid houses.

From the smoke haze, Alex had reappeared black streaked, half soot half washed in rain. Exhausted and depressed, he slumped to the wall next to Katherine, taking her hands. His own were painful and raw and extremely filthy. It was some time before he said anything at all.

Joan had many friends. They pushed around her, offering places to stay, bringing tankards of ale and smiles of sympathy. She was biting back tears but too tired to resist wretchedness for long. When she cried, it was leaning against Matt's half burned shirt, both his arms around her. Together they accepted help and a room in a friend's house nearby.

Margery had fallen asleep, the infant peaceful in a slack embrace. Joan kicked her. "Wake up. Pissed fucking slattern you are. We've a place to squat for tonight at least."

Margery grunted and rolled over, squashing the child. Matt and Joan disentangled her, hauling her to her feet. Joan approached Alex and Katherine. Alex had still not spoken. "I've friends and plenty around here," Joan said, wiping her face and her nose on her sooty fingers and her sootier apron. "They've beds enough to offer, if you'll take them. Maybe not pretty, nor clean, nor feather. Damp p'raps and the odd bug. But ready ale and a warm dip for sleeping."

Alex roused himself, as if he had been lost in dreams. "No." He smiled. "Thank you, but no. I'll go to a hostelry. Not because I give a damn whether a bed's clean or aired, and when it's kindly given it's worth far more. But I need to bathe, then sleep for a week, and first talk to my girl in private. I'll come back to find you tomorrow, if you've need of me."

Joan shook her head. "Tomorrow I'll go to the Lady Elizabeth. My Margery has friends of her own as well as making use of mine, and she and the little lad will be taken care of. When she's sane and sober again, I'll be telling her you saved her life."

Alex smiled. "She saved mine too, remember? I wish her well, whatever she decides to do with her life. Tell her maybe herbs and doctoring could be as profitable as prostitution."

"Ah, well." Joan frowned. "We all does what we does and that's as well as any of us can. What my lass has chosen, soon there'll be more the same since the new king's taxes brought in. It'll not be as easy; life under the Tudors. But we'll make do."

Katherine said, "And you're marrying Matt?"

"I am. T'was that as started the fucking fire, and I'll not celebrate again in a hurry. I'm content with the thought of a husband again, and a new job. I managed to save a few of my things. But I'm mighty sorry about the house."

"It served its purpose," said Alex. "I'll maybe buy Matthew a tilt boat instead."

Tom had made friends with the other children, all come out to watch the amazing flames and to dance in the heat. Now they slunk away, drenched and cold once more. Tom came back to Katherine. "Well lady, like I said, one adventure after the other."

Katherine sighed. "I wish it wasn't such a long walk to The Strand," she said. "And it must be near time for the gates to close. Or should I trudge up to Cripplegate? It's one or the other. I've nowhere else."

"I could go with Joan," Tom suggested. "She won't mind. Reckon there's thirty folks or forty I've talked to tonight, all offering beds."

Katherine hesitated but Alex interrupted. "Let him go," he told her. "We can pick him up again in the morning. No doubt you'll accuse me of being autocratic again, but I'm taking you to an inn for tonight, my love, and the brat would only be in the way. He's not much use as a chaperone, only as a damned infernal nuisance."

Katherine blinked. "At an inn? Together? No proprieties?"

Alex smiled. "I'm tired out, I've had enough of disasters, and neither of us really gives a damn about reputations. The hostelries close by will surely know about the fire. They'll understand the rest from the state of us, and make allowance. We both need baths, we both need food, and we both need rest. A decent inn is the only place to satisfy all that. Two separate rooms, my love, and let's hope no one recognises us."

"But you've lost all your other clothes, and I have too. What I took from the Strand house. Everything!"

"But I still have a full purse on my belt, and for the moment, that's all I care about," said Alex. "Will you come, my love?"

With his arm around her waist and after brief goodbyes to everyone, they walked down through the destruction and debris, wet embers still flying in the sudden wind gusts, down the sloping lane towards the river. The rain continued to pour and the darkness was now complete.

Then the lights, swimming up in pools from the drenched blackness, seemed magical. The shadows of the Bridge became a second roof and stretched below, with its plastered stone walls and wide open doors, The White Duck clung, determined, to the river bank. It catered mostly for Canterbury bound pilgrims who failed to make their way out of London before the Bridge closed at night, or alternatively for those staggering back blistered and exhausted, without the energy to travel further. Having been cleansed of their sins most were eager for food, for drink, and to start sinning again.

The inn keeper knew about the fire, which had been close enough to smell, and close enough to fear. "Two clean rooms," Alex said, elbows on the high bench where two cups of burgundy had been set. "And privacy for both of us. No communal chambers, nor intention of admitting anymore travellers once we're asleep."

"After what you folks 'ave bin through," sympathised the innkeeper, "I'll make sure you're not disturbed, my lord. And a late supper first is it? And hot bricks in the beds?"

"Indeed." Alex nodded. "And hot baths each too, with fires lit first. You might think we'd have had enough of fire, but it's too damned cold to be hopping from bath to bed, and a cosy hearth brings a good night's sleep."

They took their supper together in the private solar while the two baths were hauled upstairs and filled. A steady stream of maids, scullions and pot boys up and down stairs with buckets, and the faint smell of steam and herbs, echoed into the parlour. Alex sat, foot up on the half keg beside him, and watched Katherine eat. She had smuts on her nose and her eyes were crimson veined, sore from the flames. She kept her head down, aware of his scrutiny, and suddenly shy. Alex said very little.

It was when he left her at the door of her chamber that he finally spoke, his hands gentle on her shoulders. "Sleep sweet, my love," he murmured. "Since you won't take me in marriage, I shall try and understand. And you'll never lose my friendship. The offer to wed remains though, should you ever wish to reconsider. And the offer to try and overcome whatever it is that frightens you so. In the meantime, don't fall asleep in the tub. I'll see you in the morning, and not too early."

He kissed her forehead, where the little sooty marks rose up into her hairline. She tried to give him back his own fur lined coat, still damp, which he had put around her when the fire started, but he refused to take it. "You've no cloak anymore, keep mine," he said, and turned away into the long shadows of the corridor, entering the adjacent chamber and closing the door behind him.

Katherine took her candle and went into her own room, where the half barrel bath tub stood steaming in front of a small fire. She sighed, set down her candle and began to undress.

In the chamber next door, Alex was doing much the same. He kicked the fire into life, flung his filthy scorched clothes to a heap beside the bed, and climbed into the hot water. It enclosed him to the waist. He bent his knees further and immersed himself to his shoulders. The physical relief was immediate and enormous, and he closed his eyes with a deep sigh. He remained there for a very long time.

There was good quality Spanish soap and a large sponge, and until the water began to sink into sluggish and putrid ripples, black with fire-ash and flakes of soot, he did little else but soak, quieting his mind and thinking only of release. But eventually the water was nudging tepid and reluctantly he climbed back out and dried himself briskly by the high hot flames within the grate.

He regarded his hands, holding them ruefully to the firelight. They were scarred and stripped of skin and flesh across the palms, raw meat in patches, and painful. He had no salve, so dried them carefully, watching as the small blood beads rose from the open wounds. He smiled and shook his head. All the world seemed absurd, from Newgate's miseries to the wretchedness of an everyday life. And there would not, it seemed, be any salve for that either, since what he wanted, so very much, and had expected to win, seemed as far distant as ever.

A borrowed robe lay over the bed, the innkeeper's best perhaps since he'd recognised nobility in the figure of his scorched and blackened guest. Alex shrugged it on. A little short, a little wide, but serviceable blue broadcloth lined in felted wool, and laced in stout red cord. He stretched on the bed, propped up by pillows and bolster, and stared at the shuttered window and the shiver of candlelight.

The light knock on the door surprised him.

Alex stared a moment, then called to enter. He was additionally surprised when Katherine peeped, nose and damp curls only, around the crack of the opening door. He sat up at once and swung his legs to the ground, carefully wrapping the folds of the bedrobe around himself. "Kate, what's the matter?" he said softly. "Come in quick, before you catch cold."

She also wore a borrowed bedrobe, a solid affair in apple green wool with a high fox collar, far too large for her. She tripped over it, already blushing. "I shouldn't be here," she whispered. "But you said it didn't matter tonight about the proprieties. Though – well, nothing's actually the matter. Are you cross?"

"The proprieties never serve a damn between us, my sweet," he said, coming over to her and leading her into the room. There was a small uncushioned settle beside the hearth, and he pulled it closer to the warmth and sat her there. "It's only other people knowing that spoils things," he grinned. "Which is why you can share my bed, and prance around in doublet and hose, and I'll certainly make no objections. As for being cross, most definitely not, and never will be. I'm simply pleased to see you."

Her cheeks, pink scrubbed, glowed in the firelight and her blushes were part hidden. She sat with her knees self-consciously tight, looking with concentrated resolution at her bare toes, peeping beneath the heavy green wool. "I couldn't sleep," she said, small voiced. "I got more and more upset, the more I thought about things. The fire, and the panic and fear, and everything that happened before that - I didn't want to think at all, but I couldn't help it. I just wanted, more and more – to talk to you." She looked up then, with a small sniff. "I didn't wake you up, did I?"

Alex leaned against the side of the wooden bath tub, its copper hoops reflecting the firelight. He looked down at Katherine, wondering, somewhat reluctantly, whether she was wearing anything beneath the monstrous green bedrobe. He decided almost certainly not. "No, my love," he said. "I wasn't asleep, nor even properly in bed. So now tell me precisely what I can do for you."

Katherine looked back at her toes. "I want to say something," she mumbled, "but I want to explain it first. Before I say it, I mean. Does that sound too complicated?"

"I think I can cope with that," he smiled. "Even at this hour of night."

"If it gets tedious," she continued, "you have to tell me, and I'll stop. You see, it's difficult for me to explain. In fact, it's probably the hardest thing I've ever had to do. Except for marrying him, of course."

"In that case," Alex said, "you had better have a little help." The jug of burgundy stood on the small table beside the bed, and he filled a cup and brought it to her. "Now, my love?"

She took a sip, lowered her eyes and addressed the cup, beginning at full speed. "They warn you, you see. For years, over and over. Without ever explaining properly so you don't actually understand a thing, just glowering and warning. Fathers and mean old widowed aunts and the steward's wife and once even the lady brewer at the house. They warn you to be good, and how you have to be good, because of dire consequences. First of all they tell you how painful it all is. Then they say babies just happen - and if you're not married, you have to be banished or locked away in shame and your life might as well be over. They don't explain if it's any better if you are married, because after all, my mother died in childbirth, and so do half the women in England. So I don't ever want children, and you would, because you're a baron and you have to have an heir and all men want sons. They wouldn't, if they had to have them themselves. But they just sit in their halls and get drunk and the midwife comes down and says, You have a healthy son, my lord, and then they can get even more drunk. So men like to have lots of children and feel virile. But I don't. So you wouldn't want me as a wife."

Alex opened his mouth, but Katherine blinked fast and took another deep breath. "Not yet," she said. "I haven't finished." She avoided his gaze. "Edmund was – I mean, I have to be fair, he wasn't as bad as he might have been. I wasn't exactly expecting much better, so at least he didn't come as a shock. And after all, he didn't beat me, which I know lots of husbands do. He just wanted to do what men are supposed to want to do, so I can hardly blame him. And I suppose I shouldn't have hit him with the chamber pot, since my father kept telling me how I had to obey my husband in everything and be like some sort of pathetic polite cowering slave." She paused. "I expect that's what he expected," she said. "He must have been as disappointed in me as I was in him."

"Too pissed to notice most of the time I imagine," suggested Alex helpfully.

She smiled. "And that was so nice of you Alex, to do that for me. When I didn't even explain why, and you hardly knew me anyway. You put yourself at risk, and it got you into so much trouble afterwards, and you never asked anything in exchange. You even saved me from that drunken lout at Joan's, when he – that is – just another horrid man wanting what men always want – and you were sick but you still rescued me. And that's why I can't bear the thought of losing you."

Alex grinned. "Simply because I'm useful? A dog that barks at the right moments, perhaps."

"You know what I mean." She sighed. "So I have to explain first, why you really, really wouldn't want me. Because of not having babies, and not wanting to – do things. I mean, it's really nice going to bed and cuddling. And kissing is – well, I thought that was lovely. Edmund never kissed me. Perhaps he didn't know how, but he never even tried. Nobody ever kissed me before, though the swineherd tried once when I was nine. I slapped him and he ran away. But you do it – extremely well. So kissing is nice. But nothing more – degrading." She looked up at him then, still blushing and wide eyed with the slow damp of welling tears against her lashes. "But you said – before the fire – that you wouldn't ever – force yourself on me. Which was awfully thoughtful of you. And I'd promise never to hit you with the chamber pot. Or anything else either. And I'd try and be obedient like women are supposed to be, though I'm afraid I might not be awfully good at that. Like you still swearing. And like embroidery. I'm not good at that either, however much Sara tried to teach me. My stitches are terrible. And if we both tried to stay friends, without being disappointed in each other, and I wouldn't make any demands at all – if you didn't. Or at least – nothing too – horrible. Though I suppose you think I'm awfully cowardly, but I'm not a coward about most things. I'm very good at climbing trees and when I fell out, when I was only four, I didn't even cry."

The truth was dawning only slowly. Alex said, "My dearest love - "

She interrupted him, now trying absently to unpick the knot of cord in her lap, glaring at it furiously. "So, if I haven't put you off. I mean, can men go for ages without doing those horrid things? But if you haven't changed your mind, and I'd absolutely understand if you have, and – only if you're absolutely sure. Then I will."

CHAPTER FORTY-TWO

A lex paused. The fire was spitting low, the one candle had become a guttering stub and the shadows were creeping around them. Katherine remained quite still, staring resolutely at the tangled cords between her fingers. The chill had increased. Alex came beside her, bending one knee to the Turkey rug and taking her small cold hands in his.

"This is only a guess," he said softly, "but am I right in thinking that you're now accepting my proposal?"

"I didn't do it very well, did I?" She looked up at him, peeping through her tumbled curls. "But I can't bear the thought of losing you, Alex. I was just lying there in bed, tossing around and going mad thinking. I needed you so much, to talk to, to cuddle up with, all warm and cosy and safe. If you go away, I shall be so desperately miserable again. I hate the thought of going back to my father and I can't stay in Edmund's house. Is that a terrible reason for wanting to marry someone? But without you being close and kind and fun, life just wouldn't be worth living. But if you marry me, and I turn out to be cold and horrid and don't want children, will you hate me anyway? I'm so bad at everything my father says a wife ought to be good at. And especially – well, you know. Would getting married spoil everything? But if we don't get married, everything will be spoiled even quicker, because you'll go away."

He sat beside her and took her into his arms, nestling her beneath his chin, one hand cradling her head, the other smoothing the curve of her back. His voice was a murmur to the top of her hair, and she curled willingly close. "Listen, my love," he said. "I'll take your acceptance, because I might not get another chance. I want you, sufficiently to take you under any circumstances. But you must understand two things. You don't have to marry me. To agree to a wedding only because the alternative sounds even worse, isn't the best reason for a love match. But I have to go back to Mornington, otherwise I'm damned sure I wouldn't do it, knowing I'd hurt you by going. And hopefully the very fact that you want me close, and seem to enjoy being in my arms, is reason enough to hope for some happiness."

She had wriggled tighter into his arms. "Did I sound so begrudging, Alex? I didn't mean to. I'd love to be your wife, truly I would. I really want to live with you. I can't imagine anything nicer than having you near me all the time, and waking up with you, and when I go to sleep, you being the last thing I see. Having you to laugh with, and comfort me, and talk to. Having you close makes the world safe, and I look up and the smile in your eyes is always there. It's just being frightened you'll go off me because I'm so – that is - what I explained. That you'll regret asking me to marry you after all. That you'll be so sorry having no children, and start to – you know what I mean."

"I do." He smiled, then lifted her a little, tucking one arm beneath her knees. "Listen, my love. It's cold here, with the fire nearly out and the dirty bath water under our noses. I'm going to carry you to bed. Don't be alarmed, I've no intention of molesting you. I just think we need to talk a little more, and be warm and comfortable while we're about it."

She put her arm around his neck and he carried her over to the huge shadowed bed, propped her up a little against the pillows and snuggled her beneath the eiderdown. Then he sat beside her, stretching out his legs, with a respectable cocoon of bedding between them, her warm beneath the feathers and him on top. He then eased his arm behind her and took her head again against his. She curled up trustingly and closed her eyes. "Can I stay here tonight, Alex? Or would that be terribly wrong?"

"Yes, you can, and yes it would," Alex said. "But never mind about that. I need answers." But instead of speaking further, he leaned over, tilting up her face with his finger beneath her chin, and kissed her.

He felt her yield at once. She opened her lips and for the first time he was aware that she kissed him back, her desire almost matching his own. It was the answer he needed. He felt the heat, the push of her tongue under his, and the curves of her breasts swelling beneath her bedrobe. He smelled soap and fresh clean skin, the damp curls loose around her head, and the faint distance of the herbs from her bath water. He tasted the heat in her mouth and he sighed, releasing her a little. She snuggled her head back on his shoulder. "I never realised," she murmured to his neck, "that kissing would be so – special. Perhaps you just do it terribly well. You're even clever about not bumping noses. You make me tingle – in all sorts of odd places."

"Really?" said Alex with sudden interest. "Where, for instance?"

She chuckled. "Oh, I can't answer that." A sudden thought distracted her. She sat forward a little. "You can't – make babies – just by kissing, can you Alex?"

Alex paused, momentarily stunned. "No, my sweet. I promise." He clasped her back against him. "You sound very like Lizzie's son, but he's eight years old. Did nobody ever explain anything to you before you got married? Did you have no idea what to expect?"

"No, nothing." Then realising she might sound shamefully silly, Katherine shook her head. "But you mustn't imagine I'm stupid, Alex. I mean, naturally I'd never seen a man naked or anything before I was married, but I knew they were different."

"An advantage, no doubt," smiled Alex, keeping a tight hold on her in case of retaliation or attempted escape. "Though for someone who didn't know what balls are, you certainly tried hard enough to kick me in them the first time I met you."

She snorted. "Since men urinate all over the place, I do know about that. They've no shame at all. In the fields. In the streets. So I can't be totally ignorant, can I?"

"Certainly not, my love. Far from it."

"You're humouring me, Alex." Katherine smiled, looking up at him and seeing the proof of his own smiles in the lift of his jaw line. "I suppose I am horribly ignorant. I mean, I didn't even know boy babies started off already – equipped. I thought men sprouted those odd things later on. And as for - but wasn't it the same for you?" she said. "You couldn't have known what to expect – before – that is, until you did."

He laughed. "I confess boys tend to compare notes, it's a matter of interest from a very young age and discussions are more open – more frank. More bravado. But ignorance, before the fact, is always inevitable, my love." He paused, reluctant to lead her back into timidity. Then he said, very softly, "Did he hurt you, little one? So much? Your absurd husband?"

She lost her smiles and took a long time to answer. Finally she said, "I don't think he meant to. He did, but not so badly, though I had bruises for ages. Little yellow finger marks where he – squeezed – so very hard." She had curled tight to his chest, avoiding his watchfulness. "But perhaps not as much as I expected," she murmured. "They warn you, you know, telling you the first time's so terrible. And it wasn't. Although – maybe – I hit him before it could get any worse."

Alex sighed. "Your relatives – perhaps every young woman's relatives – have a lot to answer for, my love. But you had no mother, and a beetlehead for a nurse, and then just a jumble of country bumpkins around you – and whether now might not conceivably be considered a sensible moment to broach such a subject – but I imagine this story of first night torture is just a ruse to stop young girls from experimenting. There's no agony and nothing dreadful, I promise."

Katherine sniffed into his bedrobe. "That's easy for you to say, Alex," she objected. "You're not a girl. And boys don't. Do they?"

He smiled. "No, they don't. All they usually suffer the first time is the abject terror of making complete fools of themselves."

"I can't ever imagine you making a fool of yourself Alex," she sighed. "Or being frightened of anything at all." Her voice was becoming sleepy, a little soft drift of mumbled words. "But none of this matters anymore, does it? Do you mind? I mean, could you still put up with me, like this? Are you sure you'd sooner not marry me after all?"

He kissed the top of her hair. "I want to marry you, my sweet, whatever the conditions. I now consider us promised. As for everything else – well, let's see what sense we can make of each other another day. When you're less worn out."

"I am tired, Alex, awfully tired." Her head had become heavy, her hold around his waist had slackened, her voice almost lost in the shadows. The one candle stub had guttered but a faint pinkish glow still hung hazy within the hearth. "And it's – incredible – to think you slept last night in – prison. So much has happened. And then the fire."

It had been a long day indeed. He had not forgotten Newgate, but the memory seemed a year past. This would be an equally challenging night, he thought, though far more pleasant. The other two nights he had spent with Katherine in his bed, he had been ill and very weak. This time, though exhausted, the touch of her was vibrant against him. Bedrobes over nakedness tended to fall open, and he did not trust himself to enter the bed with her. So he stayed on top of the eiderdown, pulling the edges back over himself. He kissed her briefly against the slight flutter of her eyelashes. "Goodnight, my love. Remember, in your dreams, that now we're promised in marriage. And tomorrow I'll speak of it again, and explain matters a little more."

He woke once in the night. There was no more colour in the grate and the room was black and chill. A steady draught hissed beneath the door, another sneaked through the window shutters. He was bitterly cold, his bare feet trapped forward from the tangle of the bedrobe, far too short, and impossible now to rewrap without waking Katherine.

She slept deeply, her back to him, her nose only just visible above the eiderdown. Alex rose quietly from the bed, sliding one leg at a time to stop the mattress swinging. Then he stood a moment, looking down on the bed and the figure curled within it. He folded his robe as tightly as he might around himself, and with a fervent prayer, climbed properly under the blankets, curving his body to the back of Katherine's. The heat infused through his bones at once, like a long hot drink, Reginald Psalter's best hypocras perhaps, and utterly sweet. His feet tingled as the blood circulated back and warmed his toes. He tucked them deep beneath the eiderdown's feathers. Then, once again half asleep, he curled his arm around his future wife, and held her close.

She was still in his arms when they both awoke, with the sounds of the busy hostelry, the creaking of the stairs outside, the clink of pans, the horses fretful outside and the calls for the ostler. Katherine nuzzled his neck, murmuring her good mornings.

He smiled down at her. "This is what's so nice, Alex," she whispered. "Waking up all snuggled like this. You were in my dreams, and now I open my eyes, and there you are again." She blinked, as if to prove his reality. "Will it be exciting, being married, do you think?"

He laughed, bringing his own comprehension fully awake. "Perhaps. I've never tried it before. You should know, better than me. I hope for happiness, my love, for both of us. I'm not sure about excitement."

"Pooh." She wriggled upwards, tightening the cord of her robe. "As if being married to Edmund taught me anything at all. Just over a week as his wife, and except over the dinner table I only ever saw him a couple of times. Indeed, a couple of times too many."

Alex grinned up at her. He wondered vaguely if he might be committing himself to a bizarre existence where getting permanently pissed would in fact be his own solitary salvation, and the only way to cope with a wife who would not allow him to touch her. "It's true you were barely with him," he said, "and since there's to be no child of his," he paused a moment. "Perhaps, if the idea appeals to you, I could apply for a papal dispensation," he thought aloud, "and get your damned marriage annulled altogether."

"That would be lovely." She seemed to him deliciously fresh, as if she had woken with sunbeams. "I'd love to think I was never actually married to him at all."

And there was something else on his mind. "Getting dressed, in mourning or otherwise, will have its problems today. You've no wearable clothes of any kind, my sweet and nor have I. And were your earrings lost in the fire? I should go back to Draff Alley and kick through the dregs."

She had pulled the bright green wool up under her chin and now hopped out of bed, skipping over to the shaded window. She looked back at Alex as she stretched and heaved and finally lifted down the shutters, opening the room to the meagre day's light. "My mother's earrings? Fancy you noticing things like that. No, Matthew sold them for me. He bought beer for all his friends when they went off to intimidate that horrid Father Erkenwald. Money well spent. As for other clothes," she dumped the heavy slatted wood on the floor against the wall, and peered through the window. It was still raining. The light was diffused and greenish, but it was late and the sun had risen higher than the roof tops. The chamber, being a large back room, overlooked the city but the smell of the river seeped in through the plaster, the roof tiles and the window frames. "My cinnabar satin's all burned up," she said, coming back over to the bed, "and my lavender's badly scorched. Perhaps Elizabeth would have something to lend me."

Alex frowned, sitting up slowly. He felt scorched himself, and the aches of fire fighting seemed excruciating in the new challenge of a cold day. "Come back to bed, puss. Are you always so sprightly at first dawn?"

She curled on the edge of the mattress next to him and giggled and shook her head. "No. Never. It's you, Alex. Thinking I shall wake up next to you like this hundreds and hundreds of times from now on, until we both get old and rheumaticy." He opened his arms to her and she crawled into his open embrace, cuddling close. "I'm so – grateful," she whispered to his neck, "that you still want to marry me, Alex. Even after – you know – what I explained last night. I really, really, thought you wouldn't. I was sure you'd say you couldn't go without – that men have to - and I even expected you might be cross with me. You're such a nice, understanding person Alex. I'm so happy we're going to be married after all."

And Alex lay there for some time as the sun rose a little higher into the wet and mournful sky outside, with Katherine warm and trusting in his arms, wishing, wistfully, that he might slip his hands into the opening of her absurd bedrobe, his groin aching with wanting her, and feeling quite incredibly guilty.

They had breakfast brought up to them, porridge, "though not as nice as the porridge you make, Alex dear," manchet rolls and ale, still snuggled in bed and getting crumbs between the sheets. Their ruined clothes were sent down for mending and brushing with fuller's earth, their boots for cleaning, and an order for new hosiery to be brought from the market. The cold and murky bathwater was removed from their rooms and the fires lit high and warm in the hearths, while the rain continued to pound beyond the windows, and the chimney smoke turned to wet black billows outside, gushing back down with a stench reminiscent of yesterday's fire.

When their clothes were returned to them, not miraculously in perfect condition but certainly wearable, Katherine returned to her own chamber to dress and a maid servant was sent to help her pin up her hair. They met up again downstairs in the parlour for a light dinner, and to decide what steps to take next.

"Pick up your brat of a page first I suppose," Alex said, setting down his beer tankard. "Then I should take you back to The Strand." She shook her head, but he smiled. "No, don't worry, I won't leave you there. That would be far too sensible and respectable a solution. But you can pack up your belongings and get the rest of your clothes at least. Strictly speaking, were I intelligent which obviously I'm not, I should go up to Westminster and find out exactly what's happening to the earldom. Find out exactly what pension you have due, and what rights to the house and furnishings." He frowned. "Perhaps my uncle would condescend to look into it. I want no truck with this wretched king if I can help it, and I'd do well not to remind him I'm still alive."

"Well, I admit it'd be a shame," Katherine said, "if you got attainted now, after all this time. But if you did, we could live in a cottage somewhere, and keep chickens and grow cabbages. I don't know how to cook, but you do and you could teach me. It might be fun."

"Idiot," said Alex fondly. "After those few days at Joan's house, you've collected some naive idea of living in simple poverty surrounded by friends. But if you think being destitute is cosy, then I can tell you you're wrong. I intend carrying you off to my comfortable and pleasantly wealthy estates and living in unattainted luxury, with good staff, decent meals, warm beds and large fires. All the things the poor bloody peasants can't do but wish they could."

"Do you have friends too, Alex?" said Katherine hopefully.

He laughed. "Lord yes. For what they're worth. There's the Watchetts, their estates border mine over north. The Pooles and the Rastells, both successful merchants with great tales to tell of foreign lands, talking late into the evening over burgundy, with the candles burning low. There's some second and third cousins on the Talbot side, but most of them live around Herefordshire. You'd probably like Lady Mayneflete, she's a widow and has a parcel of brats. Lives nearby and gives grand parties, collecting allies for the brats' futures. And the Fabyans, and Mayor Sondle if he's still alive, and – oh, the list goes on. Some are more intimate and some more distant, but there's a certain loyalty around Mornington, both to my old man and to John. To me too, I hope." He stopped abruptly, looking into his cup. "My best friend all my life was Mel," he said softly. Then he looked up and smiled again. "And now it's you, my love."

Tom was collected, and an offer of taking Matt's boat as far as The Strand was refused. He was working out on the river, a dismal day for the wind biting up the Thames from the winter sea and a soaking from the rain, for Matt's boat had no tilt cover. "Besides," Alex said, "I have something to do first, in the market."

Joan nodded. She was nursing her grandson, feet up on a stool beside the fire, a larger house in Pudding Lane where she'd been offered rest until she made her way back to Cripplegate. Her goat was tethered by the front step, peering around the door jamb and bleating furiously. Joan was waiting only for Matt to finish his shift, ready to escort her and meet her new employer. "I'll be seeing you both, I reckon," she said. "While you're in London at least."

"And you can tell Matt," Alex grinned, "once I get my own property rights in order, I'll buy that boat for him, one with a shelter. Then he can look after you in style."

"And it's wonderful news about your coming marriage," Katherine said.

"And the same for yours, lass." Joan chuckled and adjusted the baby from shoulder to lap. "I knew that was coming from the start, and could never understand why you took so dreadful long about it. But maybe the same could be said for me. Now I'll be hand-fast afore the week's over, and would hope you do the same."

The market was busy inspite of the rain. Katherine took Alex's arm and they walked ahead, Tom skipping behind. First Alex cut up by the Walbrook to Bucklebury, the street of spicemongers and herbalists. Even in winter the shops of herbs, now mostly dried in little twiggy bunches and tied with bright ribbon, smelled sweetly pungent, a salve from the stale slink of the Walbrook. It was a salve Alex wanted. Suddenly looking around, he appeared to notice something, stared and raised his hand. Then he shook his head, turned back and ducked into the dark interior of one tiny shop, past the owner who sat in the doorway showing off her little sacks of spices, the herbs hanging upside down in swathes from the ceiling beams. With the air outside freshened by the sparkle of rain, the spices smelled heady. Katherine followed Alex inside. She peered into a huge sack of dark peppery powder, wrinkling her nose. The colours, even in the shadows, were rich and earthy. The owner knew Alex. "Bin two weeks or more, master, and me thinking maybe you was disappointed in something I'd sold you."

Alex smiled, shaking his head. "You've the best spicery in the city, Mistress Darrelby. But I've left the business, and come back only for a salve for burns. And for information."

The old woman clucked, chicken tongued, as he showed her his hands. She rummaged in a small wooden barrel and ladled a wedge of grease into a little earthenware tub, sealing it with wax and then with linen. "And the information?"

"About cinnabar," Alex said softly. "I know something myself, having been taught by an apothecary. But there might be more that you know, and more I can learn."

"Ah. Dragon's Blood," said the woman. "Then you'd best sit down and your lady too, for there's a deal to be told of cinnabar, and the terrible sulphur mines in foreign lands where slaves taken in battle will die in agony, digging for something as mysterious and dangerous as you can imagine. There's the good and there's the bad, for nothing is bad of itself but only in those that choose how to use it."

CHAPTER FORTY-THREE

A long from Cheapside where the market stalls narrowed the
road to an almost impassable bustle and the rubbish thrown
out from each stall created its own double gutters, the way widened
into unexpected grandeur. The shop windows were suddenly polished
and the glass shone, inviting glances inside, noses against the
mullions. Apprentices swept the street outside each shop and the
gutters were sluiced. The goldsmith's row here became a gleaming
pride, evidence of London's prosperity and the richest hoard outside
Westminster Palace and the Jewel Tower itself. Alex had business in
one of the smaller shops dealing in second hand gold as well as new
wrought, and took some time about it.

Then down Bread Street to Watling Street, sheltering sometimes
from the steady drenching sleet, and finally they came to the
southernmost gateway in the city's huge stone walls. Katherine,
clinging in rapture to Alex's arm, was once again wearing her
mother's sapphire earrings.

They had not left The White Duck Inn until past two of the clock,
and with winter blackening the sleety skies by four in the afternoon,
it was approaching nine o'clock curfew when they hurried beneath
the Ludgate portcullis, across the little Fleet Bridge and into The
Strand. Alex caught Tom's soggy collar and hauled him back to his

side. "Since you clearly still have some energy, brat," he said, "and the lady has not, you can run on ahead. I want no delays when we get to the house, no questioning or suspicions. You'll tell Shaddle to expect his mistress, tired and wet. Order a hot supper, and fires lit. Her bedchamber should be warmed and aired, and some other place set up for me to sleep. Not under the stairs this time I think. You can startle them all with the news of my being promised in marriage to her ladyship, and tell exaggerated stories of fires and other adventures. Oh, and you'd better point out all warrants against me are dropped. Their mistress may be marrying a Newgate pricker, but at least he's an innocent one."

Tom grinned and ran off into the night and the slanting sleet. Katherine stood a moment in the darkened shelter of the gate tower. "I suppose," she whispered, "you won't let me stay in your bed tonight, Alex. Not with all the staff knowing, and people watching what we do."

Alex chuckled. "I'd like to see Shaddle's face. But it can't be done, my love. Servants talk, and the gossip would travel quicker through London's streets than the bastard Tudor's French army."

"But no one knows me in the city," Katherine objected. "Who would gossip? Who would care? I don't know a soul in London except our own friends. Surely Elizabeth wouldn't be shocked?"

"Lizzie?" Alex grinned. "She probably believes far worse already from what she knows of my past. In fact, if she ever discovered what a paragon of virtue I've been, she'd be shocked indeed. But if you think the good people of England are only interested in gossiping about those they're acquainted with, then you're wrong. Slander runs faster and thicker than the Thames, and even more full of shit. The late Earl of Sheffield's widow, and him barely a sennight in his grave, poor soul? And the wicked Baron Mornington, escaped attaintment by a cock's spur, yet already back into his old ways."

"Oh well," Katherine giggled. "I suppose I'll sleep well tonight anyway. I'm so tired with all this walking and huddling in the rain, and after so much happening yesterday. It'll be such fun seeing your estates soon, Alex, and then I won't have to tramp all over the city day after day."

"I should have hired us some horses," Alex nodded. "It's a shame there's nothing worthwhile in your own stables."

She shook her head with a cascade of icy raindrops. She was again wearing Alex's fur lined coat, once Merevale's, but it had no hood and her veiled bonnet was dripping. "Only a pair of sumpters and that horrid old charger," she said. "Edmund hadn't got around to buying decent riding horses."

"I'll take you up to Smithfield's in a day or two and get us a palfrey each," Alex said, "now I've some money of my own at last. And I promise I don't intend us walking to Mornington. Even on horseback it's a dreary road in winter, three days if we're lucky and the fords aren't flooded and it doesn't snow."

"I like riding," Katherine nodded, shivering a little and searching for her kerchief. "I'm a country girl after all. My father may have forbidden most things, but I could always escape him on horseback."

The Strand was quiet. Far behind them the Ludgate keeper was ringing his bell for last travellers. In the distance they heard the ringing of the curfew from the bell tower at St. Martin-le-Grand. Alex carried no torch. "Come on, puss," he said, "it's quicker away from the river. We'll cut through the upper gardens."

She kept tight to his hand for it was a moonless night and even the stars were thick clouded. The rain had slowed to a misty drizzle, wetting with a cold, insidious seepage. The sounds of the river were muffled and the gulls were at rest, but the wind was high and sharp. Then suddenly there was another noise, furtive but clear, the sound of metal drawn from a leather sheath. Alex twisted, instinct honed, taught to face another man's steel. He saw nothing but heard the scrape of boots on wet cobbles. He grabbed Katherine, pushing her behind him.

"Alex, what - ?"

"Hush, beloved." His voice was almost lost, a mere whisper through the gloom. "There's danger. There's someone - "

"Just the Night Watch, Alex."

"No. Too secretive. Thieves perhaps, or they're after me. Us." His sword was already in one hand, his knife in the other. Katherine kept behind as he ordered, but pulled her own dagger from her belt.

When they came, it was from two sides at once.

At first, in the utter dark and the dizzy confusion of the rain, Alex did not know how many there were, and with Katherine too close behind him he could not swing his metal wide. He lunged outwards and parried with his knife. He felt contact, hearing their guttural breathing and the sudden clash of steel on steel. Turning and peering through the black, he positioned the moving shadows. He ran directly towards them. His thrust surprised and unbalanced them. Ruffians, not soldiers. Thieves accustomed only to club and stab the unsuspecting, their aim too wild, their weapons old. Unused to close combat or any vigorous defence, they were sluggish. No armour, no strategy. But Alex was experienced in battle. It was a game he knew.

He saw the edge of one man's steel flash close to his eye, slick in the wet. Alex ducked. His knee scraped the slippery paving, he swivelled on his heel and sprang forwards, his sword point straight up into the man's groin. It entered the flesh with a soft, yielding squelch. The man squealed. Then the body slumped and fell, rolling into the dark. The squealing became a moan, and continued.

Alex hauled back his blade and swung it high at the shadow looming from the dark. His steel cut through the falling rain like a stab of silver silk, rain diluting the blood, raining upwards in flying cascades of pink droplets, the last man's blood in the next man's face.

Stumbling into each other, one swearing at the other, two rushed him. Alex heard the low sweep of a blade slicing just above ankle height. He danced back, missing the stroke that would have taken both feet, and in effect, his life. The heavy breathing of several men, the grunting of the quick and brutal attack, boots first on stone and then the slurp of weight through mud, the clash of knife and the sudden cry of pain, but above all, confusion in the dark.

Several together jumped his back, but twisting and rolling, he threw them off, his sword sang into an arm's length circle, keeping them at a distance. Without seeing, but moving to the sounds, Alex stabbed, pivoting, springing, tripped one and sent him scuttling, then caught the next man through the neck, grinding his dagger deep. The man fell to his knees, not yet dead. Alex reached down, caught the swaying head beneath his elbow and clasped it tight to his chest. He stabbed again, his knife up to the hilt in the creature's throat. Alex let go and felt the dead body lurch at his feet.

Then he knew a sudden weakness below the ribs and the damp heat of his own blood. He pulled back, catching his breath, saw Katherine's shadow still moving behind him and shouted to her. "Get back, Kate, for God's sake. Run for the house, and call the Watch."

Suddenly a burst of bodies, not towards him but towards her, the tumbling shadows of two men grappling and grabbing, then her call, quickly silenced. Alex swirled around at once but was immediately taken from one side by a kidney dagger, from the other by a short sword. He ducked, parried and fought again. His sight cleared, his eyes adapting. He no longer saw Katherine.

There had been seven perhaps. Two he knew were dead, maybe three, two at least he thought badly injured. Two had grabbed Katherine. Now one, squat muscled, thrust his dagger point high, aiming for the face. Alex brought up his sword, clipping the dagger aside. With the next stroke he swung his blade downwards through the shoulder, splintering bone. The man fell back, gurgling and pouring blood. To his left another moved close, stabbing again to the wound between Alex's ribs. Alex crossed his steel and trapped the short knife, wrenching it from the assailant's grasp. It flew, clattering to the cobbles. Alex stepped aside, thrusting his sword low, then twisting high, bringing the point up under the rib cage into the lungs. The man's lungs burst, a bright froth of scarlet visible even in the darkness.

Alex swirled around again, looking for the next blade. There shouldn't be one, but he couldn't be sure. Both his sword and his knife were sticky, so was his own left side. He kicked a body away and called. "Kate. Kate, where are you?" He hoped she had run for the house as he'd commanded, but thought probably not. He began to search.

The club crashed heavy to the back of his head. It was unexpected. Alex fell forwards. He rolled onto his back, clearing the mud from his nose and mouth. Someone was on top of him at once, a long ballock dagger thrusting into his eyes. Someone unaccounted for, though he thought he'd killed or injured every one. Then he saw the tonsure and the pock marked skin and the crinkled glee of pale blue eyes leering inches from his nose. He'd lost his sword, the priest was sitting on his hand still clutching the knife, and for a moment a shudder of utter nausea spread from his belly to his head and Alex groaned.

"Even the devil incarnate can be vanquished by the pure in heart," squealed Father Erkenwald, the usual moderation of his voice abandoned. Alex was lying flat on mud. He could feel it oozing into his ears. A great tiredness overwhelmed him, the energy of the fighting dissipated into the rain. He didn't answer. He closed his eyes against the dancing point of the knife in his face. "Finally I have you." The priest's excitement squeaked into passion. He settled his seat on Alex's stomach, leaning over, his words spitting saliva. "God has given the power unto me, power beyond my own humble strength. Die at my hand, devil's spawn. Your hideous deeds shall never be repeated."

Alex sighed. "I can feel your erection, you foul little turd. How did you know to find us here?"

Father Erkenwald wriggled, too aroused for embarrassment. "I know where the devil creeps. God works His miracles through me. God speaks to me. He spoke through His agent here on Earth, who hired others to kill you in God's sacred cause. The Lord knows all our hearts and His vengeance is absolute. He strikes down sinners. He punishes the lewd and lustful. He will punish you now."

Alex snorted, breathing deep, building up strength, ready to free himself and throw the man off. His fingers, trapped beneath the priest's scrawny knee, clenched fast on his dagger hilt. "You hired gutter louts? And you call that God's work?"

"I? No." The priest sniggered, stabbing his own dagger point closer, hovering less than a breath from Alex's eye. "Another who hates you – who knows your wickedness. Who told me when you were coming and how to trap you."

"Who?" Alex took time. If he threw the priest sideways, he'd have steel through his eye. With the advantage of surprise, he could launch the man directly back.

"God's agent. Your enemy. One who knows your evil, as I do." The priest's breath, immediately into Alex's mouth, was sour. "You've murdered already, but I've never killed a man before." Father

Erkenwald's voice sank into gleeful whispers. "You should burn in chains, but this will suffice. It will be my greatest work. Stabbed through the same evil eye that leers at other men's wives, the eye of the devil. I cannot give you absolution, but pray now, damnable sinner, if you wish to die in a state of grace."

Then another voice, much softer, a woman's voice, sibilant and weak through the hiss of the rain. "Let him go, or I'll strangle you with your own crucifix."

The priest's face was suddenly contorted. He gurgled, his throat restricted. He was wrenched back, hauled by the braid holding his cross. The sharp wooden corner was forced tight beneath his chin, the leather thong twisted behind his neck. He was unable to speak. He made strange noises, trying to gasp, his hands striving wildly in the rain. He had dropped his knife.

Alex sat up. Father Erkenwald, still struggling, hands now desperately grabbing at the cord that strangled him, tumbled off backwards. Alex took him from Katherine, and she let him go and collapsed in the mud beside them.

Alex stood, flinging Father Erkenwald down. The priest curled on the mud, spitting bile, knees drawn up to his belly. He began to chant, words half swallowed as he choked, still gasping for breath, his hands to his neck. "The devil must be torn limb from limb and cast into the fires of hell," he mumbled. "Evil must be washed from the land in blood."

Katherine, who was still on the ground, took one deep breath and leaned over. She raised her knife and knocked Father Erkenwald sharp and hard on top of his head with the hilt. He slumped silently to the mud and was still.

She looked up into the rain. It danced into her eyes and half blinded her. She saw Alex's face coming close, his dark eyes moist and troubled. She opened her mouth to speak, but managed only a sigh. Alex scooped her up into his arms and, avoiding the bodies strewn across the cobbled path and the sloping gardens, began to walk slowly towards the house.

Something had alerted them already and they poured from the open doorway, torches flaring in the darkness, rushing across the slopes past the little hedges, calling and yelling. Alex walked into their midst, carrying Katherine tight nestled to his chest. Shaddle hurried forwards, holding up the oil lantern that turned the rain into a golden haze around him. "Master Bowyer. My lord. Is it her ladyship? What happened, my lord?"

Hewitt scurried behind, his flame torch already damp and smoking. Two scullions and a pot boy followed the cook, and lastly Tom, slipping on the wet ground, pushing desperately through the others.

Alex said softly, "Get the Watch and the sheriff. There are bodies, dead and alive, back there. But the lady's hurt. I need to get her upstairs to her chamber."

Shaddle grabbed one of the scullions. "Run to the Ludgate and ask the gatekeeper where to find a surgeon." To the other scullion he called, "Get the Night Watch and tell them to hurry." To the pot boy, "Get the sheriff, fast." He came forward, holding up the lamp, peering at the lady unconscious in Alex's arms. "My lord, her ladyship's chamber is ready warmed and aired." He turned back to Hewitt. "Hot water please, Mister Hewitt, in her ladyship's room now, and towels, and a brick in her bed." Then back to Alex. "Tom told us you were coming, sir, but when you took so long to arrive, we were worried and set out to look. But my lord, there's blood. You're bleeding."

"So is she," said Alex briefly. He knew her room. It was warmly glittering, awaiting its mistress. There were ten tall beeswax candles and fire had been lit high, the windows were tight shuttered against damp and draughts, the bed curtains open and the cover turned back. Tom held the door wide but Alex waved him away. "Go and sit with Kate's nurse, no doubt she'll be worried. I intend treating her ladyship alone, but I'll call you for whatever I need once I've examined her."

Katherine was conscious again as Alex laid her on the bed, and tried to sit up, blinking in the bright confusion of candlelight. Alex sat beside her on the edge of the mattress, arranging the bolster and pillows. "Stay still, my love," he said. "You've been hurt, but not seriously, I think. Don't be frightened, I'll soon have you mended."

"I'm never frightened," Katherine objected in aggravated whispers, shaking her head and trying to remember. "Who were those people, Alex? What happened?"

"Paid louts." Alex frowned, moving one candle closer to the bedside. Katherine's lavender gown, modest widow's jersey and higher necked than usual for a lady even in winter, was ripped at one side. The French gorget pleated into the neckline and the linen shift beneath, were torn deep and thick with blood. A knife wound from neck to breast ran like a scarlet stream and was still bleeding. Below her breasts the thick stiffened brocade of her stomacher caught the blood in pools, and there it was drying black and hard. Katherine's breathing was shallow, she seemed confused and dizzy. Alex slipped one careful finger inside the torn jersey and lifted the cloth away from the open flesh, looking beneath. "Does it hurt?" he asked gently.

"It stings – and sort of – throbs." She tried to smile. "But it's not so bad."

"Bad enough to make you faint."

She was remembering. "But I hurt him worse, Alex." She smiled, with more success this time. "A horrid brute of a man with whiskers. He stunk of sweat and his hands were filthy. He twisted my arm and stuck his knife in me. But I got away and I stabbed him right up his nose and it sort of slashed open, and he ran away whimpering. I hadn't actually aimed for his nose, but I was pleased anyway. Then the other man kicked me and I collapsed in all that nasty cold mud and couldn't get up. I managed to stab his heel as he walked over me but he had thick shoes and I don't think I was very successful."

Alex leaned over and kissed her cheek. "Brave child. Do you realise perhaps you saved my life?"

"Oh, the priest." She nodded. "Well, that was afterwards and I expect you'd have got away quite easily anyway, but I helped, didn't I? I hope he has a dreadful headache."

"I imagine he'll have more than that," smiled Alex. "A cracked skull, with a bit of luck."

"I'd have tried harder to kill him," Katherine admitted, "if it wasn't for him being a priest. I mean, even a horrid little worm of a priest, he's still ordained." She paused, groping for Alex's hand. "Should I have killed him, Alex?"

He shook his head. "Killing someone with a knife isn't as easy as it sounds. And you wouldn't want it on your conscience, my love. Better this way."

There was a knock on the door and the servants trooped in, Tom bringing wine and the others carrying bowls of steaming herb scented water, cloths, and towels. Once they had gone, Alex poured the wine and held the cup for Katherine to drink. She shook her head. "Hypocras would be better, wouldn't it? You know I don't like burgundy, Alex. It makes me woozy."

Alex continued to hold the cup to her mouth. "No my love, drink this. Woozy is exactly the way I want you." She obeyed and when she had finished, Alex filled the cup again and drank it himself. "Now," he said, "you may not like everything I'm about to do, my sweet, but you must trust me. I'm no doctor, but I've experience in battle and I know about wounds. Someone's gone running for a surgeon, but God knows if he'll find one at this time of night, and I won't wait."

Katherine sighed. "I do trust you Alex. But you said it wasn't serious."

"It isn't," Alex said. "Not as far as I can see. But I can't be sure until I open your gown. Will you mind?"

Katherine stared up at him. "My gown? Of course I'll mind. What are you going to do?"

"This," said Alex, tucked his fingers inside the torn neck of both dress and shift, and laid apart the frayed edges across her breast. The flesh beneath was ragged and bleeding, as torn as the gown. Alex took his knife once again from his belt, and began to cut further into the soft lavender wool, pulling it open.

Katherine turned her head away and took a deep breath. "Are you going to – to undress me – entirely?" she whispered.

"No, my love." Alex spread the edges of the material he had cut, then reached to the side of the wide belted stomacher and began to slip open each little hooked button. "Only what I must," he said. "You've been wounded Kate, not serious, but badly enough. You need doctoring. Close your eyes and trust me."

She nodded, winced and closed her eyes. Alex uncovered her left side from shoulder to waist, easing back the wool where the blood had stuck cloth to skin. He held one of the bowls of warm water and began to wash her. As the blood was cleansed away, he saw the injury more clearly. It was longer than he had expected but although far more than a graze, it was not deep. From the first stabbing force, the wound pierced, then wandered shallow, missing her heart and winding over the swell of her breast.

Alex was careful with the washcloth, using his fingers and the gentle warmth of the water. His hands across her breast and the rising pressure of her nipple against his palm affected him more than he had imagined. Even the concentration of his sympathy did not eradicate an awareness of touch. He blinked, controlling his fantasies. "Kate," he said softly, his fingers still warm and wet across her skin, "most of this is superficial. Only one small point, where the knife first went in, needs cauterizing."

She opened her eyes and looked up at him. "Will that hurt very much, Alex?"

He nodded. "Only for a moment, my love. I'll be quick."

She closed her eyes again and he continued to wash her, then used a dry towel to wipe away blood and water and the small floating leaves of the herbs. Her breast was pale in the candlelight, and firm, and larger than he had imagined. He had thought about it often enough in the past, watching the movement of her body and the occasional outline of her nipples as her gown clung to her in the damp and the cold.

He brought her more wine. "Drink my love. Just a little more. It'll help."

"Must I?"

"Yes, you must." He smiled. "I'm delighted at how obedient you've finally become."

She blinked up at him over the rim of the cup. "If you make me drunk, Alex, I'll probably be sick. You wouldn't like that."

"You put up with me when I was poisoned," he said. "I must have puked a hundred times, and probably into your lap."

She smiled and wiped her mouth. "Not quite." She peeped down at herself, blushed and closed her eyes. "Can't you cover me up, Alex? I'm cold."

"Not yet." He leaned over and kissed her eyelids. "First drink a little more. Then I'll cauterize the wound, and bandage it. Then I'll tuck you in nice and warm for sleep." He filled the cup again and brought it to her. After she had drunk he sat back, waiting for the wine to take effect.

Katherine hiccupped. "You won't go away again afterwards will you, Alex? You won't leave me alone, feeling sore and sick?"

"I'll send Sara to you," Alex said, frowning. "You shouldn't be left alone, but it can't be me, Kate. You know that."

She struggled to sit up, her eyes wide. "That was before! It'd be positively cruel to go away now." She leaned back again, gasping for breath and blushing. "And after all, we are going to be married, Alex. Unless you've changed your mind."

He was washing the blade of his knife in one of the bowls of hot water, but looked up at that and frowned again. "Silly puss. Why would I change my mind? I'd marry you tonight if I could – but - " He paused, then smiled. "But why not? Marry me tonight Kate, and then I'll sleep all night in your bed, and be damned. How about it?"

CHAPTER FORTY-FOUR

Alex used his knife to cauterize the small weeping wound where the assassin's knife had stabbed deep into Katherine's shoulder. First washed and dried, he then held the blade for many long moments in the heat of the flames within the hearth. Finally he came back to the bed, and sat there, summoning his own courage. "Just one brief moment," he said softly. "It will hurt very much, I'm afraid, but I'll be as quick as I can."

She'd nodded and closed her eyes, and he had touched the burning steel to her flesh with a faint sizzle of scorched skin. She yelped, biting her lip, and Alex removed his knife almost immediately and threw it to the floor. Katherine was crying silently, tears streaming like pearlshine in the candlelight, and he leaned over, one arm around her, and kissed her.

Careful of her injury, he did not pull her tight but cradled her gently, his tongue searching the rich burgundy taste on her tongue. His breath scorched her throat as her wet cheeks dried against his. She put her arms around her neck and held on until she had stopped shuddering, and lay calm. He moved away then, gazing down at her. "You're a remarkable woman, Kate," he said, "and I'm proud to take you as my wife."

She blinked, dislodging the tears still dancing on her lashes. "And it doesn't matter about me being in mourning?"

He shook his head. "Not in the slightest. I'll ask for a retrospective annulment if you want it, but that will take an ocean of time. Besides, you were hardly married at all, Kate, so to the devil with mourning. Marry me if you want me my love."

"I want you Alex, so very much," she murmured. "And Sara and Jenkins can be witnesses. But I don't want another priest. Not after - "

"We don't need a priest," Alex smiled. "But let's get you decent first." He used the salve from the herbalist's which he had bought that afternoon, and with his finger tip, smeared it very lightly along the curve of the shallow cut. Where he had cauterized, the little round mark was singed black. Knowing it would be painful for some time, he laid the salve thick. Then his finger followed the long red line down from that point and across the swell of her breast. It was more caress than nursing, and Alex realised she was holding her breath. It was not only pain. "Am I hurting you?" he said softly.

"No. Well, a little." Her eyes were squeezed shut, her lashes still moist.

His finger tingled, hardly daring to touch. Alex watched the line he traced, curving from the first firm rise of her breast, past the soft circle of her aureole, the darker tip of the nipple, and then down to where the flesh dipped again into her ribs. He smiled. "Finished, my sweet. You can breathe again."

He had torn the remaining linen cloths into ready strips, but realised that bandaging her would involve removing the other half of her dress. He sighed. It was hardly worth retaining, but meant she would be well nigh naked in his arms, making her even more timid, and demanding a resolve he doubted whether he had. Then he remembered his own wound, which continued to ache. If one of the household could be found to bandage that, then he'd need to strip half naked himself.

Katherine had opened her eyes. "Alex, it'll seem odd making pledges and taking your hand while I'm sick in bed. But I'm not sure I can stand. Do you mind? I ought to – dress up nicely – and do you credit. Instead I'll be bundled up in bandages. Even – I think – a little bit tipsy."

He laughed. "You could be roaring drunk and stark naked, I wouldn't mind."

It wasn't the right thing to say, but she simply blushed and smiled. "You – you're very patient with me, Alex."

"Hand-fast tonight, my love, and then maybe we'll have it consecrated at the church porch sometime after I get you back to Mornington." He tipped up her chin with his finger, and lightly kissed the tip of her nose. "I'll buy you a new gown and you can dress up as pretty as you like. And you needn't worry about the priest on my estates. He's a tame cleric, I promise. With my father sitting on a chair in front of the pulpit glaring at him, and John and me standing fidgeting either side, the poor man never dared say anything remotely controversial." Alex was keeping his gaze strictly on her face, but now he said, "Are you ready for the bandaging, my love? I'm afraid it'll mean removing the top half of your gown."

"I suppose it's all muddy anyway. And blood stained. And I know I shouldn't – care." She looked up at him, eyes a little vague. The burgundy was still taking effect. "I shouldn't be shy, should I?" she mumbled. "And I do feel safe with you Alex, but - "

"No buts." He rinsed and dried his fingers, then began to peel back the ravaged material from the right side of her body. Aware that he was holding his breath, Alex concentrated on what he was doing and smiled to himself. He had held so many women naked in his arms, yet now was fearful of touching the one he loved. "Remember this is medicine, my sweet," he said, "sour medicine perhaps, but nothing else." Katherine nodded and sniffed. Alex noticed her hands clenched at her sides. "Pain?" he asked. "Or timidity?"

"Can't we – talk about something else?" muttered Katherine. "Like your home, Alex, or your family?"

Alex slipped the shoulder of her gown down over her arm, laying back the torn jersey and the linen pleats beneath. "Not much to talk about my love. They're all dead."

"Oh dear, I'm sorry. Yes of course." She allowed him to remove her hand from within the right sleeve, peeped down at herself, blushed deeply, and turned away. "And we still don't know who on earth killed Merevale and Daniel."

Alex held a wad of clean linen to the small wound he had cauterized and then began to bandage her upper body, winding the cloth strips behind her back, once over her shoulder and the rest beneath her arm across her left breast. He continued working as he spoke. "Oh that," he said. "But I do know now, my love. I know exactly who it was."

The room was warm but he saw her nipples rise and harden, flushing as he touched. His hands were efficient and brisk, but he was deeply aware, and could not look away. Her eyes were shut, but when he spoke they snapped wide open. "How? Who? Mary? Or Elizabeth?"

He shook his head. "We'll speak of that later. Too much to explain. First, I'm going to take off your skirts. The bodice has gone, so the skirts will fall off anyway and make you damned uncomfortable all night. Besides, they're muddy. You can keep your shift and if you tell me where you keep your blanchet, I'll get it for you. Then I'm calling our witnesses, and we'll be hand-fast, Kate." He stood, smiling, pushing away the bowls of bloody water and discarded cloths beside the bed. He reached up to the peg where she pointed and took down her bedrobe, bringing it to her.

She blinked, suddenly startled. "But Alex, you're hurt too. There's blood all over your doublet."

"I'd forgotten." He sat once more beside her and removed the ripped lavender skirts of her gown, pulling them down over her bare feet, her legs now outlined softly pink through the semi transparency of the chemise. He helped her struggle into her blanchet and she tugged it quickly tight across her breasts, disappearing again into satisfied modesty. Alex smiled. "Better?"

Shaddle stood beside the hearth, hands behind his back and belly launched forwards, red cheeked with pride. Hewitt, though not specifically needed, hovered close, and Tom, not even invited, had to be pushed off the mattress as he attempted to sit beside the bride. Mistress Sara Whitstable twittered with delight. "My dearest," Sara said, "this is so utterly exciting. I guessed – well of course, - but so

412

much has happened, and I never thought so quickly – and after the dreadful business – and it's so wonderfully romantic."

Alex then sat beside Katherine and clasped her right hand in his. She gripped the neck of her bedrobe with the other. Alex grinned and kissed her fingers. "Ready, my love? Then I call on these witnesses to note well and recall in perpetuity, that I hereby give my hand in faith forever, in Accorder de Praesenti, taking the Lady Katherine Ashingham, known as the dowager Countess of Sheffield until such time as her previous marriage be annulled, herewith as my legal wife."

"And I take your hand," whispered Katherine, still blushing, "and give you mine as my troth."

Tom jumped up and down until Hewitt frowned at him, Sara clapped and Shaddle strode forwards. "And as principal witness, I pronounce you husband and wife. From this moment, let no man strike asunder." He poured wine for bride and groom, but Katherine only sipped hers, being aware she was already somewhat intoxicated, and Alex drained his cup and held it out for a refill. He did not in the least mind being intoxicated. It was going to be a difficult night.

He kissed her when everyone had finally gone again. It was not entirely a chaste kiss for he was vibrantly conscious of the pressure of her breasts against his chest, but the rest was only in his mind. When he released her, she still held him tight. "You've never been a husband before, Alex," she whispered. "Does it feel any different?"

"Strangely enough," he grinned, "it does."

"I was so frightened the first time," Katherine said. "So embarrassed and scared. And everything Edmund said and did made me hate him more and more. This feels so different."

"It is," Alex laughed. "With both of us wounded, and you huddled in bed? Hardly a traditional ceremony. But then, my love, we're hardly a traditional couple." He had begun to extricate himself from his doublet and shirt. The collection of bowls and cloths had been removed and Sara had gathered up Katherine's ruined and discarded clothes, but one bowl of clean water, the salve and some unused bandaging remained, ready for further need. Alex dropped his clothes and unlaced his hose from the gipon. When he looked up he saw Katherine watching him and smiled at her expression. "Don't worry, my sweet. I'm not preparing to leap on you. But I need to see whether my own injuries need attention."

She sighed. "If it needs stitching, Alex, I could try. But I'm sure I'd hurt you. I can't even stitch shirts. And as for cauterizing - "

Alex twisted his neck around, peering down and regarding the small dark hole between his ribs. "Doesn't look too bad," he said. "And doesn't hurt enough to be important. I think I'll ignore it."

"Oh, Alex, you can't. It could get infected." Katherine scrambled forwards across the mattress, losing the grip on her blanchet. "Let me wash it for you at least. I'm surely not that useless."

He sat beside her, obediently holding the bowl. She was light fingered and thorough and though the water had cooled, her hands were warm and careful. He watched the wound open a little as it was cleaned of the dried blood, and was satisfied no special care was needed. Without stitching, a thick scar would form, but he cared nothing for that. His concentration snapped back to Katherine, and the bedrobe, which had fallen open. He felt slightly dizzy and made no attempt to avert his eyes. She bandaged his chest firmly around the ribs, knotted the linen and smiled up at him. "There," she said. "Now we can both go to sleep."

Alex lay back on the pillows, hitched his unlaced braies tighter, and took his wife in a gentle embrace. He kissed her cheek. "Very proper. It's certainly late," he said. "Climb under the covers then, my love, and I'll snuff the candles."

Katherine was once more in his arms, her head nestled on his shoulder. The room was dark shadowed when she spoke again. He could feel the urgency of her heartbeat. Above them the eiderdown was a billowed cocoon, and beyond that the last small flames from the hearth danced in crimson and black reflections on the ceiling plaster between the beams. Her words tickled his collar bone. "I – I'm denying you – aren't I, Alex?" she whispered. "It's your wedding night, and I'm your wife. But I'm not – and you aren't – not like everyone else. Are you angry? Even a little bit? Do you resent – what I said?"

He took some time to answer. He was staring at the great sweep of swagged tester above their heads and beginning to wonder just how drunk she was. Finally he said, "Strictly speaking our marriage isn't legal until we do – but no matter. No one knows except us. Did you think I'd suddenly demand my conjugal rights?"

"No," she mumbled into his neck. "But I sort of wondered – I mean, wondering what I'd do - if you did."

He smiled. "And what did you decide?"

She took a long time to answer. "I wasn't sure," she said at last. "I don't think you'd be like Edmund. And I'd know what to expect. At least, I think I would. But you said you wouldn't - do anything - and I do trust you Alex. But you've been so nice. I think perhaps I'm not being – so nice."

"Listen, my sweet." He sighed, holding her a little tighter. "We're both wounded, tired and intoxicated. When the time comes, and it will come, to prove that loving me isn't in any way degrading, unpleasant or painful, I want you fully awake and fully sober. I warn you, I intend doing just that, but never by force and never demanding, nor taking advantage just because you feel guilty. Simply because I love you, and making love is part of that, and I'm fairly sure you haven't the faintest idea what you're objecting to." He smiled, slipping his arm firmly around her waist. "Now sleep, little one. Tomorrow will be another busy day."

But his hand found the opening of her bedrobe, and as she cuddled close he slipped his fingers gently inside, cradling her naked body. She was very warm. He closed his fingers across her ribs, with the enticing swell of her breasts pressed softly down against the turn of his thumb. At first she held her breath, expectant. But he did not move his hand higher and after a moment she sighed, and closed her eyes. When they both awoke in the morning, his hand was still warmly clasped there.

CHAPTER FORTY-FIVE

"Damnation," said Alex.

"But Edmund bought terribly expensive clothes," said Katherine. "You might as well make use of them until you get back to your own, or order new ones. I mean, you can't wear what you wore yesterday. What with the fire – and then all that blood!"

Alex held up the first doublet in the garderobe. "The man was keg chested, goat legged, shorter than a horse's arse and smelled like one too, with the taste and culture of a floating turd. How could I wear this?"

Katherine was dressed already, which she had insisted upon, inspite of Alex telling her to stay in bed. "Pooh," Katherine had said, "just for one tiny little stabbing? It almost doesn't hurt at all."

"You've been a shocking liar ever since I first met you," said Alex. "And I warn you, I intend being a tyrannical husband. I'll demand obedience."

Katherine had giggled and hurried off to find her dresser. When she returned resplendent in pink, her brow newly plucked and her hair pinned up in coils, Alex was glaring at her late husband's prized silks. "Do I look alright?" Katherine asked. "Sara and Sally helped me and I don't think the bandages show. And I'll keep my cloak pulled tight until we get indoors."

Alex frowned. "You look glorious Kate, but truly, you can't walk all the way to Cripplegate. Not after yesterday."

"You're wounded too," Katherine pointed out. "If you have to go there today, perhaps we could hire a carrier."

"Bumping over gutters and cobbles wouldn't be much easier than walking," said Alex. "I suppose there's no chance of you just doing what you're told and staying at home 'till I get back?"

She shook her head. "No chance at all Alex."

Another doublet, mustard velvet much pinked and pleated, embroidered with grapes, slashed in scarlet damask and trimmed in beaver, joined the pile of rich materials on the garderobe floor. "No wonder the silly gudgeon had no one to mourn him," muttered Alex. "Wasted enough money to feed half of Newgate."

Katherine offered a pea green pourpoint with collar and sleeves in gold baudekyn. "I think the king was fond of him once," she pondered.

Alex shook his head and the baudekyn joined the heap of discards. "Well, just goes to show then," he said. "Couldn't have any worse credit than that."

He finally chose a plain clean shirt and a doublet and surcoat in matching mahogany brocade, but insisted on keeping his own rather disreputable hose. "I'm not wearing anything that's been anywhere near that man's crotch," he said, and stomped off to get dressed.

Shaddle managed to find a disgruntled driver and a covered litter for hire. Alex refused to take Tom, who complained loudly, as he helped his new wife up the steps. The smell of dank wet leather and the horse's flatulence made Alex swear he'd never travel in a litter again. He was also aware of how much easier his business could be discharged if alone, and at the same time, how delighted he was to have Katherine at his side. He had become more used to seeing her covered in smuts and dressed either in Tom's grubby livery or in her own most unflattering lavender mourning. Now her gown was the colour of her cheeks, the brocade shimmered and the little miniver collar nestled beneath her chin. Her cropped box hat in starched cambric fluttered a short veil, one rich brown curl peeping beneath its crown, and her small gloved hands were clasped in her cherry pink lap. He thought she looked delicious, and grinned at her from the bumping gloom.

"If you're in a good mood again Alex," she answered his smile, "will you tell me why we have to go to Elizabeth's house today?"

"Why I have to, you mean, and you just insisted on coming along? Well, to catch the killer of course, my love. To announce my nuptials and to kiss my cousin goodbye, but principally to unmask the murderer and uncover the crimes."

"Oh," said Katherine sweetly. "Is that all!"

"Don't you want to tell Mary and Lizzie we're married?"

"Well, of course I do," said Katherine. "I'm looking forward to it. And by now Joan will have moved in there too, won't she? But about – Merevale and Daniel, I mean, how can you possibly know, Alex? It could be either of the ladies – which is a dreadful thought. At least after Daniel's death, we know it couldn't really be anyone else."

Through the Ludgate and a sharp turn north, the cart wobbled on towards the Cripplegate, lurching through puddles with a sudden bump as the iron wheels hit holes in the roads. The light rain pattered on the sheltering leathers. Alex, feet planted wide and hanging onto his seat, continued to grin. "Well, that's what I thought too. But in fact it's Mel's death that holds the clue which you discovered yourself, and the attempt to poison me even more so. Then the proof came last night. Don't worry, my love. I've everything in hand."

Within half an hour they arrived at the Burton house stables where they paid off the carter and Jenkins hurried to show them into the main hall. The fire was lit and the Lady Elizabeth was sitting beside the hearth, staring disconsolately at her embroidery. Her eyesight increasingly myopic, the stitching was now also blurred through tears of boredom and the misery of loss. She jumped up smiling when she saw her guests. "But I'm afraid your uncle Godfrey is out at market," she said.

"No matter," said Alex. "We've come to see you, Lizzie."

There was a good deal to tell her, all in excited interruptions. Joan's house destroyed in the fire, then the attack in the dark, and finally their hand-fast wedding at midnight with the bride wounded and tipsy in her bed. "It was all terribly uncomfortable," said

Katherine, "especially the fire, which was frightening. And being attacked was frightening too, but it didn't last long because Alex just dealt with it all so efficiently. Besides, I'm never frightened. And then being married, that made up for everything else. I can't tell you how lovely it is to be married."

Elizabeth smiled faintly, looking from one animated face to the other. "I remember, very well," she said with a little shake of her head.

"Shaddle called the sheriff and the Watch came and took all the bodies away," continued Katherine cheerfully. "And he told the Watch off for not having come to help us quicker. Some of the men were already known villains, but most of them are dead now anyway. And that beastly Father Erkenwald isn't dead, though I wish I'd hit him harder. His abbot came and dragged him away and promised he'd be dealt with. The abbot says they've dungeons at the monastery for miscreant monks and excommunicates, and they keep them in tiny cells for years. It didn't sound very holy, but then, that horrid priest isn't safe to have running around."

Mary crept in while they were half way through their stories. She had not been sitting with Elizabeth. With a constant atmosphere of sadness and suspicion, no friendship had grown between them. Now she sat a little away from the firelight, letting the first long shadows cover her tired frowns. Alex nodded to her. "Not thought of going back north, Mary? I imagined you'd return to your parents."

She nodded, speaking quietly. "I intend to, Alex. Indeed, I've appealed to the king for the right to keep my dower rights, and he hinted he'd approve if my father arranged another marriage for me. I'm not sure – after poor Danny - but widowhood is so - distressing."

Alex, having little regard for her previous wedded bliss to his cousin, said nothing. Katherine smiled. "I'm sure you deserve someone magnificent, Mary dear. You're the most beautiful woman I've ever seen after all."

Elizabeth interrupted. "I, on the other hand, have no intention of remarrying. I would never look at another man after my dear Edward."

"You," said the Lady Mary, "have a son with a title and wealth, still young enough to do what you tell him. And I, having been happily

419

married once, have a greater tolerance towards the prospect of other men."

"Certainly," smiled Elizabeth. "You've known enough of them my dear."

Alex laughed and stood. "If you'll all excuse me," he said, "I intend finding Joan for a quick word. I presume she's moved in upstairs? Then I've a question regarding cinnabar, and will ask it of the one person in this house who can give me an educated answer. I'll leave you to discuss your marriages in ladylike privacy."

Alex found Reginald Psalter in his own small office. The scent of mixed peppers, barks and ground spices was spoiled a little by the aroma of turpentine, bleach and camphor. The apothecary was hunched over the Latin parchments spread on the table, eating apple codlings liberally sprinkled with cinnamon, and licking his thin brown stained fingers. His eyebrows twitched disapprovingly at the interruption. "Master Bowyer," he nodded. "Or, should I say your lordship? It is still inconveniently confusing I am afraid, this matter of titles. However, young man, no doubt you have come on a particular mission. A matter of medicks or spices perhaps? No doubt I can help you with some difficult question."

"Several questions." Alex pulled a chair over to the opposite side of the table and sat, smiling at Mister Psalter. "But especially regarding cinnabar."

The apothecary frowned. "Ah, cinnabar. Dragon's Blood. An interesting substance indeed," he said, "but I am quite sure I remember instructing you in its precedence and principal uses nigh on three months past. Before leaving the house on The Strand, I believe. I fear you have a poor memory, Master Bowyer."

"On the contrary, Mister Psalter." Alex had not stopped smiling. "And yesterday I had occasion to check those facts with a professional spicemonger in Bucklebury Road, a woman I grew to trust when working with spices myself. That visit was followed by – interesting events."

"Indeed?" Reginald Psalter leaned back in his chair, his fingers steepled beneath his chin. "Then I cannot in the least see what further question I might usefully answer on the subject sir."

"A knowledgeable woman, is Mistress Darrelby," Alex continued. "You know her, of course. She informed me that you buy many of your supplies there. You might be pleased to know how she admires your skills, Mister Psalter. As an alchemist rather than a simple spicer naturally. A talented alchemist, I hear."

The apothecary bent upwards from his shadows, standing slowly as if straightening each joint separately. "I am gratified, sir." He took up a small jug that stood beneath the window, and the cup from beside it. "May I offer you some hypocras, Master Bowyer? I remember you often remarking on how you enjoy my own special recipe, and how it invigorates and replenishes the system."

Alex's smile widened. "I've considerable experience of your hypocras," he said. "Though you might call it a mixed experience. I don't think I'll repeat that experience now, Mister Psalter. The last time it worked rather more as a purge than as a tonick."

The apothecary set down the cup and pursed his lips. "You are absurd, young man. I have frequently supplied you with helpful advice, efficacious beverages, and indeed, at one time, two most valuable medicines for the bilious digestives from which you claimed to be suffering. I have never given you a purge, sir, though such a thing can certainly be medicinal in itself at the proper time."

"Ah yes." Alex was watching him closely. "You came to the house where I was staying near the Bridge, concerned for my - health. Most kind of you, Mister Psalter, and I appreciated it at the time. Unfortunately, the medicines you gave me were never tested, and were then destroyed in a fire. I've since wondered what they might have contained. But strangely, after your visit to the house where I was staying in the utmost secrecy, my whereabouts suddenly became known by the sheriff of Cripplegate parish, and also by that damnable priest. I believe I have you to thank directly for my arrest, my friend."

Mister Psalter remained standing. There was no hearth in the tiny office, but two tallow candles spat points of light into the drear gloom. The apothecary's wavering height loomed over the table, underlit by the candle flame. "I know nothing of these matters," he said. "Your words are utterly foolish, sir. It was the Lady Elizabeth herself who informed me of your whereabouts when I stated my desire to alleviate your suffering."

Alex nodded. "True. But not her ladyship who informed that damned priest, nor summoned the sheriff afterwards. You appear to have made good use of Father Erkenwald. The man of God and the man of alchemy? An odd alliance perhaps, but it served your purpose again yesterday. Only you could have set up that ambush last night."

"You are deluded, Master Bowyer, indeed, you are becoming dangerously over-excited," frowned Mister Psalter. "I must judge you positively insane. I know nothing of any ambush. I have no knowledge of your actions yesterday. How could I, sir?"

"From Mistress Darrelby," said Alex simply. He showed no inclination towards over-excitement and smiled pleasantly, but kept his hand tucked into his belt, close to the hilt of his knife. "I told the herbalist exactly where I intended going," he said, "since I ordered some packages to be delivered to the Strand house this morning. But as I entered the shop, I saw you. In fact, I turned to greet you, but you darted back under cover. It was miserable weather of course, and perhaps you simply sheltered from the rain. But I don't think so, Mister Psalter. Indeed, it was that one small action that suddenly explained everything to me. It was why I extended my visit to Mistress Darrelby beyond buying the salve I originally wanted. I became suddenly interested in cinnabar, and in who sometimes bought copious amounts of it."

The apothecary had edged around the table and was now standing closer to the door. His expression remained passive but his hands twitched, and he clasped them hurriedly behind him. "What is this nonsense concerning cinnabar? Yes, I visited Bucklebury Street yesterday," he nodded. "You are correct. Had I seen you, Master Bowyer, I assure you I would have called out. I did not see you, however. You should not imagine that my attention would be so attracted to your presence."

Alex grinned. "But as it happens," he said, "my attention was much attracted to your presence, my friend. And your dislike of being noticed suddenly made sense of everything else. When I and my wife were attacked last night, I knew you had obtained immediate knowledge of my direction from the herbalist, being the only person who knew it and who would have openly discussed it once you saw me leave the shop, and entered behind to ask. And I remembered that the afternoon before nearly dying of the poison, you had brought me a special cup of hypocras. Not to serve to everyone as is usual, or from a jug left upon the table, but just one cup, specifically for me."

Reginald Psalter took another step backwards towards the door. "You must have drunk a hundred cups of my hypocras sir. You have complimented me upon it. Now you are both insulting and deranged."

"Sunstroke perhaps?" suggested Alex, leaning back cheerfully in his chair.

"It is winter sir, and you are certainly quite mad. You accuse me of some crazed intention to cause you harm," the apothecary's voice raised in grievance. "But you suggest no motive. I have no reason to wish you ill, or indeed, not until this moment. I have many times instructed you in your business, and aided you to cast off your ignominious ignorance. I made no complaint when, without the slightest knowledge or experience, you decided to take up my profession on my departure from the Strand house. I see I have earned no appreciation for my pains."

"I know exactly what your motive was," Alex said. "Both for intending to poison me, and for causing the violent deaths of my cousins in this house."

Mister Psalter sprang back, glaring. "How dare you, sir. You are demented indeed."

"Cinnabar," said Alex, "is essential in alchemy. Dragon's Blood, the liquid power of mercury, which is one of alchemy's essential elements. You left a wet streak on my cousin's neck when you murdered him. Your hands must have been covered in it when you held the knife, since there was enough to transfer to my shoulder some hours later, far too much to come from someone else's badly dyed clothes of course. No one else could conceivably have touched raw liquid cinnabar, or even have access to it."

Psalter had begun to shiver. "Wicked words. Wicked thoughts. You have no proof, sir."

"Not much more than your filthy little priest had against me," Alex nodded. "But I know for all that, and I'm satisfied I know the truth. Only you, the Lady Elizabeth, Mary and Jenkins knew my address by the Bridge, but the sheriff was sent there after me. Only you and Mistress Darrelby knew where I was heading last night, and at roughly what hour I might arrive. Hired villains were sent to finish me off. I also know why. You imagine yourself in love with the Lady Mary. You're not the first to imagine that. She's remarkably beautiful, and quite corrupt. A fascinating combination for an alchemist who aspires to the hidden wonders of the universe."

The apothecary now had his back to the door, and his fingers on the handle. "You will not insult the lady, sir. You have no right even to speak her name."

"But as you know full well," Alex smiled, "and probably heard in detail at the time since your room was just above mine, I was once – briefly – involved with the lady. I imagine what you heard infuriated you, and you hated me then. But I learned something about Mary that night which came in quite handy afterwards. She likes to bite and scratch. She frequently left her marks on her husband, and more than once on my cousin Merevale. And then, one morning when I came to ask you about other matters entirely Mister Psalter, I was surprised to see that she'd left her mark on you. Under the circumstances, I was blind not to think of you as the culprit earlier, but I had my mind on many other things at the time. I was slow. Unpardonable. But now I know. Yet at first it was Mary I suspected, and you needed to protect her by getting rid of me. Not by the knife – too obvious, and I would have fought back. But you took Mel and Danny by surprise, the trusted apothecary surgeon. I wouldn't have been such an easy victim. Safer to kill me from a distance. "

Reginald Psalter was shaking. His body quivered, a willow in a storm. "I deny everything. You are vain and foolish, sir. You understand nothing, not of the depths of a human heart or the power of love, which is the greatest alchemy of all. And you will not mention that lady's name again, nor touch her nor sully her reputation with your foul accusations. I will not permit - "

He opened the door abruptly and darted immediately out into the corridor beyond. He turned to sprint, and tumbled straight into the welcoming arms of Joan Hambury and Sir Godfrey Quyrril, who had both been patiently waiting outside as instructed. With only one steady leg, Sir Godfrey stumbled back, but Joan hung on. Then, being considerably taller, Psalter wriggled free and raced for the stairs. Alex was behind him. The apothecary scrambled up the back stairs, then Alex, two steps at a stride. The thunderous echoes vibrated through the house and every door opened. Jenkins appeared below, gazing upwards in consternation. "Get the sheriff," yelled Alex.

The three ladies rushed from the main hall and pushed past each other, all aiming for the servant's stairs. Along the upper level where the back entrances joined the main corridor, the young Earl of Burton and his tutor flung open the nursery door and raced out in alarm. Downstairs Uncle Godfrey was hopping in fury and swearing at everyone and Joan Hambury had grabbed the sword from his hand and was following Alex.

Jenkins grabbed three of the staff and sent them scurrying out into the rain, while he stood gazing upwards and loudly ordered Mister Psalter to give himself up and come downstairs at once.

Reginald Psalter ran straight into the small earl, who was, strictly speaking, his employer, and thrust him out of the way. Stephen stuck his foot out. The flying apothecary tripped over it and fell flat on his face on the squeaking floorboards. Stephen sat on top of him and pummelled his head with his fists. The apothecary twisted, clenched one trembling hand and punched his small master very hard on the nose. It began to bleed with copious discharge of several different fluids, one of them being blood. Stephen crumpled, sobbing loudly. The apothecary flung him off and raced away.

Alex had already arrived on top of them both, but now stopped and comforted his little cousin. Stephen clung to Alex's legs, with liberal transference of blood, and Alex watched as his quarry escaped into the darkened doorway of a chamber much further along the gloomy passageway. As Joan arrived behind, Alex passed Stephen to her with a couple of curt instructions, and then raced after Reginald Psalter.

It was a small private solar, unwarmed, unlit and unoccupied. Beyond it was the bedchamber. His knife in one hand, Alex searched the solar, found nothing, and entered the other room. The shadows were heavy and the bed, curtains partially closed, was untidy, its covers strewn. A lady's chamber, and not Elizabeth's. It was, Alex guessed, Mary's room. He could not see anyone.

The Lady Elizabeth had taken charge of her son and returned him to the nursery. It was the Lady Katherine, the Lady Mary, and Joan Hambury who now quietly entered the open door behind Alex.

Mary pushed further into the bedchamber. She did not bother to lower her voice. "This is madness, Alex. What are you doing in my room?"

"Catching the man who killed your husband," he said softly. "But of course, you knew it was him, didn't you, my dear?"

"Fool." Mary stamped her foot. "How could I know? And as if I'd protect some common servant and not my own dear husband."

Katherine stood, uncertain. Alex smiled at her over Mary's shoulder. "I'm afraid you've joined a charming family, my love," he said. He turned back to Mary. "When I found Mel, his bed curtains were still closed. He loathed the dark after being in the Tower, and always slept with shutters and curtains open. But I happen to know you like them closed, Mary. You prefer the dark. For security and privacy, no doubt, when jumping from one illicit bed to another. You were with Mel the night he was murdered, I saw the fresh bite marks and the scratches. I know your predilections, my dear. But if Mel had been killed after you'd left him, he'd have opened the curtains. So you were still there, or just leaving. Did Mel insult you? Did Psalter rush in to salvage your honour? Or simply assuage his own jealousy?"

The lady stared at him, unmoving. She had bright red spots of fury on each cheek. Katherine moved closer.

"And this morning I counted back the minutes," Alex continued, "making allowance for Danny's death and your prompt discovery of his body. The main staircase not only leads directly into the hall where Danny was sitting, but it's wide enough to see the table from the curve half way up. You said you came from upstairs and found him dead. You might not have been standing at Psalter's side when he did it, but you would at least have seen him scurry away."

"You dare accuse me – my own husband - " Mary darted forwards.

"I accuse Psalter," Alex said. "But I presume he heard your quarrel and you permitted the revenge. Danny had no title anymore, no future, and with your looks, you knew you could do better. I imagine you encouraged Psalter. Is that why you took him as your lover? I really can't see much else in his favour. Or are you totally indiscriminate?"

Mary grabbed a fistful of his hair close to the scalp and twisted hard. "Indiscriminate of course, Alex dearest," she spat. "Why else would I have fucked you? And you a dirty little servant in my own kitchens at the time."

Alex reached up both his hands to hers, but could not dislodge her. She pulled harder. He winced, and putting one long fingered hand around her squirming neck, pressed until she gulped, then stamped hard with the heel of his boot on her foot. She squealed and let him go. Katherine was immediately behind her and had a fast grip on her shoulders. Taller than Katherine, Mary wrenched free. Katherine snatched Godfrey's sword from Joan behind her, bringing it up sharply beneath Mary's chin. Mary stood suddenly still.

Alex watched his wife in faint surprise. The sword was far too heavy for Katherine but she held both hands steady on the hilt, and breathed fast. "Don't you touch my husband again," she said. "You may have hurt your own, but you're not hurting mine."

Which is when Reginald Psalter emerged from beneath the tumbled eiderdown where he had been cringing in silence, and leapt between Katherine, Alex and Mary with a screech of rage.

Both startled, Mary and Katherine stumbled backwards. Alex grabbed Psalter's arm and swung him around. Katherine's wavering sword point glanced sideways, and with another yell of rage, the apothecary twisted, not trying to get away, but fingers reaching and groping for Alex's eyes. Then he stopped, teetering on the balls of his feet, confused by sudden pain. His right ear hung in a strange flapping dribble of scarlet, blood streaming down his neck onto his neat broadcloth shoulder.

Katherine stared at the bloodstain on the edge of the blade she held. She dropped it in dislike and it clattered to the rug. Psalter whimpered and clutched the side of his head, looking wildly around, lurching again at Alex.

Alex shook his head, moving back a step. "Give up, you fool. It's finished."

Psalter toppled to his knees. Blood drops spun in a slow arc as he fell, stinging his eyes. Confused, the man removed his hand from the pain in his head, and opening his palm, saw his ear lying detached there like some limp red flower petal.

Katherine, Mary and Joan stood staring down at the apothecary. He peered up wretchedly at Mary. Then he crawled forwards and fumbled for the hems of her skirts.

She stepped back quickly and kicked his hand away.

Downstairs, the front doors slammed. The sheriff had arrived.

CHAPTER FORTY-SIX

T he great carved beams and furnishings were old and heavy, the whitewashed plaster flaking, but the chamber, hugely grand and a hundred years polished, glowed in sensual warmth. A pale wintry sunshine slipped through the windows, striking one corner of the tapestry covered window seats where a small light bleached angle had faded over those long years, the richly embroidered forest scene suddenly cast in sun dipped greys and creams.

The bed was massive, its palliasse mattress new turned and aired for their lordships' return, the covers folded back to show the fresh linen. It smelled of clover and rosemary with a faint waft of mint. The bed hangings, swagged open with long gold tassels, were silk velvet in gleaming saffron, bordered with embroidery of sunbursts, black vine leaves and tiny white roses of York. Across the main swathes of blankets and eiderdowns, a fur cover was slung, wolf pelts backed in black satin.

There were forty candles at least, the small iron chandelier held the central blaze, others, sweet scented beeswax, in sconces or in shining holders, their tiny gold flame points straight and unwavering. The proof of a warm room without draughts. The firelight crackled. The hearth was mantled in dark marble and above was a silver backed mirror, age spotted, framed in scrolls, and reflecting the dance of light and heat and the whole chamber beyond so that everything was doubled, and doubly majestic.

Katherine stood in the very centre, turning a little each way. Alex stood with his hands on her shoulders. She could see his smile in the mirror. She took a very, very deep breath as she smiled back. Alex moved his hands down to her waist, hugging her tightly against him, and bent, kissing the nape of her neck. "Approval, my love? It's yours now."

She shook her head. "It's much too grand and beautiful to be mine."

He laughed and led her to the padded settle by the fire. "I don't entirely believe it either. This is the master's chamber. I was simply the impoverished younger son, never expecting to inherit more than a rusty sword and a list of my father's dire warnings to get myself by in the world. I never slept here, just crawled in sometimes to beg my father's forgiveness after some act of iniquity, once recovered from his beating."

She clutched his hands, now resting in her own lap. "I can't imagine even your father daring to beat you, Alex."

"He wasn't here often," Alex chuckled. "When he was, the whole household trembled. But he was a good soldier and a good manager. I've spent most of the afternoon riding the estates with our steward, and the land's prosperous. At this season of course the farms are quiet, but the sheds are full of grain, the animals are well fed and there's plenty stored for the villagers if the winter turns harsh. You've explored too, I believe?"

"I wasn't taught much, but living in the country taught me something. This is a wonderful place."

"I've plenty to learn as well, about the responsibilities of the estate." He was stroking her fingers, watching the play of their hands in her plum bright lap. "The younger son's lack of prospects tends to lead him more into laxity, impropriety and unadulterated vice." He laughed. "You complained when I lectured you on protecting your reputation, my love, but my own infamy made me conscious of what a reputation can mean. Now I won't limit you, and you'll do what you like whatever I say, so I won't say it." He squeezed her fingers. "There's a windbreak on the crest behind the main hall, a great line of old oak trees, excellent for climbing if I remember rightly."

She giggled. "I don't climb trees anymore, Alex."

From the Oxfordshire hostelry, they had ridden the last few miles into Gloucestershire with the light of the dawn infusing the pale skies behind them. A week before Christmas, and a good day to come home. Godfrey had left them at the inn, riding south to his own lands and family nearby, and Katherine's small party including Tom and Sara Whitstable had gone ahead with the carter. So she was alone with her husband when Katherine saw the great limestone manor of the Mornington barons nestled in its little valley, with the Cotswold Hills outlined in hazy lavender beyond and the thatches of the village cottages clustered around the wooden bell tower of the church. Away from London the land smelled fresh, of wet grass and old bark, of running water sweet enough to drink and a clear sky to silhouette the birds. No stink of refuse, of excrement, or of ten thousand smoking chimneys. The glittering points where the sun pricked the stones sparkled suddenly like dew on cobwebs or linen spread to dry on the hedges. Katherine had known then, without a doubt, she had finally come home.

Now the early winter's twilight was creeping into black night across her husband's lands outside, the sky star-spread and milky. Alex crossed to the windows to hang the shutters. A new warmth instantly enclosed the room. The light of fire and candles shone more intense, as if sharing secrets. Alex came back and sat beside his wife. "Now I'll be the town crier, my love." He grinned. "And tell you all's right with the world. That wretched priest lies in his own monastery's dungeons just a few miles away, hopefully regretting the spite of past actions. Frankly, I doubt he regrets a thing except his own incarceration, but his fate no longer interests me." Again he took her hands in his, entwining their fingers. "Mary's sitting alone and forlorn somewhere in the convent of The Holy Sisters, hearing endless sermons about the iniquity of unmaidenly lust and greed and ambition, though she'll not be listening of course. She'll be planning her next marriage, and how to go about engaging the most powerful man she can find."

Katherine shook her head. "You won't – force the law against her then, Alex? Even after what she's done?"

"There's no proof, and she'll never confess," Alex said. "The nuns'll keep her quiet for a few months, and then I'll let her go back to her parents. But she'll be careful, even well into the future. She'll be wary of what I know, and what I might do about it."

"And what might you do about it?"

"Nothing, unless I hear of the same thing happening again." He sighed. "I intend good fortune and a good future for us, Kate, and I won't concentrate on the miseries of the past. Psalter will hang of course. He's in Newgate now."

"And," she sniffed, lowering her gaze, "you know how terrible that place is."

"I don't know at all, my sweet, not really." He lifted her chin with his finger, smiling into her eyes. "Thanks to the generosity of my friends, I lived well enough in there. But I smelled the pit. Below ground level lies what they call the Limbos, just an open drain where two hundred prisoners live squashed together with rats and lice and every kind of violence. They shit where they sleep and fight over the bread thrown in twice a day. Some of the worst are kept in chains, but most roam there in the dark and squalor, kicking out their place in the new world. Some stay forgotten for years, others wait for the quick call to the gallows. Psalter may not live to be hanged. He's the wrong type for a place like that. He'll be raped. He'll have his share of food and drink stolen from him, and his manner of speaking will antagonise the mob."

Katherine gulped. "Do you pity him, Alex?"

"No. I loved Mel, and he was only just coming out from the pit of his own nightmares." Alex shook his head. "Every citizen knows the risks of Newgate. Psalter sent me there, knowing me accused of his crimes. He made his own choices."

"But Mary's getting away with everything," Katherine objected. "Perhaps she told him what to do. I hold her to be more responsible. But because she's beautiful, she'll end up married to some besotted duke. She'll eat well and get plump, shout at her servants and children, have secret affairs, and live happily ever after."

"Perhaps." Alex laughed. "But I doubt she's capable of knowing what happiness means, let alone finding it. I've no proof, and I can't be sure how involved she was, but the convent I've sent her to is strict, and the abbess knows what I suspect. So does her father, who sanctioned the move as part of a bargain for her freedom, and authorised my authority." The fire spat and a log tumbled from the grate. Alex kicked it back. "Women were certainly never blamed for anything during King Richard's reign. He pardoned and pensioned every one. Perhaps it's not such a bad example to follow."

"That's why Henry Tudor's nasty little mother never got punished for all her treachery and scheming," said Katherine crossly. "Or King Richard wouldn't have been killed and we wouldn't have this horrid new king."

Alex shrugged. "The wretched woman was only thirteen, just a baby herself when she gave birth, and the child's father already dead of the pestilence. She nearly died of course. I can imagine few things more utterly wretched. Misery breeds fanaticism. Like Father Erkenwald's fanatical belief in his miserable God of furious retribution. We all have reasons for what we do."

Katherine thought of something, and blushed slightly. "So you don't blame Mary." She sniffed, staring into her lap. "Is it because you – did – had – a relationship – with her, Alex?"

Alex pulled her firmly into his embrace, cradling her head against his shoulder. "Silly puss. I'm sorry you had to hear about that – but then, you might as well know the worst of me. As for Mary, it was just one occasion and long before you moved into The Strand, and in fact she seduced me, though I don't claim to have fought her off. But I've no fond feelings because of it. She used me, which I understood. Strangely enough, my love, most women – but enough - it's not Mary I want to discuss." He combed her hair with his fingers, his other hand firm on her back. She had already discarded her cambric headdress, but still smelled slightly weather worn with a faint memory of horse sweat. She wore the fine scarlet riding habit he had ordered from the tailor before they left London, tight sleeves trimmed in black gris, high waisted and full skirted. Alex had learned a passion for his wife dressed in red, the colour that made her dark hair gleam. But

Katherine had specified one thing, and the gown was dyed not with cinnabar, but with kermes.

"It's a little early for bed," Alex murmured, "but after three days on the road and everything that happened before, I imagine you're tired. Will you sleep here tonight, my love, or do I pass you over to Sara and your own quarters?"

She sat up straight and glared at him. "You know perfectly well, Alex. Of course I had to sleep with the women during the journey here, but that was different. Or don't you want me now we're married?"

"Depends what you mean by wanting, my sweet." He smiled rather wanly and pulled her back into his arms. "But you also know quite well. I want you in every sense. Stay here with me then." His fingers found the row of little buttons and hooks at the side of her belt. "But I won't let you sleep like this." He sighed, looking down on her. "Tonight, if you sleep in my arms, then this time I undress you first."

She stiffened. "Can I – sleep in my chemise, Alex?"

He did not answer her but began to unhook each button until the soft wool of her gown loosened. The neck opened a little, framing her breasts in dark fur, cream against the black. "Raise your arms," he commanded, and she obeyed, and he lifted her skirts over her head and flung her gown to the rug. Then he scooped her up and carried her to the bed, sitting her on the wolf pelt cover, propped up by pillows. He sat beside her and regarded her, smiling faintly. "What an adorable nuisance you are, my love," he said. "Did I really promise never to force myself on you? I must have been mad." He watched her for a moment, timid in the soft linen shift lying low across her breasts and partially transparent over her legs. Her nipples rose dark beneath the bodice, one tiny spot still visible where he had cauterized her wound, and her face, blushing, echoed the ruddy reflections from the firelight. Alex undressed quickly. Once naked to the waist but no further, he pulled her abruptly into his arms. "Now my love, if you pity me at all, tell me what the devil that absurd husband of yours did to terrify you when you married him."

She clung, sniffing reluctantly into Alex's bare chest. "You'll think I'm terribly silly, Alex," she said. "I suppose he only did what all husbands do. But he made me feel so small and ugly and it was so humiliating. I don't ever want to feel like that again, and especially with you." Her fingers absently traced down the little bumps of his spine as she sighed, forced to remember. "The first night, well, he was terribly drunk from the wedding feast," she murmured. "He just poked and prodded me. He leered and sniggered and said – well, he said in future, if I wasn't any good, and he was sure I wouldn't be, he'd go and visit the whores in the Bathhouse afterwards. He just needed to – to," she paused in desperation. "Alex, haven't you got a kerchief somewhere?"

Alex searched and discovered one in her discarded gown. He wiped her eyes and then held it to her nose. "Blow," he commanded. "And listen. The wretched man was unpleasant, ignorant and inept. Kate, you're the most beautiful woman I know, or ever have."

She relaxed a little, and giggled. "Oh, what a liar Alex, and after knowing Mary too."

He shook his head. "She's a tinted chapel window," he said. "Cold eyes. Shallow eyes. You, my angel, are vital and deep and very much alive."

"Oh, Alex. That's – sweet and kind." She sniffed, took the kerchief, and blew her nose again. "But Edmund – well – that's why I asked you to make him permanently drunk. You see, that first night when he was too intoxicated – well, he said he couldn't - . So I thought if he was like that all the time, he'd leave me alone. And it worked, Alex, it really did."

"Until you attended the coronation," Alex guessed, with a rueful smile. "I suppose he managed to stay sober that night. He wouldn't risk being pissed first night at court."

Katherine had hidden her face against the golden muscles of his arms. She was still clutching the kerchief. "That's right. He sort of – grabbed me. I panicked. That's when I hit him with the chamber pot."

"I don't think there is one in this room," Alex grinned. "Just the privy in the garderobe."

"Oh, Alex." Katherine looked away, gazing down at the wolf pelt. The candlelight shimmered, glossing amongst the fur, painting it black and gold. It was thick and very soft beneath her, but she felt increasingly hot. The luxury of the bed had become strangely uncomfortable. "I told you before," she hiccupped. "Truly, you wouldn't want me. I'd do everything wrong and I'd spoil it for you. And then we'd both feel terrible afterwards."

Alex lifted her hands and kissed both her palms. Then he kissed her on the mouth, pressing her back against the high pillows and taking her firmly into his embrace. The world immediately became comfortable again. She breathed deep, absorbing the breath and heat and taste of him, allowing his tongue to explore her and realising the pleasure of his hard nakedness against her breasts. When he finally released her and looked down searchingly into her face, she opened her eyes and gazed back. "You cannot do anything wrong, little one," he whispered, "because you need only give me permission, and in everything else, I lead. You cannot spoil what I do, because I admit no allowance for failure. I shall feel only absolute delight, because I adore you, and desire you, and long to attain the pinnacle your body already promises me. And you will feel only pleasure, because I shall bring yours before I permit my own."

She breathed a little faster but looked down again, avoiding his intense regard. His words woke something she had not expected. She stared at his knees, thick enclosed in black knitted silk, the waist cords of his hose lying loose and unlaced like leashes across the wolf pelt. "I don't understand, Alex," she said. "I suppose I never did."

"Then let me show you," Alex said softly, one arm encircling her, his hand sliding up against her cheek, the other dipping into the deep opening of her chemise. He eased the strap from her shoulder, his fingers following down across the rise of her body. She sighed and leaned in towards him, exhaling very slowly as he discovered and caressed her breasts. Gently enclosing, then teasing her into arousal, his thumb rubbed firm against the nipple. Then he leaned down and kissed her again.

"Oh Alex," she whispered, once he let her go. "Edmund never did that."

Alex chuckled, both hands now around her breasts. "If I'm to have a regular commentary of comparisons," he said, "perhaps we should start with whatever he actually did that horrified you so much you knocked him out."

She curled close, her face buried. "He was so rude. He obviously didn't even like me. And then he had no clothes on. I wasn't expecting that and I thought he looked funny but I didn't dare laugh. I mean – I'd never seen before – and he was such an odd shape. Does that sound unkind? But then he made me take my clothes off too and that wasn't funny at all." She sniffed, and reached again for the kerchief. "He kept staring and telling me off, and then he pushed me on the bed, and tried to – but I can't describe it and I don't know the words."

"Penetration?" suggested Alex, abandoning diplomacy.

Katherine blinked. "Oh. You mean - ? Is that normal then?" she demanded, scandalised. "It just seemed so horrible, and – so terribly improper –I was sure he was trying to do something quite unnatural. I just felt I had to stop him before it went too far."

Alex paused momentarily. "I think, my love, you should let me explain what is normal, and just what should happen." He kissed the tip of her nose, lifting her face up towards him. "But considering your timidity, it will be far easier shown than spoken." Without waiting for her answer, he laid his head down against her breasts and gently kissed her nipples.

Katherine gasped, curling up her knees. "Oh, Alex."

He came slowly back beside her, kissing her neck, her ears, her eyes, and her mouth. "I swear I won't hurt you, beloved. Will you trust me?"

She nodded, a little dizzy, as if not sure what she was agreeing to. Then he rose quietly from the bed and she reached out for him, missing his embrace, feeling suddenly lost. He moved around the room, checking the logs in the grate, then snuffing each of the candles. As each tiny light blinked out, the sinuous gleam of his body became blurred and muted in the glooming, then stark between firelight and shadow, the glide of his muscles caught tawny in gold. When he finally returned to her, just a flicker drifted in a red and black dance from the low flames in the hearth, but the room had become secretive and dark.

Alex sat on the edge of the mattress, facing her. He slipped his hands under the thin hem of her shift, clasping the narrow warmth of her ankles. She thought his eyes looked unexpectedly bright, and heard the fire hiss as it sank to glittering embers. His voice was just as soft, just a hint of breath as he leaned towards her. "If you tell me to stop my love, then I will." His hands moved up her legs beneath the thin linen, following the curve of her calf and up to her thighs. Then he spread his fingers, just brushing her hips, as he lifted her chemise over her head, letting it drift like a cobweb to the floor. Finally he took her once more into his arms, his hands warm and firm against her nakedness, and before kissing her, spoke again. "Now dream with me," he murmured. His kiss was more passionate than ever before, and she kissed him back until breathless.

He gave her a long time to adjust to his wandering hands and his wandering kisses, while the firelight slunk ever deeper into darkness and the dying warmth was replaced by the relentless intimacy of his loving and the flush of her response. He became the fantasy spinner and she lost consciousness of passing time. He enclosed her, wrapping her round with his own self, the feathered welter of the bed snuggled beneath and the spit of embers sparking intermittent glimmers amongst the shadows.

He whispered, kissing and tickling her ear, telling her of love and of lust. Her breasts tingled, her nipples ached and her legs throbbed as she moved where he moved her, turned as he turned her, and clung to him when he let her. She had forgotten his offer of stopping if she asked, and now had no words of her own. Accepting all sensations, she floated within layers of pleasure. His hands between her legs were gentle, his strong palms against the satin sheen of her inner thighs, long fingers sliding and tantalising. He smoothed the gentle swell of her belly down to the smaller roundness at her groin, combing through the soft tight hair, parting both the curls and her legs below, finding the smallest swelling hidden inside.

At last he whispered, "My beloved, it seems you are indeed still a virgin. Now breathe deep for me. I promise not to hurt you. This is when we join both body and mind. You become truly mine, and I give you the last part of myself."

She felt an unexpected tug and then the forced sting of his sudden entry. She held him very close, closed her eyes and grasped the back of his legs with her own. His shuddering was long and slow and mingled them both in delight.

When, a little later, he finally tucked her beneath the bedcovers and once more into his quiet arms, she was wide awake but already deep in dreams.

It snowed in the night.

Then beyond the stone gatehouse, over the pointed thatch of the mews and across to the foothills, the long rolling horizon was silver splashed by the new dawn.

Waking in warmth, Katherine tugged the fur pelt around her and rushed to the window. She hurriedly unhooked the shutters and tipped them to the floor, kneeling on the window seat to peer through the casements.

Alex hauled himself onto one elbow and squinted into the sudden daylight. "What's the excitement, my sweet? Come back to bed."

"Oh but Alex, look." She leaned over, nose pressed to the glass. "It's snowed. Just for us."

He grinned. "Silly puss. You'll catch cold."

The fur slipped from one shoulder, but she was as warm as delight could make her.

Outside on the window sill were little scratched toe marks, black etched in the white scrunch, the fragile broken star prints of a robin. Down below she saw the pad marks of a hare racing through the courtyard towards the meadows and the forest beyond. Katherine turned, looking back to the bed. "It's the first day, Alex. The first day of my real life."

"Come back over here," Alex chuckled. "I've an urgent need to make love to you again. And this time will be far, far better."

She danced across to him, swirling the fur into dark billows, kicking her toes on the turkey rugs. "How could it ever be better? It was – you were - amazing. Thrilling."

"It's never as good for a virgin." He grinned, holding out his arms. "Come and let me prove it."

The End

Dear Reader,

I hope you've enjoyed Alex and Kate's story. Once again, you may find yourself a little lost, now that you're back in the modern world. So how about another trip to the medieval, or perhaps the start of the Tudor dynasty?

In Sumerford's Autumn we meet Ludovic, the youngest of four brothers, all of whom have a secret to hide.

If you enjoyed Satin Cinnabar, then Sumerford's Autumn will thrill you. with Treasonous plot's, smuggling pirates and ghosts from the past.

And do please remember that when a reader leaves a review, it gives me a very happy face!

ABOUT THE AUTHOR

My passion is for late English medieval history and this forms the background for my historical fiction. I also have a love of fantasy and the wild freedom of the imagination, with its haunting threads of sadness and the exploration of evil. Although all my books have romantic undertones, I would not class them purely as romances. We all wish to enjoy some romance in our lives, there is also a yearning for adventure, mystery, suspense, friendship and spontaneous experience. My books include all of this and more, but my greatest loves are the beauty of the written word, and the utter fascination of good characterisation. Bringing my characters to life is my principal aim.

For more information on my other books please visit **barbaragaskelldenvil.com**

Made in the USA
Monee, IL
26 August 2021